Gold Throne in Shadow

GOLD THRONE IN SHADOW

WORLD OF PRIME BOOK TWO

M.C. PLANCK

an imprint of Prometheus Books
Amherst, NY

Published 2015 by Pyr, an imprint of Prometheus Books

Cover design by Nicole Sommer-Lecht
Cover illustration © Gene Mollica

Inquiries should be addressed to
Pyr
59 John Glenn Drive
Amherst, New York 14228
VOICE: 716-691-0133
FAX: 716-691-0137
WWW.PYRSF.COM

19 18 17 16 15   5 4 3 2 1

Library of Congress Cataloging-in-Publication Data

Planck, M. C.
Gold throne in shadow / M. C. Planck.
pages ; cm. — (World of prime)
ISBN 978-1-63388-096-2 (softcover) — ISBN 978-1-63388-097-9 (ebook)
I. Title.

PR9616.4.P56G65 2015
823'.92—dc23

2015015521

Printed in the United States of America

CONTENTS

1

REFLECTIONS

Christopher stood in front of the mirror, naked, admiring Krel-lyan's handiwork. The dents of a lifetime were erased, washed away by the power of the Saint's magic, leaving his skin smooth and unwrinkled. Too smooth: he had no calluses on his hands or feet. He'd have to be careful until he made new ones.

But now he had that ageless look that the elite of the Kingdom shared. Inside he was still a forty-year-old man. On the outside he could pass for twenty-something. The magic hadn't made him any stronger or faster than he had been. The hardness under his skin was earned the old-fashioned way, the profit of surviving the arduous life-style of this world. The reflexes he had cultivated in twenty years of amateur hobby had been honed by a year of deadly serious craft. But the scars he had also gained were gone. The regeneration had kept the good and replaced the bad.

With a trivial exception, one easily corrected with ordinary cosmetic surgery. Christopher wasn't about to suffer through that need-lessly—it was a decision he'd leave to his wife, when he saw her again. The indiscriminate regeneration spell had replaced all of his missing flesh.

And it was starting to look like *when*, not *if*. He was no longer a lonely, penniless wayfarer lost on a strange world. The lost and strange remained, but now he had allies, an army, and bags of money. Most importantly, the bargain he had made with the god Marcius made sense to him. This world needed a good shaking up, a transfer in the balance of power. The people on the bottom needed more, at the expense of the people on top, and Christopher had just the lever to do it. They had said in the Wild West, "God didn't make men equal,

Samuel Colt did." On this world, it would be Crazy Pater Christopher and his buckets of dirt that made men equal. The nobles had tael, the source of magic and unnatural vitality that made a man as hard to kill as an elephant. Now the commoners would have elephant guns.

"If you are finished admiring yourself, we have business to discuss," Cardinal Faren said from the doorway. The great Cathedral in Kingsrock had a number of plainly furnished cells for the use of traveling priests. This was not one of them. They had put Christopher in the most luxurious room in the Cathedral, normally reserved for visiting nobles recovering from some horrific disease or injury. The height of luxury was signified by the private fireplace and a full-length mirror. Other than that, the room had what a charitable description could only call "rustic charm."

An objective description would be "medieval primitiveness," but Christopher was used to that by now.

"Why haven't you had this done?" Christopher asked while stepping into trousers.

"I do not require it, save for vanity. Which is better served by signs of wisdom." The old man's crinkled face was framed by a full head of carefully coiffed white hair. This world shared the usual fetish for the young and beautiful, but it also had a strong veneration for the old. Especially old men. Not many men around here lived to be old.

"What business?" Christopher finished dressing by hanging his sword at his side. It was like putting on a necktie; he felt slightly naked without it in any formal situation.

"You're rich," Faren said. "We need to talk about how we're going to spend your money."

Saint Krellyan was waiting for them in his private chambers, deep in the heart of the Cathedral. The Saint's age was problematic. Chronologically he was about the same age as Christopher; physically he looked half of that, but his eyes seemed even older than Faren's.

"Rank is uppermost on my mind," Krellyan said. "You must

promote yourself. Your assassin still lurks, and as a lowly first-rank you are much too easy to kill. You cannot serve under Lord Nordland anymore and expect to survive your term of service. Nor would you be likely to find any friendlier assignment."

"But as a fifth-rank, you can take command of the draft levee in your own right," Cardinal Faren pointed out. "You will be a legitimate member of the peerage, vastly harder to kill, and protected by your own loyal army. I am not certain that will be enough, yet I am certain any less guarantees you will not survive the next three years. And I think your men will need your protection as much as you need theirs."

The Saint put a lump of bright-purple tael on the desk. It represented over half of Christopher's newfound wealth.

"This will advance you to the rank of Curate," Krellyan said. "It will take at least four days for your rank to fully manifest, so you should begin now. You have already lost three weeks, and I think you have little time to spare."

Christopher had not sought rank, privilege, command over others; he had only wanted to go home. But he had a job to do, and doing it would require him to accept certain responsibilities, not least of which was surviving. And the men who had stood and fought for him while Nordland fled would not be any more popular with the lord than he was.

He picked up the lump and put it in his mouth, where it dissolved like flavorless cotton candy. Over the next few days it would integrate itself into his brain. After that, the only way to get it out again would be to kill him and boil his head.

There were plenty of people who wouldn't have a problem with doing that. The people who had tortured him, smashing his legs into bone meal and driving nails through his eyes, weren't even the top of the list. His assassin, that nameless woman who had stalked him almost since he had arrived, who had illicitly interceded in his state-sponsored "interrogation" by crushing his teeth and his genitals with a hammer, wasn't the top of the list either. She wanted him to suffer too much to just be dead. But Lord Nordland, and perhaps the entire ruling class of the realm, would be more than relieved to drop his head in a kettle and finally be done with his trouble-making. They'd already tried it once.

But they had failed. Well, not failed, strictly speaking. He hadn't survived the torture. Driven to utter despair by pain, he'd used his last spell to commit suicide, killing himself with his own magic. He had his assassin to thank for that mistake on their part, but he wasn't feeling particularly grateful. After that they *had* boiled his head. And worse.

"Three weeks? But why?" Christopher demanded. A week was ten days here, so it was a whole month by Christopher's calendar.

"Why not three thousand?" Faren answered. "Knowing Krellyan's power, they should have burned your body to ash. Instead we found your empty skull on our doorstep."

"A gruesome gift, however welcome," Krellyan said.

"There is more good news," Faren said. "They did not find you guilty of treason, which would have forbidden us from bringing you back. They did not *officially* keep your body past ordinary hope of revival or *officially* mutilate your corpse. So you are legally free to continue your improbable career."

"Speaking of which, I wish to know what your intentions are," Krellyan stated. "You may rest here for a few days, until your rank asserts itself. Then you must go back into the world. What will you do then?"

"Faren is right," Christopher said. "I have to accept responsibility for the men. How do I do that?"

"You petition the King," Faren answered, in his capacity as the Church's top legal officer. "Normally the Church does not intervene in the assignment of our draft regiment, save to make sure it goes to a Bright. In this case we will."

"Nordland will be offended, again," Krellyan sighed, "when you snatch his regiment out from under him."

"It can't be helped," Faren said, dismissing the problem with a wave of his hand. "After that, you petition the King for a posting. He will send you to some county on the edge of the Kingdom. We cannot exercise any influence on that decision."

"He won't send me back to Nordland's county, will he?" Christopher asked.

"I have no idea," Faren said. "He will send you where he feels you are most needed. Or at least, he is supposed to. I am certain that politics influence the decision, and I am equally certain those political channels are open only to our enemies and not to us. Wherever he sends you, you must make the best of it."

"And try not to draw attention to yourself," Krellyan said, although his tone of voice revealed little hope. Christopher bit his tongue, unable to speak without committing blatant dishonesty. He intended to cause far more trouble than anyone could have guessed. He knew they hadn't guessed it, because if they had, he'd already be dead. Again.

2

INTERVIEWS

Christopher's regiment had long since returned to their training camp in the village of Burseberry. He was eager to join them, but the four-day wait was unavoidable, and in any case he needed some time in the Cathedral's library. He had a career's worth of magic theory to catch up on.

And of course, he had to face the King.

"You must go alone," Faren told him, angry at his own helplessness. "We dare not be seen supporting you so openly. All we have done so far is to heal and revive your men, at your own expense." That had taken another quarter of his fortune. It was an expenditure he did not regret.

It was sorrowful, though, that eighty men could be brought back from the dead for half the expense of promoting one man to a moderate rank. It put the cost of his success into perspective and revealed the sharp edge of this world: power, yes, but not without price.

He was reminded of the personal price when the carriage arrived to ferry him to his appointment. It was the same vehicle that had delivered him into torture and death, agonies still vivid and recent, only a few days old from his frame of reference. After a shamefully brief battle, his stomach betrayed him, and he threw up in the rosebushes by the curb of the Cathedral.

Faren stood by, scowling in anger, but not at Christopher. "You need not accept this insult," he growled. The coachman was careful to remain stone-faced and unmoving, and yet his smirk hung in the air, summoned perhaps by sheer inevitability.

Christopher stood up, wiped his mouth. This was not the hardest thing he had ever done. He had walked into a hospital room once and told his mother that she was going to die because the doctors had done everything in their power and failed. "You have to beat this one on your own," he had said, knowing it was impossible, knowing that she knew it too. After that, nothing else had ever seemed to deserve being called "hardest."

Ignoring the quavering in his limbs, he climbed into the down-at-heel carriage. As the coachman shut the door, the invisible smirk faded like the worn window curtains. Courage was a concrete quantity here, like gold and iron. Injury and even death could be overcome with magic, on this wondrous and distant world; fear remained obdurate.

There was a time when he had gazed up at this city with curiosity and even desire, but that allure was dead now, buried under memories of torture. The close city streets and tall buildings no longer seemed friendly and familiar. They had become hostile, wedded to the establishment that abandoned him to his enemies. Even the magnificence of the Cathedral was tainted, a white blossom lying in the dirt, spoiled by muddy footprints.

The city crammed twenty thousand people onto a spire of rock sticking up from the surrounding farmlands. Those inhabitants watched Christopher's carriage incuriously, while he watched them with silent disdain. The towns run by the Church did not tolerate this kind of poverty, uncleanliness, and petty brutality.

Every town was short on men, having buried half of every generation on distant battlefields. But here in the city Christopher saw an abundance, the detritus left over after the thresher, boys warped and twisted by violence into men who could never return to a pastoral life.

The castle was impressive, as castles go, with soldiers of precision and dispatch manning the gates, bright pennants snapping in the wind, a solid projection of strength and defense against the monsters that roamed this world. But Christopher could see only the dungeons it hid in its depths.

This time he entered by the main hall, and his escort of blank-faced soldiers took him directly to throne room. This time there would be no sudden darkness of a sleep spell. Christopher's new rank put him beyond such simple measures. If they wanted to kill him now, he could put up a fight.

But not against the King. Although tael was invisible, the King's power was palpably radiant in the graceful way his brawny frame glided across the floor, the tael-enhanced reflexes obvious even in the way his fine fur cloak draped about him. The Saint was a giddying twelfth-rank, which put him two or three steps above the heads of other Churches; the King was one above that, the highest rank in the realm. Krellyan was a healer and could make bodies whole and living from a fingernail; Treywan was a warrior and, it had been patiently explained to Christopher until he signaled that he believed it, could defeat an entire regiment single-handedly.

If you let him use both hands, they added, he could quite likely defeat every unranked soldier in the Kingdom. All at once.

At least, that had been true when men had fought with swords and shields. Christopher's regiment had rifles and cannons. He was quite certain the King did not understand what that meant, and he was equally certain that failure of understanding was the only thing that would let him walk out of here alive.

He went to one knee on the plush green-and-gold carpet and bowed his head, the most elaborate protocol demanded in this prickly world where the man in rags just might be a powerful wizard with poor sartorial taste. The King finished his discussion with the court-iers lounging around the map table before dismissing them off to distant corners of the room. It was a farce, since the hall was staffed with guards and no doubt various magical observations, but the interview could now be less formal. For the King, that is; for Christopher, frankness and comfort were unimaginable.

"You don't look that different." Treywan's voice was strong, but it had the beer-and-football bluster Christopher had always rolled his eyes at. Not here, of course. Christopher pictured the King speaking to him from atop a modern battle-tank, and decided the King could sound like whatever he wanted.

"Different than what, my lord?"

"Different than any other priest. And yet, you've caused more uproar than a sack of dragons."

"I apologize, my lord. That was not my intent."

"Nonsense," the King guffawed, with an undercurrent of menace. "Your cleverness has paid off. You've gone from first- to fifth-rank in less than a year. An impressive advance. You are to be commended on your initiative."

"Thank you, my lord," Christopher said automatically, before feeling the thinness of the ice under his feet.

"I didn't say *I* was going to commend you," mused the King. "I got no profit from your rise. That purple-tongued Cardinal of yours argued me out of my share. Said you had no commission, so I should look to Nordland and his commission for my cut. I almost did; if Nordland had taken his due from you, I would have taken mine from him. But the good Duke is too wroth to speak your name, let alone come and beg his tael from you."

Christopher could only blush in embarrassment and anger. It was not his fault that Nordland had abandoned him. It wasn't even Nordland's fault, really. The man had made the best decision, given what he knew. Unfortunately the Duke had not understood black-powder weaponry any better than the King did.

"Now that you are fifth-rank," the King said, "your Cardinal suggests that I give you a commission in your own right, so that I might never again be cheated out of my tax. To me it seems rather like closing the barn door after the horse is already at the neighbor's. Though if your meteoric ascent is not yet burnt out, perhaps I can still get some service out of you."

Christopher was not sure how to answer this. He did not want to appear to threaten the King with boasts of exploits to come. At the same time, he wanted that commission. He ignored the fact that his destruction of an army of monsters should be counted as service to the Kingdom. He knew by now that the King, indeed every noble in the land, would not see it that way. There were always armies of monsters to destroy. One more or less could hardly be counted as an achievement.

He settled on something safe and trite. "I will do my best, my lord."

"I will not be cheated again," the King said, unnecessarily. This time the menace was naked.

The conversation galled Christopher. The King could just ask for his share, instead of threatening him. Christopher could even pay it, though it would leave him penniless. But apparently the Church wielded some influence, because the King dropped the issue and turned to the map table.

"I'm sending your regiment to Carrhill. A choice assignment: the ulven hunt is a popular pastime among the lower gentry. A chance for a bit of sport, and of course, tael. Many a knight has won a rank or two that way, perhaps even to the peerage. And your boys can fulfill their commitment safely in the city, as long as they do useful work and cause no trouble. I'm sure the lads will appreciate that over sleeping in the Wild."

County Carrhill had been overrun by ulvenmen some years ago. The town had barely withstood the attack; the countryside had been devastated. Now the realm kept an army stationed there to augment the county's local regiment. Christopher thought about barn doors and horses. He was wise enough not to speak.

"Word has it," the King baited him, "that your regiment can defeat hordes of monsters entirely on its own. Without you. So I'll not deny you the hunt. In fact, I encourage you to roam the swamp, searching for wandering bands of rabid dog-men. I am overdue for some tael from your hand."

"I will do my best, my lord," Christopher repeated.

"See that you do," the King snapped, annoyed that his lure had not drawn a bite. But Christopher simply didn't know how to respond to it. Yes, in fact, his regiment had defeated a horde of monsters virtually on its own. The torturers must have told the King the truths they extracted from Christopher's mind. Clearly the King did not believe the simple facts. As usual, nobody was telling Christopher what they did believe.

He decided to change the subject, a risky proposition with kings, but still safer than the current topic. "May I ask, my lord, who commands the King's regiments in Carrhill?" He wasn't sure how far up the chain of command he had moved.

"Why, you do," grinned the King wolfishly. "Unless you can extract Baron Fairweather from whatever ulven cooking pot he's stewing in."

"There is no Marshall of the South," Faren explained, examining the parchment of Christopher's commission. "Nordland's command of the North is largely ceremonial, but the southern border cannot manage even that amount of coordination." They were eating now, the tension of the King's interview having left Christopher famished.

Returned to the safety of the Cathedral, Christopher's normal argumentativeness was restored. Jabbing at the rock-hard yellow substance in the butter dish, he said, "That's stupid. What if all the monsters attacked at just one spot? How would a defense be organized in time?"

Faren raised an eyebrow around a mouthful of trout. "Why would they do that? We are not at war with another nation; we are defending the borders of civilization from wild creatures. In any case, I presume the monsters are no more able to set aside their squabbles than we are.

"And it is precisely those squabbles we must discuss," Faren continued seriously. "Until now, you have been protected." Christopher thought of all the people who had tried to kill him, and the ones who had actually succeeded, but decided not to interrupt. "Now you are truly ranked. The tael in your head alone is a prize worthy of great violence. Your status as a member of our Church earns you our enemies automatically; your status as the head of your own chapter leaves you without our allies. Your arsenal does not include charm or diplomacy; Nordland is one of our Church's staunchest friends, yet if he saw you drowning, he would cross the road only to put his foot on your head."

The Cardinal glared at him until he gave up his abuse of the butter dish and put it down, surrendering his full attention to the old man. "But of course you already know all this. I only bring it up to put what you do not know into perspective. Much of the south falls under the dominion of the Gold Throne." Christopher had met only one priest of the Yellow, and in the very short time they had together before someone killed the man, Christopher had formed a deep and lasting revulsion for murderous pedophiles. "I know you," Faren warned, no doubt seeing Christopher's feelings on his face, "and I know that you cannot hold your tongue. But you must learn to, for the sake of your own survival. Not only is the Gold Throne wealthy and completely unscrupulous, they are also capable of intelligence and sophistication. Not all are mewling cowards who prey on children. Most importantly, their Patron is equal to our own, and power is an argument that cannot be denied. In our contest for the support of the independent lords, you cannot dismiss Dark out of hand simply because it is wicked."

"And you want me to win some of those independent lords over to my side," Christopher said. Sadly, because he knew how unlikely that would be.

"Yes," growled Faren, "you must make alliances of your own. You are in politics now. Your army exposes you to the lords; precedence exposes you to the duelists." Faren had warned him, long ago, when he had first agreed to a duel with the insufferable Hobilar, that the consequences would be unending.

"You need not try so very hard in this case," Krellyan said, handing him a slice of neatly buttered bread. "The Lord of Carrhill is a wizard of dark repute and unlikely to look upon you favorably. Nonetheless, there is something you can do to advance our cause. The wizard takes no sides in religion; thus we have a chapel there, but so does the Gold Throne. We would have the field rendered uncontested."

"But not by violence," Faren hastened to add. "You cannot simply challenge the local Curate to a duel; that would not serve our purposes, and you would probably lose. His Church can offer him much greater aid in violence than we can offer you."

"Then what do you suggest?" Christopher asked.

"Try befriending him," Faren said. "That's enough aggravation to drive any man away."

This could be a problem. Christopher wasn't sure he could walk past a temple dedicated to the sacrifice of children without burning it down.

"It is not as bad as that," Faren said, scowling at the open book of Christopher's face. "Their secret rites are just that, secret. In a town where they do not rule with absolute power, they would not dare to sink so low."

"So I can't publicly accuse them of child murder?"

"Gods no," Faren said. "To do so would invite a challenge from the Gold Apostle himself, a death sentence for a man of your rank. You must learn to avoid such easy snares. As forewarned is forearmed, I have something that might help."

Going to the door, Faren admitted a man dressed in acolyte's robes.

Christopher studied the newcomer, a face somehow familiar. The different context took a moment to sort out, because the last time he had seen this fellow was in armor and sword, on the opposite side of a battlefield, serving under the wicked Lord Baron Bartholomew. When the Baron had fallen, this knight had sensibly switched sides for the promise of a chance at pardon.

"You're the traitor knight," Christopher exclaimed. "From Black Bart's army!"

The man did not answer, bowing his head in deference.

"Speak, Torme," Faren commanded. "I warned you that you must accustom yourself to our ways, and you will find the Curate even more discombobulating."

"Yes, Curate, I was." Torme's voice was a rattling burr, with the country drawl that was comfortable and familiar to Christopher now. He had to consciously remind himself that this man was not one of his good Church peasants.

"So you're to be my bodyguard?" Christopher asked.

"More like your babysitter," Faren growled. "He knows how the Dark think, if that is the right word for their madness, from having lived under them his whole life. I figure if he survived this long, he must have good instincts."

"I would make a poor bodyguard, Curate," Torme continued, ignoring the Cardinal's suggestion that he should be lecturing Christopher instead of humbly explaining, "for I am a knight no longer. But I will serve you as best I can."

"Not a knight . . . but we didn't kill you." Dying cost you a rank, and the man had been first-rank when Christopher had captured him.

"The rank was bought with innocent blood," Torme said matter-of-factly, referring to Bart's liquidation of whole villages, "and it weighed heavily on my soul. The Saint was kind enough to relieve me of that burden."

Christopher had not yet heard anyone describe rank as a burden.

However, he was more interested in the technical details. He had thought death was the only way to lose ranks, to extract the tael from a head once it was put in.

"Such is often the price of atonement," Faren explained. "It is completely voluntary, of course, as is the atonement itself. And a waste of tael, in my opinion." The Cardinal was referring to the dismal fact that you could only extract a sixteenth of the tael you put in. "Yet sometimes necessary for the spiritual well-being of the reformed."

So Christopher had finally met someone who had atoned. He wasn't sure exactly what that meant, but he did know what not atoning meant: the noose. Christopher had sent a dozen or more criminals and thugs to the Cathedral for atonement and had never seen them again.

"Torme," Faren said patiently, "you have to learn to speak your mind, particularly around the Curate. He is too dense to guess."

It was true, of course. Christopher had not even realized there was anything the man wanted to say.

"I offered my sword to your Church," Torme said gravely, "when I turned sides against my fellows." After Bart had been defeated, Torme had surrendered and then fought to subdue the last of Bart's retainers who chose death on the battlefield over the all-but-inevitable noose. "And when the Saint showed me that there was another way, a kind of life I had not known existed, I offered my soul. But I am not worthy," and here Torme ran out of words.

"We've taught him to read and write," Faren explained, "and more theology than you've ever learned. He took to the doctrine splendidly. So we thought to make a priest of him, but he is not by nature a healer. A sword fits too comfortably in his hands."

Both men looked at Christopher expectantly. He thought he had an idea of what they were getting at, but he couldn't understand why they were talking to him about it.

"So make him a priest of Marcius," he said. The Marshall of Heaven was a war-god, and his priests carried swords.

"We can't," Faren said gently, "at least, not legally. Marcius already has a priest in our lands; if this man is to join that brotherhood, it is up to the ranking clergy to promote him."

Christopher scowled glumly. That ranking clergy was him, and he did not want this responsibility. He already had a regiment of rowdy young men to look out for. How was he supposed to pass judgment on a man he didn't know and deny or permit him a lifelong career of service to a god?

"You need not promote him right away," Faren said, misunderstanding his reluctance. "We have already paid for his acolyte-rank, so he will still be of considerable use as an assistant. But eventually your Church will require more priests than just yourself, so I suggest you start training them now."

Torme stood silently, awaiting his fate without argument. Much as he had when they had first captured him.

"How am I supposed to know if he belongs?" Christopher asked. *How am I supposed to deal with a man who used to kill people for the Dark*, was what he really wanted to say.

"That's what training is for," Faren answered. "Although I am certain he can master the skills, and as for his character, I already told you he was White. Other priests have been promoted on less." Faren's voice turned stern, as he referred to Christopher's original promotion on the strength of a single interview with the Saint.

It sounded like an order, so Christopher took the out he was given. If it turned out the man was still a homicidal maniac, it would be Faren's fault.

"When do I have to buy him a sword?" Christopher asked, immediately unhappy at how stingy that made him sound.

"Not until he has a full rank," Faren answered. "He can practice with wood until then. It seemed adequate for you, after all." He took the untouched slice of buttered bread from Christopher's plate and put it on his own, slathering it with minced fish.

As Christopher was finishing his packing for the ride home, he realized what was missing. He'd marched out with another Pater, a first-rank priest, attached to the regiment as a healer. Although the man had fled with Nordland, Christopher didn't hold it against him, since he'd only been obeying orders. Although Christopher was fifth-rank now, the regiment could still use the healing power of a Pater of the Bright Lady.

"Where's Stephram?" he asked, and the faces around him turned to stone. Once again Cardinal Faren was tasked with delivering unpleasant news.

"It is not the policy of the Church to replace healers who fall in service to a regiment," Faren said, the absence of emotion in his voice revealing just how angry he was. "One might technically argue that Stephram does not belong in that category. Nonetheless, we cannot afford to replace him."

"What do you mean, 'fell'?" Christopher asked. "Did he get killed riding home with Nordland? Can't we just revive him?" Christopher was becoming surprisingly blasé about bringing people back from the dead.

"No, he came out of the Wild alive, if not whole," Faren growled. "But you cannot revive him now. Having chosen to walk through the door, he will not change his mind on the other side."

"What are you saying?" Christopher asked, alarmed. "What do you mean 'chosen'?"

"Exactly what it sounds like," Faren snapped, exasperated at Christopher's lack of subtlety. "When your men came stumbling impossibly out of the Wild, Stephram hung his head in shame for days. And then, while you lay dead in the King's castle, he went into a copse close to the city, slung a rope over a tree, and put his head in the noose."

"But why?" Christopher demanded, stunned and angry. He'd counted Stephram as a friend. How could the man do this to him? Or himself, for that matter.

"I don't know. Why don't you ask him?"

Christopher bit back a retort. It wasn't the Cardinal's fault. And Faren had counted Stephram as a Brother, too.

"I was serious," Faren said after an uncomfortable silence. "Necromancy is barred to us, but not to you. If you would have questions, then look to his ghost for answers. The experience might be salutary for you. Not for me," Faren added sourly. "I know all I need to know. But perhaps you should test your new powers, while you are still in safe lands."

So now they stood in a little wood, on the edge of farmlands that surrounded the city. The tree they faced looked innocent enough, under the shining sun, the warm summer breeze ruffling its green leaves. It did not seem auspicious circumstances for speaking with the dead.

"His corpse is already ash," Faren said. Raising zombies was another ugly possibility in this world; burning bodies was a standard precaution. "But this is the site of his death, and you know his name and the time of his passing, so you have what you need, I think.

"Understand," the Cardinal warned, "it is not really his spirit you summon, only a seeming. The dead cannot form new thoughts or hold feelings beyond the length of your spell. Yet they retain the will they had in life, and Stephram died angry, so be prepared for hurtful words. Remember that this is only a shadow of our Brother, and not the wholeness of his life and deeds."

"What about harmful actions?" Torme asked, pale-faced. He was the only other person present and clearly unhappy about dealing with ghosts.

Faren was unmoved. This was practical theology, after all, and therefore fell under the domain of educational activities, which excused all manner of dangerous shenanigans. "It is not a real ghost," he said dismissively, "only an illusion. In any case I think my power is sufficient to deal with ghosts."

Christopher was not so sanguine, but he had to learn to master the abilities his rank had bought him. Better here with the Cardinal at his side than later. The process of gaining ranks was a surprisingly empty feeling; the only definitive change was the broader selection of fiery pictographs offered by the hallucinatory animated suit of armor during his morning trances. These represented spells, increased privileges of serving the Marshall of Heaven opened up by his advanced rank. Now he chanted the words of one of the newest ones and was unhappily rewarded with a wisp of unnatural mist rising from the ground. The quality of sunlight seemed to fade, and Christopher thought to feel a coolness in the air, as if some old and musty basement door had been opened.

The white vapor condensed into a credible vision of Stephram hanging from a tree by the neck, his hands bound behind him. The body twitched and kicked, slowly suffocating, and Christopher leaned forward automatically to help. But the Cardinal put out a hand to stop him, shaking his head sadly.

"Stephram," Christopher asked, "Why? Tell me why?"

"Because I did not make the rope long enough, so I strangled instead of snapping my neck. Hence the twitching." The ghost of the corpse spoke with unrelieved spite.

Christopher was only allowed five questions, and the witness was definitely hostile.

"I meant, why did you kill yourself. Tell me what drove you to suicide."

"I didn't drive, I walked," said the ghost. The spell compelled it to a more stringent answer. "Shame, Pater, shame at my cowardice."

Christopher had been a Pater while Stephram knew him, and the title was surprisingly painful, evoking the memories they had shared as first-rank priests in an army of farm boys.

"You were only following orders," he objected. "There was no shame."

"It is fruitless to argue," chided Faren.

The ghost answered anyway. "I abandoned a Brother in the field, at the behest of a mere lord. If I had stayed, I would have been a hero; instead, I was craven and disloyal, a figure of pity. I blamed Nordland, of course, yet I also blamed you, for the mere crime of surviving."

"But how does this equate to you killing yourself?" Christopher asked. "You knew I would forgive you."

"I did not want forgiveness, I wanted revenge. And now I have it." The leer aimed for grisly triumph. On the face of a dead man it only achieved the pathetic.

"Revenge? How?"

The ghost laughed, cruelly similar to Stephram at the dinner table telling a joke. "My death is punishment on you both. Nordland fled a coward, though no one dares to say it to his face. But my corpse cannot be denied, and many will say that Nordland should have joined me here on the tree, purely out of shame. I had the courage to name him craven by my deed.

"And you, Brother, I have also struck from beyond the grave. Now Nordland can never forgive you. My suicide will be a lasting chain that will bind his anger and guilt. I cannot be revived, so I cannot be forced to recant or induced to forgive. I stand as a bar between you and the Duke, and he must hate you for as long as I am dead. As will I."

The spell was done, the questions exhausted, and so was Christopher. The mist evaporated into the daylight, and the tree stood innocent and silent once again.

"Suicides are ever vainglorious," Faren grumbled.

"Why can't he be revived?" Christopher asked, struggling against his emotional fatigue and trying to create some room for denial. "I committed suicide, and you brought me back."

"You did not. You struck against your enemies through your act. Bringing you back let you continue your fight. Stephram can only lose his battle if he returns. And because he cannot form new desires, he cannot give up his wicked goal. Those on the other side do not change. Remember this," Faren admonished, "before you send anyone else there."

Christopher blushed in terrible shame. He'd shot a man, on the march home, for not walking. He had been irrational after two days of grueling travel and inadequate food and shelter. That hardly served as an excuse. He hadn't lost any more men to immobility. That didn't seem exculpatory, either.

Faren took pity on him. "The lad returned. He was in the act of returning home at the time, anyway, so the risk was low. The two you lost were no fault of yours. And yes, I know you dared not ask, but Karl lives also." Karl the two-time veteran was the real leader of the army, a young man of such gratuitous courage that it made Christopher's stomach ache. The release of tension made him faint-headed. He could carry on without Stephram, but without Karl he would have been utterly lost.

Climbing on his magnificent warhorse, the stalwart Royal, who had carried the dead on that march instead of Christopher, he reflected that he had gone to war and lost only two young men whose names meant little to him, boys he could not even picture out of memory. The quality of his relief shamed him.

3

RETURN OF THE PRIEST

Faren's carriage escorted him and Torme all the way to Knockford, ostensibly on its own private business, the presence of the highly ranked Cardinal guaranteeing no unpleasant surprises. They rode into town without fanfare, the guards at the gate acknowledging them with only brief formality, but inside the walls of the church Christopher was ambushed by happy faces.

"We have a lot to discuss," he told his business managers. Tom was grinning to see him back in one piece. Jhom, more reserved, was still obviously relieved; even Fae smiled at him coolly. Karl, of course, nodded a minimal greeting, as if their recent mutual deaths were not worthy of comment, and immediately countermanded his alleged superior officer.

"Not today," Karl said. "Your regiment requires your attention first."

There was something wrong with the way Karl said it, the smallest hesitation that should not have been there. Christopher wasn't sure why, until Tom spoke.

"He's a Curate, now, Goodman, not a foolish young Pater anymore." Tom made it into a joke, on both halves. In the middle the point was clear. "Mayhaps he'll not be so hurried," he added.

Christopher was already speaking. "I'll be back tomorrow," he told them, accepting Karl's judgment as his own. "I can tell you this much: in a few weeks, we have to start training the next year's draft. That means you all have to double your production." Jhom finally looked almost happy; Fae pursed her lips. That was going to cost him, he knew, but he had no idea how much, or even what currency it would be in. The woman was like that.

Then he followed Karl to the stables, where his officer corps waited for him dressed in full military regalia. At least they had polished the ugly black from the armor they had taken from Bart's defeated knights, and it shone an honest and neutral gray. The rifles attached to their saddles looked out of place next to the steel plate and chain, but only for a moment.

Karl looked at Torme and waited.

"Faren felt I needed an assistant," Christopher said.

Torme explained for him. "I am an Acolyte, Goodman, though I once served as a Knight." In a few words, Torme told Karl the information he needed that Christopher hadn't thought to convey. Now Karl knew the man's rank and his powers, and also that Torme understood what Karl's position was.

Just to make it perfectly clear, Christopher spelled it out. "Karl's title is lieutenant; he is my second-in-command." Assigning command or political power to a person without rank was unprecedented in this world. Torme, to his credit, didn't raise an eyebrow.

But Karl ignored the exchange with his customary dispatch, and Christopher was comforted.

As they rode out of town, they passed carpenters in the act of building a guard post for the handful of armored men who watched the traffic. Christopher shrugged his shoulders questioningly.

"The Vicar has made some adjustments to her security," Karl answered, with a glint of satisfaction in his eyes. Christopher was glad now that he'd escaped town without having to see her. She wouldn't be pleased with the adjustments, and she'd almost certainly blame him.

A few hundred yards from the village of Burseberry, an officer broke out of the cavalry column and galloped ahead to summon the regiment to inspection. Christopher was impressed at how closely they had timed it. Although the troops had only minutes to prepare, they were already in parade formation as he rode into the empty field that had become their drilling grounds. The barracks and barns of his military camp were unchanged, as was the stone chapel at the heart of the village just to the north, but he did not recognize the regiment before him, despite the familiar faces it wore.

Where had his rowdy boys gone? What mischievous sculptor had left this wall of stone, of ramrod-straight backs and squared shoulders? They stood in ranks, unmoving, the boisterous lads turned into toy soldiers, stiff and precise. On command, with flawless unison, they saluted, two hundred throats bellowing, "Sir!" in greeting and obedience. In the bright spring air they stood clean and firm, uniforms in perfect order, bayonets and helmets sparkling, boots shined without blemish.

Gazing over his army, he was consumed by a wave of pride. It radiated out from them, magnified and reflected by the watching village, and he was the focal point. He had taken them into the Wild and brought them out again. He had faced them against monsters and won. He had stood with them where heroes fled.

And now they stood for him, waiting.

Driven by a triumph steeped in bitter dungeons of cynicism and cruelty, he barked at the silent ranks. "You no longer serve Nordland," he told them and thrust high the commission from the King. In the perfect quiet the crackle of the parchment in his fist could be heard across the field. "Now you serve *me!*" he shouted, and the wall shattered like glass, exploding into bellowing cheers, arm-waving leaps, the deafening pandemonium of victory. And this, too, was a sigil of his power over them.

He went inside, leaving the officers to deal with the disorder, struggling to contain his own emotions. The heady wine of power made him dizzy, and he could not afford to lose his step. Perhaps here, it would not matter so much, yet even that impulsive display of his absolute command had been foolish. Who knew who was watching?

Karl was, for one. "You have something I have never seen before," he mused. "Not loyalty; a peasant's life is worth little, even to himself. To pledge it in the service of a lord is no great matter. No, you have something else." Karl's gaze pierced distant clouds on far horizons of possibilities. "You have their *attention*." He did not speak the rest of his thought, because he did not have to. He already knew that Christopher understood that with power comes responsibility. He already trusted Christopher with more than their lives.

And then the tension melted under the teary grasp of a young woman. Helga had become like a sister, and she hugged him like a brother returned from the dead. Both of them were orphans, her in the conventional way, and he in the loss of his own world. Only last year they had lived in the little stone chapel like simple peasants. Now he had an army under him, and she had her own battalion of cooks and servants to feed it.

With old Pater Svengusta, of course. "A Curate now, in less than a year! What a load of trouble that will cause. Every young buck will want to join the Church of Rapid Advancement. You'll be drowning in hopefuls, and how will I get any sleep then?"

Torme did not blush, although Christopher thought his bow was a little stiff. The poor fellow would just have to get used to Svengusta's joking.

"Pater, meet Acolyte Torme, newly of the Church of Marcius," Christopher said, just to watch how the clever old man squirmed out of this one.

"Well, that's not so bad then," Svengusta said, "at least he's quiet. If they're all like this, I suppose we can manage." He winked at Torme, offered him a mug of ale, and their friendship was sealed. Christopher wished, not for the first time, that he could lug Svengusta around to do his politicking for him.

Then there was paperwork, despite the dearness of paper. He had to look over the supplies, to see what they had left, while Karl explained how they had got on without him. Little Charles, the young man he had recruited early because of his rare ability to read, had lists of expenses to go through and disbursements to be signed, and in the process he could not help but show off his new fingers. But he didn't look any younger from his regeneration, being only sixteen in the first place.

"That's the first time a boy has come home from war with more parts than he went to it with," Svengusta cracked. The joke did not shake the adoration beaming from Charles's face.

"You're still quartermaster," Christopher warned, "too valuable to waste on any further heroics, until you teach others to read and write." And then he remembered Torme and immediately plunged the poor man into the morass.

Kennet was deeply changed by his experience, no longer a gawking teenager. In the last year he'd put on another two inches and two dozen pounds; he was now larger than Christopher, an imposing manly figure who was only barely recognizable as the village boy with the townie girlfriend that had started Christopher down the path of duels and armies. The quiet confidence in his stance uncannily resembled Karl's, but the devotion in his eyes was no less than Charles's. Even the hardened mercenaries looked on Christopher with unflinching respect. Unnerved, Christopher unconsciously sought out the one soldier who had cause to blame him, the injured man he'd shot on the march. He found him hard at work in their newest barn.

"It's good to see you walking again," he said to the young man, the humor awkwardly buried under relief and guilt.

But the soldier barked, "Yes, sir!" while the blush crept up his neck.

Christopher could not let this go, despite Karl's subtle frown. "I'm sorry, Private, that I . . . did that. I was in the wrong."

"No, sir, I deserved it!" reported the soldier before he realized he was arguing with his commander. Confused, he simply repeated his agreement with whatever was being said. "Sir!"

"He disobeyed a direct order," Karl said. "You were within your rights, both by law and custom."

"But it was an impossible order," Christopher objected.

"Since when has that mattered?" Karl replied with honest curiosity.

"It does now," Christopher said. But he could not reform an entire military culture standing here in a barn, so he swallowed his guilt and moved on.

It was late that night before he could sit down in his chapel, put up his feet, and nurse a fine light lager. The calluses were still coming in. He'd earned a really beautiful set on that terrible march out of the Wild, and now he had to start all over.

"We have to start all over," he complained to Karl. The men didn't have enough ammunition to fight a single battle, not to mention the cannonry and other hardware that needed replacing. The regiment wasn't fit for combat, and their posting in Carrhill weighed heavily on his mind.

"Food and clothing they could not deny me," said Karl, "and your witch makes bullets as fast as she can. But your shop master claimed he was busy with other things. In truth he waited for your return."

That was intolerable. When Karl had served the Saint, no one had doubted his authority.

"I'll speak to them. They have to learn you are in command."

"But I'm not," Karl replied.

The smiths had ranks, even if they were only craft-ranks. Tradition would not let them take orders from an unranked man. But they should know by now that Christopher had no patience for tradition. He tried to think of a suitable punishment for their recalcitrance and decided that the new designs he was going to dump on them would be enough.

Jhom was definitely nervous. He shouldn't be; as the manager of Christopher's machine shop, and the son of the local Vicar, the man had as much prestige as it was possible to get without a noble rank. But Christopher could tell he was nervous from the obsequious way the smith talked to him, working his new title into every sentence. To these people, that was the greatest compliment they could pay you.

"Enough," Christopher said, "I can see you were busy with useful work while I was gone." The Franklin stoves were sure to please the peasantry, once they understood that they would use half as much wood through the winter, but Christopher hadn't come here to save trees. "We need to talk about guns, Jhom. I need lots of them."

"About that, Curate. I did the experiments you suggested. I thought to suggest some changes, if you would be so kind—"

Christopher cut him off. "Yes, of course. Just get to the point."

Jhom winced but took him outside to the firing benches, where a rifle was locked down into a stabilizing block. He started to babble about it while Christopher removed the gun and inspected it carefully.

They had cut four inches off the length and thinned the barrel, reducing the weight by a third. It was in all ways superior to the weapon Christopher had designed. So this was all Jhom had wanted: approval.

"This model performs virtually the same in tests of accuracy, and the breech can stand a triple charge without bursting." Jhom was still pitching, even while Christopher smiled in satisfaction.

"It's excellent, Jhom. Better than mine. Do you still have the targets?" He had taught them the scandalous practice of firing the gun at a paper target, so you had a permanent record of the test. Scandalous because paper was almost literally worth its weight in gold. Or had been; now that Fae made paper industrially instead of ritually, the stuff was as cheap as silver.

"So we should begin producing these, my lord?" Jhom finally looked ready to be relieved.

"Begin?" Christopher complained, just to be difficult. "You should have started making them weeks ago."

"I did not know how many you would require," Jhom answered. Now that the quality had been approved, the smith seemed prepared to forget he had ever doubted it. Christopher let it go, because he had plenty of other things to annoy his engineers with. "How many should we make?" Jhom asked, already calculating his share of the profits in his head.

Christopher grinned. "All of them."

"Come again, my lord?"

"How many can you make? We need two hundred for the men; we'll retire the old rifles as soon as we can." After carrying the heavy rifles back on that long march, they deserved a break. "We need two hundred more for the next regiment. And I'd like hundreds more. Maybe we can start selling them."

The quantities made John's eyes go starry. Christopher went on. "And we need cannon, both replacements and more. And grenades. Lots of grenades."

"We do not have enough machines," Jhom reluctantly objected.

"Then you'll have to make more. Oh, and I have some new things I want you to build, too."

"We do not have enough men," Jhom said with finality. "And I cannot hire more. There are barely enough smiths to do your work and the ordinary work of the town."

This would not do, not at all.

"Can we import them? From other towns?"

Jhom was dubious. "Ask a man to leave his home and kin, just for a job? It seems unlikely that established craftsmen would respond."

Christopher sighed. He was pretty sure he knew what the solution was, because it was always the same. "Then we'll make new craftsmen." Opening the little silver vial he carried—an affectation of the wealthy, like a money belt or a watch pocket—he poured a purple pea out into his palm. It represented a fortune in gold, thirty pounds of the stuff.

To Jhom's wide eyes he said, "I can afford to make five Novices into Journeymen. Will that draw men of quality to us?"

"They'll drag their families with them," Jhom grinned, "uncles, cousins, dogs, and all."

"What about our men? Won't they be unhappy about outsiders getting promoted first?" He'd always hated that in the companies he had worked for.

Jhom considered this angle only briefly before dismissing it. "We can't promote our own men, that won't draw new ones in. It is your tael, Curate, and you have the right to spend it as you will. The men will accept this."

That excuse would get Jhom off the hook, in exchange for leaving Christopher holding the bag. Jhom was a decent man, and he took good care of his employees, but he still was ready to increase his influence at the expense of Christopher's reputation.

Or perhaps that was being unfair. These people were used to making hard choices and living with the results, and they were used to unchecked authority. "Necessary" was whatever the guy with the superpowers said it was.

"Would this work? Announce the promotions and let everyone compete for it, including the out-of-towners. Promote the five best. Then, offer the others a job, since they're already here." Christopher was feeling pretty pleased with his plan, until Jhom drilled it full of holes.

"That will just aggravate everyone, for little gain. Our men will expect to be favored, for their loyalty and time served; the out-of-towners who don't win will just go home. Those who do win will be resented and constantly challenged, since it is only their skill and not your authority that grants them their place."

Jhom took a little pity on him. "The best I can suggest is that you promote one of ours for each new man you bring in. That would please everyone, except your purse."

He shook his head. As rich as he was, he could not afford that. Now he had to choose between fairness and effectiveness, something he had never had to do back on Earth. But then, the society he had lived in was not at perpetual war with inhuman monsters.

"Do what you must," he said, closing his eyes in dismay.

"Can I at least tell them that next year, you will promote five of ours?" asked Jhom, trying to give him an out.

But the Church he served did not tolerate dishonesty. "No, I don't know that is true. If anything, we'll need even more new people. And we can't promote from within and hope that draws more, because we need them now."

"Everyone will assume that eventually you will promote your own, anyway," soothed Jhom, "so this will be almost as good."

Except that Christopher didn't want to promote anyone. Other than a handful of Seniors required for their magical abilities, the machine shop could be run by mere mortals. The men didn't need tael, just training. That was a concept more foreign than the rule of fairness.

Which brought up another point. "What about Seniors? Do we have enough of them?"

Thankfully, Jhom nodded the affirmative. "They need but do a single step, mating the breech to the block." Using the power of their craft-ranks they made the metal run like oil, forming a perfect fit between the machined surfaces and neatly solving one of the worst problems of paper-cartridge firearms. This did mean that the barrels and breeches were not interchangeable, but Christopher was the only one who thought that mattered. Mass production was another foreign concept.

"They'll need to do more than one step for these," Christopher said, pulling out his latest design. The other problem with paper cartridges was the loading time. One solution was a revolving rifle, a cylinder with six breeches mated to a single barrel. A number of them had been man-ufactured in the American Civil War just before the metal cartridge made lever-action rifles possible. But Christopher's industry could barely make enough paper and lead bullets as it was; the technology required for stamping out thousands of brass cartridges was out of reach for now, even if he could figure out how to afford that much metal.

Jhom was fascinated with the drawings of the cylinder action, so Christopher had to warn him. "We'll not make hundreds of these." They would cost a fortune, since they would require multiple steps from the expensive Seniors for each chamber in the cylinder. "We'll call them carbines, because of the shorter barrel." He'd cut a dozen inches off of the barrel; the weight of the fat round cylinder added to an ordinary rifle would make the thing unbearable.

He had another new design for Dereth. He found the Senior smith where he belonged, in front of their primitive Bessemer furnace, supervising a smelting. He had made a sword for Christopher once, the old-fashioned way, by hammering carbon into iron to make a few pounds of steel. Now he poured steel by the ton.

"Isn't it beautiful?" the smith said, watching the fiery liquid run into molds. "We rarely miss the mark now, my lord." Dereth used his craft-rank magic to get the precise amount of carbon in, though he would not tell Christopher how he did it. Just being "my lord" was not enough to make one privy to guild secrets.

"Can you double production?" Christopher shouted over the clatter of bellows and hammers.

"I am not the neck of the bottle," Dereth replied, still enraptured by the glowing steel. "Your Tom cannot dig fast enough for me."

Christopher gave up trying to talk and just shoved some papers into the smith's hands. "Only two or three," he shouted, as he lost the smith's attention to the schematics of his new toy. The little two-inch guns were nice, but having seen the quality of the monsters, he wanted something monstrous, like the five-inch Napoleon sketched out on his papers. Hopefully Dereth had enough experience with casting to bring the beasts to life.

Tom should be the easy part; all he would need was more unskilled labor. Dealing with the irreverent second son of a farmer made into the head of the Teamsters Union was always a joy, so he decided to save it for last, and steeled himself for meeting with Fae, the inscrutable and provocative apprentice witch who ran his chemical industry. Walking through town to her building, the fresh spring air did its part to undo the lock he had placed on all things amorous.

"Shut up," he told a chirping cardinal, preening from a branch in boastful glory. "You're not helping."

4

CHANGING WIZARDS

"Impossible," Fae said. "I already use my magic to the fullest to make your sulfur. I cannot do more with what I have." She was doing that subtle flirting, the kind where if you draw attention to it, people raise their eyebrows at your vanity.

Fae was only the first wizard's apprentice-rank, the equivalent of a smith's novice and thus a fairly cheap employee. "Can we hire others?" he asked, hoping she would give him a different answer than Dereth had.

"No other apprentice would surrender a career in wizardry for you," Fae said, callously dismissive of his stupidity.

"What about Flayn? Can we subcontract it from him?" Maybe the extra business would placate the man.

Fae merely smiled enigmatically, which he understood was her look of total victory, at the mention of her old master. "You can, of course, ask."

The feeling of being bested by a slip of a girl in a sensuous lace frock was enough to drive him to defiance. He resolved to do just that, despite knowing it would be totally futile. His tenacity was wasted, of course. Fae simply smirked as he rallied his forces, consisting of Torme and a few young soldiers, and marched across town. The soldiers were not his idea. Karl seemed to think he needed an escort everywhere these days.

"That is a remarkably attractive woman," Torme said unnecessarily. The man was the perfect servant, almost invisibly discreet and polite to a fault, but Fae was a force of nature.

His boys had been cowed by her profession and intelligence. His men were made of sterner stuff. They did not speak out loud in the presence of their commander, but the leers on their faces were irrepressible.

"Don't even dream about it," Christopher laughed at them. "I don't want to have to dig you out of whatever hole she buries you in." But boys made into heroes lived and breathed dreams, and they didn't even have the decency to blush.

Outside the baroque glass door of Flayn's shop, Christopher steeled himself yet again. Flayn was as creepy and infuriating as Fae was provocative, and both of them were as wily as drunken snakes.

Entering the shop, he reflected that bringing the entire squad with him was perhaps not a politic move, especially since the young men's swagger turned protective and aggressive, responding to his own subconscious discomfort. Behind the counter Flayn had already managed to be rude with nothing more than a glance, and Christopher had to bite back a snide taunt about doing his own shopkeeping now. As he was fishing for some polite opening remark, he happened to notice Torme standing beside him. The man had gone still, like a mongoose ready to strike.

Flayn's gaze faltered before settling into to its customary sneer. "What thrice-cursed god sends you to darken my door?"

"Necessity," Christopher answered, only slightly curious of Torme's reaction. It was what Christopher normally felt when dealing with Flayn, after all. "I require your services."

Panic flickered through the wizard's eyes, a curiously inappropriate response to a job offer.

"They are not for sale to the likes of you," Flayn said.

Entirely unexpectedly, Torme spoke up. "But perhaps freely offered to others?" His voice was hard now, thick, heavy iron, the peasant burr like flakes of rust. Christopher raised his hand to quiet his acolyte, uncertain why the hostility in the room was rising so quickly.

Flayn snapped out a proverb like it was threat. "Geese may quack, but the lord of the manor hears only his dinner."

"Truth is only a spell away," Torme retorted.

The two men were almost shouting at each other, a tennis match spiraling out of control. Christopher put up his other hand to quiet the wizard, a dubious proposition in the best of times, and at this juncture entirely unwise. Flayn reacted to the movement by throwing up his arms, and as Torme went for his sword, the wizard began chanting a spell.

Automatically, instinctively, Christopher began his own spell, but as short as it was, Flayn's was shorter, and all around him men fell helplessly into unnatural slumber.

But not Christopher: this enchantment no longer worked on him, a fact that Flayn could not have known yet. His own spell left his lips and his hand, the tael in his head yielding up the power it had stored, and Flayn froze like a statue, his hands in the middle of some complex and doubtless nefarious act.

In the silent shop, Christopher was at a loss, bewildered by the sudden violence in a place he had thought of as safe, and he had no idea what was supposed to happen next. He kicked Torme in the ribs while he reflexively drew his sword.

"What the Dark?" he barked, and Torme looked up, righteous anger burning the sleep out of his eyes.

"It is the wizard who slept your men at Black Bart's command!" Torme had been working for the other side, then. "I knew not his name or origin, but I cannot forget that sorry ferret face. His hatred of you was so great that Bart boasted he served for free."

That same loathing poured out from Flayn's eyes now, the only part of his body still under his control. If looks could kill, the room would be full of burnt and blasted corpses.

And looks probably could, given a few words, a gesture, and tael. Christopher's spell was only good for seconds, and time was running out the door in sheer terror of a wizard's wrath.

"What do I do?" Christopher moaned, clueless, his anxiety stuttering in impotent hands.

"Slay him now, my lord," Torme pleaded, "while you can. Who knows what devices or spells he may call upon?"

"Disarm him?" Christopher begged, still trying to avoid the obvious.

"How?" Torme said simply, and it was true. They didn't even know what to look for, a bracelet, a ring, perhaps a rock hidden in his shoe. Magic was like that.

Torme probably knew the laws better than Christopher did, even here in White lands. Flayn had attacked them, after all, and of course there was always the consolation that they could bring him back from the dead. Shooting first and asking questions later actually worked here.

Just another hard decision he had to make. Disgusted, he took it out in action, letting the cleanliness of the stroke wipe his mind. But as the wizard's head fell from its instantly limp body, emotion came rushing back, dropping him to his knees where he could not see the stump of the neck pumping out blood. He put his hand to the wall to steady himself and concentrated on not throwing up.

Torme stared at him in wonder. "He was your enemy."

"He was a human being," Christopher choked, gagging.

"Not so much," Torme said. "The only thing standing between him and the Black was courage." Torme might have atoned, but he still thought cowardice a worse vice than evil. Christopher might possibly be the only person on the planet who would disagree.

While Christopher tried to decide what to do next, Torme went into action. Awakening the soldiers, he took effective command, sending two to summon the Church officers, and two to guard the door against intrusion. Then he checked the body to make sure it was still unmoving.

"A good stroke, my lord," Torme said with approval. Christopher couldn't accept the flattery, though. He'd practiced for years on bound reed mats, designed to simulate the high point of the samurai's art—cutting a standing neck in one stroke—and had managed to achieve it on several occasions. But this time tael had guided his hand, so the credit was not his. Not that he particularly wanted it.

Skittering away from the memory of the deed, Christopher's mind found something to analyze, pinning his attention to facts and figures in defense against feeling. Tael had not bound Flayn's neck with unnatural resilience: the man could not have been higher than first-rank.

That meant he could not have been a credible danger to Christopher.

Torme's advice had made the difference. Christopher knew that was no excuse. No one would believe a Curate acted on the will of an Acolyte. He watched the man dealing with the priestess who had arrived, sending her away with casual authority, his suspicion lurking under the memory of Faren's endorsement.

The Vicar Rana was not as angry as she could have been. She was angry, yes, like a kettle boiling the last of its water away in screaming agony, but not as angry as she was capable of. She didn't threaten to kill Christopher this time.

"You swear this," she demanded of Torme again, which was gravely unnecessary since he was standing inside the zone of her truth-compelling spells. "Master Flayn aided Bartholomew in his attack last spring?"

"I swear it, my lady," Torme said.

The lady glared at Christopher from the judge's bench, obviously misinterpreting his anxiety. "No need to summon your Cardinal to this perch," she growled. "The law is clear. The violence of the ranked are beyond my jurisdiction. Your prize is safe."

"Flayn attacked me!" Christopher protested.

"You did not have to kill him—" and at first he thought he had said it himself, his guilt was so overwhelming "—but if you had not, then you would have made us do it. Honestly, we should be grateful to you for doing our dirty work." She was not grateful in the tiniest, littlest bit. "His tael is yours. As is his shop and all his worldly goods, forfeited by his stupidity and royal law."

"Can't we revive him?" Christopher asked, looking for an escape from his culpability. "I can pay for it."

"Why in the blazes would we do that?" the Vicar thundered. "In any case, I cannot believe he would come at our call. Would you go to the summons of a Dark priest?"

She shook her head in disappointment at his childishness. "Not every broken pot can be mended. If you do not like the consequences of your actions, then I suggest you act more carefully. In any case, now you must clean up the shards. Dispose of that body, at your own expense, and take possession of his demesne. I leave it to you to disarm the traps he doubtless left there, without causing harm to my town or my people." The subtle emphasis left room for him to cause all the harm he wanted to himself. "Should his master come seeking vengeance, do not look to me for defense."

Court adjourned, the small crowd spilled out into the street. Karl was deeply satisfied and did not hesitate to give due credit to Torme for the profitable outcome. "Once again they put a weapon in your hand and you strike unerringly," he said to Christopher. Lowering his voice, he went on. "I almost suspect the Cardinal of suspecting . . . but no matter."

"Master?" Christopher bleated. "Vengeance?"

"True enough," Karl mused. "I don't suppose the wizards will approve."

The Lord of Carrhill was a wizard. Christopher's program of diplomacy seemed poised to sink in the harbor.

"Burn it," Torme suggested. "Just burn the accursed shop to the ground, body and all." Nothing had been touched, yet. The crime scene investigation had consisted of the Vicar looking in the shop and shaking her head in disgust. After that, the door had been barred, and now the place was Christopher's problem.

"Perhaps it would be safer that way," Karl said, "yet on the other hand, you must learn to deal with wizards and their craft. This may be the only time you can plunder a magic shop at your leisure."

Hadn't he already hired someone to do his wizardry for him? "Fae. She was an apprentice—she was *his* apprentice. Shouldn't she be able to help?"

"Flayn's traps are probably less dangerous," Karl said. "But as you wish."

The arch of her pretty back broadcast her triumph. Subtly, of course, as was her nature, although the effect it had on her décolletage was not so subtle. Hat in hand, metaphorically speaking, Christopher petitioned his putative employee.

"Flayn shared few of his secrets with me," Fae demurred, "and even if he had, I am of little use to you as an Apprentice. To separate the wheat from the chaff, and the harmful from the insignificant, would require a true wizard."

Torme frowned. "No wizard is going to help the Curate sack another's shop," he quite logically objected. Christopher sighed as the man played directly into her hands.

"If I make you a wizard," Christopher said, giving up the argument entirely, "can you increase gunpowder production to the levels I require? And dispose of Flayn's shop? You won't have time to run it." Killing a wizard was bad enough, Gods forbid he should bankroll their direct competition.

Fae wanted to savor her victory, but the lure was too great, the dream she had thought forfeit within unexpected arm's reach. The habits of a lifetime asserted themselves, and she dropped to one knee, spreading her arms in supplication. "I swear my service, my lord. I will bind my future to yours, for as long as you will have me." The shining in her eyes made it hard for him to concentrate, and the abject surrender of her pose completely unbalanced him.

The women working in the shop grew still and quiet, while Torme struggled not to stare. Karl, of course, was just Karl.

"I suggest you accept, Christopher," he said conversationally. "Wizards rarely pledge fealty beyond apprenticeship."

"Then—why?" Christopher could not fathom this sea change in the woman.

"Your advance is rapid," Torme softly explained, "and your purse is generous. Many will kneel to clutch at your cloak, to climb up the ranks in your shadow.

"Not all will pledge to your cause, as I have," he added with only a very little defensiveness, "but there is no shame in pledging to your rise. The crumbs from your high table are fortunes to the low." The cost of rank doubled every step; for the price of Christopher's last promotion, they could have made thirty-two first-rank wizards.

"I'm not going to be promoting people willy-nilly," Christopher objected in plain contradiction to the fact that he had been promoting ordinary craftsmen since he'd first gotten his hands on tael. "I've got big plans, and I need all the tael I can get," he said with just a little defensiveness of his own. After all, craft-ranks were a fraction of the price of a professional one, and their skills were necessary to his schemes.

But Fae was part of his plans, too. He needed her magic, and she knew it. He had already made this commitment and accepted responsibility for her career when he'd hired her away from Flayn. "What does this bind me to?" he demanded angrily.

"You are bound to promote her as her service warrants," Torme said, "or so is the rule in my experience." Torme had the most experience, having been both warrior and priest now. "Of course, there is sufficient wrangling over the niceties to strangle a pig. I cannot imagine it would be less so with wizards."

"Do with me as you will, my lord," Fae said, and arched her neck in submission, exposing her fine white throat. Christopher had the very concrete experience of being trapped between a rock and a hard place.

"Get up, Fae," he growled in defeat. He wanted to lather on the disclaimers and exceptions, but he knew it wouldn't matter. No speech he could give would trump their ancient customs. In the brief flash of her eyes as she stood, he thought he saw something like genuine happiness, and his tongue was stilled.

"You should probably promote Torme, too," Karl suggested that night over dinner in the chapel. The stone hall, still the biggest room in the village, no longer served as sleeping quarters for a gang of boys or as a chemical refinery. Without conscious intent on Christopher's part, it had become the center of his empire. For a medieval lord, that meant it served as reception, lecture, and dinner hall. Mealtimes were not such simple affairs here; a lord showed who mattered and who didn't by who got to sit at his table. For Christopher, this had grown to be a very large table. "A first-rank would be adequate to the ordinary scrapes and bruises the regiment sustains on a daily basis."

"Cost," Christopher grumbled through a slice of bread. His lurking distrust made the argument seem more compelling, at least to him.

"A strange Church you have, Brother, that promotes wizards ahead of priests." Christopher couldn't tell if Svengusta was really objecting or just bringing the topic up to be dealt with before it rotted into something truly ugly.

"I do not question," Torme said, alarmed that anyone might think he did. This annoyed Christopher even more. Living under the likes of Black Bart had left the man with a far too healthy dose of respect for authority.

"You should," Christopher told him. "I'm not going to cut your head off for asking questions, but if you let me walk into snake pit without speaking up, I might. After all, Faren sent you to me to give advice." Advice he wasn't sure he wanted to take.

"The regiment normally has two priests of the Bright Lady," Karl continued. "Whose time is not consumed by the duties of command." Damn it, whose side was he on? Well, the regiment's, of course.

"We have an entire new regiment to outfit, come this winter," Christopher countered, "and an old one to almost totally reequip. Plus I'm having some new, more expensive toys made. So, cost."

"Speaking of new recruits," Karl changed the subject, his opinions having been made known, "I am surprised they are not here yet."

"Who?" Christopher asked, confused. The new boys wouldn't start training until midsummer.

"The hangers-on, my lord," Torme explained, "the shiftless, the landless; free-booters and mercenaries. Because you are White, and a priest, they know they can expect healing and fair treatment."

"Because you spent a fortune reviving commoners," Karl said, "they will flock to you like fleas to a dog."

Svengusta tried to rescue him. "Because you will not pay them, they will flee just as quickly." The men currently under his command were draftees, compelled to service for three years. Only Karl and the senior officers drew pay.

"I want to start paying the men," Christopher admitted sheepishly. "Not much, a few gold a year. Just some pocket change."

"Which they will squander on women and drink," Karl objected.

Nobody had paid him for his two draft terms. "Do not waste your money."

"It is not entirely without profit," Torme intervened. "A salary excuses the Curate from expectations of sharing the spoils."

The man was sharper than he had appeared. And apparently taking to heart the command to raise unpleasant questions.

"It's true," Christopher sighed, though he hadn't exactly thought of it in those terms until now. "I am not going to promote any warriors." Tael was too valuable to waste on mere physical strength. He had guns for that.

Torme looked at Karl with obvious concern, and perhaps even sympathy. Karl was pretty clearly the kind of guy who normally got promoted to warrior-ranks. But Karl's face was bland, and Christopher knew that the young man wholeheartedly approved of his policy. It was a position far too foreign and difficult to explain, so Torme would just have to deal with it on his own.

Everyone else, of course, already understood. Even the officers, the men who had come to him as mercenaries and now served as draftees, had long ago unconsciously accepted that they would never rise in Christopher's service. They could not climb over Karl, and Karl was not going anywhere, not even to the first craft-rank of the warrior profession, a relatively trivial expense. In fact, several of the men had gone down the ladder, having died and been restored to life but not to their craft-ranks. Although they weren't complaining about it.

Torme papered over the awkward pause in the best possible way, by changing the topic. "Some of those who seek to serve will already be ranked," Torme suggested. "One can rent for cheaper than one can buy."

"And buy you must," Karl said. "It is unheard of that a man of your standing should be served by none lesser. Tongues will wag and for good reason: you are exposed. The love of your men is little buffer against the powers of rank." The Invisible Guild had powers that confounded common sense, or so people kept saying.

"Get me Gregor," Christopher said. "We know we can trust him. Maybe we can finally afford to hire him."

"I do not think a knight of his stature will serve for salary," Karl said. "You may have to accept fealty from more than just your witch."

"You are going to take her with you, I hope," Svengusta said. "A sharp bird like that should be kept under a close hood."

"Erm, no," Christopher said. "She still has work to do here." Also, he wasn't sure he wanted to find out which bond was stronger: her oath to him or her loyalty to the wizards. Specifically, the wizard of Carrhill.

Svengusta shook his head in dismay. "As if she wasn't enough trouble before, when she was just a nose-in-the-air shopgirl. Now she is a Darkling wizard."

"Pater!" objected Helga. She did not tolerate that kind of speech at her table. Also, she seemed to like the woman, which mystified Christopher completely.

"She won't be a wizard until tomorrow," Christopher said, as if that were any solace. "But she's going to help me go through Flayn's shop. Maybe he left us a surprise."

"Oh, I'm sure he has," Svengusta laughed. "Just as sure as I am that it won't be nice."

Fae bowed to him with rigid formality. She had always held herself above ordinary folk, despite having been born one, and now she exuded the reek of power. Christopher was of half a mind to throw a snowball at her head. But he did not have the heart to deny her the playacting that went with her new status. He had not spent all his life in dreams of this moment. Fae was no worse than a starlet with her first international blockbuster, or even just a community theater celebrity with her first rave review.

"Mistress Fae," he said, knowing the title would please her, and seeing his reward in the thin smile that threatened to become genuine, "are you prepared?"

"Yes, my lord," she replied, and he supposed he would have to accept that title in return.

"Good. Then tell me what we do." He only had so much formality in him.

"We may enter the shop," she said. "I am certain that much is safe. If your men could undo the door. . . ." They had nailed it shut with broad wooden boards and now came forward with crowbars. Once they had pried it free of obstacles, Christopher reached for the handle. Torme leaned forward and stopped him.

"You are not expendable, my lord," he said. Before Christopher could rebuke the man for his gracelessness, Fae opened the door.

This is what Faren had sent the man to do, but Christopher didn't have to like it.

He followed her inside, at a distance of ten feet, which seemed acceptable to his sentinel.

"We will require no others," Fae announced, and Torme closed the door behind them, staying outside. At least he didn't throw a motherly glare at Christopher.

"You have prepared your detection spells, my lord?" Fae asked.

"Yes, and stop calling me that." There was no audience here.

"Of course, my lord," she agreed, ignoring him completely. "Let us examine the body first. Here in the public area of the shop there should be no dangers."

She coolly gazed down on the decapitated body of her former mentor and paramour. Christopher still found the scene sickeningly unreal and had to struggle not to look away. Fae chanted a brief spell, knelt to the body, and passed her hands above it in a searching manner. She tugged open garments, obviously looking for something specific, and her impassiveness was not enough to block the satisfaction when she found it. From a loose sleeve she withdrew a thin wooden wand with a sparkling red gem affixed to the end.

"What is that?" he asked, already guessing it was what Flayn had been reaching for.

"One of the few secrets he did reveal to me. Men are so boastful." She laid the wand across her arm, admiring it.

"And it is?" Christopher prompted.

"It is only because I have sworn fealty to you that I may tell you my secrets. It is only because Flayn is dead that I may reveal his. Do not blame me for not having told of you this before, Christopher." Funny how when she wanted something from him, she was able to remember his name.

But she still hadn't told him what it was. He pointed at the wand and shrugged his shoulders, trying to drag information out of her with his bare hands.

"A wand of fire," she said, and though he did not know exactly what that meant, he understood from her tone why she had to seek forgiveness for not telling him.

"It is old, though, and close to exhaustion. Otherwise Flayn could not have afforded it. He did not know how many charges remain, and I cannot know either. There is at least one; quite likely that is all there is."

"How dangerous is it? Could he have killed me with it?" Christopher asked.

"You are only fifth-rank," she said dismissively.

That was a resounding yes, and he looked at the wand with appraisal. Something like that could come in quite handy on the battlefield.

Fae saw his glance but stopped herself from defensively covering the wand. She was going to at least pretend she might let him have it.

"You cannot use this device," she said. "Only wizards can."

"And the Invisible Guild," he said, mostly because that was about the only fact he could offer to the conversation.

"Yes," she grimaced, "I suppose they can too. But they do not know the command word, and I do. I beg of you, give it to me, for my defense. I will make many enemies in your service, and you will not be here to protect me."

"How do you know the command word?" he asked, curious.

"I convinced Flayn to tell me, once." The brief flash of disgust on her face convinced him he didn't want to know more.

"About enemies," he said, conceding. "What about Flayn's master? Will he come after either of us?"

"Wizards are not servants of a common cause, like you priests," she said, dropping the flattery now that she had won her argument. "They are bound only by power and knowledge, and Flayn had little of those to offer." The wand disappeared inside her sleeve, like a hermit crab into a new shell. "You have made no threat to the guild. They will not trouble you on the account of a first-rank shopkeeper."

"What about you?" Christopher asked. "Is your promotion legal?" Even the craftsmen had rules about promoting people.

"I can read his spell-book," she smiled in triumph, "and I have the tael from his head. Killing one's master for rank is time-honored and legitimate, if not particularly auspicious. No one will deny me."

"Actually, we don't have the tael yet." No one had harvested it, and he was hoping Fae would offer to do it.

"A technicality, which I will now remedy." She chanted the words that drew the purple essence from the severed head and gravely handed the nugget over to Christopher. She didn't ask for a share, which he suspected meant she either wanted something else or the wand was worth more than she had let on.

"You get his spell-book, too?"

"Yes," she answered, "for without it I am but a glorified apprentice. It is of no value to you; you could not sell it, nor could you buy its replacement for me. Had I earned my rank in the usual way, he would have given me a selection from it. Now I get it all." But she was gloating out loud, so she changed the subject.

"It is most likely protected by a ward. But Flayn was only first-rank. He could not cast his own wards or afford much from others. You should use your spells now, to search the general quarters, in case he put up something new after I left. I will save my remaining magic for his bookcase."

With her guidance, they swept through the back of the shop and then up the stairs to the living quarters. The mess was substantial, including dirty dishes in the sink. Flayn had not replaced his house-maid *cum* apprentice.

"I thought you told me once that every man you had slept with had a wife," Christopher asked, too curious to realize how impolitic the question might be. "Where is Flayn's?"

"I was not counting him as a man," Fae replied absently, studying the bookcase carefully. They had found no other traps or magic.

The bookcase was in plain sight. Fae had explained that the Invisible Guild could find anything hidden, so there was little point in bothering. Instead, the heavy leather-bound book lay there invitingly, right next to what looked suspiciously like a coin-box, just begging to be picked up.

"Isn't that dangerous?" Christopher asked.

"Ridiculously so," Fae said. "But if anyone were to be accidentally vaporized, even the Vicar could not hold Flayn accountable. Every child knows not to touch a wizard's spell-book.

"The potential thief must decide if Flayn is bluffing. Either he wards with a spell so powerful he need not bother with anything else, or he pretends to. If the book were chained, or otherwise restrained, then it would be obvious that no fatal magic protected it."

"Does it?" Christopher asked.

Fae cast her detection, touching her hands to her elbows before holding her left hand in front of her face and peering through the circle made by her thumb and forefinger. Christopher thought he saw a glint of light, as if she had palmed a lens. The wizard's arts seemed far more elaborate than his own magic. By know he knew better than to ask about guild secrets, though, no matter how intensely interesting.

"It claims to. There is magic, though I cannot tell if it is illusion or death, which is the entire point of this kind of ward. One version is cheap and harmless, one is expensive and fatal, and both look the same by design."

Wizards were definitely a nasty lot.

"Flayn never boasted of it?"

"No," she agreed, "he warned me, of course, as if I needed warning, but he did not boast. Still, that is a slim bridge, and this gorge is deep."

"Maybe I can break the enchantment," Christopher suggested.

"It should at least be safe to try."

She stood back at the stairwell while he chanted the words of his spell. For him it was a simple matter of reciting the name of the Celestial glyph he had memorized this morning, plus the basic hand maneuvers necessary to direct the spell to its target.

The simplicity often left something to be desired. In this case he could not tell if his spell had any effect; the faint light that suffused the area and then faded merely told him the spell was done.

Fae immediately cast her detection again and then casually walked over to the book and picked it up. "Your god is strong," she said, tracing her fingers on the spine of the book. "No magic is left," and then, betraying her confidence, she closed her eyes while she opened the tome. But nothing exploded, and she relaxed again.

"The money-box?" Christopher asked, and she shrugged indifferently, turning the pages in covetous ownership. He opened the box, shook out a handful of gold. At least she was going to let him have the coins without an argument.

"You'll need to make an inventory, of everything. Use what you can in our industries, but I don't want you trying to run the shop." He didn't want to advertise that she was a wizard; her oath of fealty to him seemed likely to annoy other wizards rather than impress them.

"It would be profitless," Fae agreed. "My time is better spent on your custom than others." Now that she had everything she wanted, Fae was returning to the helpful person he had first hired.

On the way out, he realized that she had helped him in another way. She had made it clear that killing Flayn really had been his only option. Unfortunately, he probably couldn't explain that to anyone, since the wand should probably remain secret. But then, no one else was looking for an explanation.

5

MAJOR TOM

He finally got to talk to Tom, and as always, the man proved to be a font of inspiration.

They were discussing Dereth's complaint about the ore supply. "Shovels are plentiful, my lord," Tom told him with a grin, "but fools to put behind them are becoming scarce. With all the wizards and craftsmen you're making, not many are willing to settle for the honest labor of ditch-digging. Not to mention the heroics," he added, sliding a little seriousness into his tone. "Were you to raise a private company, you'd tempt even our sober townies back to the sword."

"I've been warned that a rabble will be arriving soon," Christopher said. "Could you hire some of them?"

"They'll not see much chance of glory at the end of a shovel. But yes, there should be sad sacks in that lot hungry enough to work for a living. I can probably double my crew, if that is what you desire."

"Triple it," Christopher said. "The more iron you make, the cheaper it gets. And we haven't sold a stove to everyone yet."

"A nice stove it is, too," Tom agreed. "The wife loves it, and loves me the more for it. Your iron toys are fascinating to us all. You can't imagine how hard it is to keep the lads working when your smiths are testing their guns."

And thus the proverbial light went on, although in this world it was a carved lump of rock instead of a glass bulb.

"What if the men who worked for you got a rifle?" Christopher asked. "Wouldn't that make the job more attractive?"

Tom was mystified. "And sure it would, my lord, but what is the meaning of this?"

"Militia," Christopher said, gratified to see there was a word for it in this language. "What if we raised a militia? Armed citizens, for emergencies. Is that allowed?"

"We're not a March county," Tom objected. "There are no emergencies here. But yes, on the border of the realm, even ordinary men tend to keep a weapon close to hand."

"So we tell them they can have a rifle, if they join the militia for five years. They can keep it after that. In the meantime, they have to stick around and serve, and that means they need a job."

"But that means in not very many years, you'll have a blooming lot of men with rifles running around loose." Tom seemed to think he was protecting Christopher's source of influence.

But Christopher didn't care. An armed citizenry was no threat to his plans. Heck, it *was* his plan. He pretended nothing had been said and went on with his scheming.

"Could you run this? Organize the men, impose some discipline and practice? I'll work your men into our schedule, for the rifle training, at least, but I don't really have any officers to spare to run the outfit." Not that it would be a problem. Tom was a veteran soldier, like every man over the age of nineteen in this county, and he ran his crew with a competence so effective Christopher had never even noticed them.

"You mean on top of managing your wagons, my lord?" Tom was saying yes, in his own charming way.

"About that," Christopher said. "How much do you know about building roads—no, scratch that. Learn what you need to know about building roads, and then start with that travesty that pretends to lead to Kingsrock. And you already know the new regiment will require more wagons."

Tom leaned on his shovel and contemplated Christopher, who was secretly pleased to see he had finally thrown the man off-balance.

"That's a lot of arranging you're asking one young fool to do," Tom said.

"I guess it is," Christopher said, pretending innocence. It was something he needed practice at. "I guess I better give you a pretty high title to go with it. How does Major sound?" Of course Tom had no idea what names Christopher had invented for his army organization, but it clearly sounded good.

Tom didn't ask for a raise; he merely stood, dumbfounded. He already knew Christopher would give him one. That wasn't the point. He was going to have a lot of heavily armed men doing what he told them to. On this planet, pretty much as on any other planet, that kind of status was its own reward.

"You won't be needing this again," Christopher said, and with deep satisfaction he took the shovel from Tom's limp grasp.

The first of the oncoming crowd was someone he'd tried to hire before, and failed. The troubadour Lalania had refused to work for him, preferring her status as a free agent. Christopher was shamefully happy to see her anyway, and not just because of her long blonde hair and pretty smile.

"My lord Curate," she curtsied deeply, "I like what you've done with your face." His nose was no longer slightly crooked, his skin now smooth and unblemished, but her flirtations were only for fun. Christopher surprised them both by hugging her.

"Help," he begged. "Tell me everything I'm supposed to know."

"A mortal life is too short for that, but I did not come without presents." She introduced the Baronet Gregor like she was displaying a trained bear, a treatment the armored knight bore with patience.

"You've done well by yourself," Gregor said. He had helped Christopher fight Black Bart several times, including the last and most desperate battle, any of which would have been lost without the blue knight's sword.

"Um," Christopher said, less concerned with past success than current dangers. "I couldn't have got here without your help."

"I can see I should have stayed and helped you more," Gregor said. "I had no idea you had the capacity for so much mischief. I'm sorry to have missed all the fun." The destruction of Black Bart had been somewhat eclipsed by the battle with the goblins, at least in terms of sheer slaughter.

Karl never let niceties get in the way of business. "It's not too late to fix that. The Curate is hiring."

Gregor was a man of action himself. "Partners, or fealty?" he asked.

"Salary," Karl said, and Gregor shook his head in disappointment.

"But if you'll allow me, perhaps I'll hang around and freelance for a bit. It's worked out for me in the past." Though Gregor made a joke of it, Christopher was sure it meant there was a real need for his presence.

"You are always welcome, Ser Gregor," he said. "More than welcome."

"Not many of those who are to come will find salary acceptable, either," Lalania warned.

"Then maybe they'll go away," Christopher said. "Can you tell me what's coming? Are they ranked or just commoners?"

"Some of both, though mostly the latter. Still, I suggest you find a more courteous way to disappoint them."

Christopher latched on to her. "That's the first thing you can tell me."

"You truly do not seek associates?" she asked. "You would travel all but alone?"

"I'd love to have Cannan and Niona." Cannan was the most physically intimidating person he'd met, outside of the monstrous Black Bart. Having him onside was quite comforting. And his wife was a druid of amazing skills and more amazing equanimity. Christopher had become quite attached to both of them while they were all marching around the country, trying to lure the Invisible Guild into an attack.

"An unlikely match to your Church that would be," she laughed, "but they are still in the Wild, and beyond my trace."

"How about Baronet D'Arcy?" he suggested. Lord Nordland's Ranger would be the perfect addition, short of the magical Niona, and he had enjoyed teaching Christopher's scouts his woodsman skills. Lalania just rolled her eyes.

"You would hire away Nordland's liegemen? Have you not done enough to the man? No, Christopher, I will not even inquire."

"Can we get any others like him?" Christopher really wanted an experienced woodsman to keep training his own scouts, but he wasn't even sure where they lived. Niona had merely described her home as being east of Knockford, and Cannan wasn't even from there.

"No Ranger will serve you for salary," Lalania said. "Why do you insist on assuming money can buy everything?"

A difficult question to answer. *Because it can where I came from* introduced topics he did not care to discuss with the bard, like, for instance, where he came from. Helga saved him by announcing lunch and then monopolizing the troubadour with topics feminine, like dresses and fashion. Only afterwards, when Torme and the officers returned to their duties, did they get the chapel to themselves. Helga brought them beer, and Christopher finally got to explain the militia plan to his informal council.

"A clever ploy," Svengusta complimented him. "You cannot raise a paid company without the Saint's consent, which he cannot grant you for reasons political. But you pay your ditch-diggers with jobs and arms, not gold."

"They will be of little value to you," Gregor warned. "You cannot take them into the Wild or deploy them in other counties."

"I don't need to," Christopher said. "I just want them for defense."

"Against what?" Lalania snapped. An awkward silence ensued, so Christopher changed the subject.

"Have my rifles made an impression? Do you think I could sell them to other people?"

"I confess even I am dubious of their value," Gregor answered. "It seems too incredible to be true, though I know it must be."

"The Church of the Bright Lady will buy your arms," Karl promised. "Their police," Karl refused to call the retired and soft men soldiers, "already favor crossbows, and your weapon is in all ways superior."

"But that amounts to only a few dozen," Svengusta said. "In any case, why would you want to arm the regiments of other lords?"

In the new silence, Christopher tapped his thumbs together patiently. Sooner or later they would stop asking him questions he could not afford to answer.

"If Gregor can't even believe it," he asked Lalania, "then what do people believe? Why did the King send me to a choice assignment, if it really is one?"

"They believe you have a Patron," she said. "A powerful entity that aids you in secret, perhaps invisible, perhaps remaining in the Wild to come at your summons."

"He does have a Patron," Svengusta objected. "He serves a god."

"Gods do not intervene so blatantly," she countered. "One does not need to be a theologian to know that."

"It *is* a choice assignment," Gregor said. "So much so that my accompanying you there will arouse no questions at all. Who wouldn't want to do a little hunting in the company of a healer?"

"Especially one with such a powerful, albeit unknown, ally. I think this is the mark, Christopher." Lalania said. "They seek to test the power of your guardian. After all, it might have been an artifact with a single use that saved you before. Hunting ulvenmen is the sort of low-level constant danger that reveals true rank. Why not try the wood with someone else's ax?"

"And if you get eaten by an ulvenman, then their problem

is reduced to someone else's indigestion," Svengusta pointed out helpfully.

"If that's what they want me to do, then I should do something else," Christopher said.

"You mean we aren't going to hunt ulvenmen?" Gregor made a sad face.

"What a perfect opportunity that would be for an assassin," Karl said. "Or an angry lord, with a small but mobile band of knights and an impeccable woodsman for a guide."

"You don't think Nordland would stoop to that?" Gregor said, slightly alarmed.

"No, I don't think so," Lalania said, "but Karl is right. It would be foolish to ignore the possibility."

"So what else do I do?" Christopher asked. The King had all but ordered him to the hunt. "Didn't somebody tell me cavalry was the monster's weak point?"

"Yes, it is," Gregor agreed. "But you have none."

"I have money and soldiers. Isn't that enough?"

Karl actually looked pained. "That is out of my expertise, Christopher. I can only teach boys to ride; I cannot train them to fight from horseback. That is the province of the knights."

Christopher made a face, annoyed by yet another socially imposed restraint on knowledge. Gregor waved it away with one hand.

"It's not that special," the knight said dismissively. "The only thing standing between Karl and knighthood is tael, not ability. I can teach him everything he needs to know."

"A service I can pay you for," Christopher suggested, and the blue knight laughed at having been outmaneuvered.

"Will you charge me, then, for Karl teaching me what he knows? If these rifles of yours are here to stay, then I suppose I should learn how to use them."

"I have no secrets from you," Christopher said, and then had to modify his statement to remain within the bounds of strict honesty. "On that score, I mean." This made yet another uncomfortable silence, but Lalania was back on her game and smoothly changed direction.

"That dispenses with the commoners. Now what of the ranked? Strong alliances keep the peace, Christopher. To be perceived as standing alone invites assault. Because you are not of the Bright Lady, some may think that the Church will not defend you as it would its own. Because Gregor is bound to you only by friendship, they may think that he will not be bound to vengeance."

"We have a saying here," Svengusta interjected, before Christopher had time to register his confusion, "that perhaps is not known to you. *Tael is thicker than blood.* Your retinue would be expected to avenge you, even more so than your kin, and that expectation would keep you safe."

No one had told Svengusta the secret of Christopher's origin; nonetheless he had clearly guessed more than he had ever told anyone else. He had been the first person to speak to Christopher, and he alone seemed to remember that Christopher was truly foreign to this place, needing even ordinary convention explained to him.

But if Lalania was given any more time to think about it, she might be making guesses of her own. Quickly he lurched ahead with the conversation.

"I just can't afford it." Although he didn't know how much tael he needed to get home, it was safe to assume it was going to be a lot. Also, he wasn't trying to make a new group of aristocrats; he was trying to empower the ordinary folk. "And I don't think I can trust anybody who shows up here, anyway."

Lalania sighed. "So you will force us to protect you out of pity and friendship, at our own expense, and make it as hard as possible in the bargain."

"Oh no," Svengusta said. "He could make it much harder. Trust me on that."

The laughter masked, though it could not erase, the blush that crept up Christopher's neck.

"Lala, you're smart," he said. "Figure out a way I can give you some money, too." He'd offered her a salary every time he'd seen her, but she was as prickly about her free-agent status as the knight.

"That's not so hard," she said. "First you open your purse, and then you hand me the coins."

"Will you sing for us?" asked Helga, excited. Christopher was embarrassed at the mercenary transaction, but Lalania smiled indulgently.

"Of course I will," she said, "and I will write Christopher a pretty speech to give his petitioners." Turning to him, she lectured. "The commoners you can defer to Karl, but because I am not your servant, I cannot represent you to the ranked. This you must do yourself, and though they are low, you cannot afford discourtesy. You will say the words I tell you to say, and spend the money I tell you to spend."

Christopher nodded his grateful surrender.

The days that followed were difficult for Christopher. Not physically: the technical details all went well. Every day one or two people would present themselves in his chapel, kneeling before him while he recited Lalania's speech. They ranged from the ragged to the heavily armored, the academic to the muscular, men and women, young hopefuls and aging has-beens. He disappointed them all and then fed them a banquet while Lalania sang and played her lute. The food was fabulous, because Lalania was directing Helga's kitchen; the speech was effective, because Lalania had written it; and the music was elegant and graceful, perfectly suited to an air of sorrowful but necessary refusal. The petitioners went away satiated, if not satisfied. The troubadour turned Christopher's military lecture hall into a refined court of nobility, through genius and unending labor. All he had to do was sit there and act the part.

Which was the difficulty. He did not like playing nobility, even when he knew it was merely an act. And it would be graceless to complain when everyone else was working so hard, so he couldn't even vent. Most of all he worried that Karl might come to think of him as actual nobility. He dared not broach that topic with the young veteran; Karl would be offended at any doubting of his loyalty, and in any case, openly discussing the democratic leanings of his army officers was probably a bad idea in general.

"No," said the latest applicant, a young woman with curly black hair. She was Mary Ann to Lalania's Ginger, cute, petite, and stubborn. "You may not turn me away, Brother."

"Huh?" he said, confused.

"Yes, Brother," she repeated, politely ignoring his gibbering idiocy, "I am entitled to the word, though it is impolite to use it in mixed company. But I am a priestess of the Bright Lady, I am reporting for duty, and you may not turn me away."

"We have not heard of this, Sister," Svengusta smoothly intervened. "You are among friends of the Church, so you may speak freely."

The girl looked dubious, but she had a case to make, and it spilled out of her in a rush.

"Your regiment has no healer. It is the duty of the Church to send two healers with each draft."

"Two were sent," Svengusta gently interrupted her. Christopher was relieved that the old priest was going to handle this, so he just shut up and listened.

"Of which I should have been one," the priestess answered. "I had already received my orders and made my peace with my family. I was to go to the draft. But Brother Christopher was sent in my stead. As unfair as that was, I did not complain." In the way of these priests, she amended her statement so that it conformed to the truth.

"Much." Then she continued, uninterrupted. "But now the regiment has none instead of two. The draft is not optional. One is not allowed to choose to leave it, once sent. Though the Cardinal rules otherwise, I am bound by honor to replace the one who failed you." It was obvious who she meant, even if she did not name names, for fear of speaking ill of the dead.

"Unfair?" Christopher asked, too surprised to remain quiet. "You *wanted* to be drafted?" That seemed highly irrational.

She at least blushed. "I do not seek war. But it is an open secret that promotions go first to those who served most. All of the men have been drafted once, before they became priests. All of our senior clergy served as healers in a draft, and most of them are men because some fools think war is easier the second time around. I would not have my career crippled merely because I am a woman."

Christopher was openly grinning by the end of her speech. A true feminist polemic, delivered from a perky college coed. But she was right, of course. Even Christopher could see that. Vicar Rana was the highest-ranking woman in the Church, and she was crusty enough to have served in ten drafts.

"We must dance the steps we draw," Svengusta said placatingly. "What the Saint rules, he rules for the good of us all."

"On the other hand, I could really use some help," Christopher said. This would get Karl off his back about promoting Torme. "Can we argue this? Can we win this case, Sven?"

"We?" said the old priest, subtly reminding Christopher that they now served different masters, before he took the sting away by laughing. "I suppose I could use the help, too. Your boys are several times the number of clumsy but heavily armed bravos that I normally am responsible for."

"I will press my own case, Brothers," the priestess said, "if you but give me leave to do so."

Christopher was sure he'd changed the nature of the service the draftees normally endured. He didn't expect to lose half his men over the next three years, so the economics that had driven the Church's first decision didn't really apply anymore.

"Yes, Sister," he said, "I do, and I will give you arguments to take with you. Tell Faren I will pledge to revive any of his priests who fall in my service, so he risks little."

"Will you also restore them to the priesthood?" asked Svengusta. The old man never failed to see to the heart of the matter. Raising a person to the first-rank cost five times as much as returning them to life.

"Sure," Christopher said, blithely promising to pay debts he might never incur.

The priestess looked slightly surprised, as if she hadn't expected to win so easily. "I will take your words to the Cathedral, my lord Curate," now that she was done arguing with him he got his fancy title back, "and return to do my duty. I am the Patera Disa, of Samerhaven." Now that they were all in agreement, she would give her name.

"Isn't that next to Carrhill?" Christopher asked. He'd spent a lot time looking over the Cathedral's map collection, such as it was.

"Yes, my lord Curate, it is," she answered.

"Stop calling me that," he said automatically. "Tell Faren that, too. I'm being sent to Carrhill, so I can use all the local knowledge I can get." But of course Faren already knew that.

"My knowledge of that county is limited." She blushed. "Mostly peasant's gossip. But I will serve you faithfully, no matter where your regiment is sent." He had forgotten that Carrhill was considered an easy posting, and so his comment made her look like she had only come forward once it looked safe.

"I'm sure you will," he said, trying to be diplomatic and certain he was failing. She'd just have to get used to him, like everybody else. That wasn't as unfair as it sounded. After all, he'd done his share of getting used to them.

The headaches of trying to get his army back on its feet consumed him with long lists of costs, schedules, plans, and schematics, and he barely noticed when Disa returned and took up her post. Svengusta undertook to teach her what was expected of a combat healer, as he had once taught Christopher. Gregor and Karl were always out looking at horses, Lalania promptly disappeared with the last of the ranked visitors, Charles was thrilled with the task of educating Torme on the bookkeeping, Kennet had wrangled some kind of duty that left him in Knockford town every day and Dynae's bed every night, and even Helga had too many girls to boss around to waste time in chitchat, so two whole weeks flew by until the flow of strangers and problems fell to a trickle, and he could seriously begin to consider marching to Carrhill to take up his own post.

Karl had efficiently dealt with the influx of ordinary rabble, swelling Christopher's industrial payroll and Tom's militia by the dozen. But now he had something he needed Christopher's personal attention for, a group of rough-edged older men standing in a poorly disciplined line.

"Christopher," he asked, "how close to the line do you wish to walk?"

Christopher eyed the gang and answered, "Pretty close. What did you have in mind?"

"These men are leftovers from previous drafts, gone to drink and petty villainy." Karl was unsparing. "But I think I can refurbish them, and I think you can accept them as draftees, since they are still technically citizens of our lands. You cannot pay them outright, but if you put gold on account for them, then I believe they will serve you well."

"How much?" Christopher asked, getting right to the point.

"A pound of gold a year would be generous. Although there is no chance of booty or advancement," Karl was repeating this for the benefit of the men, "you will also be providing them with food, shelter, arms, and the possibility of revival." Raising the men who fell on the battlefield made one very popular with soldiers. "It is better prospects than they deserve and, not incidentally, a chance to serve their Church and Saint."

Another twenty hardened veterans would be quite welcome in his army. But this seemed suspiciously close to breaking the rules.

Karl misread his concern. "You need not pay them anything until the end of their term," Karl said. "They'll take your word for it, as I and the others have. You wear the White, after all."

Those were terms Christopher found hard to turn down. He nodded his acquiescence, but Karl wasn't done with him.

"Then you should see what color they wear."

"You really think that means that much?" Christopher asked, surprised at Karl's reliance on magic.

Karl cocked an eyebrow but was unwilling to argue in front of the men. Christopher sighed and did what was expected of him.

Speaking a phrase in Celestial, he pointed to each man in turn. As he did so, an aura around each swam into view, a magical revelation of the man's current moral development. They were all green, as he had expected: men of honor, if not necessarily principle. One was aqua, halfway to blue, a welcoming sense of rectitude to Christopher's eyes but probably a source of aggravation to his fellows. Many had streaks of yellow, glittering like pyrite in copper, yet not enough to brand them as concerned solely with their own gain.

"I accept you," Christopher told them, "based on Karl's recommendation, and in case it wasn't perfectly clear, I will reject you on his word as well."

Karl dismissed the men, sending them off to find quarters. Before he followed them out, he spoke to Christopher.

"Of course it means that much. Though affiliations can be disguised, it is impossible that such measures would be available to these men. We must guard against changelings and the weakness of ordinary human nature, but that is always true. I do not understand your objection, or why you took from Master Flayn what you will not take from Saint Krellyan."

Christopher had to think about it before he realized that Karl was referring to a loyal servant.

"I know what motivates Fae," he said. "I'm teaching her new things."

Karl shrugged. "The same applies to these men. They should be paying you for the chance to face the monsters of the Wild with a rifle in their hands."

"I don't think they would see it like that," Christopher laughed.

"No," Karl said, almost cracking a grin, "I don't suppose they would either. But they will cost you less than the horses they ride, so do not begrudge their pay."

That would be another bucket of money shoveled out the door. And now it was time to go to town and see how much he was spending on guns.

Karl was impressed with the carbines and immediately filched the entire production for his cavalry. "They'll be our shock force," he said, "firepower on demand. When can you make forty more?" The cavalry regiment had already doubled, filled out by promising candidates from the draftees.

"I was just going to make them for the officers," Jhom objected.

"That's an excellent idea, too," Karl agreed. "One or two in each squad of twenty will stiffen the line against sudden charges."

Christopher had nothing to add. "What he said," he told Jhom. The horsemen would need shorter-barreled guns, anyway. "Put the carbines in the front of the production line."

"Even ahead of the new machinery?" Jhom was just a barrel of problems.

"Yes," Christopher decided. "Delay the new rifles for the current regiment. But you cannot stint on guns for the next regiment, or grenades. Especially not grenades."

"Those come off a different line," Jhom explained. "Now that we smelt iron faster than we can cast it, there will be no delay there. Your cannons will also be on hand in a timely fashion."

"Ammunition?" Karl prompted.

"For that you must see to your witch," Jhom sniffed. "Casting lead into molds is simple enough for even women to do, so I have transferred that entire operation to her."

Christopher couldn't complain. The machine shop needed all the relief it could get, and Fae could certainly take care of herself. It was probably her idea anyway, an expansion of her empire at the expense of the clueless smith.

And how her empire had expanded. The women in her employ had tripled, she was having a new building erected to match her existing one, and she had turned her old workshop and apartment into more industrial space. She was living in Flayn's shop now, and Christopher had to admit the downstairs made an impressive corporate office, even while he flinched at how much she must be spending on all that fine furniture.

"We need to do another bond issue," he told her, trying not to be nettled by her cool professional air.

"I can print them in three days," she promised. "It would be efficient, however, to print the second run at the same time, if you do intend to do one."

"That is a lot of valuable paper to leave lying around," Karl frowned.

"I have asked for soldiers," Fae answered him, "but your officers have turned me down. Perhaps you should personally inspect my security arrangements and decide for yourself?"

Christopher was hard-pressed to imagine anything more boring or less suited to his talents. And he was eager to escape. Fae, always provocative, was more so today. Maybe the romance of spring was affecting her, too.

"I've got to see Tom, so can I leave you two at this?" he almost begged.

"As you wish," she said.

As he stepped out the door with relief, he briefly considered if this was fair to Karl. But the man was made of steel. Not even Fae could break him.

Tom, on the other hand, was only human, which explained his unfortunate relationship with the witch. The man was out at the moment, so Christopher stood in Tom's fine house and awkwardly tried to chat with Tom's homely wife. The woman seemed far more relaxed than the last time he had seen her. Back then, she had been impressed to the point of muteness with his lowly first-rank. Now that he had a serious title, she wasn't awed at all.

She'd been eating pretty well, too, he privately observed, and then it made sense.

"Are congratulations in order?" he asked her, and she blushed in pride.

"Yes, my lord, and thank you."

Christopher unconsciously shook his head, thinking of the trouble Tom would be in if he got Fae equally prideful. In one of those moments of feminine intuition, perhaps empowered by her expectant state, the mother-to-be read his mind with uncanny accuracy.

"Never you mind that," she said with a sly smile. "I've given him something that tart never can. My Tom's a handsome man, and I can't blame him for a bit of pretty, but he'll be home tonight, and every night." She patted her belly with serene confidence.

Christopher was too surprised to think about being polite. "You mean wizards can't get pregnant?" he blurted out. Had Fae traded away the possibility of a family for her power?

"Not off a mortal man, my lord. Everyone knows that."

"Oh," Christopher said, and then stood there stupidly until Tom came home.

"Light of my life, mother of my dynasty, what's for dinner?" the young man cried and lifted the woman easily into the air for a kiss.

"And my love to you, too, my lord Curate, though I'll withhold the kiss if it'll not offend you." Grinning irrepressibly, he bowed to Christopher in his kitchen, while his wife clucked happily, tossing things into boiling pots.

"I wanted to see how my roads were coming along," Christopher said, "but obviously you've got other projects in the works."

"I can do two things at once," Tom laughed, and his wife threw a carrot at his head in outrage. "But let us retreat to the main hall of the glorious mansion you've bought me and discuss manly things over a beer.

"All is in hand, my lord," Tom assured him somewhat more seriously after draining half a mug in one shot. "It turns out that roads are mostly comprised of labor. Which I no longer have a shortage of. My men would like to know when they get their guns, but for now they'll do with just your word."

"Probably not for a year or more," Christopher winced.

"They'll hold as long as you need. In truth it's me that drives the eager wagon. I've always wanted to be a High Commander, with swaggering bravos under my heel."

"So if I give you the command of the militia of the entire town, you'll swell up and explode?"

Tom smiled happily at him. "Like a puff pastry in the wrong oven. But will you really give away rifles to just anyone?"

"Not yet," Christopher admitted, "but eventually, I would like to see at least half the men in the town able to rally to its defense."

"If these weapons are what your lads say they are," Tom said, "that would be a stout defense indeed."

"And probably under the command of the Vicar," Christopher said, "instead of me. Is that going to be a problem for you?"

"I can charm that old dragon as easily as I can whistle," Tom smiled, "or more honestly, I can certainly charm her better than you."

That was undeniable, and Christopher had to grin.

"Speaking of charming," he lowered his voice, "are you still being a fool?"

"The weather's cooled off as of late," Tom admitted, "not that I've minded. But I've been careful not to provoke any wrathful scorning, so I think you have nothing to fear on that account."

"That's good to hear," Christopher said, although Fae in Tom's bed was probably less likely to cause trouble than any other place she could be.

"I'll not ask," Tom said seriously, "why you'll take fealty from a pretty bird but won't hear her sing. It's not my place. But others take note, and an answer might be handy to have."

"I have a wife," Christopher said.

"That's not entirely an answer. Yet you wear the White, and your word is your bond, so I suppose it will do. Why you gave your wife a vow of chastity is another question altogether, one men will likely not ask. Questions like that have a way of sparking foolish notions in others," he said with a broad wink, as his wife brought a plate of rolls to the table. She would have thrown one at his head, but bread was too expensive for that.

6

HARD DUTY

After a long and cheerful dinner Christopher rounded up his posse at the church to head for home. But Karl was missing. A ghost of a worry brushed through his mind. Without any purchase in fact, it drifted away.

Until he got to the shop, to see Karl standing in front of the glass door, the handle still in his hand, and a peculiar look on his face.

"Not you, too," Christopher said. Not that he really had a right to complain about what adults did in their free time.

But Karl did not answer. He let go of the door and stepped into the street, only to stop moving again.

"Rethinking the wisdom of that choice?" Christopher asked. It seemed awfully early for buyer's remorse.

"It does seem foolish, my lord," Karl said. "I apologize. It won't happen again."

The ghost came back with a vengeance, a banshee howl accentuating the unprecedented form of address that Karl had just used.

"Since when do you call me that?" Christopher said, angry and unhappy.

"Since I behaved so stupidly," Karl said, before his face betrayed his confusion.

Anger bled into suspicion, driven by Karl's uncharacteristic indecision. Almost without conscious thought, Christopher cast a detection spell, having had them on his mind since the looting of Flayn's shop.

The lingering trace of magic on Karl erased all misgivings, replacing them with a towering rage. Christopher threw open the door so violently a glass panel shattered, and he blew into the shop like a storm front bellowing thunder.

"FAE!"

She did not answer the summons, and in Christopher's mind her guilt was now clear. Behind him Karl followed, eyes narrowed and jaw set in a grim scowl.

"Fae!"

They went up the stairs, two at a time. Christopher knew he should have felt worried or frightened, but he was too angry.

"Fae."

She sat on her disheveled bed, in a silk nightgown, and tried to answer him.

"Why do you—" but her voice broke, and she looked down at the floor, unable to continue.

"What have you done, woman?" Christopher growled.

"What did you do to me, witch?" Karl snarled.

"You have no cause for complaint!" Fae cried, shocked by Karl's anger. "I gave you only pleasure."

Christopher tried to put a check on his wrath. *Do not let her compound the crime*, he felt more than thought, and so he cast the spell that bound tongues to truth. She watched him silently, her face pale and drawn like a frosted glass vase.

"Did you use magic against Karl?" he demanded, when the spell was live. "Did you lay an enchantment on him?"

"What of it?" she cried, defiant now. "Am I a hideous crone, to sicken him with the deed? Any man in town would gladly take his place. I placed no bond on him, laid no further demands at his door. What man can honestly say I wronged him?"

"I can," Christopher said. "That's rape, Fae. Rape! What would the Cardinal do, if Karl had held you down and done the same to you?"

"He would hang me for the deed," Karl answered, "even for the sake of a foul witch."

"I did him no violence!" Fae sobbed.

"You did violence to his mind," Christopher said. "You did violence to his rights."

"The Church will hang you for this," Karl proclaimed in righteous wrath. "Commoner though I be, I am theirs, and not yours to trifle with. You will hang."

"You dare not!" she screamed. "He needs me. I alone will keep his secrets and make his sky-fire. I am his, and your Church will not touch me, for he needs me."

Even in the midst of the red fury in his eyes; even in the grief and shame he felt for his part in the making of the witch, and thus this terrible ordeal; even through all of that, Christopher could not help but notice that these people spoke in terms of property, not rights. Drawing a deep breath, he put aside his ethical indignation and answered in their language.

"I need you as an apprentice," he told her, "not as a wizard. What I put in your head, I can take out. I can hang you, revive you, and reduce you to just an apprentice again."

"You would not!" she cried, outraged at the expense he dared, but he was standing in the zone of truth too. Her eyes danced wildly, seeking escape. Though her hands did not twitch, Christopher said it anyway.

"If you reach for that wand, I will cut you down and burn your body next to Flayn's."

The pretty face quivered and then cracked, blubbering, all pride and will vanquished in an instant. "Forgive me," she cried, tears falling like lonely raindrops, "please forgive me. The power went to my head. All my life to be a toy, but once to hold another in my hand.

"I am sorry." She wrenched the words from her torn and bleeding heart and then collapsed in a weeping heap, her black hair in disarray, her fine white skin red and crumpled.

"I cannot forgive you," Christopher said heavily, astonished at the hard scales on his own heart. "You must ask Karl for that."

"You'll not get forgiveness from me," Karl laughed barkingly, as if the very concept were absurd. "But I will withhold my judgment, for as long as you serve our master. Should you ever fail him again, I will have my vengeance, and no amount of rank will protect you."

Fae's tears washed her face and Christopher's anger, the flame in his heart slowly quenching under the deluge. Karl stood like iron, revealing neither pain nor sorrow. Christopher wanted to avenge the proud young man, to honor him, but Fae was just a foolish child with a dangerous toy. Flayn had not seen fit to promote her. Christopher had. He could not escape his share of the blame.

"I'm sorry," he said, but Karl would not understand. The soldier would hold only Fae responsible, and Christopher could not even argue with him. Karl had been severely wronged, and he had the right to deal with it as he chose. The truly guilty would just have to accept it.

"I will not fail you again, my lord," she sobbed. "I will earn my pardon, and even Karl the Cruel will not begrudge me. You will see, I am still valuable to you."

Christopher could not afford to feel sympathy for her. "See that you do," he growled, and left the room and the cloying stench of shame.

Outside, in the street, he tried to apologize to Karl again. "I am sorry for the harm you suffered from me and mine."

"Do not trouble yourself, Christopher," Karl said. "Now the witch is truly bound to you, for you can take her head whenever you please. As for me, I am a soldier. I have had worse duties." Christopher was wounded by the perfect normalcy in the young man's voice. He watched helplessly as Karl put his suffering in an iron chest and locked it with chains of unyielding discipline. Not that he expected tears, but Karl would not even acknowledge that he had been touched.

Late that night, finishing the long day in his chapel, he observed a subtle interchange, a brief glance from Karl and a well-disguised flush from Helga. So the man would dress his wounds, refill his self-esteem, and restore his manliness at the girl's expense. Christopher was saddened to see the damage shared around, but what could he do? If he ordered Karl to leave her alone, he surely would, though Helga would hardly thank him for it. Who was he to deny them solace and pleasure, simply because it was driven by hurt instead of love?

He had been disappointed, many years ago, to discover that words could not fix everything. Now he was disappointed again, discovering that even magic could not fix everything.

"You haven't hired the new men yet?" Standing in the machine shop yard, Christopher struggled not to snap angrily. He understood that things moved more slowly in a world without clocks and telecommunications; still, he paid Jhom to take care of things. After Fae's betrayal, he was in no mood to countenance failure on the smith's part.

The smith was unsympathetic, meeting Christopher's glare with a mulish frown of his own.

"I cannot lure men away from ditch-digging when rifles are given as freely as shovels. And my own men glance askance. They ask why they may make rifles but may not wield them."

"So you want a militia program for your shop, too?" Christopher let himself think it all the way through. "But not so much under Tom's command."

"My men do know and trust me best," Jhom suggested humbly. "They already work as a team under my direction."

A chance to recruit the Vicar's son into his militia was too good to pass up.

"I have given Tom the ultimate command. But there will be too

many men for him to oversee them all. The militia will have to be organized into platoons and companies, and he will need other officers."

Jhom was considering it. "What position would I hold, under this
scheme of yours?"

"Second only to Tom," Christopher promised. "Captain of your
own company." He tried to ignore the twinge of conscience at the promotion of officers based on politics instead of ability. Jhom was, after
all, an effective leader.

And a reasonably honest man. He did not try to usurp Tom,
instead nodding his head in approval. "You reward your man's loyalty
with your own. I was second in your service, so I will be second in
this."

Dereth was arguably the second man Christopher had hired, but
it didn't seem politic to bring it up. Fae was certainly the second
employee he had ever had, and that topic seemed safer.

"What about Fae?" he asked.

Jhom dismissed the suggestion with a shrug. "She is ranked,"
the smith said. Professions were a different world. Unfortunately, the
two worlds were not equal; the mundane one that Christopher was
equipped to deal with was so insignificant to the other as to be nigh
invisible.

Just as Christopher was feeling marginally optimistic about facing the
wizard of Carrhill with a smoothly running industrial empire at his
back, Lalania showed up again. He wondered how she managed such
excellent timing. Before he could ask about it, she frowned at him.

"That was not wisely done," she said.

"What now?" Christopher asked in alarm. He had thought the
plan to distribute rifles to the peasantry was subtle enough to evade
attention.

"To slay a shopkeeper is no great matter; to deny a dozen a significant portion of their income is altogether different. The Wizard's Guild seems unlikely to turn a blind eye to yet another offense."

"What are you talking about?" Christopher exclaimed.

"Paper, of course," she said, annoyed at his denseness. "I realize you do your Church a good turn, and turn a profit for yourself, yet the damage seems unworthy of the gain."

"I only sell paper to this Church," he objected, "because there are no wizards here."

She cocked an eyebrow at him. "But I saw your product in Samerhaven and at the Cathedral to boot."

He was completely lost until Lalania set him on the right path.

"Just how much paper do you sell here?" she asked, and he went to saddle his horse and face down his latest betrayer.

The Vicar received him in her office, as cool and urbane as the Sphinx with its secret smile. She answered his garbled accusation with calm precision.

"When a Church has an oversupply of any particular item, it generally shares it with the others. Paper is only a single example. No one can fault me for giving my excess to our sister Churches." Paper that cost her a fraction of the usual cost, now that he made it industrially.

"But how do you profit from this?" *Other than stirring up trouble for me*, he wanted to add.

"I spend what I always have spent, while the other Churches spend nothing. I aid my brethren at no cost to myself. Would you deny me this?"

"The cost is to my reputation," Christopher said sourly. "The wizards will not approve."

"Poor Christopher," she said pityingly. "The wizards cannot hate you any more than they already do. Consider: what do they despise the most? The holy symbol, for our magic competes with them, and the sword, for its power frightens them."

"But my holy symbol *is* a sword," Christopher said, stupefied, as she gently shooed him out of her office.

Disa only made it worse. Having promised to tell him what she knew of the master of Carrhill, she regaled the dinner table with tales of darkness.

"He only comes out at night, draped in black robes. Those who have seen him, a glimpse under the hood or a hand out of a sleeve, claim his flesh is more leather than skin. Few who go into his tower ever come out of it, and those who do speak of a crypt, not a castle. He perfumes himself with saffron, to the point of a cloying stench, and once, when there was no spice to be had, he resorted to garlic. This is taken as proof that he douses himself not to attract but to disguise the reek of decaying flesh. It is said the wizard has ruled from the tower for over two centuries."

"Is that possible?" Christopher asked.

"No," Svengusta declared. "No magic can extend a man's natural life."

"Nobody said anything about extending his *natural* life," growled Gregor. "I have heard a word whispered in connection to his name, but I confess until now I thought it only rumor."

"I have no firsthand knowledge," Disa was quick to remind them. But she had also lived next door to the county, which was more than any of them had ever done.

"What word?" Christopher, as usual, had to ask what everyone else knew.

Lalania could never resist a dramatic moment. Leaning forward, pitching her voice softly so that the word would not escape the table, she whispered the dreaded phrase. *"Lich."*

A collective shudder went around the table. Except, of course, for Christopher. He sighed, and waited like a particularly obtuse child for an explanation.

"Your performance is wasted on our good Curate," Svengusta laughed.

Lalania was too surprised to counter. She stared at Christopher, worried, and causing no little worry in him. If he kept making mistakes like this, he would never have to tell her that he came from a world without magic. She would figure it out on her own.

Torme did his job and rescued his boss. "No doubt they are called differently in your homeland. She means the ultimate creatures of darkness, the masters of the soul-trapped, the ministers of death. They are akin to a zombie, but they trap their own soul in their own body."

"Doesn't that mean their body has to be dead?" While Christopher didn't know much about zombies, this much seemed fundamental.

"Yes, it does. The wizard is so enamored of life that he kills himself to gain eternal undeath."

Then Torme undid all his good work. "What do they call them in your land?" he asked Christopher innocently.

Christopher dodged, answering with a question instead. "Is it possible we didn't have any?"

"Probable, even," Lalania agreed. "They are extremely rare. And I don't believe any decent Kingdom would tolerate such a creature. Surely the King would view a lich as a hunting opportunity, not as a vassal. Our good King might have his flaws, but his dedication to the cause of Men cannot be questioned. And a lich is no longer a man."

Christopher, who had recently spoken with the King, was not so certain of the strength of his principles.

"I would think the fact that the wizard of Carrhill tolerates a

White chapel in his lands is proof he is not a monster of the Dark," Svengusta said.

"It does seem uncharacteristic," Disa conceded. "Still, who knows how a mind like that would work?"

Christopher couldn't help himself. He immediately looked at Torme. The table followed his gaze. The man seemed to take their stares as simple curiosity rather than reflexive accusation.

"How long has the chapel been there?" Torme asked.

"Since the war," Disa answered. "Ten years or so."

"Then it seems unlikely," Torme said. "For the Black to have that much patience is unprecedented. Either he only pretends to be Black, or . . ."

"Or what?" Christopher demanded.

"Or he is a fiend beyond all our experience," Lalania finished sourly. "And since we have no experience of liches, we must now consider it a possibility."

Only Gregor found her words heartening. "This could turn out to be a really interesting trip," he said with a grin.

The cavalry was still in training, so it would have to catch up later. This meant Christopher was marching without Karl or Gregor, and the prospect daunted him. He'd lost a chunk of his officer core, too, staying behind to run the training camp for the boys who would be arriving soon, leaving him responsible for the organization of a two-hundred-man march. Even Lalania deserted him, saying she would make her own way to Carrhill and meet him there.

His worst concern was that without Karl or Lalania, he would commit some inexcusable faux pas.

But of course, that was what he had Torme for. The man would need an officer's title. "I'm making him a lieutenant," he told Karl, "and you a major. I'll make myself a colonel." The names meant nothing yet. Captain was the only title that translated, meaning the head of a company, and you were supposed to be at least second-rank for that. The head of his company could only be himself, so to avoid long and potentially difficult explanations he just skipped that one for now. At least the militia was not taken seriously, and he could assign titles there without raising eyebrows in anything other than gentle derision.

Finally he realized all this self-promotion was just a way of avoiding his nervousness, as was the constant planning. Time to go. "We march in three days," he told Torme, "whether we are ready or not." The deadline made real, things and people and horses fell into place, and on the third day he set out again, like he had only a season ago.

Except this time it was different. The men did not march so much as strut, yet they managed more efficiency and orderliness than he would have thought possible. The road took them through Knockford again, and the mood of the town was also changed. Not a festival, with people admiring the fine uniforms and pretty young men, but a deep and quiet pride. The older men nodded to the young soldiers like they were equals, the women smiled and flirted with grave dignity, and the children stared in open awe.

Christopher could feel the tension generated by this wholly unusual atmosphere, even though the scene seemed normal to him; this was how he was used to people treating men in uniform, after all. But he could not stop glancing around in false alarm, as if a dark and mysterious panther were stalking him from the back-alleys and side streets of town.

The Vicar pounced on him from one of those side streets, where she stood watching the parade go by. Her lips pursed in dismay, she scowled at him, but when she spoke, it was with a soft voice.

"They will follow you to Hell," she told him. "Through the very gates of the lowest plane, singing all the while. Watch where you walk. An army cannot back up."

After this cryptic advice, she pointedly ignored the men and horses clogging her highway, pretending that nothing out of the ordinary was occurring. It was a pretty good act, he judged. It would probably fool the lower gentry. But if there was anyone in this crowd with Lalania's talents, he would be setting off fire alarms across the entire realm. The thought spurred him, so he spurred his horse and his army, and they spent the night on the open road, a few miles south of town, under the brilliant stars and the cool spring air.

7

WELCOME TO THE JUNGLE

They traveled south through two counties friendly to the Church though not under its direct control. He recognized some of the countryside, having chased Black Bart this way on a desperate hope and enchanted horses. The speed he missed, since everything takes forever with men and wagons. The desperation he would have been happy to have not met again. The danger he faced now was less immediate, but it was also unlikely to be solved by a bag of dynamite.

The receptions they got in the towns and villages along the road were not much comfort. No one stared like they had in Knockford, though every so often he saw curious glances, as if a community orchestra, long loved despite its haphazard attention to melody, had suddenly managed to play a piece flawlessly. Too much exposure to this, and those quirked eyebrows might turn into questions.

But then he realized the crowds were only commoners. The local lords and professional classes did not even bother to notice his army. Once again, inconceivability was as good as invisibility, and he finally started to relax.

Samerhaven was a Church fief, and a quarter of his men were from there, but the town met them with the same simple joy that Knockford had shown the first time around, merely admiration for clean uniforms and snappy marching. No dangerous visions slept here, behind inscrutable eyes. Or perhaps they were all just better actors. Except for the local Vicar, a middle-aged man who exuded competence, caution, and the smell of a man under siege. He viewed the army with barely concealed disapproval.

"You continue on the morrow, I assume," he said to Christopher.

"We'll not trouble you, Brother," Christopher replied, without perhaps as much friendliness as the appellation suggested. "We brought our own supplies."

The Vicar did not appreciate his tone, and returned it. "So many pretty frocks cannot fail but to draw the attention of mad wolves, who exist solely to despoil. And my own people will be emboldened, demanding that I patrol my borders with a finer comb."

"Perhaps you should," Christopher said, before he thought about it.

"A man who lives next to a hungry bear does not roast over an open flame," the Vicar answered. "My nest is not safely in a forest of birch." Unlike Knockford, Samerhaven shared borders with counties ruled by the Gold Throne.

As usual, Christopher had to apologize. "I'm sorry, Brother. Yes, we make haste to Carrhill. But my wagoneers will be regular travelers on your roads. Will security be a problem?"

"Send nothing worth stealing in them, and no." The Vicar accepted the apology, though it didn't make him any happier. "Food and ale should be safe enough. Your treasure you must personally accompany."

"What treasure?" Christopher asked, mystified.

"Your winnings from the hunt." The Vicar was almost as mystified. "Unless you plan to keep them for yourself?"

Torme spoke up for his boss. "We serve our own chapter, Lord Vicar, not the Saint's."

"So you do," the Vicar mused, rocking back on his heels. "I am not entirely certain what that means."

"Neither are we," Christopher had to admit. But he could see reflected in the Vicar's appraising eyes how much it would shake up the local politics.

Carrhill itself was a pleasant surprise. The town was girded in stone walls fifteen feet high, and more than one layer of them, all dominated by a tower that was the tallest structure Christopher had seen in this world. Narrow and straight, it reached at least a hundred feet into the air, and at the peak illusionary torches burned permanently.

The local regiment seemed reasonably professional, with plenty of crossbows, pikes, and chain mail. Their commander introduced himself as Captain of the Wizard's Guard, with the respect due to Christopher's superior rank.

"Your men are surprisingly well dressed for the Lady's draft," he observed.

"Thank you," Christopher decided to say. He wanted respect, yes, but the covetous look in the Captain's eyes was a bit unsettling. "Now perhaps you could fill me in on the current situation." He knew practically nothing. The feudal system did not generate intelligence dossiers.

"That idiot Fairweather got himself eaten," the Captain complained, "and his regiment dissolved before the week was up. We hung a few deserters, but then someone claimed we didn't have the right, being as they had no lord, and so the rest slipped away. We were already short the other regiment, for reasons never explained, so your arrival is duly welcome."

"There are supposed to be two regiments here?" Christopher asked. Were they going to send somebody else?

"Usually," the Captain said. "But your Lady's draft regiments are rather larger than normal, and so they count as both from the bean-adder's point of view. Not that I am complaining. A few years ago we had one of yours out here, and the boys were relatively well-behaved and quite helpful at our perennial hobby of wall-building. I presume these fancy clothes will not alter that?"

"I hope not," Christopher said, although he didn't think he wanted his army put to use as free construction labor.

"I confess I would prefer an armored regiment," the Captain said. "And those half-spears they bear are too short for wall-work. You must at least supply them with pikes."

That was one good point about this place. "You need not worry about that," Christopher grinned. "They're more like crossbows than spears, and behind a good stone wall my men are undefeatable."

"I had heard some rumors to that effect," the Captain acknowledged. "But I dismissed them, as I do all rumors. No offense intended, Curate, but I will continue to do so. I am charged with the defense of this town, and I must see to it to the best of my capacity."

Just as Christopher was about to be impressed by the integrity of the man, he continued. "Our local weapon-smiths can fulfill your needs, at a reasonable cost despite the urgency of the order. I know which ones are competent and which ones are charlatans, so you need not worry on that score."

"Indeed," Christopher said, trying not to be too sardonic. "Perhaps you could give me an estimate?"

"I'll send someone to your quarters," the Captain replied. At least he wasn't going to hold his hand out for the bribe here at the gates.

"When do I see the Lord Wizard?" Christopher asked.

The Captain boggled, caught by surprise. "Never, if you're lucky. Why the Dark would you want to?"

Torme came to the rescue. "My lord merely intends courtesy."

"Then let him inflict it upon the Gold Curate," the Captain suggested with a sly smile, a man anticipating a good cockfight.

Christopher had been hoping to win over the wizard, or least see the lay of the land, before facing the competition. But after his dealings with the King, *not* dealing with the wizard was probably the best option.

Their quarters turned out to be huge stone halls attached to the inner set of walls. Although sparsely furnished with tables and bunks best described as firewood, they at least had ample space for the men.

The walls appeared to be made of layered stone blocks, but this was deceptive. The blocks were just a patterned facing carved into a solid piece of stone. Christopher searched the wall for dozens of feet but could find no seam or joining. Just another reminder that nothing here was what it seemed.

The men were settling in well enough under their officers, so Christopher decided to pay the one courtesy call he could count on to be both friendly and genuine.

"I'm going to the White chapel," he told Torme, and slipped out before the man could protest.

The weather was warm, sometimes unpleasantly so. Despite the heat the city did not stink as much as Kingsrock. Perhaps it was because this city was spread out more, not being confined to the top of a rock, or perhaps it was merely that this city had fewer people. Some buildings even looked empty.

Those buildings were of normal construction, made of brick and thatched roofs, rather than the solid rock of the barracks and walls. The people were browned by the sun and favored muted colors and light, loose clothes. They were polite enough when Christopher asked directions, but they were not friendly and gave him as wide a berth as they dared.

He could hardly blame them, walking around with a sword on his hip. It was still uncomfortable compared to Knockford, where he was a local hero, or even Kingsrock, where there were enough swordsmen to render him anonymous, so it was with relief that he slipped into the wooden chapel at the end of a short alley.

The building didn't look like a chapel; it looked like a warehouse that had been repurposed into a sick ward. At the moment most of the two dozen beds were empty. A stout woman sat at one bed, talking to a patient, while a much younger woman intercepted him at the door.

"Please, Ser, put your sword aside," she said earnestly enough, although from her face he could tell she did not expect success.

"It's okay," he said.

"By law, Ser, but our custom is different. We ask that you respect that if you wish to make use of our services."

"No, I mean, I'm one of you." He had worn the thing in front of both the Saint and the King. How could it not be acceptable here?

"Then all the more reason you should respect us," she said gravely.

She was a very small woman, barely more than a girl. He could have squashed her with the flat of his hand. Christopher suspected this was why she had been given this job; there were a few men in the room wearing the white aprons of an orderly, but they were careful not to look his way.

With a sigh at his own ineptness he unstrapped and disarmed. She smiled brightly, almost making up for how graceless he felt, and put the sword in a wooden chest by the door. By then the older woman had made her way to Christopher and greeted him with cautious optimism.

"Do I have the honor of addressing the Lord Curate Christopher?"

"Prelate Oda, I assume?" He reached out a hand to shake with, while she looked at it perplexedly.

"I am, and good welcome to you, Curate."

This was far more formal than he expected. "Is there someplace we can talk privately?" he suggested.

"Of course, Curate." Oda led him through the room to double doors on the far side. Along the way he wondered at the patients lying in bed. What was the point of a hospital when spells cured you in an instant?

After passing a storeroom, a kitchen, and what looked like a dormitory, she finally settled in a small, cramped office lit by a solitary light-stone. Black slates were stacked on the desk and shelves, this world's reusable answer to expensive paper. Apparently Rana's generosity hadn't extended quite this far. Oda offered him a stool and waited until he was seated before taking one herself.

"Can we dispense with all of this, Sister?" he said, his tolerance for protocol already exhausted. At the last word her face lit up with a genuine smile.

"My apologies, Brother. I had been told you were . . . unusual, but I thought it wise not to assume anything."

"Surely you don't treat Faren this way."

"Faren would not wear a sword into my chapel," she said with a twinkle in her eye. "But to fairly answer you, the Cardinal has never stepped foot in this city, nor would he dare to without leave from the Lord Wizard."

So Christopher was more alone than he had realized. Faren wouldn't be rolling up in his coach and bailing him out anytime soon.

"Is permission hard to get?"

"I wouldn't know," she said. "I've never seen the Lord Wizard either. I was born here, so after I served in the Cathedral for a while, I took it upon myself to return. The good Captain frowned but did not arrest me, and after a few years it became obvious that he would not. From this we deduce that the Lord Wizard at least tolerates my existence. But then, I am hardly a threat to him, being only fourth-rank."

"Wait," Christopher said. "I showed up with an army. Will he view me as a threat?"

Oda shook her smiling head. "You are only fifth-rank."

Apparently an army counted for less than a Cardinal.

"And," she added, "you have the invitation of the King, do you not?"

The lady was better informed about Christopher's mission than he was. He decided it would be safe to level with her.

"I have his express orders. I also have instructions from the Saint, to—"

He stopped talking because she had put her finger on his lips.

"Say nothing you would not repeat in public," she said.

He scratched his head and tried again. "I understand there is a Curate of the Gold Throne here. The Saint suggests that's not . . . helpful."

"There is indeed," she said, "and it is not particularly helpful. Although the summer season produces more fevers than I can cure, Lord Joadan only heals those who can pay his fee. If they paid me instead, I could build a bigger hospital to serve the ones who do not require magic."

"You don't get paid?"

"I am paid what they can spare. But I choose my patients on the strength of their affliction, not their purse."

Basic triage. Christopher could be certain that Oda was doing the right thing, just as he could be certain that there would be those who didn't like it.

"If I'm going to get Joadan out of the city, I need to know how he got in."

"The gold proving, of course."

"Um . . . pretend I don't know what that means."

She raised her eyebrows. "The Cathedral is slack indeed if it does not teach the most basic elements of the other theologies. Who is Master of Novices these days?"

"I don't know. I mean, I didn't learn anything at the Cathedral."

Oda sat back and clasped her hands together in her lap.

"I'm a special case," he said weakly. Finishing his education was what they had given him Torme for. He was using the man as a supply clerk.

"It is a doctrine of the Gold Throne that its priests are worth their weight in gold. Thus Lord Joadan paid the Lord Wizard a hundred and forty-two pounds of gold for the privilege of the city. If you were to compete with him, no doubt the Lord Wizard would expect the same from you."

Christopher couldn't raise that much gold. He paid his bills in paper, a currency he was certain the Lord Wizard would not even find amusing.

"I don't want to compete with him."

"Good. Because you could not. Our faith will not allow you to make back such a huge sum from the pockets of the poor. Your commission from the King is as a regimental commander, not a healer. Perhaps you had best respect that distinction for now."

Oda was all but telling him to keep his distance. He couldn't blame her. She would have to live with Joadan, and the Lord Wizard, and the Captain for decades; he would be free to leave in a few years. Whatever trouble he stirred up would be hers to settle. With a grim nod he conceded the point and took his leave.

But it seemed fate had other plans. He had barely turned the corner outside of the chapel, a little bit lost but intrigued by the sights and sounds of the city, when he caught a flash of yellow from across the street. A trim, handsome man in gold robes stepped out of a doorway, followed by a pair of servants in yellow livery. Instinctively Christopher shadowed him from his side of the street, pretending to look at the shop fronts while surreptitiously watching them.

Joadan—for it had to be Curate Joadan, wearing rich clothes and a long, straight sword with glittering jewels in the golden hilt—walked purposefully, but Christopher felt the man was also looking for something without wanting to be obvious about it. Apparently it wasn't enemy priests, since as far as Christopher could tell he hadn't been noticed. After half a block Joadan turned down a narrow alley. The servants, laden with packages, followed awkwardly.

Christopher hurried across the street to the mouth of the alley. Masked by the servant's package-bearing width and occasional stumble into a trash bin or puddle, he slipped far enough in to see Joadan's destination.

A small group of boys, wearing little more than loincloths, had been playing a game with balls and sticks. Joadan spoke to them sharply, and the boys, with the courage of the young, jeered at him, chattering some odd nonsense syllables like screeching monkeys.

Then the boy closest to Joadan collapsed, coughing. The rest fled in abject terror as Joadan reached down and caught the boy. He stood up, the lad in his arms, and looked around to see who was watching.

Christopher pressed himself into a doorway. Miraculously he appeared to have escaped detection; after a few seconds he peered out to see Joadan and his servants disappearing down the far end of the alley.

His heart racing, Christopher pondered his options. Faren would seem to have been tragically misinformed; apparently the Gold Throne was not above stooping so low in broad daylight after all. The imprudence of pursuing the matter at this immediate juncture was obvious to him, even as his feet quickly followed down the alley of their own accord. There would, after all, be no other juncture for the boy.

He began to hustle, and then run, reaching the end of the alley and looking around wildly. He only saw them because of the servant's livery; they were both clinging to the back of a coach that now bumped its way down the road. Christopher almost called out, but to whom? Even if there were a guardsman about, he would be just as likely to support Joadan, or at least look the other way. And involving ordinary townsmen would be irresponsibly dangerous, a fact that the townsmen no doubt already understood.

So, alone with his fear, he ran after the coach, which seemed to be in some haste. He struggled to keep it in sight for several blocks, gradually falling behind as exhaustion gained on him. But when the gap had opened up to a hundred yards, the coach stopped in front of a handsome building, and its occupants disembarked and hurried inside.

Brown and square and three stories tall, with thick oak double doors and bay windows on the upper floors, it looked surprisingly like a good New York brownstone. The thought of storming it to rescue a child about to be sacrificed to dark gods momentarily seemed absurd.

Christopher stood in front of the steps, checked by sheer normalcy. It was a calm, sunny day on a busy city street; how could he single-handedly assault somebody's house?

"My lord," called a voice from the nearest intersection. Torme and a squad of hard-breathing soldiers came jogging up. "You should not have gone out without an escort. You should not have come here alone."

"But I'm not alone. You're here, and just in time. It's happening now, Torme. I saw the Gold Curate grab a kid off the street! They're in there, *right now*. We've got to do something."

Torme frowned at the building, glanced over his squad, and looked up and down the street. "There," he said, pointing at a wagon full of cabbages. The squad of soldiers descended on it, pushing it onto its side while Torme intimidated the driver into silence. The men knocked off the wheels and liberated an axle. Gathering around their newly acquired battering ram, they prepared to charge up the steps.

"We will necessarily lose the element of surprise," Torme said.

"Or not," Christopher said, and cast one of his new spells on the axle. He had memorized it as a joke, intending to use it on the bard the next time she lectured him on his many failings, which he assumed would be minutes after the next time he saw her. Now it would be put to serious use.

He touched the battering ram, and silence washed out from it, pooling around them. ". . . ," Christopher said, intending to say *let's go*, but the silence was complete. The noise of the city was blanked out, along with the sound of his own breathing. He grabbed the front end of the axle instead.

Torme gestured, and the men surged forward. The axle slammed into the door, visibly shaking it. The men struggled a bit to get into rhythm without any verbal cues, falling into unison only on the third swing. After the fourth the door sagged. On the fifth the left side fell back into the hall, landing at the feet of a wide-eyed butler.

The butler tried to scream, but the men threw the log into the hall. His voice cut off, the butler turned to flight. Christopher sprinted after him, catching him by the back of the neck. He pulled the man back, handed him off to Torme, and ran down the hall. Torme passed the butler down the line, each soldier in turn passing him to the last and youngest, who pushed him up against the wall and threatened him with his rifle.

A few meters from the entrance the noise of the world broke over them like ocean spray. Their footsteps boomed in Christopher's ears, and he wondered how the household remained unaware.

Torme was still not speaking; he sent a man down each hall or door they passed with a wave of his hand. Christopher instinctively looked for a basement, and when he threw open a door and saw stairs down, he shouted, "Here!" Assuming he was followed, he went down three steps at a time, and now his footfalls truly rang out, accompanying the jingle of his mail and his scabbard knocking at the wall as he tried to draw the sword.

He burst into the bottom room and a terrible scene. The lad was hanging upside down from his knees, his shirt off, the Gold Curate striking him on the back barehanded. A servant knelt in front of the child with a bowl and rag; several others stood in the background, watching mournfully.

"Get away from him!" Christopher shouted, which he realized was a singular waste of words when Joadan answered by casting a spell. There were better things to do with speech than threaten people; you could use it to kill in this world. Christopher's self-recriminations were cut short when a huge black panther leapt out of the shadows on the floor—not that there had been shadows on the floor an instant ago—and tried to bite his face off.

He went down on his back, both hands locked around the beast's throat to hold it off. The animal had unnaturally glowing yellow eyes, but its hot, fetid breath in his face felt terrifyingly real. He could see its fangs, yellowed and fearsome. Once it realized it could not bite him, it latched onto his shoulders with its front paws and proceeded to rake his belly, trying to scoop him out like a melon baller.

He could feel its claws scrabbling on his chain-mail, links catching and bursting off to tinkle across the room. In another few seconds the dribble would become a deluge and his mail would cease to exist. Even now claws raked through rents, burning lines of fire down his torso. His tael, though vastly greater than when he had been first-rank and thus only twice as hard to kill as a mortal man, would still only last seconds under this sustained assault.

Torme leapt into action, straddling the beast and grappling its head with both hands. At that precise moment Christopher truly felt the sting of his penury; he still had not bought the priest a blade, which would have spared him the sight of a man wrestling a panther barehanded. The two of them were strong enough to immobilize the cat's head, though they could not dislodge its grasp on Christopher or stop its raking attack. Then a soldier stepped up, put his rifle into the cat's mouth, and pulled the trigger.

The animal burst like a pillow into a thousand gold rose petals, which slowly faded into gray and then nothingness after landing on the ground. Christopher was lifted to his feet by his men, who faced him in the right direction and put his sword in his hand. He ignored the steel rings still dropping from his armor and pointed his blade across the room.

Joadan's servants were readying themselves for a desperate defense, several with daggers and one wielding a footstool. Joadan was pushing a servant toward the back of the room, uttering harsh commands, his sword drawn and already softly glowing. The servant was carrying the boy, and the boy was reaching out to the Curate, with both hands, crying out. Once Christopher's hearing recovered from the rifle shot, he understood the boy's plea.

"Daddy!"

Christopher opened his mouth and closed it. There were no words appropriate to the situation. Instead, he dropped his sword and raised his hands in surrender.

"My lord?" Torme asked, clearly astounded.

"Drop your weapons," Christopher said. "Everybody drop your weapons."

"He was attacking the child," Torme argued.

"No," Christopher said, "he was saving his son's life."

At that Torme threw down his wooden sword and raised his hands. The other soldiers looked around nervously before setting down their guns and imitating their officer.

"Pick up your sword," Joadan said. His voice was tightly controlled, like he paid for every word and meant to get his money's worth. "I would not have it said I killed an unarmed man."

"No," Christopher answered. "We were wrong. *I* was wrong."

"You burst into my house, assault my servants, terrify my child, and you think *I was wrong* suffices? Pick up your sword and prepare to die."

"You're a priest," Christopher said. "Why don't you just heal him?"

"Oh," said Joadan, clapping his free hand to the side of his face in comic surprise. "Why didn't I think of that? Why did it never occur to me to use the power of the gods to undo the fate the gods had bestowed upon my child? All my life I have stumbled in confusion, needing only your brilliant insight to set me free."

Christopher felt his facing turning red, but he did not let it distract him from Joadan's words.

"If you can't, then let me."

Joadan put his hand down and stared at Christopher with incredulity. This was a comforting development, as it was by now a response Christopher was used to.

"Do you truly take me for a lackwit?" Joadan said, when it became clear Christopher wasn't going to say anything more. "Would you trap me so easily?"

"I don't understand?"

"What price would you have me pay?" Joadan said. He didn't seem to think it was funny anymore. "The Gold Throne has forbidden commerce between our Churches. Should a single coin pass between us, the Apostle would have my head."

Silly politics. "Then I'll do it for free."

Joadan's sword sagged, as if it could not bear the weight of so much stupidity.

"Surely you must know, I took a vow: to pay for, and be paid for, every transaction; to neither give nor receive charity; to be only what I can be, not what others make of me. The Yellow Emperor would have my ranks for the sake of that vow. You offer me a choice between death and impotence."

Apparently his metaphysics were even sillier. As a priest, Joadan was naturally bound to a certain code of conduct derived from the precepts of his Patron's affiliation. Christopher hadn't expected that code to be cripplingly stupid. His own religious vows were vastly less confining.

"And yet," Joadan said, his sword rising up again to point at Christopher's throat, "you do me even further insult. Did you think your own power greater than mine? Does your god favor you with miracles instead of mere spells?"

"Sometimes," Torme said. "This is the Lord Curate Christopher, whose mere survival is a miracle. You would be wise to reconsider your threats."

Improbably, Joadan's face fell, and he turned to the side in disgust. "Go," he said. "Begone."

Despite this welcome change of attitude, Christopher could not leave well enough alone. He had to ask. "Why?"

Joadan glared at him while answering. "The consequences of

intemperate oaths. I swore to spare the hand that brought low the Baron Black Bartholomew, regardless of its color. That odious stain on my Church's honor is now expunged. And with this, my oath is expired. Our next encounter will not be similarly constrained. Now leave, as you entered: in silence."

Christopher had to bite his tongue to stop himself from apologizing again. Instead he picked up his sword and sheathed it. His men followed him out quietly, Christopher not even trusting to speak to the poor butler, still standing against the wall. He settled for patting the man on the shoulder and grimacing an apology.

Standing on the street, watching the butler try to stand the broken door back in its place, and surrounded by a group of cautious but angry cabbage-sellers, Torme was the first to speak.

"I confess myself confused."

"That makes two of us," Christopher said. He took out his purse and started counting gold coins into the wagoneer's hand, until the man's face brightened. He added a few more, for good measure, and then led his squad down the street in a random direction, since he still didn't know which way was home.

"That seems unlikely," Torme said, "as you are the author of my confusion. Why did you condone the Curate's child-beating? It is legal, of course, yet you spoke of life-saving."

"That's the part that confused you?" Christopher said. "Okay, look, the kid has cystic fibrosis." The words sounded wrong to him, and he realized they were in English. "Basically, he's drowning in his own snot. Joadan was clearing his lungs."

"I have not heard of this disease. It must be in the advanced studies."

That was nice of Torme, although of course Christopher had not actually undergone advanced studies. He wasn't even sure they existed.

"It's a genetic thing," Christopher said, and again the word was in English. Torme nodded, pretending to understand, but Christopher stopped walking.

"Wait a minute. Maybe that's why Joadan can't cure him. The spell for diseases—it doesn't fix allergies, right?"

"One must treat allergic reactions as a poison. But of course you knew that," Torme said, managing to look only a little alarmed at Christopher's ignorance.

Christopher backed up and tried a different tack.

"What spell cures birth defects?"

"You mean, like Charles's missing fingers?"

"Yes! Joadan's boy is like Charles, except what he is missing is, uh, not fingers. Something internal."

"This would not seem to help. Only the Saint can regenerate, and Joadan can no more deal with him than he could with you."

"Well, then, maybe he should switch sides."

Torme frowned. "It is not perhaps as easy it seems. Particularly for a man already so far advanced in age and rank, and learned in theology."

"Ah . . . sorry," Christopher mumbled. Torme was not just the only person he knew who had switched teams; he was the only person he'd ever heard of switching. Making light of it was incredibly rude.

Torme acknowledged his apology by smoothly changing topics.

"Perhaps you were confused why he would loathe Black Bart. I can shed some light. Bart of course did not take his knights into his counsel. Nonetheless we detected hints of disagreement. At the time I took it for mere rivalry, but perhaps it was a sign of schism."

"Schism?" Christopher couldn't imagine how that could occur. He was under the assumption that if he were screwing up, Marcius would appear and set him straight. Wouldn't it work the same for everyone else?

"Your own existence has caused division in the White. Imagine how much more so if our affiliation did not command us to humility. In other faiths, where personal power is a direct sigil of divine favor, there is somewhat less . . . cooperation."

"Don't the gods have anything to say about that?"

Torme looked at him askance. "A priest expects to meet with his god but once, at his initiation, and that is a rigidly formal affair. Even a mere conversation with a god must be hedged on all sides by limits and restrictions, else risk violating the sacred compact."

That didn't really describe his interaction with Marcius. Christopher felt it might sound like name-dropping to bring it up, though.

"Well, if there is a split in the Gold Church, maybe we can use it to drive out Joadan."

His assistant didn't look very happy with the thought, but he held his tongue.

"What is it? Damn it, Faren told you to be frank with me. You defer too much to my judgment. I need you to be more assertive. You need to tell me when I'm making a mistake."

"I completely agree," Torme said, perhaps thinking of the most recent debacle, though still too polite to mention it.

Christopher took out his little silver vial, opened it, and poured out a precise amount of purple.

"I'm sorry I took so long to do this. Write to Dereth and tell him you'll need a sword."

Torme was polite and grave. "As you will, my lord."

But the man was not invulnerable, and he had to ask the question that preyed on him, as it must on anyone in his position. "What if the Marshall does not accept me?" Acolyte-ranks did not require the direct approval of the god, but a full rank did.

Christopher shrugged, unconcerned. "I don't expect that to be the case." He did not consciously realize they were the same words the Saint had said to him, over a year ago. "Now tell me: what's wrong with my plan?"

Torme put the pellet of tael in his mouth before answering.

"It seems profitless to wash the walls with mud."

That was an excellent point. It would not be an improvement to replace the likes of Joadan with the likes of Black Bart. He would have to think of something else. And soon—Joadan would likely be eager to provoke another confrontation, one that Christopher wasn't sure he could win and was even less sure he wanted to.

"You should not be seen in this state," Torme said, unbuckling the remnants of Christopher's chain mail. His shirt came away with it, having been reduced to rags. "Your dignity would suffer for it."

Torme took off his own shirt and handed it over. Christopher objected, saying, "What about your . . ." but he trailed off into shocked silence when he saw the scars on Torme's back. Old and long healed, but the sight still sent a sympathetic twinge down his spine.

"I am a commoner for one more day. And commoners have no dignity," Torme answered. Hefting the tattered mail over his shoulder, he took the lead, and Christopher and the men followed him home.

8

A NIGHT ON THE TOWN

The army loved him, but they were young men. For the first few days, just cleaning and settling into the barracks sufficed to keep them busy. Inevitably, though, the town they were embedded in began to lure their gaze and drain their attention. Christopher stepped up the busywork, but he knew that very soon someone would slip and do something foolish like sneaking out. And then he would have to dispense real punishment.

Torme knew it too. "'Tis hard to tell the men they cannot venture out at night for a drink or two, especially when you are paying them drinking money."

"Do you think we can hold out till Karl gets here?" Letting this pack of boisterous young men loose on this town would create problems Christopher had no idea how to handle.

"No," Torme said, insensitive to Christopher's desire for an easy answer. "My suggestion would be to put them under the command of the Captain, building walls and training with pikes." The pikes had started arriving, and Torme had declared them to be of acceptable quality and only twice as expensive as they should be.

But Christopher was not going to turn command of his army over to anybody else. He had a brief moment of sympathy for the UN Peacekeeping forces, who were routinely expected to do just that. Back when he was a civilian, it hadn't seemed like a big deal, and he had authoritatively shaken his head in dismay at the foibles of military officers. Now the shoe was on the other foot, and it pinched.

"Pick the best ones, and give them a night's leave. Make sure they understand that if they misbehave, there will be no more leave for anyone." He hoped that would buy him a few nights.

As he sat brooding in his office that night, awaiting the roar of a riot or some other disturbance to reveal his incompetence, the dreaded knock came.

"Sir, permission to enter," a young sentry said. Christopher had been training his men how to talk to him, and he much preferred "Sir" to the ostentatious "my Lord Curate."

"Granted, Private," he answered. His men had also been training him how to speak to them, and he felt like he was making progress.

The door opened to a slightly flustered young soldier and a strikingly attractive woman dressed in peasant's clothes somehow arranged to give the distinct impression of harlotry.

"She said you would want to see her, sir," the soldier apologized, as Christopher began shaking his head in anger.

"What an absurd breach of protocol," he began to lecture, but then the woman interrupted him.

"Take it easy on them, Christopher. I had to work to get this far." The woman shook out her hair, changed her posture in some subtle way, and suddenly was Lalania again.

The soldier stood, waiting for release or blame. Christopher could hardly give him the latter, so he made the best of it. "Very well, Private. Dismissed." Damn it, if he had known the man was going to exit with that lascivious grin, he wouldn't have let him go so easily.

"Where have you been, and why are you dressed like that?" he demanded of the girl.

"The answer to both of those questions should be self-evident," she replied, rolling her eyes. "Do you see me reproaching you for your whoring around?"

"But I don't," he said automatically.

"I am so tired of hearing that," she said, but not really to him. "Peace. You asked for my help, now take it."

He really did need help, so he shut up and listened.

"Your wizard is a careful man. And yes, man he is, despite the rumors. Once a week he takes a woman into his tower for the night. Very discreetly, I might add. It took me days to find out where and when the selection was made."

"Oh, Lala!" he exclaimed. "You didn't . . ."

"This is my job," she answered, angry now. "Do not dare to look down on me. When I am done with my appointed tasks, there are not headless bodies lying everywhere."

If it was a rationalization, it was a good one.

"But it's not your job to take such risks," he said, because he could always find something to argue. "If he had suspected you were working for me, he would have burned us both."

"Or worse," she agreed, jaunty again now that the topic was mere danger. "But he has great confidence in his power. Each morning he wipes the girl's mind, so she can recall nothing of what occurred the night before."

"So you gained nothing? Why even try, then?"

"Because trying costs nothing. If I cannot remember, then I can hardly complain."

Christopher tapped the desk in annoyance. Either she was talking metaphysics or justifications; either was a waste of time.

"Because I am not a credulous peasant girl. That kind of magic is beyond his reach," she said, sitting on his desk and stopping his hand with hers. "If not, it would be a fact worth knowing. I prepared myself against the more probable but lesser spell, and was proved right."

"More danger," Christopher complained. "What if he noticed?"

"Not with magic," she laughed. "I am only first-rank. And magic is all he sees. The foolishness of the high; they forget that common sense and cleverness can oft slip thaumaturgical puissance. So now I can tell you what he would rather you did not know."

That sounded dangerous in and of itself. But knowledge was power, and he wasn't going to turn down Lalania's sacrifice.

His face must have revealed his concern, because Lalania grinned at him. "The first and most important thing he does not want you to know is that he is a balding, paunchy, middle-aged man of a thoroughly pedestrian nature. The only unpleasantness I faced was boredom. My skills were wasted on him; clumsy peasant girls are all he can conceive of."

Christopher did not want to know what skills she was referring to.

"He wears Black to frighten and cow, but he is too wedded to personal gain to be anything but Yellow. He never leaves the tower unless cloaked in robes and illusion intended more to disguise than to terrify. He lives and breathes plot and counterplot, scheme and stratagem. He is desperately lonely, up there in that tower with nothing but his magic and his baleful contingencies, yet so subsumed by paranoia that it has never occurred to him he is his own jailer.

"And most important, he is not immortal. He was an apprentice of the previous lord of the tower. In tried and true fashion, he murdered his rivals and then his master." Fae had said that was an acceptable way to become a wizard. "It was the tael from the war ten years ago that made him a power and not merely a shadow hiding behind a reputation and a handful of magic looted from his predecessor.

"So you must trim your interactions with him to this pattern. He has true power, so do not be dismissive; but obsequiousness is not necessary or helpful. The promise of friendship may draw him to you against his will, but flattery will only make him suspicious. Though he will not be moved by charity, he can be impressed with hard bargaining."

"I don't think I'm going to have any interactions with him."

"Not unless you improve your social graces. I understand you paid a call on the Gold Curate? The rumors are amazing. Apparently you smashed down his door and walked away unscathed; yet the Gold Curate still lives. Do you know what that looks like?"

"Um. No?" Christopher had assumed that everyone else had seen the shame clinging to his shoulders.

"It looks like a superior chastising his recalcitrant servant."

"What? Joadan threw me out!"

"Without murdering you? Even Faren would slay a Dark priest who broke into the Cathedral without a second thought. How utterly unlikely that a Gold would let you walk away from his house unharmed."

"This is not going to look good for Joadan," Christopher said.

"You think?" Lalania said, with wide eyes and an exaggerated tilt of her head. It was uncomfortably close to the way Joadan had looked at him.

"I mean, he was already talking about trouble at home. Some kind of schism. So if they think he's working with me, the Gold Throne is going to come down on him."

"What do you know of schism?" she said rather more sharply than he would have expected.

"Joadan was apparently an enemy of Black Bart. He let me go because I was the one who killed him. Torme seems to think it means the Yellow Church is in some kind of conflict."

"And indeed it is," Lalania said. "Joadan, whom you have been sent to destroy, is the lighter side of that bronze coin. There is dark, and then there is Darkness. The Gold Throne is under a shadow. I came here and did what I did not for you but to see if the wizard cast that shadow and if Joadan was his tool. Now I find my suspicions a-jumble, and all because of you."

"Why didn't you tell me this before?" Christopher asked.

The bard paused, and it occurred to Christopher that she did not, in fact, work for him. There was no particular reason she should share her secrets.

"An oversight," she said, "and unworthy of our alliance. I won't let it happen again."

"I don't understand what you mean. How can a whole Church be under a shadow?"

She paused again, considering her words, trying cover it up by adjusting her blouse. Which was an admittedly effective distraction.

"There are intrigues among the gods, just as among men. The Iron Throne, in particular, does not work by daylight. Instead it infiltrates other Churches, turning their priests one by one to the Black, until it inhabits the shell of the church like a rotting carcass under a carefully preserved skin."

Christopher thought of Bart's priest and the black robes that had been hidden under his yellow cloak.

"That's not . . . good."

"For once, you are a master of understatement. But I have had my fill of banality for now. I am going to take advantage of your washroom, and quite possibly one or two of your young peacocks."

"We saved you a room in the officers' quarters," he hastened to tell her retreating back. She had just said that last part to tease him.

Probably.

In the morning he had other things to worry about. None of the men he had given leave had returned. Like with any dog that goes missing, he feared the worst, but resolved not to panic until he had at least checked the local pound.

He and Torme walked through the town until they found the jail, where he discovered his men lounging around, battered, bruised, and caged.

But not demoralized. They snapped to attention without a trace of shame when he stood outside their bars.

"What happened?" Christopher asked. He recognized a face in dismay. Charles, his quartermaster, still a short and skinny kid, was the one he'd thought of as a paragon of reason compared to the average teenager.

"What else? They got drunk and started a fight," answered the jailor.

Christopher ignored him, frowning at Charles's black eye and split lip.

"It is true that we had plenty to drink, sir," Charles said. "But we did not start any fights. We can't help that the local girls are interested in real men, not smelly simpletons."

"You Darkling rat!" barked the jailor, and lunged at the bars, raising his club. The soldier didn't flinch.

"Please don't do that," Christopher said to the jailor. The man immediately cowered, properly terrified of Christopher's rank. "Please don't do that, either," Christopher sighed futilely. Fear he could evoke instantly. Understanding took time.

"If they really were just defending themselves, is it still a crime?" he asked the jailor.

"That's not my domain, Lord Curate. For that you must speak to the Captain."

"Is it permissible for my assistant to see to their injuries?"

The jailor really wanted to say no, but in the face of Christopher's exalted rank, he wilted.

Christopher started to leave, but he didn't want to deal with the Captain without Torme at his side. Then he thought of something else he should do before that meeting.

"Where are the others?" he asked the jailor. "The ones my men fought?"

The jailor stared at him, carefully blank. "I would not know, Lord Curate. We were unable to identify any of them."

While Christopher was busy fuming about the unequal treatment, Torme explained from inside the jail cell.

"The Curate only wishes to heal your fellow citizens, Squire. He has no desire to punish."

The jailor did not look convinced. "All the same, Pater, we cannot give what we do not have."

Torme came out of the cell while guards locked it behind him. "I doubt it is necessary, my lord. These men have only bumps and bruises." Christopher could see he hadn't bothered to heal any of the men. Torme didn't consider mere pain worth worrying about. But then, neither did the men.

"So there were no weapons involved?" Christopher asked.

"No, sir," Charles answered. "They apparently felt outnumbering us three to one was sufficient."

If his men had really faced such odds and come out with so little damage, they were tougher than he had thought. On the other hand, bar fights were mostly about spirit, not skill. He could see how his men would have had a huge advantage over the ordinary peasant. He could also see how so much arrogance would be insufferable to the locals.

On the way to the Captain, he asked Torme about it. "Do you think they are innocent? Did they really not start the fight? They seem awfully cocky."

"They did not need to start a fight," Torme answered. "They were doomed from the moment they walked into the tavern. They hold their heads like lords, the girls react accordingly, and the men react to that."

Christopher's concerns about what the rest of the Kingdom would think caught fire and burned.

"We've got to get them to stop that. We can't afford the attention right now."

Torme shook his head. "You cannot. It is no longer in your power to take away the pride you have given them."

No, Christopher thought, *and I wouldn't if I could.*

"Then what do we do?"

Torme responded like the soldier he had been.

"More discipline."

The Captain was not in his office. Rather than wander around the city at random looking for him, Christopher decided to go back to his barracks. Torme volunteered to wait. It seemed unfair, but Torme assured him that was what assistants were for.

He spent the day drilling with the troops, trying to keep them occupied. They built an obstacle course and had races through it, with the natural enthusiasm of young men sparked by Christopher's promise of a gold coin to the winner. He was defeated in his purpose, though, when a squad ganged up under their junior officer, each individual throwing away his chance on the course to hold back the faster runners, while their corporal surged ahead. The sign of cooperation was welcome; the corporal's promise to spend the gold on drinks for his squad as soon as they were allowed out on the town was not.

Torme returned at nightfall, and Christopher had to order him to eat something before issuing his report.

"The Captain invites you to join him at The Hanging Tree, a local tavern." Efficient as always, he already had directions and led Christopher through the town, the darkness reduced to a comfortable dim by the plethora of magic streetlamps.

So Christopher would finally get to see the nightlife of a medieval town. In the village, it consisted of men sitting around drinking and discussing the weather, every bit as exciting as an English pub. Not something to write home about. On the other hand, he hoped it wouldn't be a seedy, smoky bar with topless dancers and the reek of sweat and alcohol.

His hopes were dashed.

The outside of the tavern was his first warning. The windows in the huge stone building were boarded shut, muffling the sounds of voices and music. The bouncers at the door were his second warning.

Large, beefy, wearing executioner's hoods, black leather pants, vests, gloves, and armed with wooden clubs.

They asked for Christopher's sword. He had it half off before Torme stopped him.

"You are ranked. You do not disarm for anyone."

Torme threw the bouncers a glare, and they stepped aside.

The door led to a large, open room, ringed by a balcony, with flickering light-stones hanging from the ceiling. There was a small orchestra on one side, but without electronic amplification it could barely be heard over the din of drunken laughing and shouts. Scantily clad women, or in some cases unclad, floated about, advertising their services.

More annoying from Christopher's perspective was the smoke. It wasn't tobacco, which didn't surprise him—he had not seen any New World crops here—but it was just as unpleasant. Not as thick, but twice as cloying, it made the air feel heavy. The source seemed to be a myriad of hand-carved pipes, which were being passed around at some of the tables.

The Captain was in the center of the room, at the edge of a large table, a mug in one hand and a woman in the other. The small crowd around him were cheering and jeering at a man with three oddly shaped blocks in his hand.

Christopher did not identify them as dice until the man threw them on the table. They weren't cubes, and they didn't seem to have any symbols he could recognize painted on them. They weren't even all the same shape.

A shout went up from the crowd, and the man hung his head in defeat. The croupier raked gold coins from his side of the table to the Captain's side.

"Ah, Curate. Welcome to our table, and many thanks for leaving the door on its hinges." The Captain greeted him with alcohol-fueled camaraderie and a crude smirk. "Would you care to wager on a throw?"

"I'm afraid not," Christopher said, striving for politeness. "I have no idea what the game is."

"You've never played *Dragons, Knights, and Angels?*"

"No," Christopher confessed, "I've never even heard of it."

"Did they raise you in a monastery?" laughed the Captain. His crowd laughed with him.

"No, it's just personal." He'd never understood the point of gambling. If you couldn't control or at least influence the outcome, why bother?

The Captain, like all bullies, moved on to an easier target.

"What about you, Pater? You have the look of a man who appreciates a good wager." The Captain pushed the dice toward Torme, who was careful not to touch them.

"I fear not, Lord Captain. My Patron grants me Luck as a domain, and I do not wish to taint your game."

"Bah," the Captain grumbled. "You two are as meek as nuns."

"Speaking of meekness," Christopher said, "you've got some of my men in your jail. I was wondering if I could have them back."

"Meekness? Your boys are as arrogant as dukes. And as pretty as peacocks, the way you've dressed them in all that finery. For the sake of our young women's virtue, they should all be locked up."

The young woman he was currently groping didn't look all that virtuous.

"You know what would cure them?" the Captain continued, coming around to what Christopher suspected was the real point. "Shoveling mud. Put them to work on the walls, and the discipline problems will go away."

No doubt. If his army was reduced to dirty, simple-minded laborers, they really would lose their appeal. And the spirit that made them an army.

But Christopher was distracted by a technical question. "Mud? What has mud got to do with wall-building?"

"Ha!" the Captain chortled. "Everything. In fact, everything you see here was made out of mud." He waved his hand at the stone walls, spilling ale on a well-dressed man standing next to him. The man carefully ignored the accident.

Christopher couldn't decide if the Captain was making fun of him or was just too drunk to understand the question. He decided it would be polite to not press the issue. The Captain was still sober enough to detect his suspicion.

"You don't think we cut those miles of stone out of the ground by hand, did you? I don't know how it goes in your county, but in this one, the lord earns his keep."

"Hail to the Lord Wizard!" someone immediately shouted, and everyone took a healthy drink from their mugs.

So there was magic involved. Christopher had never seen a wizard in action. Except for Master Flayn, who hardly counted, being only first-rank. Well, and Fae, but he preferred to forget about that.

"That's an impressive feat," Christopher agreed. After the hordes he had seen in the Wild, he felt every town should have these kinds of defenses. "I'd like to see that."

"Then you're in luck. I was just on my way to a setting." The Captain drained his mug, looked into the empty bottom of it, and took a fresh mug from the person standing next to him. "One for the road," he muttered, draining it in a single go as well, though not without spilling some down his bearded chin.

The Captain did not present a particularly impressive figure at the moment, being drunk, disheveled, and stinking of sweat and smoke. Christopher found his appearance so unusual that he spoke without thinking.

"Are you sure you're ready to meet your boss?"

The Captain glared at him. "Unlike your peacocks, I know when not to act above my station."

That was not altogether heartening.

"Besides," the Captain said, with a grin that was supposed to be manly but only came out lopsided, "there's no shame in fortifying your courage to meet the Lord Wizard."

"Hail to the Lord Wizard!" came the automatic refrain. The Captain reflexively raised his own mug, even though it was empty.

Outside, he and the Captain walked through the well-lit streets, Torme following a respectful distance behind. The Captain did not make small talk, however, lost in his own thoughts.

On the edge of the city, there was a work gang milling around a long wooden form of a concrete mold. The scaffolding reached fifteen feet into the air and went on for thirty yards, where it joined a section of already finished wall.

"Wait here," the Captain growled, and went to join a fancifully dressed man standing on the stone wall that abutted the wooden extension.

"I wish Lalania could see this," Christopher told Torme. "She might understand what's happening."

"If wishes were wings, then beggars would fly," Lalania whispered, stepping out of the shadows. "And if I were Joadan, you would be dead. Why don't you have a guard detail with you?"

"He cannot display his army so brazenly," Torme said, answering for him, although the truth was he just hadn't thought about it. "And in any case a squad would only show weakness."

"Fortuitously, his corpse will not care about other's sensibilities," she said. "In the future take more precaution, lest you stop caring altogether. Now try not to draw any attention. I do not wish to chance the wizard's recognition." Discreetly she pointed at the wall.

A black-robed figure moved slowly through the air, stopping to hover next to the Captain and his associate. Christopher gaped, impressed and diminished by the authority of a being that tread on air. Which was, of course, the point. Lalania could make a grand entrance when she wanted to, but flying in trumped everything.

There appeared to be a brief conversation, too distant to hear, and then the wizard turned his attention to the wooden wall. Christopher saw the wizard flick something outward from his hand, and then there was the sound of wood groaning and creaking as the load it bore changed. The wizard flew off, disappearing into the night sky above the illumination of the weak streetlights. The two men on the wall relaxed, and the work gang began carefully tearing down the wood.

"Wow," Christopher said. He had not seen magic used on the scale of buildings before. Could they build a fort on the march? Could his enemies build a fort against him?

Stone masons fell to work, hammers banging, cleaning the flashing from the cracks in the mold and continuing the decorative grooves from the wall it was attached to.

"Why are they doing that?" Artistic license didn't really seem likely to be the explanation here.

"I'm not sure." Lalania was unhappy about not being sure. "I'll find out."

"I have a better idea," Christopher said, seizing on the chance to shield Lalania from further dangerous investigations. "Let's get them to tell us." He started walking toward the Captain, but neither of his companions moved.

"Perhaps you should tell us your plan first, my lord, so that we might not foil it through ignorance." Torme was being nice. What he really meant was, so they could stop him if it was hopelessly idiotic.

"Good idea," Christopher agreed. This was what he had promoted Torme for, after all. "I'm going to suggest to the Captain that wall-building is more important than I thought. Therefore, I would like to assign the men he has in jail to the wall crew. But only if they are required to learn all aspects of the job."

Lalania was impressed. Christopher was a little embarrassed by how much that meant to him. Torme agreed, too, but his approval just didn't carry the same effect the pretty blonde's did.

"I'll explain it to your men," she volunteered, "in such a way as to keep their eyes open without betraying their curiosity. And I'll tell them they do it for me, so if they are questioned, they cannot implicate you as a spy-master."

That was a good idea, too.

Torme volunteered, as well. "I'll explain to the rest of the army that if they get in any more trouble, they'll be out there digging mud too."

"And I'll talk to the architect." Christopher figured talking shop with a civil engineer was something he could handle. The Captain and the fancy-dressed man from the top of the wall were heading their way.

Lalania gave the architect a dismal glance. The closer they got, the worse he looked. Christopher wasn't that certain of local costumes, but he was pretty sure the man was wearing his vest inside out. He was considerably overweight—which was a rarity in this world, given how expensive food was—and unkempt, with what little hair he had left straying in all directions. "Fair enough," Lalania muttered, and disappeared into the darkness.

Torme covered Lalania's departure by taking his own as soon as the Captain arrived. "By your leave, Curate," he said with a salute, and strode off.

"Impressive work," Christopher said to the architect. "Did you also design the tower?"

"No, the tower has stood forever," the architect burbled. He was drunker than the Captain. "And though I have thankfully seen it up close only once, it was made by a different process. No need for peasants to labor, or men to oversee their labors."

"If he did that for the walls, he could spare us this nightly ordeal," the Captain grumbled. He meant himself and the architect, of course, not the men who dug in the mud.

"But then we could not build walls so fast. Transforming mud to rock must be less taxing than summoning it out of nothing."

"How fast do you build them?" Christopher asked.

"One every night, for the last ten years. And the presence of the wizard never gets any easier to bear. Did you know, tonight he asked me about my wife?" The architect grimaced.

"You're married?" The Captain was surprised.

"No," the architect said. "But if I was, I wouldn't want my family to come to his attention."

"Captain," Christopher interjected, "I think an appropriate punishment for my men would be to assign them to the walls. Just the ones who are in jail, I mean."

The Captain shrugged, no longer concerned with petty details. "Settle it with Alstanf," he grumbled, and stalked off.

"Pleased to meet you," the architect introduced himself. "I style myself Esquire Alstanf, though I confess I have no rank of any kind. Only skill, for what little it is worth."

"I am apparently the Lord Curate Christopher. You can just call me Christopher."

Alstanf quirked an eyebrow but accepted the informality. "Well, Christopher, would you like to join me in a drink? I feel the need of relaxation."

The architect didn't look like he needed any more drinks. But Christopher wanted to talk to him, so he said yes. "Just not The Hanging Tree, please. That place scares me."

"I've no desire to haunt the Captain's company any more than I have too," Alstanf agreed. "I know a quiet tavern. The girls aren't as pretty, but they're twice as friendly and half the cost."

The girls weren't as pretty. They weren't girls, either, being closer to thirty. But they were friendly instead of brazen, the dozen patrons in the tavern were talking in low voices, and the ale was a fair price. Even for the pale lager that was the only drink Christopher found potable.

"So how did you get into the wall business?" he asked Alstanf, leaning back on the padded bench and getting comfortable.

"My father was a stonemason, but I didn't have the hand for it. My eye was good, though, so I made a living laying out lines and drafts. I went where the work took me, living a free and easy life, if a bit thin at times. After the war, I knew there would be work here, so I came. And now I am trapped."

"Trapped?" The man was comfortably wealthy. The clothes, the weight, and the way he tipped the waitress attested to that.

"It's true the wizard pays me well. But I dare not think of leaving. He would send some Dark spell after me, to fetch or punish me. And I am so very sick of building walls. I laid out the plans years ago. Now there is nothing for me to do but oversee the labor, which never changes. All I have to look forward to is some unimaginable catastrophic failure, for which I will no doubt be blamed."

"Well," Christopher said, trying to be helpful, "the ulvenmen could come back. Then people would appreciate your walls."

"Perish the thought!" Alstanf exclaimed, and upended his mug. "With my luck, they'd throw down the walls with magic, and we'd all be dog food within the hour."

"Is that possible?" The walls were raised by magic. If they could be lowered by magic just as easily, that would rather severely reduce their value.

"Not according to the wizard. He claims the scrollwork we do on the face of the walls prevents the spell from being reversed. But I worry all the same. It is my nature." He called for another drink.

"What about ordinary siege efforts?" Christopher was wondering how big he should be making his cannons.

"The stone is not granite, for which the masons are most grateful. Still, it is stone, ten feet thick and fifteen feet high. It will hold for many days against trebuchets. And because each piece is a solid block, it will hold against undermining. But I ask you the question I ask everyone: How high can an ulvenman jump?"

Christopher had to admit he didn't know.

"Neither does anyone else. If it is sixteen feet, my walls are as wasted as my life."

"Another layer, then?" Doubling the blocks would make the walls absurdly high.

"It's not as simple as stacking blocks. The bottom would have to be wider, to support the weight."

They spent the rest of the evening talking about stress-to-weight ratios. All in all, the best evening Christopher had spent out in a long time. Alstanf even paid for the drinks.

When he went to leave, he found Torme and a squad of soldiers patiently waiting outside.

"Why didn't you just come get me?" he asked, chagrined that he had kept them idle.

"It's not our place to, sir. Weren't you engaged in espionage?"

He had been, and successfully, too. He now knew far more about wall-building than his men would learn at the end of a shovel.

"Also," Torme added, "I put the men in lockdown. So being here means I don't have to listen to their complaints. We can sneak you in tonight, so you won't have to listen to them either, but tomorrow they will be hard to contain without direct orders from you."

Which he was unwilling to give, since it struck him as cruelty to keep them all but caged in the barracks. On the other hand, letting them out was only sending them to the Captain's cage, and from there to the mud-pits.

Though he was prepared to siege, assault, and storm the fortifications of a thousand monsters, he was wholly inadequate to the task of disciplining two hundred rowdy young men. This whole leadership thing was harder than it looked from the outside.

"We've got to come up with a plan," he said.

"But not tonight," Torme suggested.

Christopher had found the lager a bit too agreeable, so he had to concede the point. In fact, he had to lean on Torme for a minute, until he got his bearings.

"I miss my wife," he said, overcome by a deep wave of longing.

"I'm sorry, sir?"

He had spoken in English. "Never mind, Torme. Just take me home. And make absolutely certain Lalania does not disturb me tonight." He did not think he could trust himself in this condition.

9

DEFEAT FROM THE
JAWS OF VICTORY

Christopher's entry into town had gone largely unnoticed. Gregor's did not. When the knight came trotting through town on his giant warhorse, swathed in gleaming blue armor, and at the head of a column of twoscore smartly dressed cavalry, everyone came out to see. They lined the streets, with work-stained hands and happy faces.

"He's getting quite a hero's welcome," Christopher said to Lalania. They were waiting for the horsemen inside the barracks ground, but they could see the parade reaction through the gates.

"Of course they are. Another lord, come to kill ulvenmen. Who here would not find that salutary?"

A little girl sitting on her father's shoulders cheered, and Gregor waved his hand at her in majestic acknowledgment. Lalania sniffed in exasperation.

The troop cantered in between the blocks of riflemen standing in formation on the grounds. They brought their horses to a stop or, rather, made a credible attempt at one, only a few of the animals needing to be pulled back into line. Horses don't like standing still any more than schoolchildren do, and the cavalry was still learning. Christopher didn't care how they looked on parade, anyway.

Karl walked his horse over, slipped off it, and snapped to attention in a single movement. His horse stood perfectly still, of course.

"Reporting for duty, Colonel!"

"At ease, Major. Dismiss your men." Christopher's only guide to military talk was a healthy dose of WWII movies.

Gregor nodded hello at Christopher, but his eyes were only on Lalania. Suddenly she dashed out to the horses and gracefully sprang in the saddle in front of him. But facing the wrong way, so she could smother him in kisses.

So much for military protocol.

The cavalry dismounted and promptly followed Torme out of the gate again to be stabled in town, as their quarters did not account for the needs of a cavalry regiment. Christopher had reserved a stall in the officer's barn for Gregor's horse. Karl and Gregor rode that way, and Christopher went to wait for them in his office.

Karl showed up twenty minutes later. Like all cavalrymen, he fed, watered, brushed, and cared for his mount first. His superior officers came second. His own needs came a distant third.

But in the privacy of Christopher's office, the two men could be friends, not fellow officers.

"Any trouble?" Karl asked, and Christopher brought him up to date.

"Yes, you must have an escort at all times," Karl said, agreeing with Lalania's judgment, and "No, we cannot keep the men caged here," he said, agreeing with Christopher's. "Let me go out with a few tonight and see if I can find a solution."

"And what about Gregor?" Where was the knight, anyway?

"I left him in the stables. He had more than his horse to care for."

In the stables? The girl was unbelievable.

"But," Karl continued, "that is a partial answer to your question. As long as you hold the troubadour's attention, you hold his."

Another delicate balancing act for Christopher to perform.

"Let's talk about guns," Christopher suggested. He wanted to know if there were any problems with the carbines. At least those would be problems he could solve.

⚬⚬⚬

Gregor and Lalania joined them for dinner in the officer's mess, the knight in an irrepressibly good mood.

"I owe you a favor, Christopher. Riding at the head of your column like a captain was an exhilarating experience."

An experience that should have been Karl's. Not that they would have reacted to Karl that way. He had no title. But Christopher already had Karl's loyalty. It was Gregor's he needed now. Wincing inside at the necessity of politics, he made the knight another offer.

"If you really enjoy it, I could make it permanent."

Lalania cut him off at the knees. "No, you can't. They were not cheering Gregor. They were cheering Duke Nordland. A blue knight with a cavalry troop, and one whose name is linked to yours."

"How could you possibly know that?" Christopher was incredulous. He was pretty sure he knew how she had spent the last few hours, and it didn't leave room for intelligence-gathering.

"I deduced it. Then I went outside your barracks and asked." On the other hand, people would talk to her, openly and easily, in a way that Christopher's rank would never let them talk to him.

Gregor was crestfallen but shook it off. "All the same, they cheered."

"I only bring it up," Lalania said, "to prepare you. Any minute now the Captain will come to pay his respects to the Lord Duke. I think we should disappoint him politely."

A sentry entered the room and snapped to attention, and Christopher rolled his eyes in disbelief. Lalania's absurdly precise timing had to be a product of her tael. He'd never found exactly what her profession's powers were, and he was pretty sure she would never tell him all of them.

"Acknowledged, Private." Christopher said. "Show him in."

The sentry opened his mouth before realizing the question he hadn't asked had already been answered. "Yes, sir!" he finally got out, and a few seconds later he returned with the Captain in tow.

Christopher was immediately struck by the change in the man. The Captain was clean, neat, and sober. More noticeably, he was deferential. But then, Nordland was a Duke, a terrifyingly eight ranks high.

"On behalf of the Wizard, I would like to welcome the Lord Duke to Carrhill." The Captain apparently had a short speech memorized, but Gregor didn't let him finish.

"Though I appreciate the compliment, I cannot accept it." He stood and bowed to the Captain. "Baronet Gregor, at your service."

The Captain scowled.

"I'm sorry," Christopher said, even though it couldn't possibly be his fault. "Just a case of mistaken identity." They didn't have newspapers, magazines, or televisions here. Probably no one in this county had ever seen Nordland face-to-face.

"May we offer you some refreshment, Ser?" Torme asked.

"No thanks," the Captain grunted. "I prefer my own stock. Good night, Curate." He bowed to Christopher and stiffly left the room.

Christopher sighed. What goodwill he had built up with the man seemed to have evaporated in an instant, and he wasn't even sure why.

Lalania smiled, however. "That went well."

"How do you figure?" Christopher demanded.

"Nobody issued a challenge to a duel. And you can relax, Christopher. The Captain won't hate you for seeing him humbled at your table any more than he hates you for seeing him humbled at the wizard's wall."

"But why was he so rude to Gregor?" The Captain hadn't even acknowledged his existence after the first sentence.

"As he said," Gregor said, "he prefers his own stock. And frankly, so do I. Tell me what taverns he frequents, so that I can avoid them."

Instinctively these people could tell who was Bright or Dark, like Scotsmen could spot a Catholic from a Protestant at twenty yards. That must be one of Lalania's skills: she could convincingly act like either, fitting into a person's expectations, giving off the subtle cues they didn't know they were searching for. Not magic, just Oscar-caliber acting.

"Speaking of taverns," Karl announced, "I'll retire now to do my own research. If we're going to spend two years here, we must come to an agreement with the locals."

Christopher hadn't thought of it in those terms. "We won't get reassigned next year?"

"Probably not," Gregor said.

"Not unless you provoke the Wizard, the King, or the Captain. Or any of the Gold Throne's allies," amended Lalania.

"In that case . . . don't get too comfortable," Christopher sighed. Then he went to deal with the mail Karl had brought him, and spent the rest of the night engaged in merely technical difficulties.

The next day at breakfast he was surprised to see Karl's face black-and-blue.

"I thought the goal was to prevent fighting?"

"The goal was to prevent our men from being arrested and to come to an accommodation with the locals. I believe I can report success."

"How?" Christopher wanted to know what magic Karl had worked, for the next time Karl wasn't around.

"By victory," Karl said. "Charles's problem was that his group lost."

So Karl's great plan had been to go into a tavern with a handful of picked men and beat the living daylights out of anybody who objected to their uniforms. Not a solution Christopher could ever implement. Or even Gregor. This was an issue between commoners. Rank had no place in it.

"Shouldn't I be healing somebody? Like, for instance, your victims?"

Karl shook his head. "They started it. If you heal their pain now, they'll just do it again all the sooner. Better to let them nurse their wounds until the lesson sinks in."

Christopher knew Karl was not irresponsible. If anyone had been severely injured, he would have mentioned it. And of course, this town already had magical healing. No one would die from Karl's victory.

The morning inspection counted all the men present, and as long as that was the case, Christopher really had no right to complain about Karl's methods.

"We've got to get out of the city," Christopher said. "We're supposed to be hunting ulvenmen." There was also the consideration that every day outside was a day he wouldn't bump into Joadan.

Karl seemed to think he was concerned for the men. "Foot patrols will be safe enough, within a few miles of the city. Our cavalry is prepared to range farther afield. Although only half have carbines, their firepower and the mobility of the horses should be enough to defeat ordinary ulvenmen."

"And for the unordinary ones?" Whatever those were.

Karl looked away and spat, deflecting as he always did when the topic turned to the need for rank. "Blood and flesh the men can face, but I do not know what battlefield sorceries to expect."

"Neither do I," Christopher said with an unhappy shrug. His fellow clergy focused almost exclusively on healing and truth-magic, neither of which seemed likely to be employed by their long list of foes.

"Then we should ask Gregor for advice. He has been in the councils of the ranked before."

"You want to ask me about magic?" Gregor was surprised. "Better you should ask Lala."

"Not entirely," she disagreed from her perch on his lap. "The Church of the Aesir is a combative one. The stories you have heard from your father's knee are perhaps as instructive of clerical warfare as anything I know."

"Your father is a priest?" Christopher hadn't known that.

"Was," Gregor said sadly. "But not much of one. It was our tradition that a man takes four ranks of warrior, before becoming a priest of war. My father only made it to the first-rank of priesthood before old age claimed him."

"It's a bad tradition," Lalania said, frowning delicately. "It is no good use of tael to split ranks. You only wind up half-competent in two professions."

"Nonetheless, it has always been my desire to join the priesthood," Gregor said with a grin. "I hate waiting on you healers to get around to me. Better if I could heal myself."

"The Aesir now favor making their women priests, and their men warriors." Lalania ignored Gregor's joke.

"A tradition they learned from us," Disa said. The young priestess had stayed behind to finish her education with Svengusta and had come out with the cavalry. "In another few generations, they may even see their way to becoming healers."

"I doubt it," Gregor argued. "Our fiefs are on the border, and danger is constant. We cannot afford to promote people to positions of power who cannot also fight."

"Healers can fight," Christopher said. The Vicar Rana had frozen Black Bart like a statue. But Gregor and Disa were having an ideological argument, so they weren't interested in his facts.

"Not all power comes from fighting," Disa said. "And I am not arguing against fighting. One healer and three knights can defeat four knights, a thousand tries against one."

"But you confess a healer cannot beat anything his own rank, do you not?" Gregor thought he had a good point.

"Yes, I confess it. But that only makes my case."

Gregor was confused.

Lalania explained. "She means to say that healers chose service to the cause over personal power. And frankly, I am half-minded to agree. The efficiency of the healer profession is commendable."

Poor Gregor was beset on every side by clever women. Then Christopher realized he was in the middle, too.

"Hey," he protested, "I didn't choose to not be a healer. It was Marcius's idea."

"I chose it," Torme said challengingly. "I thought it the best way to serve my cause."

"Enough," Lalania ordered. "We need no theological arguments to divide us. Leave such discord to the enemy. We serve a common cause, each as we see right. And right now our question is plain: should Christopher ride outside the walls and expose himself to the enemy?"

"Or our erstwhile allies," Karl pointed out. "A battle between Nordland and Christopher produces only victory for the Dark."

"Let us test the waters, then," suggested Lalania. "Send the patrol out, but without Christopher. If Nordland does pounce, he will leave empty-handed. He will not murder mere servants, no matter how much he hates Christopher."

"And if . . . others attack?" Christopher didn't want to see his prize cavalry obliterated by some kind of infernal magic while he wasn't there. Well, he didn't want to see it while he was there, either. He was assuming he would make a difference. Given how little he knew of magic, that might not be a good assumption.

"One sleep spell and half the company is down," Karl said.

"Your horsemen are too spread out for that," Lalania corrected him. "And Gregor's rank would be a stiff defense against that spell."

"I don't fancy riding into combat without healing," Gregor said. "I will be a prime target, at least until they learn that your peacocks can spit fire."

"I can heal," Torme said. "At the Curate's command, I will put your life above the lives of our own."

"I will also go," Disa volunteered. "This is why I came, after all, to serve in battle. I will not shirk my duty." She didn't even have a weapon.

"I will go, too," Lalania said with an uncharacteristically sour glance at Disa. "As eyes and ears, if nothing else." But Christopher had seen Lalania in action. She was deadly with a crossbow. "Yet you must stay behind, Christopher. Here, in your stone barracks, surrounded by your footmen, even the Gold Apostle would hesitate to engage you."

"Great," Christopher said. "The King orders me to hunt ulvenmen, and so I'm sending every person I know except myself to do it." A supreme irony; he had locked down his men until Karl's arrival, and now that Karl was here, he was the one confined to barracks.

"It's only for a little while," Gregor grinned. "You can come out to play once we've made sure the sandbox is safe."

Late that night Christopher had an unexpected visitor. Gregor came to his quarters, a mug of ale in each hand and a troubled look on his face.

"I thought you might like a nightcap," he said, although clearly that was not the reason he was there.

"Sure," Christopher agreed, and tried to give the man time to come around to it on his own. They drank in silence for a few minutes.

"If you can ask me about magic," Gregor said, "then I can ask you about women."

"You can ask, Gregor, but . . ."

"It's Lala," the blue knight said, ignoring Christopher's disclaimer. "Whenever we are apart, she is all I can think of. I'm not a fool; I know she does not feel the same. Yet when we are reunited, she showers me with such affection that nothing else matters, and she tolerates no other woman's glance at me. Until the days begin to drag, and then she goes away again, to leave me to stew on my own while she . . ." Christopher understood the troubadour's comment about whoring around now. Gregor, true to his love, was faithful, even when he knew she wasn't.

"Yes," Christopher agreed. That was what the woman did.

"What do I do?" the knight moaned.

Psychological counseling was not really part of the priestly training he'd received, mostly because he'd received virtually no training. But he had fifteen years of life experience over the knight. He thought of something he'd seen on TV once.

"Maybe you should stop sleeping with her."

Gregor was extremely dubious.

"I mean it, Gregor. See if there is anything to your relationship besides sex."

He could have made a joke. He could have said something like, "What makes you think I want more than that?" He could have passed it off the way any virile young man would have, without a second thought. But he didn't.

"Why is it the good answers are always the last ones you want to hear?" He finished his mug and took his leave.

Only after the knight was gone did Christopher realize how impolitic his advice was. If Lalania was the chain that kept Gregor bound to him, then he had just smashed at it with a sledgehammer. The only person who could possibly profit from his advice was Gregor.

He sighed, recognizing that even understanding that beforehand he would have said exactly the same thing. The only people he could bring himself to take advantage of were the volunteers for that duty. Like Karl, who did all the work and accepted none of the reward. Or Torme, who stood behind him with a broom to sweep up his every oversight.

Or Disa, who would put her cute little body in the jaws of slavering monsters, for no better reason than duty.

It was a solid week before they let Christopher out of his prison. He did kata and paperwork, alternating between sweaty sword drills and inky-fingered supply lists and mechanical drawings, but his strolls back and forth under the tall gray walls of the barracks ground were becoming longer and more frequent, to the point where the men edged out of his way when he got near, as if shying away from a tiger pacing in a too-small cage.

Only Alstanf saved his sanity. The architect came by most nights for a chat and brought his own bottle. They talked about the limits of engineering and the hazards of imperious bosses who issued dictums and left the technical details up to their subordinates. Christopher described flying buttresses, which Alstanf found fascinating; the architect in turn taught Christopher the many, many details of magic wall-building, such as how to mix mud without injecting bubbles that would weaken the structure later. True, he mostly provided this education as a series of complaints about the day's difficulties, but Christopher was still grateful for the conversation.

Now Christopher was along for a ride. The days were hot, muggy, and insect-ridden; the night was spent on soggy, uncomfortable ground after eating salted meat and hard bread. Worse, he was clad in the heavy plate he'd won from Bart, his chain mail still a disassociated pile of links.

"Brave peasants this county has," Gregor said. They'd seen farms and villages ten miles south of the city.

"It is good land," explained Karl. "Ulvenmen are in their past, but a rich harvest is in front of them."

"They've spread too far from safety," Disa said sadly. "If the ulvenmen come again, many will die."

"There are no ulvenmen within a hundred miles," Gregor

answered. "If there were, they would've already heard this cavalcade of horses and fled."

"You want a smaller patrol?" Christopher barely felt safe with the twenty carabineers behind them.

"It should be just us," Gregor explained. "You, me, and the girls. Quick and quiet, like a knife in the dark. We'd have a lot more fun that way."

"Men and their absurd fantasies," Lalania grumbled. She was surlier than he had ever seen her. She shared a tent with Gregor, but Christopher suspected sleep was all she was getting.

Disa was still bright and cheerful, if gradually becoming more disheveled with each day. Karl and Torme, of course, were in their element.

"I fear Ser Gregor is right," Karl said. "Our troop makes too much noise and dust to trap anything unawares."

"Was there anything here to trap?"

"I have little skill at this," Lalania said. "Lady Niona could tell you the color of their shoes by their tracks. All I can say is that Fairweather must have traveled farther south."

"Then so should we," Gregor said.

"And follow to his fate? No, that is not wisdom." Lalania brushed a clod of dirt from her shoulder, an act she repeated throughout the day. The heavy destriers churned the ground so furiously that the boundary between earth and air became blurred by a soup of mud, gravel, and rotting vegetable material. Christopher had combed half a beetle out of his hair last night.

"It does feel like a trap," Christopher mused. "They lure us so deep that once we do fight, we can't fight our way out. And all they have to do to set the trap is not be here. Our own frustration and greed drags us to them."

"Yet drag we must. We get no profit out of sitting in that city. And some of us have bills to pay."

Christopher was surprised at Gregor's mercenary finances, until he realized the man was talking about him. Christopher was the one with bills to pay; specifically, thousands of gold pieces of bonds to redeem.

"Then let's bring the whole regiment out here."

"The Captain will never let you strip his city of its defenses—which now include your men. He would probably lock you in your barracks if he thought he could get away with it. No, Christopher, if you would hunt ulvenmen, you must do it the way it has always been done. Rank by the handful and daring by the bushel." Gregor was smiling at the prospect, which tempted Christopher to question his sanity.

But danger marched into his barracks. Right through his soldiers, and his advisors, and the hard stone walls, and the thick bronze-braced double doors. He'd barely shaken off the dust of the road and stopped looking around warily for an ambush when the Captain, a squad of city soldiers, and Joadan stomped into the courtyard.

"To what do we owe the honor?" Lalania asked, interposing herself between the intruders and Christopher.

"A simple question, which the Curate can easily answer, and send us on our way." The Captain was pretending to be friendly, which could only signify true menace.

"I—" started Lalania, but Joadan cut her off.

"—have no place here, troubadour. I speak rank to rank, to the Curate only."

Gregor folded his arms across his chest. Christopher felt things were getting out of hand, so he stepped forward.

"Thank you for not knocking down my door. But I have to say, this feels hardly less friendly, so ask your question and go."

"Very well," said Joadan, with a glitter of triumph in his eyes. "Were you not sent to dislodge me and claim my place?"

"Um . . . yes?" Christopher was still struggling with the syntax of that completely spurious "not," so he did not notice Lalania biting her lip.

Joadan turned to the Captain and spread his hands, framing Christopher's answer like a show-pony.

"Indeed," the Captain said, "a clear and present challenge to your station. By royal law you may respond with a challenge to your person."

"Now hold on a minute," Christopher said.

Joadan and the Captain ignored him, continuing their little play.

"I do so."

"As Captain of the town and charged with maintaining the peace, I will oversee the terms," the Captain said. "This is a personal challenge, between men of equal rank. There will be no secondaries and no stakeholders. Weapons shall be swords only, and all parties are forbidden from seeking revenge, whatever the outcome. Lord Curate, are you prepared?"

This was directed at Christopher, and now the entire yard fell silent, waiting for his response.

"No," Christopher said. "I'm not prepared now or at any time in the future."

"You assert cowardice in front of your own men?" The Captain tilted his head back, as if presented with a bad smell. "Then present your ransom and depart the city."

"I cannot leave the city," Christopher said. "The King ordered me here."

"He ordered your regiment," the Captain answered. "In your absence I will assume command of it. The city remains protected."

Christopher floundered, reduced to desperation. "I'm not sure the King would agree."

"I am sure the King would not let a coward lead a regiment." The Captain looked like he was ready to duel Christopher himself. "But you can ride to Kingsrock and take it up with him. Just as soon as you present your ransom. One hundred and two pounds of gold. Or tael, as you prefer."

That was a ridiculously large sum, even though it was only a fraction of what his last rank had cost. But that wealth was long spent; promoting Torme to first-rank had all but bankrupted him.

The Captain shrugged at his silence. "If your pockets are empty, then we must withdraw from your head. Kneel, and I shall make it quick." The Captain put his hand on his sword.

Christopher had finally had enough. "Unless you're trying to get in line," he said to the Captain, "you can knock it off." He turned to Joadan. "Do me the courtesy of answering my own question first. You know my reputation. What makes you think you can win?"

"Reputation? A sword of lies and an unwitnessed miracle are less probatory than you might think. But the answer is simple: I have something worth fighting for. This is not the first risk I have engendered, and it will not be the last. The cause that drives me is worth any danger; the need I have for power and wealth cannot be tarried."

"I could be an ally in that cause."

"Perhaps you already are," Joadan said. "The wealth from your head may lead to the final cure. If not, be assured it shall not go to waste."

"Then it's settled," the Captain said. "Here will do," and he started scratching out a square in the dirt with his foot.

"Krellyan's law requires twenty-four hours before a duel. You cannot ask me to violate that."

"This is not the Saint's land," the Captain objected.

"But I am his man. And I don't want to have to face him after I've faced the lot of you. So go away and come back tomorrow."

The Captain did not want to give up. "I could arrest you for failure to pay. I don't have to wait a day for that."

Joadan put out his hand to stop the Captain. "No. I accept the delay. It matters not; the portents will be as good tomorrow as they are today. And if not, then let the gods decide."

The Captain frowned at this betrayal, but he seemed to run out of threats. With an ill temper he marched his soldiers out again. Joadan followed them out, pausing at the gate only long enough to give Christopher a contemplative glare.

"Shiiiiiii—" said Gregor.

"Oh, hush," Lalania said. "It is too early to panic. Wait until tomorrow. Then we can panic."

"Don't you have work to do?" Christopher said to the gawking soldiers. They quickly resumed their tasks or invented ones if they happened to not have any.

"What the hell was that all about?" he asked, once his little group had regained some sense of privacy.

"If ever there was a time to lie, that was it," Lalania said. "Against no other would Joadan march in here and demand they indict themselves out of their own mouth. And yet the blame lies with you, Christopher. You have been indiscreet. Someone has heard of your instructions from the Cathedral and carried the tale to your enemies."

"Wait," said Christopher, "how did you know what Krellyan said?"

"Because you just told me," she snapped. "Now you have indicted the Saint as well. Can you not learn the virtue of silence?"

This would have been the perfect time to cast the spell of that same name. But he hadn't memorized it again, having been too ashamed of the echoes of the first time he'd used it.

"You assume the Curate is displeased with this turn of events," Torme said. He was trying to defend his boss. Christopher knew he didn't deserve it.

"Nope, I blew it." He tried to think of whom he'd discussed the matter with. Oda, but only in general terms, and she would seem to be above reproach. Other than that, he'd hardly spoken to anyone from this town, except . . .

Alstanf.

He'd thought of the man as a friend. He had forgotten that in feudal politics, there were no friends; only vassals and rivals, only the subdued and the soon-to-be subdued.

"Okay, what do we do now?"

"There's not a lot we can do," Gregor said. "Unless you're hiding a fortune in your pants, and even then, I would council against it. You cannot let a challenge like this stand unopposed, or every sellsword from East to West will be here on the morrow looking for their payout."

"Joadan's not stupid. He wouldn't challenge me if he didn't have an ace up his sleeve."

"Oh, he does," Lalania said. "A dirty trick, and probably more the source of Krellyan's law than gentleness. He cast an augury. He's probably been casting them for days, waiting for one that was unambiguously favorable. And thus he bravely walked in here knowing that the gods had predicted his victory—at least for the next hour." Despite the scorn in her words, she sounded like she approved of the strategy.

"So why throw it away by accepting a delay?"

"Because you earned his respect," Gregor suggested.

"More likely, he realized that he had already won his victory—by winning the argument to force a duel. Thus, the augury was expired," Lalania said.

"Or he just hates you *that much*," Torme said.

Christopher looked to Karl, the man he always turned to for the final decision.

"Ser Gregor is right: you must fight. The Captain is also right: you must win."

He had armor now, and rank, and a strong body unencumbered by old injuries. But Joadan had armor as well—the Yellow priest had been wearing a beautiful golden breastplate with elaborate curlicues and matching greaves—and the same rank, plus years more experience with magic despite being a decade younger. His sword looked a lot more expensive than Christopher's. The only advantage Christopher could see was that he was a few inches taller than the other man. Having been routinely trounced by short Japanese sensei for decades, he didn't feel that was an edge worth betting on.

"I need to think," Christopher said.

But he couldn't think about Joadan without thinking about Alstanf. Finally, to clear his mind, he went in search of the traitorous weasel. Lalania let him go with only a small squad; there was little danger that anyone would try to kill a man who was already under a death sentence. She had used her wonderful intelligence skills to determine that the city generally assumed he was doomed. While Joadan was not notorious as a duelist, he was famously unimpeded; many other problems had been plowed through in the young man's quest for fame and fortune.

Christopher could relate; he understood the impetus.

He found Alstanf in front of another brownstone, overseeing several shirtless young men loading a wardrobe into a wagon. When Christopher spoke his name from behind, he leapt into the air like a startled rabbit and cowered behind the furniture.

"Just tell me why," Christopher said, his anger evaporating in the face of such terror.

"Flying buttresses," Alstanf squeaked.

Christopher turned up his empty palm to show that was not an answer. But only his right hand; these days his left stayed hitched onto his sword hilt.

"I want to build flying buttresses. And I will never, ever build them here. The Captain promised to let me go. He said he would grant me release from the Wizard's service. Forgive me, Christopher, but that was a boon that all your wealth and knowledge could never buy."

And so it was. Christopher left the man in peace, thinking.

He could name at least one drawback to Krellyan's rule. Spending twenty-four hours contemplating a fight did not make it easier to face.

Lalania and Gregor had quizzed him over his first encounter and then given him the benefit of their tactical wisdom when it came to selecting his spells. For instance, he had assumed that the panther or whatever it was would not be an issue, having seen it blasted into smithereens. Gregor had gently set him straight while Lalania stared at him, and Torme had found a defense suggested in one of his novice-training books.

So now he stood in his barracks courtyard, arrayed in plate and mail with a head full of spells and a heavy heart. The Captain had sent over a man earlier to lay out a dueling square in red ribbon. At least there would be no crowd of townsmen; the only audience would be his own soldiers. Playing a home game should have been an advantage. Somehow it didn't feel like that to Christopher. These men weren't just expecting him to win; they required it. Failing would not only get him killed but would put them back into the peasant's harness. Just keeping his head seemed like enough of a burden to carry on his shoulders.

The Captain and his plate-clad squad of halberdiers waited outside the gate until Joadan's party arrived. The Gold Curate had brought a pair of servants with him, wearing livery but apparently unarmed. Christopher's soldiers stood at attention in steady rows along the walls. They were also unarmed. They had left their rifles indoors, at Karl's specific order.

Gregor had been aghast. "No wonder Joadan challenges you in

your lair. Not only do you command your men to meekness; you disarm them. When Joadan looks out over these ranks, his knees will not tremble, and he will not be weakened by the fear that if he wins, a hundred angry men might descend on him. Even such a tiny edge can turn a duel. Why disarm yourself?"

"Because they might well do something," Karl had said. "It will be hard enough to keep them alive if Christopher falls; should they commit treason by firing on the Curate, the entire regiment will hang as a body. The Captain wants them for slaves; the Lord Wizard only wants them for the tael in their heads."

Torme had memorized a detection spell, the one aid he would be allowed to render. He would verify that Joadan had not come into the duel with pre-cast magic. Christopher wasn't entirely sure why those rules should apply to priests, but Gregor explained that was what made it a duel.

"This way at least pretends to be fair. If you load up on magic and then jump somebody, that's just an ambush."

The enemy now paraded through the gates, or at least the soldiers did. The Captain sauntered, and Joadan walked with simple, purposeful steps. Christopher took his place inside the ring opposite Joadan, and the Captain walked between them.

"Do you both declare yourself free of outside magic, as per the well-established rule?"

"I do," both men said, which Christopher would have found hilarious if he hadn't been so nervous.

Torme cast his spell, but neither of Joadan's servants approached Christopher. Apparently the Yellow priest would take his word for it, just as Bart had done.

"He is free of enchantment," Torme reported, "but both his blade and armor are ranked." Then Torme retreated from the square, unable to even wish Christopher luck without creating the suspicion of magical interference.

The Captain backed up, grinning widely.

"Then begin," he said, bringing his still mail-clad hands together in a ringing clap.

The duel started somewhat anticlimactically, as both men immediately began chanting spells. The panther appeared, as expected, and sprung ten feet across the ground at Christopher. But he had raised his protective spell, and the beast bounced off an invisible wall and fell to the ground. It landed on all fours, hissing and spitting.

Joadan did not react to this setback, instead launching into another spell. Christopher charged him; the panther intercepted. It could not touch him, but neither could he force his way past it. If he tried, the act would shatter his protection.

Balked, Christopher started another spell of his own. He felt a bit of sympathy for the audience; this chanting could go on for quite a while yet. But Joadan apparently felt he had enough advantage. The panther circled around Christopher, blocking his retreat, and Joadan leapt at him with rather more alacrity than one would except from under so much armor.

Christopher sidestepped and parried, hoping the action would disconcert Joadan as much as it had Karl, back when they had practiced for Hobilar's duel. Whether or not the gambit succeeded was rendered irrelevant when Joadan's sword sliced neatly through his own. He had not yet cast the sword blessing; mere steel could not stand against the permanent enchantment on Joadan's blade.

To be fair, it had also been a clumsy parry.

Though he had not expected the duel to end so quickly, it was still the anticipated outcome. He dropped the ruins of his sword and raised his hands in surrender. Again.

"I yield."

Joadan paused in mid-stroke, a remarkable feat of discipline given the battle-lust in his eyes.

"You have your ransom now?"

"No," Christopher said, "and neither am I willing to vacate the city."

Joadan raised his sword.

"But in lieu of that, I offer you a service. I shall perform a single task at your direction, and we will call it square."

Intelligent man that he was, Joadan paused his killing stroke to satisfy his curiosity.

"What service could you possibly render me, short of your head and your absence?"

"I can write a letter."

Joadan's eyes narrowed, and his sword slowly inched up.

"To the Saint."

The Yellow priest froze like a statue, finally anticipating what came next.

"To cure your boy at my expense."

Joadan spoke through clenched teeth. "I have searched across the realm for a cure. I came here, to serve the Lord Wizard, solely to convince him to search across the planes. And yet you claim it lies under my nose all along?"

"It's a birth defect, Joadan. At a—" there was no word for *molecular*, "structural level. A regeneration should fix it. I can buy that service, even if you can't. But you can claim it from me on the field of battle."

Complete silence, for uncomfortable moments, while Joadan stared at him. The audience held their breath—amazingly, even the Captain stood without jeering, although the look on his face was more dismay than anticipation.

The silence was broken by a popping sound. The cat had turned into golden feathers again, and was now gone.

"You have earned my respect for your acuity," Joadan said quietly. "You may find in the future that you regret that status."

Well, Christopher hadn't exactly expected a thank-you card.

Joadan sheathed his sword, turned on his heel, and marched out of the ring with squared shoulders.

The Captain spat in disgust. "Dark gods, you White priests can't even do this right."

"Peace is restored," Torme said, "and a boy is saved. The goals of the White are advanced, even though you are denied your entertainment."

The Captain stared at Torme, rolling his tongue behind his teeth. Christopher expected a threat or at least a reprimand, but the Captain spat again and stalked off.

"Praise the gods," Lalania said. "I have never seen a better match of winning by losing. But you took a terrible risk, Christopher. The likes of Black Bart would have cut you down before you finished speaking."

That Joadan was not the likes of Black Bart was the entire reason Christopher had done this. He preferred a Gold Throne to an Iron one, and he was certain the Saint would too. But for once, he took Lalania's words to heart and kept his mouth shut.

"Your sword," Torme said, handing him the pieces sorrowfully.

Christopher shrugged. He had a spell for that.

He stood at the city gates the next day, watching Joadan's servants drive a pair of heavily loaded wagons through it. The Yellow Priest was leaving immediately for Kingsrock and was making plain his intention not to return.

Christopher walked into the road next to Joadan's horse and handed up the letter.

"You don't have to go," he said.

"I have what I came for," Joadan said. "There is nothing left for me here."

His horse cantered out of the gate, withers and head high. Despite that, and Joadan's fine words, it was retreat all the same, and everyone knew it. To stay and act as if Christopher's act of mercy meant nothing would rub against Joadan until it broke his vows.

The townsfolk did not take the lesson to heart, however. Where Christopher saw goodwill, they saw only incomprehensible metaphysics. They would freely grant him the quality of cleverness. A reputation for kindness he would have to earn the old-fashioned way.

And without Lalania's help. Her patience for standing still had finally run out, and she was on the road again. The consolation prize was that Gregor was staying behind. "You promised me ulvenmen heads," he said, "and I'm not leaving until I get some."

But Christopher found himself disappointed, watching Lalania and Gregor discuss her departure. There was no passion. A subtle thing, but he had become used to it, so it was remarkable by its absence.

10

TROUBLE IN BED

The privilege of the city was a grand thing to have. He strolled into Oda's clinic, leaving his squad of troopers and his sword at the door. She greeted him with a warm smile and assigned him his first patient, a cherubic two-year-old girl with whooping cough. Or, at least, *a* whooping cough. Christopher didn't know precisely what disease she had, and he didn't care. He invoked the spell, speaking in Celestial and placing his hand on her head, and her eyes cleared instantly. The child giggled at him, grabbing at his hand, while the mother made grateful beacons of her eyes.

His duty done, he was free to leave. Walking to the door, he felt the eyes of the other patients on him. He was spared the burden of diagnosis and triage. Oda made all those hard decisions. He just showed up, snapped his fingers, and basked in adoration. Then he swaggered off in his fancy clothes, followed by his heavily armed and high-spirited bravos. What happened next should not have surprised him.

As he was retiring to his quarters for sleep, he thought the two guards on duty were grinning more than usual. Since people had been smiling at him all day, he did not pay any attention to it, just as he ignored the bits of cloth lying on the ground at their feet.

These little details nagging at his consciousness were not enough to alert him. Only when he saw the body lying in his bed did they come boiling to the surface, screaming of wrongness and danger.

The spell left his lips instantly as he clutched out at the figure, and it froze. Now that he thought about it, the figure hadn't been doing much in the first place. Mostly lying around languidly and provocatively.

He had his sword halfway out of its sheath before he realized that there was a girl in his bed. Whether that was a testament to his reflexes or his paranoia wasn't clear.

Resheathing the sword, observing the paralyzed body, he finally had time to recognize that it was a fresh-faced girl, sixteen or seventeen years old, with long black hair, a lovely figure, and no clothes.

She was stark naked. The significance of the pile of cloth outside his door chimed in. And the leers on the faces of his guards.

He spoke the release word in Celestial, freeing the girl from his spell. She gasped a little in shock before opening her arms invitingly. Or trying; she was too nervous to manage actual seductiveness.

"Who are you, and why are you here?" His tone was perhaps more brusque than the situation demanded, but she was quite attractive, and it had been over a year since he had seen his wife.

"My name is Ugewne, my lord." Her voice was trembling between schoolgirl sweetness and harlot-level huskiness. "I am here to serve you."

"Who sent you? And how did you get past my guards?"

She was wilting under the interrogation, pulling her arms in to cover herself. "No one, my lord. And I walked past them. Do I not please you?"

"I'm sure you're a nice girl." Or an extremely accomplished actress, pretending that perfect mix of hesitancy and desire that spelled innocence. "But you should go." She made him feel like a teenager. He did not want to feel that way, right here, right now. He did not want to act on those kinds of feelings.

Stunned by his dismissal, she burst into tears and fled the room, not even stopping to collect her clothing. Christopher followed her halfway, helplessly.

"What the Dark do you mean letting her in here like that?" he barked at his guards, relieving his frustration in anger.

"I'm sorry, my lord. It is their custom. And a fine custom indeed. We did not know it would displease you."

In the face of his anger they reverted to the most flattering of titles. Deflated, unable to lash out at anyone, Christopher spun his wedding ring with his thumb.

"I made a vow, Private. I can't accept this custom. Whatever it is." Massaging his temple, he indicated her clothes. "Catch up to her, give her my apologies. And her clothes. Please, explain it to her." He almost handed the soldier a gold piece to give the girl but decided that might be taken the wrong way. He couldn't solve every problem with money.

The soldier had already saluted and departed by the time he was done with these ruminations.

"What custom?" he asked the other one.

"It's considered good luck for a girl to spend her first night with a man of rank. And begging your pardon, sir, your generosity and kindness are well-known. We did not understand, sir. We do now. It will not happen again."

Christopher put his hands to his face in dismay. The old right of the lord, to sleep with the bride on her wedding night. Here it had been institutionalized into a custom perpetuated by the commoners themselves. Giving it voluntarily reduced the instances of having it taken. And plying superheroes with pretty girls to keep them happy and close was in the community's best interests. Christopher, flocked in White, healing children and raising commoners, and wearing the face of a twenty-year-old, would be considered easy duty.

As much as the sight of the girl had aroused him, the depths to which these ordinary people had sunk sickened him. Pretty young women were always drawn to rich old men, in every world, but here it had gone from mercenary biology to self-imposed subjugation.

He went into his room and shut the door, to find his own private peace with his turbulent feelings.

The next day he thought to detect a subtle change in the way his men treated him. He would have expected derision, confusion, or even suspicion at his turning down a nubile girl. He could have accepted jocularity or slackness, since he had not punished the guards in any way for their failure of protocol. But it was none of those.

If anything, they were more friendly and personable, even while their salutes were crisper. If only Lalania were here to tell him why.

Karl, surprisingly, had not yet heard of the incident. But the young man looked drawn and tired. He trained as hard as he drove his soldiers, and he partied as hard as he trained. Still, his instincts were intact. When Christopher described the events of the previous night, he immediately seized on the one significant word.

"You told them you had taken a *vow*?"

"Yes," Christopher said. "My marriage vow. I promised I would be faithful to my wife, and I aim to keep that promise."

Karl shook his head in derision. "A foolish thing to promise, especially with your wife so far away. But I have always honored your decisions. Now, I fear, it is no longer your choice."

"What do you mean?"

"You told them you made a vow." Christopher nodded for him to continue; they'd already established this. "They have finally found an explanation for your meteoric rise and fantastic good luck. You made a pact with some power, some extra-planer entity. Possibly even a god. And chastity is the price you paid."

"But that's not true." Well, he had made a pact with a deity, but it was only the ordinary arrangement of priesthood. Nobody here found his spells to be worthy of special comment.

"Truth is less important than comfort." Karl shrugged. "Now your entire army views your virtue as their lucky charm. You will need to warn Lalania. If they think she aims to seduce you, they will shoot her."

Christopher's shock received no sympathy from Karl. "You have given a name to their hopes, a concrete fact to hold against the unknown. And one they can hope to affect, through their diligence. It will do the army good and save me the need of babysitting you." Karl had already had to intervene once, when Christopher had been seduced by magic.

That new quality he had detected in his soldiers was protectiveness. And they were ennobled by it. No longer merely servants under the protection of his political authority and magic but partners in protecting him the only way they could.

Perversely, he spent the rest of the day annoyed by it. She really had been a very beautiful young woman.

But by the time he retired to his quarters, he had come to terms with the arrangement. He was asking a lot from these men. It was only fair that they could expect him to pay a price, as well. Spotting the same soldier outside his door, he asked about the girl.

"As per your orders, I gave her such comfort as I could, sir. Which explains why I was away from my post for half the night. Not that I am making excuses, sir."

Not excuses, Christopher laughed to himself, but bragging. Still, that result seemed more appropriate; they were at least of an age.

It didn't make his empty bed any more comfortable, though.

When he walked into Oda's clinic the next day, eager to see another patient, he immediately knew something was wrong. The crowd shrank back from him perceptibly, and Oda's face was a mask of pain.

"I appreciate your help, Brother. But someone does not. I think it best that you reserve your magic for your own men, from now on."

With great sadness, she produced a cloth from her cupboard. Unwrapping the object it contained, she handed him a crossbow quarrel of white wood, fletched in goose feathers.

"This was found next to the body. Although we did not understand it, we knew it could only be a message for you."

Christopher understood it. His assassin had found him.

"What body?" he demanded. This was going to cost him a hundred tael, a veritable fortune. "We need to send for Faren, immediately." It was a long ride to and from the Cathedral.

"We will not send for him, Brother. He would not come. It is of no use."

He wanted to yell at her, to demand that she talk sense. He wanted to shout loud enough that he could not hear the words in his head, the memory of what Svengusta had told him once, when he had first discovered the power of revival. And its limits.

It is reckoned futile to even try with a child under three.

He crushed the quarrel in his hand, but it did not yield. Its power, like the power of evil, was obdurate.

The giggling face of the little girl swam before his vision. The first person he had ever cured of disease, the first person he had made whole and healthy for no other reason than that he could.

And now dead, because *he* had healed her.

"None blame you, Brother. But they fear you."

Why were the only people who ever feared him the ones he tried to help?

"I understand," he said through gritted teeth, though he would never understand what useless spite drove a person to such lengths. The assassin gained nothing from this, risked herself for no profit, only for the harm it did him. That she was a woman and used a child as naught but a stone to throw against his window baffled him. But confusion crumbled before a tide of anger.

Stiffly he bowed to Oda, turning to leave like a wooden toy soldier. She sensed his fury and clasped him in a tearful embrace. "Do not blame your-self. We are not responsible for what evil chooses. Do not blame yourself."

"I know who to blame," he growled.

The people of the town parted before him as he stalked through the streets, every boot-fall a warning of violence, his soldiers marching now stone-faced and double-time behind him, their cheery insolence evaporated without residue. But their advance broke on a wall of stone and a servant in black livery.

"I'm here to see the wizard," Christopher announced to the chubby, sleepy-eyed gateman at the foot of the high stone tower.

"Not during the day, you aren't." The man shook his head in denial. "My job is a simple one, suited to a man of my simple abilities. My job is to tell people to come back at night."

"This is about murder. Let me in."

"If I do, it will be, about mine. It's worth more than my life to open that door in the daytime. Come back at night."

Shouting up at the barred windows seemed too undignified, even for Christopher. And he was coming to ask a favor. Defeated, he turned away and retreated to his barracks, the one place in town where his law was absolute and his people were safe.

Karl was confused as well. "I did not think her so wicked as that. You have a way of bringing out the worst in people." Christopher almost said something snappish, before he remembered Fae. Karl had earned the right to talk like that.

"Not always the worst," Torme demurred. "But, my lord, con-sider your next action carefully. You do not want to drive the wizard to extremes."

Gregor shook his head, too. "Lalania thought you safe from the assassin, and in a way you are. You certainly outrank her now, and in any case she must know the Saint can revive you from a single hair. She cannot hope to destroy you directly. But no one could expect her to strike like this."

"Could Lala find her?" Christopher had failed to catch the woman when she was hiding on his own Church lands. Finding her here would be ten times as hard.

"No," Gregor said. "Because of the duty of wall-building, almost every man in the city is tracked. It would be hard for a man to live here without attracting the attention of that ravenous labor press gang. But nobody keeps track of women."

A thousand times as hard.

"Maybe the wizard has magic that can help."

Disa shook her head. "I doubt it, Brother. The governance of society is the domain of priests, not mages."

"I'm going to ask, anyway." Christopher could not bear to do nothing.

Gregor and Torme accompanied him to the tower in the dark, along with Karl and a dozen soldiers. They didn't expect trouble, but they could still hope for it. A vicious, poison-edged ambush was preferable to the assassin's current tactics.

The same servant met them at the door.

"Don't you have a replacement?" Christopher asked.

"No, my lord. The wizard does not care to squander more gold than necessary."

"So you are always on duty?" When did the man sleep? Or do other things, equally biologically necessary things.

"The duty is not that burdensome, my lord, although I thank you for thinking of me. Hardly anyone ever wants to see the wizard. Indeed, you have been so kind that I wish to advise you, exalted as you are, no doubt fully aware in your omnivorous perspicacity of all salient facts, yet nonetheless embarked upon a course of action whose dreadful outcome is acutely expected by myself, not through any contemplation or faculty of thought, I assure you, but merely brute, raw experience."

That was the biggest word salad Christopher had heard on this planet. And like salad, completely devoid of calories. "Advise me of what?"

The doorman quirked his eyebrows, perhaps surprised Christopher had followed his entire speech.

"Why, *not* to see the wizard, my lord."

"Not an option." Christopher would leave no stone unturned to exorcise the creature that haunted him.

"As you wish, though you must hazard the tower alone."

"If you're not out in an hour, we'll come in after you," Gregor growled.

The blue knight was only third-rank. The wizard was at least ninth, or so Lalania had claimed, based on the magic she had seen him do. It was not a credible threat.

"If you're not out by daylight, we'll knock the tower down," promised Karl.

Even though Karl had no ranks at all, the threat was serious. Karl had a dozen cannon back at the barracks. Christopher grinned wolfishly, thinking of how surprised the wizard would be to see his tower smashed from a thousand yards away, until he remembered he would still be in it.

The doorman bowed deeply before turning to crank open the heavy iron door. It squealed on its hinges, flakes of rust drifting down, finally coming to a stop halfway open. With an apologetic smile the doorman threw his body against the door, trying to move it, in vain.

"That's okay," Christopher said. "By the way, an excellent performance." He had the distinct suspicion that the doorman loaded the hinges with rust flakes in between each visitor.

"A last detail, my lord," the doorman said. "You must rely on the wizard to provide illumination."

Christopher took his light-stone out of his pocket and handed it to Torme, ignoring the doorman's outstretched hand. Stepping around the edge of the door, Christopher entered the tower.

The room inside was completely dark, not even allowing the light from outside to enter. Shadow, solid and monolithic, started at the edge of the door, a black fog impenetrable and featureless save for the glow of magically illuminated paving stones leading into the tower. Stepping into the darkness was unearthly. He could see nothing but the stones. He could only see his hand if it were in the path of the stones, a blank silhouette.

"Knock three times when you've changed your mind," the doorman called. Christopher looked back, but he could see nothing outside of the tower, either, the intangible fog cutting off all vision. He could hear the door cranking shut, however, and the solid thud when it meshed into the stone lintel.

When the hairs on the back of his neck stood up, he discovered he was not immune to superstition and spookery.

But the vision of the little girl came to him, and in an instant the theatrics were wasted. Striding across the glowing stones brought him to a spiral iron staircase, every other step illuminated like the path. Unwilling to endure any cruel tricks, he took the staircase two steps at a time, until it deposited him on what he guessed was the third floor, a room of only ordinary darkness.

This room was dressed like a crypt, with rough stone benches and a handful of light-stones flickering from iron candelabra sticking out in regular intervals from the wall. The color they shed was black, a feat Christopher found wholly inexplicable, until he realized they must be in the ultraviolet spectrum. His skin shone with an unnatural reflection, as did cobwebs draped around the room. He reached out and touched one. Brittle with age, it crackled in his hand.

"Why do you disturb my rest?" The voice was sonorous, and Christopher turned to see where it came from.

The wizard sat on a stone throne, draped in black robes. Christopher could not see his face under the hood. But remembering Lalania's description rendered the illusions ineffectual.

"For good reason, Lord Wizard. I have come to report a murder."

"Isn't that what I pay the Captain for?" The querulousness of the question diminished the effect of the grave tone.

"This is beyond his ability," Christopher said. He had completely forgotten to even mention it to the Captain, but he knew it would have been a waste of time. "The murderer is a professional assassin."

The wizard tapped long fingernails on the stone arm of his throne. "I presume the assassin stalks you. So why does this concern me?"

Christopher came straight to the point. "I want your help in finding her."

Leaning back, the wizard shook his head gently, so as not to disturb the careful folds of his hood. "You fail on two points. First, I have no incentive to help you, and secondly, I could not if I wanted to. Hunting down an Invisible Guild rat is a job for dogs and policemen, not wizards."

"Then give me permission to search the city." He would funnel every adult woman through a zone of truth if he had to.

But the wizard anticipated him. "I will not let you turn my city upside down and shake it until everything falls loose. I would hear no end of complaining, and I cannot bear it. Have you not done enough already?"

"Then what are you going to do?" Christopher demanded.

"The obvious solution would be to remove the attraction. Banishing your army would be easier than banishing one invisible woman."

The wizard's tone was ironic, but the truth of it washed over Christopher like fresh water.

"Yes. Banish me. Build me a fort to the south, and I will take my army and my person away from here. For the small cost of a week of your time, I will extend your southern border twenty miles, giving your farmers the protection of at least an early warning." He was making up plans as fast as he talked, all the pieces tumbling into place easily. "They will flock to those empty lands, raising your taxes. My soldiers will only trouble your tavern keepers every few weeks, when their pockets are full of silver. And I may be able to find some ulvenmen, which will make the King happy."

The wizard stopped his improv with a raised hand.

"I see your point. Indeed, it makes so much sense one wonders why no commander has ever volunteered it before. I confess a certain curiosity as to your motivation."

Because life in this city had lost its allure, slain by a single white quarrel. And also, paradoxically, because it had too much allure. Not just the teenage girl in his bed, but the desire to upend the entire social order, which the wizard would probably interpret as a threat to his rule.

"Because I am haunted by too many women," he said, trying to give an answer that was reasonably close to the truth. The luscious body of his young seductress, still fresh in his memory, brought him not even a shred of guilt-tinged arousal. In his mind she wore the face of the young mother he had so terribly failed.

The wizard laughed, forgetting his role as undead overlord. Then he caught himself, and tried to cover it up with a fit of coughing.

"It's okay," Christopher said. "I know it's just an illusion."

"How?" Then, again, in the graveyard tones. "How do you defeat my magic?"

"What incentive do I have to reveal my secrets?" Cheeky, yes, perhaps even impertinent in the face of so much rank, but Christopher was buoyed by his sudden plan. Though escape was no victory, it was better than despair.

"To earn my favor. Does that mean so little to you?"

A sense of relief washed through Christopher. The mere fact that the wizard was arguing meant Christopher had room to negotiate.

"Now that you mention it, I would like to ask a favor of you. Can you teach me to fly?"

The wizard was taken aback. "I thought you a priest."

"I am, but of a god of Travel. I can memorize the spell, I just don't know how to use it."

The wizard hesitated, and then came to a decision. He pulled his hood back, so he could look Christopher directly in the face. The transformation from figure of dread to middle-aged insurance adjustor was more unbalancing than any of the theatrics had been.

"You would be a most unusual apprentice."

"Not exactly an apprentice. After all, I'll be showing you something new, too."

"You would be an odd choice of partner, as well."

"It's true, I'm just plain odd." Geek humor, but the wizard smirked, and then said the most unexpected thing possible.

"Would you like a drink? I've got some imported wine around here, somewhere."

The emotional depletion of the entire day sagged at Christopher. "Yes, actually, I would."

When the wizard stood up from the throne, he was a head shorter than Christopher. He started pushing at the lid of a stone coffin, and Christopher went to help him. Inside the coffin was a pile of hay and a number of bottles.

"Keeps it cool and dry during the day," the wizard said. "These blasted summers are unbearable. Now . . . some glasses." He stared absently into the distance, and Christopher could hear glass tinkling. Straight out of the stone wall floated a pair of huge goblets, suspended on thin air. This was spookier than anything else Christopher had seen in the tower, sending an involuntary twitch through his shoulders. The wizard seemed oblivious, absently snatching one of the goblets while he rooted around for a bottle.

Christopher steeled his nerve and plucked the remaining goblet out of the air. It came away in his hand with only the slightest resistance, and then it was just a glass.

Not just a glass. When he looked inside it, a huge beetle crawled out and fell to the floor.

"Blasted bugs," the wizard snorted, and stomped on it.

"Um. Do you have a sink?" Christopher stared at the remains of the huge insect that had just been in his drinking vessel.

"Yes, this way." He walked through the wall and disappeared. Christopher could not help himself; he extended a hand and watched it disappear into the wall, feeling nothing. It was, as he expected, mere illusion. He still closed his eyes as he stepped over the barrier.

On the other side was a staircase, circling up the side of the tower. The wizard was already halfway to the next floor, almost as if he had forgotten about Christopher.

"Sorry about the mess," he mumbled, when Christopher came out of the top of the stairs into a fiendishly untidy room. A huge table dominated the center, and bookshelves lined the walls. Much to Christopher's amazement, there were books on the shelves. Perhaps a hundred volumes.

"Your library is impressive."

"It's mostly junk," the wizard said. "That whole set over there are just tax records. Why would anybody write that stuff down? You get what you get. Writing about it doesn't make it more. Oh, right, a sink." Across the room, to another hidden doorway, and they walked through an illusionary bookcase to the next flight of stairs.

Living quarters, and if possible, even more untidy. But there was a sink in the corner, and water flowed from the tap when he depressed the lever.

"There's a tank on the roof," the wizard said, "and I leave the phantasmal servant running at night to fill it. Cheaper than feeding an apprentice to do it."

Christopher washed out his glass, moved a pile of dirty laundry from an old and faded armchair, and sat down. The wizard made a grand gesture, and the table swept itself clean, all of the junk sliding off the edge and floating gently to the floor. Almost all of it. There was sound of crockery shattering.

"Clumsy servant," the wizard grumbled. "But watch this." He said a word in a language Christopher had never heard before, and the cork popped out of the bottle and flew across the room.

"That's my limiter. When I can't remember the magic word, I know I've drunk too much."

Christopher smiled at the attempt at humor. The wizard really must be desperately lonely. And no wonder: not only was he isolated by social class and profession; his paranoia was justified. His head was the most valuable thing in the county; boiled, it would yield enough tael to raise a commoner to Christopher's rank and still have enough change left over to buy a new suit and a haircut.

So Christopher held his glass out for wine and put his grief and anger aside.

"A toast to whatever peasant trod these grapes, so that we might have a moment's respite." The wizard raised his glass, and Christopher joined him. It was the kind of toast Christopher could drink to.

"And to your god," the wizard added politely, raising his glass again.

"Why? He didn't pick any grapes," Christopher said. The wizard laughed, they took a long drink, and it was time to talk business.

"How?"

"You bring in a woman every week, but your mind-spell can be defeated." Christopher was nervous about giving away Lalania's secret, even though it was necessary. He needed allies. He needed this ally.

"I knew that girl was too good to be true. The blonde, right?"

"Yes." Thinking of the buxom girl in bed with this seedy little man was an uncomfortable image, so he took another long draft of wine.

"Dark take it, I know the spell landed. How did she undo it? Or was that your work?"

"No, she did it on her own, with paper. She wrote down her intentions and gave it to an innkeeper to return to her the next day. Reading what she had set out to do the night before apparently jogged her memory and let her remember everything."

"Ah," the wizard said. "I got lazy. Should have used two compulsions, one about coming here, and one about what happens when she does come here."

"Or you could just avoid literate women."

The wizard laughed again, a rusty sound, like he'd forgotten how to do it in front of company.

"That would be easier, I agree. You're just full of easy answers. I think I like your religion."

Christopher had to laugh then. "Don't look to me for conversion. What I know about religion is less enlightening than your tax books."

"Then I'll fulfill my part of the bargain. But before I tell you how to use the spell, I should tell you how to not kill yourself with it."

That was a promising start.

Christopher pounded three times on the huge iron door. Then he did it again, just for the sound of it.

"Patience, my esteemed lord. I crank as fast as I can," the doorman said. But Karl and Gregor were already pulling the door open.

Christopher staggered forth into their arms.

"Priest, heal thyself," Gregor muttered, as Torme leapt forward in concern.

But they all relaxed once they realized he was just drunk.

"I take it things went well," Gregor said.

"They did indeed. I got us banished." Christopher, never politic, was utterly inept when he was three sheets into the wind.

"Grave news, my lord," Torme said, but Christopher waved him off.

"No, it's great news. That wench won't be able to hide in a fort full of men. The wizard's going to build us a fort, see. He's not such a bad guy."

"I'm certain it is only the liquor talking," the doorman said, shaking his head at the last comment. "He is most assuredly nothing but that."

The sun was just coming up, light creeping into the dark sky.

"I would like to take a nap now," Christopher said. He looked around for a comfortable place to lie down.

"This way, sir," Torme said, guiding him home. Karl and Gregor fell in behind, the squad of surreptitiously yawning soldiers following.

"This would be the perfect time for her to strike," Gregor muttered.

"Unless he only fakes his impairment." Torme always cast Christopher in the best light.

"Is that possible?" Gregor said, prepared to be impressed.

"No," Karl admitted. "The man can't hold his liquor. But she doesn't necessarily know that."

"Hey!" Christopher mumbled. "I heard that." He turned around to find Karl and give him a sound thrashing, got lost, and had to wait for Torme to point him in the right direction again.

The men were careful not to show their dismay. They were not insensitive to the death of the child, but they were still young men. The town, with its rowdy taverns and accommodating women, still held plenty of allure for them.

"You can come back every few weeks, and be party animals then." The idea of a weekend pass was another one of Christopher's innovations. "In between times, you're going to be soldiers." They perked up at that. They were at that improbable age where fighting sounded like as much fun as chasing girls.

His army poured out of the gates, a long column of wagons and men. The cavalry was already in the field, scouting the advance.

Karl approved, of course. "It was good for them to live a hero's life, for a while. But it is better for them to have to earn it again."

Gregor had already registered his delight by leading out the cavalry. He'd been gone from the city since daybreak. No doubt Royal would rather be with them, tromping through the countryside, but like Christopher, the big warhorse was saddled with other responsibilities. Disa rode on a gentle mare, looking uncomfortable and out of place.

"How do you usually get around?" Christopher asked, when it became obvious she had never ridden before.

"The poor walk, Brother," she said. That was no longer an option. Her magical skills were too valuable for mundane transportation.

The thought made him grin. Just as soon as he got the chance, he was going to travel in a wholly new manner, too.

But today he had an army to oversee, a thousand trivial decisions to make, and a logistics nightmare. The wooden wall-molds occupied most of the space in his wagons, so they would be making multiple trips over the next few weeks for the rest of their supplies. In the meantime they had to pack only what they could not do without.

The locals came out to cheer them as they marched past villages and hamlets. Christopher wasn't sure if that was because his men had already made friends with them, or because they were just relieved there would now be soldiers between them and the ulvenmen.

After the second day they were out of the farmlands, and the roads ended. Now it was hard slogging through unbroken swampland. Just finding a path would be work, and finding a destination would be impossible. He wanted to build his fort on a hill, but the trees were so thick that visibility was limited to a few dozen yards.

Karl sent a soldier up a tree, to no avail.

"Well then," Christopher said. "I'll just have to do it myself."

Handing the reins of his horse to Karl, he stepped into a clearing, closed his eyes, and cleared his mind. He spread his arms and chanted the words of the spell, waiting for wind beneath his wings.

When the feeling came, it was immediately exhilarating. He drifted upward, slipping through gravity's fingers like water, elevated by desire alone. It was the same feeling as a heavy sigh, the same release of tension, that moment of weightlessness as you sink into your leather easy chair. Only the direction was different.

Opening his eyes, he soared. Arms outstretched, crucified on a shaft of air, he moved *up*, past the tops of the trees. He dared not look down, dared not to respond to the sudden shouts and cheers of his men. He did not want to chicken out.

So he went higher, without letting himself think of how high. The wizard had told him the chief danger of the spell was that it only lasted a fixed amount of time—for Christopher, it would be slightly less than an hour—and when it did fail, it did so with little warning. If you were within sixty feet of the ground, you would be safe, the spell letting you down gently for at least that far. But after that, it could disappear at any moment, dropping you like a stone.

As long as he didn't lose track of time, he would be fine.

He couldn't hear the noise of his army as clearly now. There was nothing in his peripheral vision but blue sky. Still he went up, figuring that a thousand feet would give him a good view. He was afraid that if he looked down now, he would not have the courage to go higher.

When he finally let himself stop pushing upward, he brought his hands in and forced his gaze toward the ground, so very far away. He hung in midair, standing on nothing. He had expected it to feel like skydiving. He was wrong. It felt like flying.

His army snaked out below him like a string of ants, tiny brown dots barely glimpsed through trees. He laughed wildly and spun in a circle. Then he leaned forward and began to fly in earnest.

The wind rushing past his face was still light, so he wasn't breaking any speed records. Without the passing ground as a reference it was hard to guess, although the wizard had described it as half-again as fast as a man could run. Royal could put a stiffer wind in his face in a hard gallop.

But Royal had to work for that, and this was effortless. All of his duty and grief had been left on the ground, discarded like a rumpled night-robe. For these few moments he was simply, ecstatically happy.

The wizard had warned him of another danger. If he went too high, he ran the risk of attracting a passing elemental, some mythical magical beastie that lived in the winds. The creature would undoubtedly take offense at such an unnatural intrusion into its domain and might punish him by dispelling the magic. His sixty feet of graceful drifting would not be much comfort then. And he could only do this spell once a day, so even if he had the concentration to cast it while falling, he couldn't.

Since the stakes were so high, he had resolved to take the wizard's words seriously, no matter how much like superstition they sounded. He wouldn't be setting any altitude records.

Going any higher would not be profitable, anyway. Already the land below him stretched out unbroken and smooth, a carpet of flat, scrawny green with patches of brown mud splattered liberally across it. Beginning to descend, he searched for a lump worthy of his plans.

With a start he realized he had no idea how much time had passed. It couldn't have been long, but the euphoria of the experience distorted everything. What he would give for a wristwatch! Instead, he swooped down and circled around, searching for his army. Flying over their heads would make them look up to him. It was hard not to respect a man whom even gravity deferred to.

When he found them, their startled cries alerted him to one last danger. They might shoot him by accident. He went lower, until he could see their faces and they could presumably see his, and found the head of the column again. Then he floated in, like the witch in Oz, and once his boots touched the soil, he let the spell dissipate. He didn't dare risk a second ascent, not having any clue how much time was left.

The men gaped open-mouthed at him, except for Karl, of course.

"Did you find a suitable location?" Karl asked, the pure normalcy of his tone more grounding than the earth beneath Christopher's feet.

"No," Christopher admitted. "All I saw was more trees." All of his cares and burdens scrambled up from the mud, climbing onto his back where they belonged. But they seemed lighter now, unreduced in number or import but nonetheless robbed of their crushing weight. "We'll keep going south, and try again tomorrow."

Gregor and the cavalry finally rejoined them, trotting in as the sun set.

"No ulvenmen," the blue knight reported, "but we found a good camp."

"What makes it good?"

"Why," Gregor said with a grin, "it's next to plenty of mud."

They only had a week before the wizard would come out to find them and start the magic. The men had a lot of shoveling to do, and easy access to the raw materials would count highly. But Gregor was joking, of course. Everything out here was next to mud.

11

FORTRESS OF SOLITUDE

In the morning, as he was eating breakfast and ruminating on how badly the quality of his victuals had fallen in the last three days, his sentries brought him a visitor.

The young man was dressed in green leather, with a six-foot bow on his back and a short sword on either hip. He went to one knee as soon as he saw Christopher.

"Get up," Christopher said, annoyed at the formality. "Have some porridge." That seemed like punishment enough for far worse crimes, so he put his annoyance aside.

"You do not even know my name, and yet you offer me food from your table?"

Christopher shrugged. "It's not food. It's porridge."

"I see your reputation for generosity is not unmerited."

He had to think about that one for a while before he decided the young man wasn't mocking him.

"So what's your name, and why are you here?"

"I am Ser D'Kan," the young man announced, and then muttered under his breath, "and not for the porridge," looking sourly at the bowl after his first spoonful. Christopher's men were very good at many things. Cooking was not one of them.

"I am here for a job, my lord." He squatted next to the small campfire that Christopher and a few others were sitting around.

Christopher was trying to remember the speech Lalania had written him for dismissing applicants and petitioners.

"Not a partnership, my lord. I do not pretend to be so significant that you would take me into your retinue. No, I desire a job, for pay, a simple quid pro quo."

"I don't need archers, really." Not with two hundred riflemen.

"I offer my skills in woodcraft. I am ranked as a Ranger."

Now Christopher remembered where he had seen green leather before. "You mean like the Baronet D'Arcy?"

"Not so very like him." D'Kan's face flashed a hint of distaste. "For instance, I am only a Knight. Still, I believe I can lead your hunt in vastly more profitable directions than you have hitherto experienced."

That wouldn't be hard.

"Are you willing to work with my scouts, and teach them what you can?" D'Arcy had seemed to enjoy doing that. But this fellow looked scandalized by the idea.

"I suppose that is not unthinkable." Apparently it was not that scandalous. He must want the job pretty bad.

"So how much is this going to cost me?"

"In salary, my lord, not a single coin. Though I ask that you feed and shelter me, I will be glad to contribute to the rations with my hunting. And naturally if you choose to share some of the spoils of the hunt, I will be grateful."

Christopher put down his empty bowl.

"You haven't actually said what I will be paying."

D'Kan bowed his head in acknowledgment. "Only this. If I aid you in your hunt, I would ask aid of you for mine."

"I don't think I can find anything you can't." Only after he had spoken did Christopher guess the obvious.

"It is not the finding I require assistance with. It is the laying low of the prey I cannot do alone."

Which is what he wanted an army for. Killing a dragon or some other nonsensical monstrosity with gods knew what obscene powers.

"I think you better tell me what kind of monster you expect me to help you with."

"The worst kind, my lord. A brigand, a traitor, a murderer, a killer of women, a thief of children, a kin-slayer."

Only a man. A very bad man from the sound of it, but Christopher was pretty sure his army could take a lone man. Conveniently he ignored the fact that his army had just retreated from a lone woman.

"That sounds like the kind of deal I could make. But maybe you should tell me who he killed, first."

"I will, with great regret, for it brings me great pain. His victim was my dear sister. You knew her as the Lady Niona."

Christopher leapt to his feet. Instinctively, irrationally, his hand went to his sword.

"What the—what is Cannan doing about it?"

"I imagine Cannan is doing nothing about it, my lord."

Christopher stared at D'Kan, waiting for him to make sense.

"This is why I came to you. Because you know of Cannan and have dealt with him in the past."

"So what?" Christopher growled. "Get to the point." They should be out finding her body to revive, not sitting around chatting.

"The point, my lord, is that Cannan is the murderer."

There was, of course, no urgency. Nothing in this world was hurried; news traveled one footstep or horse-step at a time. The trail was long cold, the deed many weeks in the past.

D'Kan explained that the Rangers had tracked Cannan as far south as they could and had lost him. "We cannot rely on the Wild to serve justice on him. He travels without fear, walking openly where we must skulk, protected by some powerful enchantment that foils mortal creatures."

That would be the ring Christopher and Cannan had won in their joint duel with the terrifying Black Bart. Only their enchanted blades had cut through its protection. Cannan had claimed it as his share of the spoils, and Christopher had agreed, because Cannan had fought the better part of that duel. At the time it had seemed a small price for Cannan saving his life.

No, D'Kan explained, they had no knowledge of why Cannan had killed his wife. Nor did they care. All they knew was that their kinswoman was dead.

And ashes.

"Our woodcraft is strong. We found where he did the deed and searched for her body. We do not revive our dead, considering that a violation of the cycle. But we reincarnate them, allowing them to finish their life in whatever guise the Mother cares to give them. For many years, my favorite aunt was a cat. But Cannan denied us even this, burning her remains with savage thoroughness. All he need leave us was a single strand of hair. No doubt he learned that fact from Niona. Her trust sealed her doom."

That was what the Saint needed, too. Despite the fact that Christopher personally knew two men who could raise the dead, it was still possible to die on a permanent basis.

"Something has to have happened," Christopher argued. "An accident or a misunderstanding. Cannan was a good man." Despite his prickly exterior, Christopher had seen how gentle the knight had been with Niona, when he thought no one was looking. Christopher had recognized the signs of true devotion, the kind that bound across time and space. It was inconceivable that Cannan had turned from such love to foul murder.

D'Kan shrugged stiffly. "I did not come here so that you could defend him. I came here to enlist your help in destroying a monster with a heart of darkness and a protection that renders my arrows useless."

"Not useless," Christopher sighed. "I saw a crossbow quarrel hurt him once. You just need a bigger weapon." Like a rifle.

D'Kan seemed mollified by the new information. "That is good to know. Then you will help?"

"I will bring him to justice, yes. But if I can do that without killing him, you must accept that."

"I will agree to that condition," D'Kan said, "because I know it is impossible. He chose to embrace darkness, whatever the reason. And now that he has, I do not think any power can compel him to choose otherwise. Your Saint does not atone the Black. It is a waste of time to even try."

"This is an army," Karl said. "You'll do what the Colonel tells you to, or you'll go your own way."

D'Kan glared haughtily. "I am a Ranger. We swear obedience to no man." His face changed again, grief replacing anger. "But I will swear obedience to your Curate, for as long as vengeance takes. Before I was a Ranger, I was a brother."

Exhausted with the grievous topic, Christopher asked what he thought was an innocent question. "Then why does D'Arcy serve Nordland?"

"For love" was the cryptic answer, but D'Kan made a face when he said it, which rather undercut the nobility of the sentiment.

They slogged south, while Christopher bottled his impatience. D'Kan had only come to him after losing the trail. There was no guarantee the druids would ever find it again, and what they could not find, Christopher could not even begin to search for. Cannan could disappear into the Wild and never come back. He could flee back to the barbarian tribes he and Niona had visited, or presumably there were other Kingdoms he could go to. Although no one seemed to know the names of those other lands, they all took it for granted that men built cities elsewhere on this world.

Those unknown people might find a murderer equally undesirable and mete out an appropriate punishment, which in this world invariably meant a death sentence. While that would serve the interests of dispassionate and druidic justice, it would leave Christopher uninformed and unfulfilled. He wanted to talk to the man, to find out what had happened. He wanted to know why. He wanted to believe that Cannan had saved a piece of Niona, just the tiny sliver the Saint would need to bring her back. He needed to believe that miraculous reuniting was possible.

Those answers and possibilities lay deeper in the wilderness, where Cannan and the ulvenmen were hiding. He tapped his heels into his mount, trying to hurry the crawling column of men forward.

That column came to a halt, jerking to a stop in pieces like a Slinky running into a wall. Impatiently, he rode to the front.

Several soldiers were engaged in rescuing a cavalry horse that was knee-deep in quicksand. The horse, panicked and frustrated, was not helping.

"Get more ropes. And can anyone calm that poor beast down?" Christopher's commands were unnecessary. The men knew how to handle their animals.

But the horse's fear rose steadily, despite their efforts. Christopher tried to guess how close he could push Royal without getting him trapped in the mud as well, since the big warhorse usually had a calming effect on other horses. That's when he noticed that Royal had his ears flat, the equine equivalent of balled fists.

Royal's perspicacity was wasted. The ambush happened before Christopher could utter a single word. The bushes on the opposite side of the mire exploded, and a truckload of striped leather, shaped vaguely like a giant naked chicken, sprung across the gap, landing on the horse like a piano dropped from a rooftop.

The horse broke with a sickening thud, dying so quickly it did not even have time to squeal. The massive creature squatting over it on two legs flicked its impossibly long tail, bent its serrated maw to the dead animal, and tore out a chunk of flesh, swallowing it whole. Then it reared its head and bellowed, the sound unnervingly different than a lion's roar but no less impressive. It waved a pair of huge sickle-shaped claws at them, like a cat telling the world to stay away from its mouse.

The rest of Christopher's cavalry bolted, taking their hapless riders with them. Only Royal stood firm. Christopher drew his sword, although he could not honestly imagine what a yard of metal could do against two tons of angry theropod. But he was tired of running away.

The creature noted his defiance and gathered itself for another tremendous leap. The dead horse was not an entirely stable launching platform. This time the beast fell short, landing ten feet away from him, sinking immediately up to its knees in the mud. It bellowed at him again, so close he could feel its hot breath, smell the carrion rotting in its teeth. Stupefied, he pointed his sword at it and waited for Royal to charge to their certain death.

Men, sans timorous horses, came running up on foot. Then the roll of thunder, over and over, as they emptied their rifles into the thrashing creature. The noise disturbed Royal, and the steed trotted back behind the lines, while men reloaded, advanced to point-blank range, and fired again.

"Hold your fire!" Gregor shouted, dismounting. With drawn sword the blue knight approached the dead beast, poking it to see if it would move.

From the mud rose two men, completely covered in black goop. They had been closest to the horse when the monster attacked and had demonstrated their extreme sensibility by simply sinking under the surface and not moving until the thing forgot about them. Then, they had even more sensibly not moved while the panicked riflemen were firing.

"A brave act, Christopher," Gregor said. "To hold your ground and stall the monster till your men could finish it. Braver than I might have been; this is a fearsome beast indeed." Then he laughed at the muddy cowards and threw out a rope to pull them in.

Christopher wondered at the fact that his standing still and doing nothing was counted as courage, while their lying still and doing nothing earned them a ribbing from their fellows. It didn't seem fair.

"What in the Dark was that?" D'Kan exclaimed, finally forcing his horse to the front. The Ranger's horse was not a great destrier like Gregor's Balance or Christopher's Royal, but it was as superbly trained.

"It's a dinosaur." Christopher was amazed to discover that word in this language. "Megaraptor, I think." Bizarrely he remembered being humbled by a nephew with a picture book, the five-year-old expert carefully explaining how the huge single claw on each forelimb established its identity.

"Not that." D'Kan rolled his eyes. "I know what that is. What was all that *noise?*"

"Rifles!" a grinning young soldier said, carefully reloading the six chambers on his carbine.

Christopher could see the wheels turning in D'Kan's head as the Ranger put the pieces together. Many unranked men, a thunderstorm, and one dead dinosaur. And no blood on Christopher's sword.

Gregor grinned in sympathy, no doubt remembering the first time he had discovered the effect of rifles. "It's something to think about, isn't it, Ser?"

D'Kan looked back where the long column of armed men stretched into the jungle. Then he looked at Christopher, with an entirely new attitude. Christopher wasn't sure if it was respect, fear, or disgust. He suspected the young Ranger wasn't sure, either.

"You've seen dinosaurs before? There are dinosaurs here?" Christopher wished somebody would tell him these things.

"They are not uncommon to the swamp," D'Kan said. "Although

I confess I have never met one face-to-face. If I had, I would hardly be here to tell about it. This breed is considered the equal of a sixth-rank."

"So it should have tael, then." Gregor poked disconsolately at the creature's head. It was bigger than any of the pots they had brought.

"I'll do it," Christopher said. Placing his hand over its forehead, he used an orison to draw the tael out, a tiny purple grain.

"That's not a sixth-rank's worth." It was a fraction of the expected amount. Immediately Christopher regretted how greedy he sounded. Then he regretted even knowing such a gruesome fact.

"It's only an animal," Gregor said, when it became clear D'Kan was not going to answer but merely stare in amazement at the village idiot.

Karl had ridden up by now. He stayed only long enough to make sure there were no casualties and to toss out a helpful comment. "He's always like that, Ser D'Kan. Best you get used to it." Then he went back down the line, restoring order and chastising the gawkers.

"If you are so eager for tael, my lord, we could search for its fellows. Although likely that dreadful noise has warned them away for miles." D'Kan had finally found his voice again, and it was sour.

The little purple dot was worth three pounds of gold. Gold was worth less to him than horseflesh, out here in this blasted swampland. And it was sheer luck that the creature had not killed any of his men.

"No, the King didn't send me out here to kill dinosaurs. But Gregor, make sure the scouts are warned. We don't want to be surprised again."

"This will keep them on their toes," the blue knight grinned. Then he set to guiding the column around the mud-hole.

"Can we eat it?" Christopher asked.

"If you're really hungry," D'Kan said. "For my part, I'm not that hungry yet."

From a distance, Christopher could hear Gregor's angry bawling. The treacherous mud had blocked his new line of advance.

"We need to get a visual on this, see if we can find a way around this muck." Thinking about flying made him both excited and nervous. It was tremendous fun, but it was also nerve-wracking, and he'd had enough wrackery for a whole week, even one of these absurd ten-day weeks. He might as well share.

"I need a volunteer," he announced to the men within range of his voice. He looked around, but Kennet had already leapt forward and saluted.

"Don't you know you're not supposed to volunteer for anything in the army?" Christopher asked him.

"Yes, sir," Kennet barked, with a perfectly straight face.

"You're not afraid of heights, are you?"

Kennet's eyes widened, just barely enough to betray there was a young man under that severe countenance. Apparently something other than combat and Dynae could still stir his emotions.

As usual, Christopher worried, even after having burdened the young man with rules, procedures, and threats. "Don't go out of sight of the column. Don't go over a thousand feet high. When you hear the gunfire, come immediately back. If you break any of these rules, I'll never let you fly again." Kennet took it in silently, either absorbing it or ignoring it, in either case waiting eagerly for the spell. When Christopher spoke the words and touched him, he looked up, without hesitation or fear, only a calm rapture on his face. Then he launched, fists clenched and jaw squared, a bottle-rocket aimed at the sky.

Charles the quartermaster counted silently under his breath, the closest they had to a clock. Christopher remembered seeing hourglasses in Flayn's shop, but at the time he had not identified them as one of the ten thousand things he desperately needed. So he passed the time nervously, until Charles aimed his rifle at the sky and fired the signal shot.

Only moments later, Kennet swooped down to issue a salute and a report of a hill to the south, and the possibility of drier ground.

"Any trouble, Corporal?"

"No, sir," Kennet said as calmly as if he'd been asked to walk around the block. "Although I did see some movement to the east, I did not investigate too closely, as per your orders."

"Probably the rest of the herd," D'Kan offered. "Your ranks should go after them, lest they assault the common men."

"If we go running off after those, what else will attack while we're gone?" Christopher answered. "Until the men are in a fort, they won't be safe. We march south."

They made better progress the next day, though not without cost. Gunfire erupted toward the rear of the column, and Christopher launched himself into the air, swooping over the heads of his men as he flew to the sound of trouble.

By the time he got there, it was mostly over. Another pair of voracious dinosaurs had been tempted by the pungent odor of horseflesh, springing out from a bush and tearing a scout in half between them. Ironically, the horse escaped with minor injuries, bolting forward to safety, but in the battle another infantryman was flung through the air by a savage flick of a monster's tail. It took many bullets to bring down the dinosaurs, and the infantry rifles only held one shot.

Christopher knelt over the injured man, looking at the shattered bone sticking out from the shredded meat of the left shin. The situation was familiar: he had done this with Royal once.

"Hold him down," he ordered, and when they did, he took the leg in both hands, snapping the bone back together while the man shrieked in agony and Christopher said the words in Celestial.

The bone knitted itself together, growing at incredible speed like

a time-lapse movie, the flesh layering over it. The man whimpered and
went limp, deserted by the shock and pain that had been flooding his
system. Absently Christopher pulled the ripped trouser leg together
and mended it with a minor spell, restoring the young man to what he
had been moments before, except for the covering of blood.

He could not restore the horse's rider. They gathered the halves of
the scout, wrapped him in his great leather coat, and Christopher sent
someone to find an empty barrel.

He would not be able to cast the spell that would preserve the body
until the next day, and it would have to be renewed every five days until
he could send the grisly package to the Cathedral. The revival would
cost him a hundred tael. Pulling the purple stone from the monster's
skull with another minor spell, he weighed it in his palm.

The faces around him were careful not to betray the question that
hung unspoken on every lip. They would not presume his generosity.
It grieved him that they dared not expect revival as their right, but
he could not afford to salve his conscience. He needed them alert, not
comfortable to the point of sloppiness. More importantly, he needed
them aware that a day might come when he could not afford the cost.

Holding the lump of tael up so they could see it, he stated the crassest
calculation he could imagine at the moment. "As long as you kill three
dinosaurs for every man we lose, I can afford to keep raising you."

They were too proud of their manliness to cheer and too used to
insignificance to be offended. But he could feel the electricity sweep
out from him, a subtle ripple that ran up and down the column, galvanizing even those who did not know the facts yet.

The flight spell was still live, so he went into the air, ostensibly
to scout—he'd used the spell for the day, so he could not send anyone
else up—but really to escape the pressure of so much expectation. All
military commanders must feel this terrible burden, knowing that
they held lives in their hands, knowing that they must send some to
their deaths so that others might live. Surely being able to bring some

of them back to life was an improvement. But it didn't feel that way. It just felt like a second chance to fail them, when cold accounting would force him to bury men he could have revived.

Even the man they were stuffing in the barrel might not return. If his last emotion was fear and flight, he might carry that with him to the other side and continue to flee, even when the Saint reached out a beckoning hand. Floating high above the army did not help to relieve his burgeoning sense of isolation, so he skimmed to the head of the column. The scouting effort was wasted: D'Kan had kept them on a steady course despite the lack of any visible guideposts, hewing to the direction Kennet had pointed to the previous day.

"A Ranger's skill" was D'Kan's explanation when Christopher asked him. Christopher hoped it wasn't a tael-bought skill. His men would never have tael to spend on skills like that. And scouts who got lost weren't worth the price of their horses.

They made the foot of the hill by nightfall, and a sense of relief could be seen on the faces of men who knew they would not spend the next day crawling through a swamp. Christopher shook his head sadly but said nothing. He wouldn't be on the idiot end of a shovel for the next week. Might as well let them enjoy the illusion of labor's end.

Bright and early the next morning, he addressed the squad of young men assembled before him. They were the ones who had spent their time in the city working on the wall, having been caught in the Captain's trap after a single night of freedom.

"I hope you were paying attention in the city," Christopher told them. They looked with dismay at the boxes of shovels and baskets being unloaded from the wagon. "Because now your job is supervising the rest of these lazy bastards. They'll work in shifts, three a day, and I expect you to keep those shovels moving at maximum speed. Wear out a group and get the next one in the trenches." He couldn't afford enough shovels for everybody. Metal was too expensive.

The men grinned and fell out to inflict on their fellows the fate they had thought themselves doomed to. Karl had insisted that Christopher make this announcement, as he insisted that Christopher hand out all rewards and praise, while he dealt out punishment and discipline. The division meant that Christopher got their loyalty; it also meant that Karl got their obedience. A standard arrangement in any modern army, though not one that feudal lords could emulate or even understand. The typical Baron wanted his men's obedience as well as their loyalty. Christopher's willingness to channel their obedience to commoners, an officer corps, an *institution*, was simply inconceivable.

On the other hand, he hoped it meant his army would keep fighting even after he was incapacitated. His record for finishing battles on his feet was mixed, at best.

The other consideration was that he intended to turn over command of this army to someone else, someday. Preferably a democratically elected president, or at least a republican senate. This vision of freedom was the only relief that made the burden of command bearable. It was the only way he could duck inside the tent others set up for him, accept the cup of tea that others brewed for him, sit and discuss plans that others would implement for him, and not cringe.

Outside the sound of obscenities mixed with the blows of axes, as the scraggly trees began to fall. They would clear the ground within fifty yards of their hilltop fortress. This part of the plan they could start on right away.

"We need to scout the hill," D'Kan said. "It is a natural strong point. I would be surprised if it were not already occupied."

"What are we waiting for?" Gregor said. The blue knight remained stung at having had no part in the destruction of the dinosaurs.

The trees were unusually thick on the solid ground of the hill. Combined with the steep angle and the usual coating of slick mud, just climbing the mound would be a challenge. Standing impatiently as they draped him in the heavy full-plate that was his battle gear, Christopher dreaded the next few hours. Heat, humidity, hill climbing, and plate armor were not a pleasant mix. But it was his job to be in front. He was the one most likely to survive any attack.

At least he wouldn't be alone. Gregor's armor and rank also marked him out as a principal, so with drawn swords, D'Kan at their side, and two dozen men at their backs, they started up the hill. They made it almost all the way to the top before something large, black, and furry slammed into Christopher like a freight train, knocking him flat on his back while it reared over him, roaring its ownership over this territory.

Karl shot the bear between the eyes, and it fell over backward without another sound. Two minutes later they shot its mate to death while Gregor pinned it against a tree with his sword.

"Bear stew," Gregor said. "A blasted relief from porridge. Your men will love you. Dark take it, I'll love you."

"And the skins will make a fine rug for your tent." D'Kan wasn't being supercilious. He really meant it. A professional hunter, he saw nothing wrong with the events of the day.

Christopher was upset at dispossessing the bears. But there was nothing else he could have done. He couldn't share the hill with the bears, and he couldn't have merely driven them away. The hill was the only place to hide from the dinosaurs. From the top of the hill, they could see how the marsh flattened out on the other side, a vast soggy plain that could not support even the scraggly trees.

When the rest of the column began scrambling over the hill, the danger gone, Disa joined them and watched in dismay. Gregor was happily assisting D'Kan in transforming the dead animals into provisions, lending his strength to the Ranger's skill in butchering. "Does it make you feel like a man to murder those poor animals and steal their home?" she snapped at Gregor, before breaking into tears and fleeing back to the wagons.

"What the Dark was that about?" Gregor asked, but no one could help him. Disa was the only woman in the camp. No doubt the presence of so much testosterone was a constant burden for her. Christopher went to talk to her, anyway.

"We had to, Disa. You know that." It was the only decent site they had seen, and they were running out of time.

"Soldiers must kill," she answered. "But they need not grin about it."

"He's just making the best of a bad situation." Christopher couldn't quite figure out how he had become Gregor's advocate, but he told himself it was because he wanted peace in his camp. Guilt over destroying the blue knight's relationship with the beautiful troubadour surely couldn't be part of it.

"He could make better, if he cared to try," Disa said cryptically, and then she changed the subject to other matters.

In only five days, they had changed the landscape. Like a cloud of locusts they stripped the hill bare, stacking logs in neat piles to dry while the overseers marked out trenches for the molds. Like a nest of ants, they dug mud from the swamp, carried in long lines of men with baskets up the hill, and filled the wooden structures. It was a small hill, which was just as well, since Christopher had only committed the wizard to ten walls. Still, that was nine hundred feet of circumference, which would cover the hilltop. With another fifty yards of swampland cleared behind, and the flat, open plain in front, Christopher would not fear *Tyrannosaurus rex* himself.

The tenth night since they had left town, he had his men light a massive bonfire. D'Kan was perplexed.

"Won't that risk attracting attention before we are ready for it?"

Christopher had almost forgotten about the ulvenmen. But there was a specific attention he needed to attract.

"I'm expecting an air drop," he grinned, anticipating it would baffle the Ranger. But D'Kan nodded sagely and refused to be surprised when the black shape of the wizard glided into the firelight.

"Lord Wizard," Christopher greeted him, remembering the night they had spent drinking. Christopher's men, having no such protection, shied away from the sinister robes dangling in midair.

"You were right," the wizard said. "I could see your bonfire from the city, once I'd gone high enough. Yet it is nigh twenty miles."

There was nothing else in the swamp making light, so there was no competition. Christopher knew that, having sent Kennet up just the night before.

"What about the journey?" Christopher asked. Even without superstition, flying at night through this crazy world would be terrifying. Who knew what would spring out of the nearest star-lit cloud?

"I was hidden until I reached your camp," the wizard said matter-of-factly. "So do not expect me to come out here and rescue you. Not only does the trip take an hour, it depletes me of spells."

"I don't," Christopher answered. "Your job is defending your people. Losing a whole city is far worse than losing a regiment."

The wizard shook his head, a negative motion that somehow still signaled approval. "Your greed is as lively as a Yellow. I am well aware that you left my domain so you would not owe me taxes on your gains, but I am surprised to see you turning down my share from ordinary combat."

Christopher blushed. He hadn't realized this secondary motivation was that obvious. Technically being outside the borders of the realm, he would owe a tael-tax only to the King.

"Fear not." The wizard sounded like he was laughing, although the illusion he wore wasn't really consistent with humor. "I have never claimed a tael-tax on ulvenmen, and I'll not start now. If people want to risk their lives killing monsters, I'll not dissuade them, near or far. Nor will I come to your rescue and steal your thunder. That's the King's job. The only thing you need fear from me is admiration for your sharp practice. I would think a White priest to be shamed at words of praise from a Black wizard."

"I don't mind being shamed, as long as I'm richer for it," Christopher said with a grin. He knew the wizard wasn't really Black, but he could hardly compromise the carefully constructed false persona in public. "Speaking of which, I saved a bottle of wine for you, in case turning mud to stone is thirsty work."

"Just one," the wizard said. "I still have to find my way home." He glided off to work his magic on the wall. His flight spell lasted considerably longer than Christopher's.

Only after they had finished the bottle, while Christopher was trying to explain to the wizard why you could see a fire from the air when you couldn't see it from the ground—apparently these people did not know their world was round—did it occur to Christopher how much trust the wizard had shown in drinking his wine. Karl would have had an apoplectic fit over such a security breach if Christopher had done the same. Though the wizard was highly ranked, he could still be killed, and poisoned wine would be an ideal opening shot.

This was the price of a life of paranoid solitude—once you did trust someone, you trusted them too much. After the wizard had zoomed off into the night, Christopher discussed it with his political officer.

Torme dismissed his speculations. "You are White, Brother. Of course he trusts you. He knows that should you become his enemy, you will send him an invitation before attacking, and you'll probably heal him after the battle to boot."

"Are we really that inept?" Christopher asked. No wonder the Church didn't have an army.

"So I have always been taught," Torme said. "Always the Dark crows about the stupidity of the Bright. And yet . . ."

"Yet what?"

Torme shook his head. "I have seen more power in your train than in any place I have looked in this world. I cannot explain it. But I believe it. And in any case, I am now White myself. If you did not send that invitation, I would deliver it by hand."

"Not to worry," Christopher laughed. "He's on our side."

"For now," Torme said. "For now."

The wizard had departed for the last time the night before. Now Christopher surveyed his new fortress.

The stone walls were being carved, not merely in decorative swirls. Men were drilling narrow firing ports instead of the wider sawtooth crenellations necessary for crossbows. Inside the ring of stone, buildings were being raised. Crude ones, made out of the scraggly lumber from the marsh, with tent-cloth roofs, but still a marked improvement over sleeping in the open. Regular latrines, stone hearths, storage pits, and stables dotted the grounds. The best lumber went into making the gate, bound with strips of iron brought from the city in wagons. The men had complained about carrying thick bars of metal and heavy barrels of nails. They weren't complaining now.

Nor had they complained, even once, about dragging the cannons through the swamp. Seeing them ensconced in regular intervals around the walls gave everyone a deep sense of security.

The single greatest difficulty in supplying a fort was their easiest achievement. Instead of trying to dig a well in this muddy sinkhole, they had their magic water bottle, a gift from the Saint. The thick bronze vase shot out clean, cool water like a firehose on command. It had been invaluable in turning dirt to mud. Now it supplied them with uncontaminated water for drinking and cooking.

"We'll need to send the wagons for more supplies tomorrow," Karl said.

Christopher sighed. Having created a safe haven for all of them, it was already time to split his forces and send men into danger.

"Do you think we can exterminate the dinosaurs?" he asked

D'Kan. "Or at least teach them to fear our guns and stay away from our horses?"

"Probably not." D'Kan was merciless. "And if you could, then something worse would just move into their place. At least the dinosaurs are mostly interested in your mounts. Ulvenmen would always aim for your men first."

Perversely, Christopher felt the loss of the innocent animals more than his soldiers. He couldn't revive the horses.

D'Kan must have guessed his feelings. "You still mean to revive your common soldier?"

"Of course," Christopher said.

The Ranger shook his head. "No wonder they banished you to this miserable swamp."

It was an echo of the sentiment Captain Steuben had voiced in the Cathedral. The head of the Saint's bodyguard and loyal to the cause without question, Steuben had nonetheless frowned dubiously at Christopher's mass revival of common soldiers. Thanks to the hateful speech of his assassin, Christopher understood why. He wondered if D'Kan did.

"Pretend I don't understand that, and explain it to me."

D'Kan looked at him in surprise but gave a pragmatic answer Christopher had not considered. "What man would serve another lord if he could serve you? You force them all to revive their own or lose them to your banner. Instead they chose to put you where your policy will bleed your coffers dry with petty deaths."

Karl had a counterargument. "Why would any lord care if common men chose to serve Christopher instead of them?"

D'Kan laughed. "Then who would groom their horses? But they should care, more than they know. If they understood what your rifles could do, they would kill you out of hand." He was still grinning, so he couldn't be that attached to the established social order.

"Let's not tell them, then," Christopher suggested.

"You need not fear my tongue," D'Kan answered. "You know what binds me to you. For the rest, I care not a fig. But surely you understand they are not completely stupid. Sooner or later, they will understand your advantage. What will you do then?"

"I'll sell them guns."

Finally D'Kan was startled. "I know you do not jest, but I do not understand. You would put a weapon in the hands of your rivals? Truly you wear the White too tightly, a blindfold across your eyes."

"It's not my rivals I will be arming," Christopher muttered, nettled, even though he knew he should keep his mouth shut. But his secret was safe. D'Kan simply could not envision a world without feudal privilege, and he merely stared at Christopher in wonder.

"Ser D'Kan, I would have you accompany us as guide. At least for this first trip." Karl was returning to business, and Christopher only had one comment to offer.

"You don't have to ask him, Karl. You outrank him." Karl was second-in-command, by Christopher's rules.

D'Kan stiffened. But after a few deep breaths, he relaxed.

"Let this be another fact we do not tell them. To place the ranked under the command of the common is an insult of staggering proportions. I bear it only for the sake of my vengeance; I ask you not to compound my burden with public shame."

Christopher couldn't leave well enough alone. He never could.

"That's not true, D'Kan. That's not the only reason you bear it."

The Ranger frowned at him.

"You bear it because you know it's right. Because you know Karl is capable. Because you know that command should come from ability, not tael."

He was afraid he'd made the Ranger angry, but after a moment the young man grimaced.

"My lord, living with the unvarnished truth is your burden, not mine. Spare me your insights and leave me my illusions."

Despite his original reserve, D'Kan had proven unable to resist imparting his knowledge to an eager audience. Christopher's scouts were shaping up nicely under his tutelage, and the Ranger was almost as proud of them as Christopher was.

"Do you want me, or Gregor and Disa?" Christopher asked Karl.

"The latter, and Torme as well. You do not need political advice out here in the wilderness, and we may need more healing than one priest can provide."

That was Christopher's entire staff in one tasty horse-basket. But Karl was not reckless. He also took all of the cavalry and three platoons of infantry. And he took Christopher's flying privileges.

"You simply cannot risk leaving the fort while we are gone. If you were laid low outside the walls, who could succor you?"

"You see," Christopher said to D'Kan, "it's not only you who bows to the will of Major Karl. You get to go have a drink in the city, and I get put under house arrest."

D'Kan smiled at the joke, but in his eyes Christopher thought to see a hint of confusion, a glimmer of a distant vision of how things *could* be.

12

DOGFIGHT

After two weeks, the challenges seemed over. On the open marsh, the cavalry could destroy the dinosaurs with little danger. The smell of horseflesh would lure the predators out of the scrubby woods, where the range of the rifles could tear them apart before they could run a horse to ground. Christopher knew that sooner or later somebody would stumble and fall, and then he would be sending another barrel to the Cathedral, but after six more of the huge beasts the supply seemed to dry up.

Building a road through the swampland gave the men plenty of physical exercise and kept them too tired to complain. D'Kan and the scouts crept through the marsh and brought home alligator tails and odd bits of edible plants, bright-blue beans, and fiery red peppers. The camp was stuffed with supplies of oats and gunpowder. The walls were finished and seemingly impenetrable. Tael from the predators of the swamp trickled in slowly, even ordinary—although exceedingly large—alligators yielding a tiny speck. No women haunted his steps or his bed. Disa called him Brother and argued only with Gregor.

The present was a paradise, but the future promised only violence once the scouts found ulvenmen, the druids found Cannan, or Lord Nordland found Christopher. He stood next to a cannon and waited for misery.

Karl came up to hurry it along. "I do not think we should splinter our strength anymore. From now on the supply wagons must be guarded only by common soldiers."

"You'd send them through the Wild alone?" Christopher remembered when Karl had asked very much the same question of D'Arcy.

"We can afford to lose men. We cannot afford to lose you." Now Karl sounded like the gentry he hated. But Christopher didn't point that out. They both knew it was true.

He thought the conversation was over, but as he turned to leave, Karl spoke again.

"They are not afraid to walk in the Wild with no tael, as I was. They are proud to do so."

Now Christopher found himself speaking as cynically as Karl usually did.

"Only because they don't know what you do."

Karl acknowledged the reversal of their standard roles with a brief grimace. Christopher began to appreciate Vicar Rana's warning. His army could not back up; it couldn't even back down. Once infected with pride, these men could never again live as helpless dependents. If rifles and discipline were not enough to defeat monsters, then the men would die. Either in the maw of unspeakable horror or of simple broken hearts.

Their test came two weeks later. In the height of summer, the air muggy and sleepy, the sun merciless and heavy, a cavalry patrol thundered across the plain with all speed. Within sight of the fort, they fired a single gunshot into the air, and men leapt into action.

Purposeless action, since they did not know what the news was, but they reacted as if the legions of Hell were hot on the horsemen's heels.

For all Christopher knew, they were. He went to his command tent and waited for the report.

Kennet strode in, filthy from the ride and drenched in sweat. He snapped a crisp salute and a single word.

"Ulvenmen."

"Fire the signal rocket," Christopher said. Charles ducked outside, relayed the order, and returned instantly.

Seconds later the rocket boomed in the air. This would alert all the patrols, and the men attempting to create a road through the swamp, to come back to the fort in haste.

"You might as well save your report until Karl and Gregor return," Christopher said. "Unless we are about to be overrun in the next thirty minutes."

Distressingly, Kennet looked like he was calculating. "Not in thirty minutes, sir."

"Go see to your horse and get something to drink for yourself." Christopher sent him out of the tent.

Then he let Charles help him into the clanking plate armor.

"We saw only a dozen," Kennet reported to the staff meeting of ranked nobles and mercenary officers. "However, they moved with organization and purpose, and I felt they had to be scouts, not raiders."

"Did you bag any?" Gregor asked.

"No, Ser. Because the situation was so fluid, I decided not to reveal our full capabilities. When they fired on us with bows, we retreated." One man had taken an arrow to the thigh and had lost a lot of blood on the ride home. But once inside the fort's walls, Disa had healed him before he even dismounted.

"Saving all the tael for us, are you?" Gregor grinned, while Christopher gaped in awe. Where had this military wisdom come from? Somebody had been training his army very well.

"Sir," Kennet said, "I request permission to return to scouting."

"Why?" Christopher asked. "Does it matter how many are out there? Will it change what we do? I'd rather make use of the fort, if we can."

"We need to make sure they don't bypass us and simply head for Carrhill. If they are only raiders, such will be their goal." Karl never hesitated to point out any weakness in Christopher's plans.

"I don't want to risk horses," Christopher argued. "Let them pass us, and we'll cut them off from the rear. It's still miles before they can reach any peasants."

"Sir, I could fly."

Kennet was volunteering to face an unknown danger, completely alone. But Christopher was even less willing to risk men.

"What if they have shrikes?" He remembered the black wings that had torn apart Lady Nordland's giant owl and hawk.

"Ulvenmen don't use shrikes," D'Kan said. "It is more likely their shamans would just shape-shift into eagles."

"Right," Christopher said. "Flying's out. Now we wait."

It was hours before anything showed itself on the plain. The men spent that time preparing for a siege, bringing firewood into the fort, carrying out refuse, taking the protective covers off the cannons, topping off the fire buckets with water, dismantling the wagons and stacking them neatly in a corner, and counting their ammunition. Karl kept them too busy to think about why they were busy.

Gregor stared at the dozen figures to the south. Christopher and Karl joined him on the wall. Once again Christopher wished he'd invented telescopes, but he never seemed to have the time.

"I think they're baiting us," Gregor said. "It's just the dozen, still."

"Then we won't fall for it," Christopher said.

Karl shook his head. "We need to go out there and kill them. Otherwise they will ignore us and simply march north."

"If we go out there, we'll be walking right into their trap."

"Not likely, Christopher. They do not think as you do. The ulvenmen will gladly throw away a dozen no-ranks to test your strength. Certainly most lords would not hesitate to do the same."

"He's right," Gregor agreed. "Any ordinary lord would take this bait, dash out there and claim those easy heads for his purse. The ulvenmen know that. But that doesn't mean their high-ranks are ready to commit themselves without seeing us in action first."

"How can they convince the low-ranks to take such a terrible risk?"

Both men looked at Christopher with curious expressions, perhaps envious of his naïveté. Karl answered. "Because any low-rank who survives will likely be promoted. This is the blade of the thresher in action."

"At this point we want to give them what they expect," Gregor continued. "The later you spring your surprise, the better."

"Are you suggesting we ride out there and fight them with swords?" Christopher wanted to be outraged at the stupidity of the idea, but sheer logic prevented him.

"Indeed I am," Gregor grinned. "Assuming you thought to bring any of the old-fashioned things along."

They could mount nine swordsmen. His original mercenary officers, minus two who had stayed behind in Burseberry to handle training of the next batch of recruits. Karl with Black Bart's huge magic sword, and Gregor with his own glowing blue blade. Despite the shortness of his swords, D'Kan was already in the saddle, so apparently he considered himself adequately armed. And Christopher and Torme had their katanas, the latter's having finally shown up in a supply shipment from Knockford.

Armor was more problematic. D'Kan had his leather, and Christopher had the monstrous plate he'd been lugging around because everyone made him hang on to it. Gregor had his own plate-mail and the only shield in the entire camp. The rest of the men had nothing but their helmets and coats.

They did have two hundred useless pikes, which Christopher, having paid so dearly for, had hauled out of the city in the last supply run. Cutting down half a dozen of them into light lances gave the unarmored horsemen a way to attack from a safer distance. As they formed up at the gate, Disa joined them with a terrified but determined face.

"Absolutely not," Christopher said. "Your job is here, inside the walls. If we all die in a trap, you will be the only healing magic these men have. They will need you."

"How can one first-rank priestess matter to them then?" she asked plaintively.

Christopher shrugged, unsympathetic. No one had given him any sympathy when he had been the only healing magic in a wooden fort, facing a thousand goblins. "Ask the men," he told her, and rode out.

Their gate faced north, so they had to ride around the hill to reach the plain. Along the way Christopher tried to marshal his emotions. There was a pit of unaccustomed fear in his stomach. In all his previous battles, he had been following someone else's lead; now he was the high-rank. He would be the prime target of the enemy.

Responsibility sat squarely on his shoulders, as well. His decisions would be obeyed without hesitation. If they were the wrong ones, then they would all die.

And finally, under all the turmoil, whispered a voice of disquiet. What crime had these creatures committed? They had fired on his men, true, but had caused no real harm. And it seemed entirely reasonable that Christopher might be the trespasser here. If he had strayed into their lands, weren't they entitled to shoot first and ask questions later? But now he came to meet them, arrayed for war. No questions would be asked, no negotiations would be engaged. Only violence and death could result, and he could see no way to prevent it.

Karl, with his preternatural leadership skills, assessed the morale of his companions and found only Christopher's flagging. Riding in close and pitching his voice so only Christopher could hear, he said the words that would put Christopher's mind on the task at hand, stowing away all doubts and fears until they sat at campfires with ale in their mugs and no more than the long, dark night to face.

"Think of a little girl, frightened of carts," he said, calmly invoking Helga's terrible childhood nightmare, when she and hundreds of others had been captured by the last ulvenman horde and spared only because the King's cavalry outran the monsters' appetite.

Then Karl dropped back to his place in the cavalcade, behind the ranked men.

Christopher was angry at Karl, angry that the man would so casually manipulate his emotions, and angry at himself that it worked so well. Angry that he had to do this to himself, angrier still that he fell into the righteous wrath with so much relief.

As they came out onto the tundra, he felt himself hyperventilating. Royal responded to his mood, stepping higher, with sharp precision. Gregor looked over at him and grinned, the fire in his face that came with every battle, the conflagration that turned the gentle, friendly knight into a single-minded predator. Torme was grim and quiet, but then, he always was. D'Kan and the mercenaries laughed, the wind in their faces, the enemy waiting for them in a rangy line a few hundred yards from the walls of the fort. Behind them, the army watched, and on someone's signal, gave a unified cheer.

"Hold your charge until we are close," Gregor called. The great warhorses could pace the creatures all day, but they were only good for a hundred yards of attack speed.

When they were two hundred yards out, Christopher drew his sword, pointing it to the sky. He stood in the saddle and cried out in Celestial, while they cantered forward. The twinkling lights of the blessing fell around his party like snowflakes. From the fort came a spontaneous cheer.

The men grinned, the power of the spell flickering at the edge of their consciousness. Christopher could feel it there, whispering its promise of supernatural accuracy in every blow he would aim at the enemy. For the common men, it would be a noticeable boon; for Christopher, the effect was somewhat muted, as his rank already boosted him to Olympian levels. Gregor, although lower ranked, was a warrior, and his tael made him Christopher's equal in a sword fight.

But in battle, every edge counted. Gregor swelled as much from the spell as anyone.

A hundred yards, and Christopher could begin to see the details of his foes. Larger than a man, oddly bent. The dozen showed no inclination to flee. Several of them began unlimbering curved bows.

"Cursed archers," Gregor growled. "Let Christopher and I take the fore." He spurred Balance out ahead, and Royal matched the other horse pace for pace. Behind them D'Kan drew his own bow. With an undulating yell, he loosed an arrow. It flew high through the air, dropping with deadly precision. At the last minute, the targeted ulvenman stepped aside, and the arrow sank into the grass behind him.

"Magic and archery from horseback," Gregor exclaimed in pride. "If they have no ranks, may the gods have mercy on them." Men said the strangest things before combat.

The ulvenmen responded to D'Kan with a flight of half a dozen shafts. Gregor leaned forward and batted one down with his shield, saving Balance from taking a hit. Another arrow struck Christopher in the shoulder, glancing off his thick armor without effect. The rest fell around them and disappeared into the sea of grass.

Seventy yards, and he could see them bending their huge bows, guess which ones were aiming at him. As the arrows sang through the air, he dropped the visor on his helm, and held his left arm over Royal's head, trying to protect the horse as much as he could. The arrows slithered through the air around him, absurdly accurate, and one sank into Royal's shoulder.

The warhorse snorted in disdain and did not break stride. Though

Christopher flinched in sympathy with every jarring step, he could see the wound was only painful, not fatal.

"Go ahead," Gregor told him. "We'll need the horse."

Relieved, Christopher leaned forward and pulled the arrow from his horse's body. It was barbed, and ripped flesh and blood followed it out. The horse grunted in pain but would not allow himself to fall behind Balance. A second later Christopher touched the wound, spoke a word in Celestial, and the wound closed itself, not even leaving a scar.

Fifty yards, and the arrows came again, two clattering off his armor, one sticking in Gregor's shield, and another impaling itself in the joint of Gregor's right arm. His half-plate was not as complete as Christopher's.

Gregor pulled the shaft out with his teeth, gnawing clumsily at his arm through the open visor of his helmet. He spat it on the ground, the only blood on its barbed tip. His tael was sufficient to deal with such a minor wound.

Thirty yards, and Christopher could make out the shape of their bodies. Dog-legged, with hunched backs almost as high as their heavy heads stuck out on short necks. Massive shoulders, draped in some kind of hide armor, leather straps and bits of metal wrapped around them. The arrows flew straight from the bows now, no longer dropping in lazy arcs from the sky. He felt their impacts, felt one pierce his shoulder, then fall out. His tael closed the wound, but he could feel the insubstantial hollowness of its absence. Only a fraction of the tael he could draw upon today, yet a reminder that he was not immortal. Enough damage, and he would bleed and die like any man.

The last salvo fired, Gregor shouted his battle cry and spurred his horse. Royal took the call and burst into a charge. Behind him the men shouted, their horses pounding the turf like rolling thunder. The ulvenmen answered with their own howls, long and savage, and rushed forward to meet them, drawing axes, swords, and maces from sheaths and belt-loops, an entire armory carried on their backs.

Ten yards, and Christopher could see their faces. Like wolves, long snouts and huge fangs, snarling and flicking spittle. Black noses under yellow eyes, gleaming hatred and fury. Their long jaws snapped in eagerness for the coming fight. Christopher remembered that these creatures thought of humans as *food*.

Fear now, in earnest, in Christopher's stomach, but the blessing still held and it calmed his momentary dizziness. Behind him the shouts of the men reminded him of why he had come. He raised his katana to high guard and let Royal bear down on one of the monsters, a yelping horror with eyes that rolled in wild frenzy, a long straight sword in one hand and a spiked ball on a chain in the other.

They clashed like titans, the ulvenman stabbing and flailing in one smooth motion, Christopher sweeping his blade down at the same time. Plate armor turned the point of the ulvenman's sword, but the iron ball bounced from Christopher's chest to his faceplate, rattling him like a can of peanuts. He wasn't sure he'd even hit the creature, and then he was past and Royal was already angling to charge the next target. Leaning forward in the saddle, he ran an ulvenman through from behind, the body sliding off his sword, still moving. Some skill on either the part of the horses or Gregor narrowly prevented a collision between their mounts, and then Christopher was out in the open again, Royal thundering in a tight circle.

An arrow sank into his back, between the plates on his shoulder. Again his tael closed the wound, although the barbed head remained stuck in him. Knowing he would not bleed to death allowed him to ignore the pain.

The ulvenman in front of him dodged left, then right, then left again, playing a guessing game. But a cavalry mount blew past him from behind. Avoiding that put him in Royal's path, and the warhorse rammed into him like a snowplow.

The ulvenman was twice as heavy as a man but still a fraction of Royal's size. Its body disappeared under the flashing hooves while Christopher clutched at the pommel with his left hand.

The loss of momentum was not inconsequential. Royal came to a stuttering halt and seemed to be catching his breath. An ulvenman took this opportunity to run up and chop at Christopher with an ugly crescent-shaped ax. Parry, thrust, and strike followed while Christopher wondered why his damn horse was just standing there. The ulvenman ducked under his attack and sidled up next to the horse, reaching out with one hand to grab at the reins. Christopher reversed his grip and stabbed down. With all of his weight on top of it, the sword sank into the ulvenman's shoulder, pushing it to the ground, where it howled and beat at the steel blade with knobby claws.

Royal reared on his front legs, lashing out with his rear hooves. The ulvenman he had trampled had gotten up and come running after him. Christopher felt the force of Royal's kick though the rising saddle.

As the horse came back to earth, Christopher leaned over and stabbed at the ulvenman below him again and again until he found a chink in its armor, and its ridiculous vitality finally failed it. Sitting up, he kicked his heels at Royal, trying to get the horse in motion again. Too late he realized that grabbing the pommel for support had signaled the horse to stop for a dismount.

From the other side came a staggering blow. A massive ulvenman clobbered Christopher with a two-handed ax. Metal squealed and his shoulder twinged in fire. As the ax blade withdrew, his flesh closed up again. If not for tael, he would have lost the arm.

Christopher put his hand to his chest and cast a healing spell, replenishing his tael's effectiveness. Perhaps selfish, since he was not completely drained, and some other man might need that magic not to die. On the other hand, it would be false economy to let himself fall.

The ulvenman, outraged at being cheated of any effect, dropped its axe and sprung on Christopher. Together they fell off the opposite side of the horse.

He had thought of himself as a reasonably strong man, at least according to ordinary civilian standards. Karl had worked him into a leaner strength with a year of constant training, and his height and weight normally gave him an advantage. But this creature knocked him around like a rottweiler with a rag doll. It simply ignored his fumbling, clawing his arms out of the way with savage force, and biting down on his throat.

His armor saved him, the gorget squealing under the pressure of fangs. The ulvenman worried at him, yanking him around by his head, trying to break his neck. Its hot, foul breath choked him more than the clamp of its teeth. The slobber of a hungry animal dripping onto his face, the sense of utter impotence as it mauled him, the primal terror of being devoured battered his mind as savagely as the creature battered his body. He curled up in a ball, clinging to the beast, supporting his fragile neck from its own bulk. Once he got his legs tangled around it, he started punching it in the head with one gauntleted fist.

Finally hatred instead of fear. His tael still absorbed the ulvenman's brutal thrashing, while he beat on its skull, trying to dislodge it. He felt its jaws move a fraction of an inch, and punched harder.

Suddenly, it released him, threw back its head, and howled. A terrible sound, evoking pity and dread in equal measures. Christopher punched at it in a blind panic, making contact only with air. Nonetheless it flopped over and stopped moving, pinning him under its dead weight.

Gregor stood above him, bloody blade in both hands, the blue glow eerily illuminating the red.

"Clear!" Gregor yelled, and answering shouts came.

"Casualty report," Karl called, while Gregor pulled Christopher to his feet.

Men and ulvenmen lay in bloody heaps. A few moments later, the men stood, mostly healed. Torme and Christopher had exhausted their spells, but they had turned fatal injuries into minor scrapes. All the ulvenmen were dead, with swords, lances, and D'Kan's arrows sticking out of them. With some dismay, Christopher noted that the pattern of bodies showed no attempt at retreat.

Gregor was lopping off heads with an ax. They didn't have magic to waste harvesting them, so their future lay in a kettle.

"The expected showing," Karl said with satisfaction. "Save for your poor horsemanship. The ulvenmen won't know what to make of that."

"How could they have learned anything from this?" Christopher could see nothing else on the plain.

D'Kan could. He snapped off a shot from his bow. Christopher happened to be looking in the right direction, so he saw the arrow impossibly strike a hawk fluttering up from the grass twenty yards away.

More impossibly, the arrow bounced off the bird like a straw blown at a stone.

The hawk was sixty yards out and moving fast before D'Kan got off a second shot. This was apparently the limit of possibility: the arrow was wide by at least six inches. D'Kan lowered his bow.

"That's how," he said.

The count of the tael confirmed what they had already suspected. Most of the creatures they had fought were not ranked, despite the incredible fight they had put up. Only their leader, the one that had unseated Christopher, had been first-ranked. Christopher found it deeply unfair that the ulvenmen should have such a natural advantage in size and strength over his men.

"It's a good thing you invented rifles, then," Gregor laughed at him. "You can imagine how facing those horrors down on foot would be a daunting task, no matter how long your pike."

It explained why the last army had hid in the city, letting them devastate the countryside.

"From their armor, they were merely scouts." D'Kan was dissatisfied, the pieces of the puzzle not fitting into place. "Such a large scouting party is unusual. And they were lightly provisioned, yet well-fed. They could not have traveled far from their supply lines."

"What do we do tomorrow?" Christopher asked. There wasn't enough left of the afternoon to accomplish anything more today. And Christopher was not about to blunder around in the dark with those things. D'Kan swore they saw as well in the dark as they did in the day.

"See who blinks first." Gregor grinned wolfishly. "They'll send out another scouting party. It will either be backed up by their principals, or it won't. If it is, then us riding out there alone will be fatal. If it's not, then us taking a platoon out there will give away all our secrets."

"They saw me heal. They must know I am a priest."

"Good point," Gregor said. "They know they won't be able to wear us down with repeated low-scale attacks. So I predict their next move will be to deploy their real ranks, in a contest of strength."

Gregor turned out to be right, in a way no one could have expected.

"My lord Curate, wake up." Torme's voice was graver than usual. But the tone of his voice was less important than the fact that he had used Christopher's full title.

It had to be bad news.

He rolled out of bed and washed his face in the bowl Torme had brought him.

"What time is it?" It was still dark out.

"Dawn is but a few minutes away, Brother."

They had woken him early. He hated that, and they knew it.

It had to be really bad news.

Torme led him out of his cabin and up on the south wall, where Gregor and Karl stood looking out over the plain.

Gregor didn't crack any jokes.

It was still dark, and Christopher's night vision hadn't adapted from the light-stones in the fort. He couldn't see anything.

"What am I looking at?"

"Another call for a miracle," Karl said.

The rising sun tinged the gloom a lighter shade. Christopher could sense movement, hear growls and the distant clatter of metal.

"D'Kan is over there, trying to avoid the torchlight. He might have a better estimate." Karl pointed down the wall.

The sunrise promised to render all estimates moot in only a few moments. It also promised to reveal a terrifyingly large crowd of monsters. Christopher was beginning to hate sunrises.

D'Kan came over and joined them. The Ranger seemed unfocused and disoriented. Christopher finally recognized the symptoms as fear, an emotion he had not seen on D'Kan's face before.

"There are at least five hundred ulvenmen out there," D'Kan reported, "not counting a smaller but indeterminate number that have flanked us in the swamp. We are surrounded, cut off, and severely outnumbered."

Gregor whistled through his teeth. "Five regiments of ulvenmen would make even the good Captain of Carrhill knock his knees. And that's with a wizard at his back. If you really are protected by some secret entity, Christopher, now would be the time to call upon it."

"It's just us and the men," Christopher said. "But this time we have a stone fort, not a wooden one. I'm not worried yet."

D'Kan looked at him as if he had lost his senses, but Gregor's face was restored to the grin that normally lay there. "You are a cool one, priest. I'd think you mad if I hadn't seen what you did to those dinosaurs."

"I did see, and I still think you are mad," D'Kan said. "One of us can probably escape with your flight spell and carry warning to the town."

Christopher had a cage of pigeons for that duty. He had to use a minor spell on them to get them to fly to the right place, though. "Let me pray and I'll send a message. But I don't think they will come out here to rescue us. At least, not in less than a week."

"Speaking of magic," Karl said, "what can we expect from the ulvenmen?"

D'Kan shook his head dismissively. "Normally, very little. They rely on strength more than craft."

That was excellent news. No amount of strength could make up for guns.

"But," D'Kan continued, "you saw the hawk deflect my arrow. That is magic. So I can only tell you to expect anything."

Reflexively, they all looked at the brightening sky.

"I'm no woodsman," Gregor said, "but I'm pretty sure that a dozen hawks hanging over our heads is unnatural."

"Put our best sniper on it," Christopher said. "One rifle won't give anything away. They'll just think it's magic." Then he went back to his cabin to prepare what little real magic they had.

An hour later he stood at the pigeon cote, with a pinch of biscuit in his hand. One of the pigeons finally decided it was better than scratching in the straw at the bottom of their crate and came over to peck half-heartedly at the offering.

"A pox on picky birds," Christopher muttered, and then said something rather different in Celestial. Now the bird tamely let him tie a scrap of paper around its leg. The message was short and sour: "*500 ulvenmen. Send help.*" There didn't seem to be anything else to say.

A half-dozen rifle shots had cleared the sky of hawks. Their best shot turned out to be Gregor. The blue knight had taken his lessons from Karl in earnest, and his tael-enhanced accuracy gave him an edge over the ordinary men. He'd only killed one hawk, but after that the rest had retreated out of sight.

Christopher threw open the lid of the crate and chased all the pigeons into the air. Watching the dozen birds flutter up, he felt the burden of responsibility settle on his shoulders. If he felt this bad about dispatching a dozen pigeons as decoys, knowing most of them would die to the hawks, how would he feel about sending men to their deaths to save others?

As long as they were in the fort, trapped in a siege, he might not have to make a hard decision like that.

Karl came to give him an update.

"No change. As best we can tell, they are sleeping. On the bright side, all of them are in merely hide armor. They are poorly equipped, and that usually means poorly disciplined as well. Even D'Kan is beginning to think we have a chance."

Christopher would have asked why they hadn't attacked yet, except he already knew the answer. As usual, they were waiting for the cover of darkness. Just once, Christopher wanted to fight monsters that weren't bigger, meaner, and able to see in the dark.

"Then I'm going back to bed," he told Karl.

He woke with a start, not knowing how much time had passed. Groggy and stiff, he forced himself to do a dozen deep knee bends and a few lunges with his sword before he went out of the cabin.

It was late afternoon, and the fort was quiet. Karl wanted the men sleeping, and to facilitate that he had ordered complete silence. Even Torme whispered when talking to Christopher, asking his advice on what magic he should prepare.

"The weapon blessing," Christopher told him, "as many as you can. And remember it works on cannons as well as swords." The spell had already saved his army once. Ordinary guns weren't much use against creatures that could only be harmed by magic.

Royal wanted to go for a ride, pushing at Christopher's shoulder with his huge head. Apparently the warhorse had enjoyed yesterday's excursion. The coming siege would not be fun, however. The inside of his fortress was the size of a football field, but it was cluttered with buildings and supplies. Hardly enough room for the big horse to break into a gallop before he had to slow down.

Gregor was as impatient as the warhorse, although he didn't nudge Christopher with his head. He just twiddled his thumbs.

"Nervous?" Christopher asked, before realizing that was not a very complimentary question.

"Bored," Gregor answered. "When are you going to let me start shooting ulvenmen? The cheeky bastards are sleeping less than three hundred feet from the walls."

That was about the limit of effective range for a recurve bow. Even if you could hit something that far out, the shaft would have lost so much energy it wouldn't do much damage. D'Kan's long bow and the heavy crossbows that were popular back in the civilized world had twice that range, so either the ulvenmen had forgotten how humans fought, or their bird-spies had told them there were no bows in the fort.

Christopher's rifles had a killing range of a thousand feet. But the ulvenmen had no way of knowing that yet. He wasn't going to let them know, until it was too late.

"How are the troops holding up?" he asked, trying to pretend he had not just questioned Gregor's courage.

"Better than our stalwart Ranger," Gregor said, but he wasn't smiling. "Honestly, I would think them enspelled if I did not know otherwise. Even high-rank lords would look at that ocean of fangs and quake. But your boys seem to think you'll pull a dragon out of your pocket and kill everything. They're more concerned with whose turn it is to cook dinner than they are with the coming battle. If it is possible for an army to be overconfident, yours wins the prize."

"Is it?" Christopher asked. "Is it possible for an army to be overconfident?"

"An over-tempered blade may hold a fine edge, but in the face of setbacks it can shatter where a less keen blade would only be notched."

Remembering the battle against the goblins, Christopher shook his head.

"They won't break and run. We don't have anywhere to run to, anyway."

"I noticed that," Gregor said. "Most high-ranks leave themselves an escape route, in case something unexpected happens. That's how they live long enough to become high-rank. Did you at least prepare your flight spell?"

"No," Christopher admitted. He'd chosen different spells, intended to counter the effects of enemy magic.

Gregor sighed. "Don't tell D'Kan. He is under the illusion that after everything falls apart, you will cut a finger from his body before you flee, and he will at least have a second chance at life. Truly, Christopher, you mystify me. You chose actions that increase the morale of your unranked at the expense of the morale of your ranks."

"Don't they have as much right to life as we do?"

"You could fit a lot of fingers into one sack."

Christopher hadn't thought of that. He felt his face flush.

"I wasn't serious. You couldn't possibly afford to revive everyone. Nor do you have need to apologize. Both D'Kan and I understood our place when we joined you. You have treated us like ordinary men at every turn. We cannot expect different now."

"I'm sorry," Christopher said, because he was. He knew he had taken advantage of both men, accepting their service without paying the usual price.

"I confess," Gregor said with surprise in his voice, "that I find it refreshing."

The two men stood together for a moment, sharing a feeling that had no place in the iron hierarchy of rank and privilege. Indeed, it might never have been felt before in this world. Gregor was discomfited by its strangeness at last and went off to find Disa, saying that he'd best mend his fences with her before the battle.

"I don't want her remembering our theological arguments when she's deciding where to put her last healing spell," he said. His smile showed he was not serious. She would do what was right.

They all would.

13

A SHOCKING EXPERIENCE

The night passed fitfully, but peacefully. Even though the sky was heavily overcast, screening out the starlight and leaving the world in deep darkness, the enemy did not attack. D'Kan suggested it was too dark. Their foes were not magical, only flesh and blood, and they needed some light to aim their bows by.

Another unhappy sunrise told the truth, however. The ulvenmen had simply been waiting for the rest of their army.

D'Kan stood open-mouthed, gaping at the plain beyond their wall. Christopher found his confidence equally shaken. He had never seen anything like this. Worse, none of the veteran soldiers around him had ever seen anything like it.

"The King needs to know about this," D'Kan hissed. "You must select one of us as a messenger. Already we could have saved one man yesterday."

"I don't think so," Karl answered him. "They had already invested the woods as of then. And the hawks would have led them to you. Once the spell failed, they would be waiting underneath you with sharpened knives."

"It's true," Christopher told him sadly. "My flight spell won't get you all the way to the town. And anything less would be certain death."

The ulvenmen did not have cavalry. They had worse—or better, depending on whose side you were on. Two dozen Megaraptors, bred for size and overstuffed. Their armored riders glinted with metal, coats of overlapping scale that would still turn a blade or bounce an arrow, if not quite as swaddling as the fancy plate-mail of knights. The creatures moved in bursts of speed out on the plain, their long legs eating up the ground. Christopher wasn't sure his horse could outrun them. He knew his magic could not.

Instead of supply wagons, the ulvenman army had more dinosaurs. Eight massive *Triceratops*, the size of houses, with baggage piled twenty feet high on their backs. And one carried a howdah that glinted gold even from a mile away. The enemy commander rode to battle in considerably more style than Christopher's warhorse.

"He must feel pretty safe to reveal his position so openly," Gregor said. Another joke from the blue knight. The enemy commander was perfectly safe, since he was sitting in the middle of approximately two thousand warriors.

And not lightly armed, like the hide-wearing scouts. Most of the new troops clanked with metal coats that looked just as effective, if not quite as shiny, as the dinosaur riders' armor.

"They will destroy the town." D'Kan was not giving up. "They will sweep over us tonight, like a child stepping over a stone, and they will devour the entire county in hardly less time. The King must be warned, not for the sake of Carrhill, but for the sake of the entire realm."

"Warned by who?" Gregor asked. "They wouldn't even need to wait for the spell to fail; those hawks would tear you apart. The only person who has a chance of surviving the trip is Christopher."

"Then why won't he go?" D'Kan asked.

It was a good question, and Christopher didn't have a good answer.

"You can start over," Karl told him. "Sacrificing this regiment is worth saving the next two."

"No," Christopher said. "I can't start again. I don't have the energy. The smiths will keep the factories running. The sergeants will train the next regiment. Sooner or later the lords will see the value of guns, and everything will take care of itself. I am no more important to this process than anyone else, now. If I run, it's only to save myself, not for the cause."

"Why will you not save yourself?" D'Kan asked, genuinely curious. "There is no shame in fleeing from certain death."

Because retreat meant exile from his wife. *Forever.* He would never have guessed it, had he been asked in his old life, but now that he was faced with it, the prospect seemed indistinguishable from dying. He couldn't tell the difference, except that one would be long and miserable, and the other would be miserable and short.

He did not want to live out the rest of his life a broken and useless old man, robbed of even dreams. Better to die here, with men he called friends.

And women or, rather, woman. Disa joined them on the wall, under Gregor's protective arm, her eyes red from weeping.

"If I could save one of you, I would," Christopher told them. "But I do not think I can. And I cannot abandon you."

"You could save Gregor," Disa said urgently. "His strength will defeat the hawks, his word will move the King. Send him, now, while there is still time."

Christopher didn't understand her change in attitude. Not that it mattered. Gregor shook his head with a snort.

"Not a chance. I left you once, and you had way too much fun without me. I won't make that mistake again."

"Then we are all doomed?" D'Kan said, and the young man's face trembled.

"Every ulvenman we slay is one less to harry the Kingdom." Karl spoke matter-of-factly. "We will do our duty. If we die, it is so others might live."

D'Kan breathed heavily, and Christopher felt sorry for him. It was one thing for the hard-bitten Karl, the professional Gregor, or the old and worn-out Christopher to face death. It was something else for a handsome young nobleman with a life of glory still ahead of him.

"I will not fail my honor," D'Kan resolved, stiffening his shoulders through an act of will.

"I know you won't," Gregor told him gently. "We will make an end worthy of heroes."

Torme joined them, eating a bowl of porridge. The ordinariness of the act was insulting, but he shrugged off their stares.

"I have earned my death many times over," he said. "If the gods come to collect it now, I have no room to complain."

In the fort below them, the young men went about their business with only an edge of tension. Still protected by their absolute faith in Christopher, they seemed unaware of the hopelessness of the situation. Christopher decided it would be the better part of mercy and wisdom not to tell them.

People should talk more, Christopher thought. Specifically, the ulvenmen should have talked to the goblins. If they had, they wouldn't be making the same mistake.

Out on the marsh, several hundred armored ulvenmen were advancing, carrying crude ladders—a reassuring sight, since it suggested that ulvenmen could not in fact leap fifteen-foot walls in a single bound. The army behind them was picking itself up, getting ready to march on, sunset the signal that had roused them. Distant figures were repacking the supply dinosaurs. Obviously, the ulvenmen expected their advancing regiments to take the fort by frontal assault inside the next hour.

If Christopher's men had pikes, swords, and bows, they probably would. An ulvenman was worth two men in strength, hardiness, and ferocity. In the close press of combat, where density mattered, that translated into certain victory.

Another two hundred of the light troops fanned out before the assault, armed with bows. The fact that they weren't firing flaming arrows meant they wanted to capture the fort largely intact, the better to loot it. They were attacking only one wall, the south one, and had been so obvious about their plans that Christopher's men had time to redistribute the cannons, putting fully half of them on the front line. In every aspect, the assault was hurried and overconfident.

Just the way Christopher liked it.

At one hundred yards the ulvenmen broke into a trot while their archers loosed a shower of arrows. The arrows fell harmlessly on the fort, the men safely ensconced in their firing ports. Even the horses were protected by wooden slatting over their stalls.

At fifty yards the ulvenmen began to yelp and howl. With any other army, Christopher would have had to give the order to fire or watch his men dissolve into mindless fear. Staring at the advancing creatures, knowing that in seconds they would be swarming at the foot of the walls and over the ladders, was nerve-wracking. But these men had complete faith in their commander. They waited, calmly sighting down the barrels of their rifles like it was just another drill.

When the ulvenmen were twenty yards from the wall, Christopher gave the signal, and Charles fired a rocket out over the marsh. It burst into a very pretty green and yellow star, and while the ulvenmen paused to look at it in confusion, mystified by an attack that did no damage, the riflemen began to fire.

The ulvenmen were not cowards. Seeing their fellows fall like dominoes sparked them to rage, not fear. Rushing forward and slamming the ladders in place, they scampered up them at a full run.

But as fast as they came over the top and into view, the cavalrymen shot them down with their carbines and threw grenades after the falling bodies.

Many of the ulvenmen futilely tried to protect themselves from the hail of bullets by holding up shields. After a few minutes the survivors threw them down in frustration, and the ulvenmen fell into retreat, snarling and barking in hatred.

Much to their surprise, the bullets didn't stop coming when they were more than twenty yards out. Or thirty. Or even fifty. At one hundred yards, the guns fell silent, only because there was nothing left to shoot at.

Inside the fort there was still gunfire, however. On the north wall several ulvenmen had appeared from nowhere, stabbing at shocked young men. The ulvenmen were equally shocked when other young men shot them at point-blank range, knocking them down with blasts of fire and smoke.

"Invisibility," Gregor growled, and ran to protect Disa while she healed the wounded. How the ulvenmen had gotten over the wall was unclear, but their lack of armor suggested they had been boosted up by other invisible ulvenmen in a canine pyramid. Or maybe they just had invisible ladders.

"How many invisible ulvenmen can dance on a wall?" Christopher asked no one in particular.

Returning to the south wall, Christopher looked out at the enemy army. They were staring with perplexity at the complete failure of their frontal assault. Hundreds of bodies littered the ground, mostly within a few yards of the fort.

"We need to harvest those," Gregor said. "Or they will, and be the stronger for it. Yet the ground is not safe." He pointed out onto the plain, where a head was detaching itself into thin air and then disappearing, presumably into an invisible bag.

Christopher sighed, because he knew what that meant. Time for heroics. With Gregor, it was always time for heroics.

"The question is whether we want to spend our magic now or save it."

Gregor was practically salivating over the fortune in tael the corpses represented. "There is a fourth-rank lying at your feet, if only you would bend to pick it up. Give it to Disa, and within four days she will be able to out-heal you and Torme put together."

Put in those terms, Christopher saw the attraction of the idea. If this turned into a siege, which he certainly hoped it would, then all of that healing power would be invaluable.

The only alternative to a siege was immediate defeat, in which case whatever decision he made here would be irrelevant.

"Get ropes," he told Gregor, and the blue knight ran off grinning fiendishly to organize their insanely dangerous adventure.

Karl approved, only because they still had some surprises for the ulvenmen. They hadn't fired any cannons yet. "As long as we have tricks up our sleeves, we can act as they would expect. Any ordinary lord would have already jumped from the walls to collect that booty."

Moments later, twenty men with axes and bags stood on the edge of the wall. Another ten with carbines were going along with the party, mostly for the sake of morale. The real protection was the hundred riflemen watching over the edge.

And Christopher and Gregor, of course. Going outside the wall was a ludicrous risk, but if it tempted the ulvenmen into another impetuous charge, it was worth it.

He did not cast the blessing spell; it only lasted a few minutes, and the ulvenmen might not attack right away. But mindful of his previous experience, he cast a new spell and felt strength quicken in his arms and legs. Springing to the top of the wall, despite the immense weight of the plate-mail he wore, he finally felt like a hero. For the next few hours, at least. It appeared simple strength was not without its use, after all.

"Down!" he shouted, and he and Gregor went over the edge, rappelling the fifteen feet to the ground. The rest of the men followed, setting to their grisly harvest as soon as their feet hit the ground, while Christopher and Gregor stalked about, looking for trouble.

The men worked fast, unhindered by opposition or armor. One man would yank on a monster's head while the other struck at the neck with an ax. Then into the bag and on to the next. They were halfway through the mess before the first guard fell silently, an ulvenman popping into view above him with a bloody blade.

Christopher shouted the words of his revealing spell as he sprinted toward the trouble. The visible ulvenman was already dead, cut down by rifle fire from the wall. The men on the ground stared wildly in random directions, fearing the next unforeseeable assault. As Christopher came up to the area, ulvenmen started appearing from nowhere, howling in outrage that their invisibility had been compromised.

Quite intelligently, they recognized Christopher as the source of the problem. Not so intelligently, they charged him as a body, hoping to destroy his effect. As they entered the radius of his spell, they became visible, prompting fire from the walls. Christopher stood still in one spot and tried not to flinch as the rain of bullets fell around him, splattering ulvenmen and spraying blood everywhere.

Something smashed into his leg, knocking him to one knee. As he looked down to see the cause, his thigh extruded a bullet and closed up the wound. If not for tael, he would have been a friendly-fire casualty. The damage would have shattered his leg and severed an artery.

Instead, he cast a healing spell, restoring his tael to its full strength. Around him, the rest of the men stood up from where they had cowered and began harvesting the new bodies.

"Your failure to die has revealed you as a principal," Gregor shouted gleefully. "The ranks are interested." He pointed out to the marsh, where a dozen of the Megaraptors were thundering toward them.

"Up!" Christopher shouted, and everyone scrambled to the ropes, while men pulled from the top.

The dinosaurs were fast. Even with his new strength, yanking himself up hand over hand, Christopher had only made five feet by the time the first cannon fired. He did not need to look over his shoulder to see the danger. The faces of the men above him, and the sounds behind him, were sufficient. He clawed at the rope in deafened silence after the cannon to his immediate left spoke. Rifles sprouted from the wall, and he saw a cavalryman above him empty his carbine as fast as he could pull the trigger. At the edge of the wall, helping hands grabbed his arms, shoulders, helmet, and dragged him over, even as something massive slammed into stone where he had just been.

The dinosaur was only a ton of flesh; the wall shrugged it off. The creature snapped with flashing teeth before falling away. It struggled to right itself, but bullets pinned it down. Within seconds the wall was wreathed in white smoke, rendering even the ground invisible.

When the smoke dispersed, six dinosaurs lay dead. Their riders were strewn about the field, identifiable by their silvery armor. The rest were in full retreat, a hundred yards out and running fast.

"More for the kettle," Gregor shouted with a demonic leer. And the party went back over the wall.

When they came back up ten minutes later, there was no danger, so Christopher let the men on the rope pull him up. His spell gave him strength, not endurance. Half an hour of sprinting and climbing in plate-mail had left him limp.

Leaning on the wall, he looked back at the enemy camp.

"What do you suppose they will try next?"

"I don't know," D'Kan panted, "but, as one of the men on the wrong side of that rope, may I suggest you cast your flight spell next time?"

Their victory had restored the Ranger's spirit. The young man was cracking jokes again, basking in the ridiculous bravado exuded by the soldiers. Even the men slain by the invisible ulvenmen did not distress them. The living stuffed the dead into barrels, joking about how lucky they were to escape kitchen duty so lightly.

Christopher had promised to revive them if they brought in enough tael. And the wealth of heads going into the kettles was staggering. The dinosaur riders were moderately ranked, judging from the number of bullets it had taken to bring it down. Each of them was worth a fortune alone.

He reached up to clap D'Kan on the shoulder, to share in the glory of the moment. Out of the corner of his eye he saw a flare of light, bright and hot and heading directly for him. Instinctively he dodged, throwing himself out of the path, which in this case meant off of the wall and into the fort. As he fell a bolt of lightning streaked past him, its glowing halo galvanizing his body and setting the sleeve of his shirt on fire.

Along the wall he had abandoned, men transformed into charcoal statues of corpses, their clothing bursting into wreaths of flame as the stroke ripped a blinding line through them.

Christopher landed heavily on the ground. His helmet protected his head from the stunning impact, for which he was duly grateful. Even though it had only barely touched him, the electricity had evaporated his tael and cooked flesh through his shoulder. He could not feel his left arm. With the last of his strength he looked up. An ulvenman, glittering with gold- and silver-scaled armor, stared down at him from the wall. The alien features did nothing to disguise the annoyance on the creature's face. Christopher was absolutely certain there hadn't been any ulvenman there a second ago. How it had gotten there he didn't know, and it wasn't telling, but the way the creature was pointing its hand told him it meant to finish what it had started.

Christopher had time for only one act. He chose to use it casting a defensive spell. Torme had come running to his aid, already kneeling at his side, oblivious to the doom crouching on the wall. When the next bolt came crackling down, slamming into the ground, Torme writhed like a hooked fish and burned.

But a golden haze flared around Christopher as his spell countered the lethal damage intended for him. Astonishingly the spell faded away, spent; he had been counting on it to be good for several strokes, but the ulvenman's magic was terribly potent.

His soldiers were already reacting. They pretty much reacted to every unusual event the same way. Gunfire rattled the camp again.

Distressingly, the bullets bounced off the monster as easily as D'Kan's arrow had bounced off the hawk. The whine of ricochets sounded like defeat. But as the firing reached a crescendo, every gun in the fort turning to face the new threat, one shot got through. The monster's metal coat of scales jingled, a scale popping off to spin through the air, and blood spattered in its wake.

Growling in frustration, the dog-man transformed into a giant eagle and threw himself off the wall. Men rushed forward to point their guns over the edge, only to shout in dismay. The creature had disappeared into thin air, it seemed.

Gregor arrived and stood over him protectively, his glowing blue sword pointing out and sweeping from side to side in defensive arcs. He called to Disa, but she sobbed in frustration.

"I have no magic left." She had spent it all on the men attacked by the first set of invisible ulvenmen.

"I do," Christopher said, and started healing himself. It took several of his lesser spells to undo all the damage. But there was no point in saving any. The men who were struck by the lightning were beyond healing.

Karl issued an order from thirty feet away.

"If you cannot aid him, Ser, then get away from him. Let us not put all of our eggs in one basket."

The blue knight and the priestess retreated to a different part of the camp.

"Get these corpses in barrels before they suffer more damage," Christopher ordered, watching in horror as Torme's left hand crumbled into ash.

"They are already past raising but not beyond resurrection," Karl said. "Just more expense for your purse. We can fit them all in one."

Christopher blinked, trying to understand the man's strange comments, before realizing they were supposed to be reassuring. Karl was dispelling the shock by focusing on the task at hand.

"How many?" Christopher asked, and immediately changed his mind. "I don't care. Collect them all. Don't bother to identify the parts." He would revive them all. He would not single out Torme and D'Kan.

Assuming, of course, that anyone survived to take the barrel home.

An hour later, Christopher stood in his cabin with what was left of his staff, listening to a damage report.

"You owe your architecture a note of gratitude," Gregor said. "Because the wall curved, only twenty men died in that first stroke. Had the wall run straight, we would have lost forty." The second stroke had been aimed down, at Christopher, and had killed only Torme.

One of the small cannons had shattered under the first blast, though, and several of the dead men's rifles were warped and torn. Their ammunition had caught fire with their clothes. Luckily, since it was only contained by paper, it had burned instead of exploding.

"Because you live, the men hold firm," Karl reported.

"We have no magic left," Disa whispered. "We cannot renew until the morning."

"I still have one spell," Christopher corrected her. "If that thing comes back, I'll show it what an enchanted cannon can do." It had saved him against the goblins, in the end. It might save him here.

"What else will they throw at us?" he demanded.

"Flesh and blood only. Amazing that such a high-ranked shaman came alone into the camp in the first place. He must have been very sure of his power, yet he failed to kill you. Instead you sent him packing with a bullet wound." Gregor spoke confidently. "No other ranks will risk themselves now. Instead, they will overrun us with their unranked."

"Speaking of rank," Karl said, "I suggest you consider this." He handed Christopher the results of the boiling operation, a purple stone the size of a golf ball.

"A profitable day," Gregor said weakly. He apparently found it harder to crack jokes in the face of staggering wealth than in the face of certain death.

"If you do not count the ones we lost," Christopher answered. The resurrection was three times as expensive as a simple raising, and he now had twice as many who needed it.

"I do not think we should count them," Karl said. "If we do not survive, they remain dead. If we do survive, we will no doubt gain more tael to spend on them. Let us spend what we have while we have need of it."

Gregor nodded his approval. "Promote Karl," he urged Christopher. "Within the day he will be a knight and twice the strength he is to us now. In fact, you could promote a gaggle of knights with that rock."

Karl frowned. "A knight with a gun is not twice a man with a gun. We need magic, not strength."

As always, the young soldier was right. Carving off a large flake, Christopher handed it to Disa. "Your second-rank is worth more to us than anything." Looking at what he had left in his hand, he calculated. "Ser Gregor, how close are you to fourth?"

"Halfway, Christopher. But I find myself swayed by Karl's wisdom. Better you should gain a rank of healing than I should gain a rank of fighting."

Christopher understood this world well enough to know Gregor was wrong. The blue knight's high rank meant he was the only other person in the camp who could pretend to have a chance of surviving the lightning bolt. And his skill with his magic sword might be necessary to penetrate the shaman's arcane defenses; the guns had been surprisingly ineffective. As much as he hated to admit it, he still needed the knight's raw strength.

He chipped off another, much larger, chunk, and handed it to the blue knight. Then, before he could question himself, he ate the rest of the tael, shoveling a veritable fortune into his mouth. It would be enough, just barely.

"If they let us live another day, we'll each have an extra rank to face them with."

Gregor held his share in his hand, his face troubled.

"Go on," Christopher told him. "It's not charity, or even pay. Just simple necessity."

A ghost of a smile on the blue knight's face. "Terms I can agree to." He put the chunk on his tongue and closed his mouth.

Then they went back to their posts, to wait for whatever came next.

What came next was startling. The wizard's voice, in Christopher's head.

"Got your bird yesterday, but took a while to fire up this spell. I see you're still alive, so I assume things aren't too bad."

Christopher could feel the wizard's attention waiting on him, and he knew he had only a few words before he lost it. *"Three thousand ulvenmen, two dozen dinosaurs, and a shapeshifting shaman. Warn the king,"* he thought as loudly as he could, and then the presence was gone.

No point in asking for help. It would take the Kingdom days to mount a force that could hope to challenge this horde, and days more to get it here. By then, the monsters would have either gone over Christopher's fort or around it.

Then Gregor's voice outside his cabin, a real sound, though a less encouraging one.

"They're coming."

Christopher closed his writing case and shoved it under his cot. The letter he had been writing to his wife was unfinished, though it could not matter. There had never been anywhere to send it to. And she already knew everything he was trying to say.

Outside, mounting the walls, he took a deep breath. This would be the final push. He was physically whole and fresh, having been restored by his healing magic, but he had only one small spell left. Their last remaining secret was the six-inch Napoleons, as yet unused.

"Fire arrows!" came a sentry's cry, and a moment later a flight of burning shafts fell among the camp. Kennet had the water bottle in his hands, and he dashed around putting them out. But if one managed to land in an ammunition store, it would get ugly.

Looking over the wall, he saw the archers preparing another volley. They were three hundred feet out and obviously thought they were safe from counterattack. They should have been; at that range, with nothing more than starlight, the men could not possibly pick out targets. But the ulvenmen were holding flaming arrows to their chest.

"Shoot them," he ordered, and rifles barked. The dancing lights in the distance began to fall to the ground and stop moving. Then they all fell, as the archers cast away their arrows and fled.

If that was the extent of the attack, the ulvenmen must be getting desperate.

Then he felt the ground tremble slightly under his feet and realized the ulvenmen had a surprise of their own planned.

Because they were so large, the *Triceratops* became visible much farther away. They trundled toward the fort, gradually picking up speed.

"Stop them!" he cried, and the small cannons began to fire.

"Faster," he muttered, as his crewmen reloaded their guns. The dinosaurs were easy to hit, but one shot from a two-inch cannon only made them angry.

The six-inch guns were loaded with grape-shot, for short-range slaughter. Their crews started unloading the rounds, intending to replace them with solid cannonballs that could hit the big dinosaurs at long range. Christopher swore at their foolishness until they emptied the guns the easy way, by firing them into the darkness. The explosion was tremendous. If nothing else, it was good for morale.

Finally the big guns were properly loaded. They belched, spitting tongues of fire ten feet long. Christopher saw a huge dinosaur stumble and fall, and he started breathing again.

As the herd approached, Christopher could see small figures swarming around them. The entire ulvenman army, advancing on foot.

The small cannons fired another salvo, and another *Triceratops* trumpeted and fell, crushing ulvenmen as it rolled over. Christopher could see the dinosaurs were blindfolded, with huge swaths of cloth over their eyes. The *Triceratops* weren't just baggage trains; they were mobile siege engines. Ten-ton battering rams. And they would be here in heartbeats. Time for only one more salvo.

"Double powder, and don't fire until you are sure," he shouted. Then he looked for something to hang on to.

At point-blank range, the cannons shot the beasts in the head. The huge bony plates shattered, and several *Triceratops* collapsed. But three sailed on, driving head first into the wall. He could feel the section of solid rock lift up slightly, vibrate, and then crack.

One of the dinosaurs fell over, stunned, one horn snapped in half. One blundered off in a different direction, blind and angry, trampling ulvenmen under its feet. The third went berserk, pounding the wall like a jackhammer. Dust sprayed in the air as the stone began to disintegrate.

Ladders were slapped up, and again a horde of ulvenmen scampered over the top. This time they would not be dispensed with by the time the carbines had to reload.

Christopher opened a box of hand grenades and threw them with both hands, pulling the pins out with his teeth. He didn't look where they went. As long as it was the other side of the wall, he didn't care. Other men followed his example, a profligate consumption of expensive objects. When life was measured in minutes, the price of things had a different meaning.

When he reached the bottom of the box, he tucked the last two in his pocket, drew his sword, and stood to face his doom.

A lull in the fighting. Thick white smoke masked everything more than a few feet away, and the ringing in his ears was unbearable. The wall had stopped vibrating, which told him someone had killed the last *Triceratops*. Blind and deaf, he stood uncertainly, waiting for a cue. Beside him a man reloaded his rifle.

Christopher felt the threat coming, tael-fueled instinct or perhaps just the pressure of air. Kneeling just in time, he let it sail over his head. Claws, leather, and a long tail whipped over him.

The Megaraptors leapt into the camp, using the dead *Triceratops* as stepping stones. They landed heavily, gathered themselves, and staggered forward to make room for more. Wading through men and wooden buildings, they smashed everything in their path.

Most of Christopher's men were on the walls, however. The Megaraptors had to stretch to reach them, yanking the unlucky ones by a leg and tossing them over their heads, where others snapped them out of the air and bit them in half. But the dinosaurs were only flesh and blood, if three times the size of warhorses. Under the withering fire, they began to fall. In their agonized death throes the dinosaurs demolished everything, including the stables. Horses panicked and fled, but it was for a good cause. The disoriented and angry dinosaurs snapped at the tasty horses, ignoring their riders' demands to focus on the real danger.

The riders wielded curved bows and lances to deadly effect, but their surprisingly effective armor and advanced rank only bought them four or five extra lives. They fell, one by one, and the problem began to reduce itself to manageable.

The south wall clattered with ladders again as the ulvenmen regrouped. Christopher worried that he had not brought enough grenades. But the six-inch guns opened up again, full of grape-shot, and the ulvenmen staggered back in confusion.

A pike tapped at the inside lip of the wall. Christopher leaned over to see what was up.

Charles drew his attention to Kennet, who was standing on a ladder and trying to hand up a box of grenades. Christopher pulled the heavy box in, stowed it against the wall. This time, when the ulvenmen came back, he only threw them one hand at a time. The pace of the battle had slowed, the wall and the smoke reducing everything to a series of individual encounters on a narrow stone path. His knew that his army survived because of the constant drumbeat of rifle fire, punctuated by cannons and grenades; he knew the ulvenmen were still there, because the only thing he could hear over the gunfire was their barks and howls.

More importantly, he knew that the ulvenman shaman had not committed himself to battle yet because the only flashes in the night were fueled by gunpowder. If he did see the streak of lightning, it would be his duty to run toward it.

Sometime in the night, he felt his magical strength desert him. That bothered him less than realizing he was out of grenades again.

Now a ladder poked up in front of him, and he had only his sword. He had finally run out of tricks. All the ulvenmen had to do now was keep pushing, and his army would crumble away in this acrid, thick darkness.

The man next to him attached his bayonet to his rifle and joined Christopher in front of the ladder.

"Don't be stupid," Christopher shouted at him. "Go find some ammunition."

Nodding, the soldier ran off into the smoke.

An ulvenman head appeared, and Christopher poked at it. He had a significant advantage here. The creature could only fight one-handed, since it had to use the other hand to hold onto the ladder. It decided to ignore him and tried to clamber over the top. Christopher's tael guided his thrust between the scales of its armor, and the sword sank deep into its belly.

He had to pull the sword out and beat the thing over the head a few more times before it fell off the ladder. By then the next ulvenman was climbing onto the lip of the wall.

He killed that one, ignoring the ax blow that cracked his helmet and diminished his tael. He killed the next one, too, but not without suffering another hit. They were coming too fast, the ones behind scampering over their dead and dying kin.

A soldier with a carbine walked up, shot the current ulvenman, leaned over the edge and fired five more times. Then he left, reloading as he went.

Before new ulvenmen appeared, the first soldier came back. Now they alternated shooting and stabbing the creatures, and Christopher fancied they could keep up. At least until he fainted from exhaustion. Leaning against the wall, panting, he tried to catch his breath in the acrid smoke.

After a few minutes, he realized something was wrong. He'd been resting for an unseemly length of time.

His companion was slumped, unmoving. Terrified that the sleep was magical, he kicked the man. But the soldier sprung wildly to his feet, ready to fight. He'd only been dozing.

Rifles still barked, intermittently. The cannons had gone silent, their crews waiting for something worth firing on.

Karl appeared out of the slowly thinning smoke. Glancing over the shambles of the fort, the bodies of men and animals strewn like spilled and bloody beans, he smiled at Christopher.

"I think we won."

They waited anxiously for the next attack, the next wave of ulvenmen, the next surprise. When the air began to lighten, Christopher's heart skipped a beat, convinced for a second that this was some terrible magic that would grow until it blinded them and left them helpless.

But it was just the sunrise. This one, for a change, revealed a pretty sight: the plain in in front of them was bare save for corpses. The ulvenmen had withdrawn from the walls in the night and had apparently kept running.

Another twoscore of his men had been lost in the final assault. Finding what the dinosaurs had left of them was not as gruesome as Christopher had feared. The blood and gore was so uniformly spread over the ground that it lost its power to shock.

"You need to get some sleep," Karl ordered. "And Disa too. We need your magic ready as soon as possible." Not to cure the wounded; there were hardly any of those. The attacks had been so powerful that ordinary men either lived or died. Karl was expecting the ulvenmen to return.

And so was Christopher. Tossing and turning on his cot, he had nightmares of invisible, snarling wolf-men hiding in every corner, waiting for a secret signal to pounce.

Late in the afternoon he gave up trying to sleep and tried to meditate instead. Alone inside his tent, he was unable to shake off the fear of sudden attack. Eventually he moved outside, under the watchful eye of his soldiers, where he finally felt safe enough to pray.

His head full, he went to find their few wounded, but Disa had beaten him to it. After that terrible, brutal night, there were only the dead and the cheerfully whistling. He thought about an old *Star Trek* episode. War was supposed to be painful, so people would be encouraged not to do it. Even the winners were supposed to suffer.

But on this world, victory was complete. Your wounded would be healed, your dead would be revived, everything would be made bright and shiny again. As long as you kept winning, you might never even guess that there was a downside to perpetual violence. Well, unless you were a commoner; for them, war still meant pain and death.

And the upside, at least from the nobility's point of view, was presented to him fresh from the kettles, the product of the corpses strewn inside and outside the walls. A rock of tael as big as a peach.

He'd bet the farm and won. In one day and night he had doubled his fortune, taking from the field of battle more tael than he had begged, borrowed, and stolen in his entire career as a priest. In his hand he held enough tael to make him seventh-rank.

"I never even got the chance to call you Vicar," Gregor laughed. That was the title for Christopher's sixth-rank, which hadn't even manifested itself yet.

Since Torme was otherwise occupied, Karl had to be the voice of gloom.

"Do not forget the tax you owe the King."

That wasn't the only expense that came before Christopher could think about another promotion. "Can I deduct what I spend to revive the men?"

"No," Gregor answered, rolling his eyes like Lalania always did. "The King comes first. He takes his quarter off the top."

And Christopher had to add in the tael they had taken the night before. Even the tiny specks from the alligators had to be counted. A truth spell would not be fooled by accounting tricks.

There was another expense he knew he was going to make, so he might as well do it now. He went looking for Disa and found her in the camp kitchen. She was making herself useful trying to sort the crockery into heaps that could be mended and piles that couldn't. Breaking off a large lump of tael, he handed it to her.

"We still need you fourth-ranked. Some of these men are going to get infected, and I might not be able to cure disease quickly enough." He could only do two a day, and that was only if he wasn't doing other things, like finding invisible ulvenmen or nullifying lightning bolts.

She stared at his generosity, holding the fortune as gently as an egg. Then she made an unexpected complaint.

"Ser Gregor served you as well as I did." She looked across the fort, to where Gregor was helping the men lift and move rubble.

Christopher shrugged, annoyed at having to explain his mercenary finances. "This is not a reward, it is an investment. You will be serving me for another two years. Gregor is a free agent. He can leave anytime he wants and take my tael with him. In any case he already got a promotion out of me. So why are you arguing?"

"Because I do not wish to profit at the expense of others."

It was a fair comment. It was the nature of those who wore the White to be scrupulous. But Christopher was in charge now, and he had to bear the burden of choosing pragmatism over fairness. Disa, having made her argument, acquiesced and swallowed the tael, reveling in the sensation of power even as she looked at him with reproach.

He was beginning to feel some sympathy for the hierarchy of the Church. The Saint and Cardinal Faren had carried this load for all their lives. Even Vicar Rana had to make these kinds of decisions, controlling other people's fates for the good of everyone else.

Anything that could make him feel sorry for that old harridan had to be bad, so he spent the rest of the day being grumpy, on principle.

After a peaceful night, Christopher had to make another decision. They had a lot of bodies to deliver to the Cathedral, and only six days to do it. They were all but out of ammunition, much of their food stores had been ruined, and half their horses were dead.

"Do we abandon the fort?" he asked his staff.

"No," Gregor answered. "It is a strong position."

"We paid too high a price for it," Disa said.

"Morale would suffer from a retreat." Karl always had his finger on the pulse of the army.

"Then I have to go. I have to personally deliver this tael to the Cathedral, to pay for all those raisings. And I have to accompany the corpses, to keep them preserved. But I can't bear the thought of leaving the army defenseless."

"I'll stay," Gregor volunteered.

Karl shook his head. "If the men cannot stand on their own behind stone walls, then we have accomplished nothing. Best we tell them how worthless they are before they make the mistake of thinking themselves soldiers."

Christopher winced, but he had deserved it. "Point taken, Major."

"I'll still stay," Gregor said. "I'd rather be here than in Carrhill. If that's all right with the Major." He softened it with a smile.

"You're welcome as a guest, Ser. Under our protection." Karl tried to smile back. Because he was deadly serious, it didn't work.

"Terms I can accept," Gregor said with a genuine smile. He had fought with these men when all seemed lost. They treated him like a comrade-in-arms. Only Karl seemed to remember he was a nobleman.

"Then we better start making a list of things we need." Charles the quartermaster had disobeyed Christopher's explicit order and gone and got himself killed again. Probably doing something heroic.

He took a piece of paper from his writing box, dipped pen to ink, and scribbled out the first word.

Grenades.

14

KING'S CROSS

They didn't leave until the next day. Gregor had wanted a chance to patrol first and was disappointed to find no sign of ulvenmen within five miles of the fort. He was the only one who felt that way.

What was left of the cavalry rode out with Christopher, escorting what was left of the wagons. But he didn't need very many; the only load they carried were barrels of dead men.

In the hot, humid summer weather, their cargo quickly acquired an unbearable stench. Christopher used his magic to preserve bodies as fast as he could, but it would take days before he got to them all. By the time they reached the city of Carrhill, their clothes seemed permanently impregnated with the odor.

But that was not the reason the gate sergeant goggled at them from on top of the wall.

"I thought you were dead," he said. "But you only smell like it."

"I'm not, so open the damn gate already," Christopher growled.

"Dark Hells, no," the sergeant said. "It's worth my neck to let that stink in here. And we're officially under siege, so I wouldn't open that gate for anything less than the King. How do I know you aren't a changeling? And no, I'm not going to wake the wizard, so don't even ask."

"Sell us some food, at least," Christopher said. They'd had cold porridge the night before, unwilling to light a fire in the deserted countryside.

"That I can do," the sergeant agreed.

Half an hour later they lowered baskets of fresh bread, broiled ham, skins of beer, and bags of oats for the horses.

"Thank you," Christopher told him, feeling much better after a decent meal. He threw a handful of gold coins into a basket, and the troop climbed aboard their wagons and horses again.

"Where are you going?" the sergeant called after him.

"To the Cathedral," Christopher shouted back. They could make another ten miles before the horses would need to rest. And tonight, safely inside settled lands, they could have a fire.

Two days later, he met an army coming the other way.

It was glorious, with shining armor, colorful tabards, and pennants snapping in the wind. Well-ordered troops of cavalry marched at the fore, followed by several hundred armored footmen with ranks of crossbows, pikes, swords, and shields. They put Christopher and his dozen smelly, muddy cavalrymen to shame. A pair of horsemen came galloping up to order Christopher's wagon train out of the way.

"The King's army makes haste. Get your damn wains off the road, fool."

Christopher wasn't wearing his armor. Still, the horse he was on should have given away his status.

"That's Vicar, if you don't mind." He'd paid a high price for this promotion. Or rather, his men had.

The knight took a second look, but didn't much like what he saw. "The King doesn't care if you're a bleeding Prophet. County Carrhill is overrun by ulvenmen, and you are in the way of his retribution."

"About that," Christopher said. "You better take me to the King." Over the last few days he had become increasingly worried about the reaction to his raising so many commoners. If he could make his report and pay his taxes beforehand, perhaps he could avoid dealing with the King afterward. Captain Steuben would be bad enough.

"He doesn't have time to banter with overdressed merchants! Now move your sorry-arsed mules."

The other knight was more pragmatic. "If he truly is a Vicar, the army will want his healing. Go down and tell the King we are coming." Turning to Christopher, he said, "Please allow us a moment, Vicar. Bad news is afoot, and men are on edge."

The first knight galloped off in great annoyance, while Christopher and the remaining knight tried to convince their horses to ignore each other.

"The news isn't that bad," Christopher said, making conversation. "I've just come from Carrhill, and as of five days ago the ulvenmen had retreated into the Wild."

The knight's horse snorted in response to his sudden change of attitude. "Why didn't you say this before?" he snapped.

"I hardly had a chance to get a word in edgewise."

The knight impatiently waved for Christopher to follow, and together they galloped down to meet the King and his party in the middle of the road.

A small group of riders had pulled ahead of the army column. Treywan looked magnificent in his armor, inspiring respect and confidence. Christopher would have been overjoyed to see that riding up to his fort six days ago. But now he was just nervous.

"Why are those wagons still blocking my path?" Treywan shouted.

"Begging your pardon, my Lord King. This man claims to have come directly from Carrhill, and he says the danger is past." The knight pointed at Christopher, and then discreetly sidled a safe distance away.

Treywan aimed his full fury at Christopher. Before he could loose it, he recognized his target.

"You!" the King exclaimed. "What in the Dark are you doing here?"

"My lord," Christopher said, trying to be deferential. Royal's prancing made it difficult. All the warhorse could understand was the challenge, and he was ready to answer it in kind. "I am coming to report and to resupply. The ulvenmen are gone, at least for now. Although I am extremely grateful to see the army coming to succor us, it is not necessary." He was actually surprised that they had responded so quickly.

A different member of the royal party spoke up. "We had reports of three thousand ulvenmen. Perhaps those reports were exaggerated?" Lord Nordland glared at Christopher. According to Lalania, Nordland had spent months suggesting Christopher was quite the extravagant raconteur. Christopher had promised himself that he would be contrite with Nordland, but being called a liar to his face threatened to make him hate the man all over again.

"Indeed," growled the King. "I do not think I like this jape. You cannot cry wolf and summon an army because a handful of ulvenmen snapped at your heels. I am prepared to be quite wroth." He looked prepared to dispense a whole wagonload of wroth.

"My lord," Christopher said hastily, trying to regain control of the conversation. "There were many ulvenmen, but we slew at least half of them. After that, the rest fled."

"You expect us to believe that lie again?" Nordland's voice was no longer angry. It had moved beyond that into deadly calm.

"Not without proof, my lord," Christopher said quickly, while the King's hand was moving up to give some signal.

Treywan stopped his hand and stared hard at Christopher.

"What proof?"

The men had been repairing the fort and cleaning up for days. The bodies of their enemies had gone into bonfires, leaving behind nothing but ash. Disa assured them that the dead ulvenmen could not be reanimated as walking skeletons once their heads were removed, but the men found the nightmare prospect of fighting the horde all over again too much to discount. They had denuded the scraggly forest for miles for fuel, their fear driving them to labor far harder than their officers could have commanded. Even the dinosaurs went into the fire. The golden howdah was revealed as mere paint over wood and was quickly added to the funeral pyres; the armor and weapons were piled in a heap outside the fort, destined for recycling at the forges back home. The King would not be impressed by a mound of rusting iron, and the ulvenmen had brought no other treasure with them.

Save, of course, for what they carried in their heads. The only proof the King really cared about was in Christopher's pocket. He pulled out the ball of tael.

"Your share, my lord," he said, and carved off a fortune.

"Blood and thunder." Treywan was impressed. "Dismount, priest, and bring that over here."

"How do we know he is not a changeling, my lord?" Another knight forced his horse forward, between the King and Christopher, voicing the ever-present security concerns of taking strange glowing balls from people you had just been threatening.

"You need not fear your loyal servant," said an unexpected voice. Cardinal Faren had worked his way up the party, on foot. Christopher could see his carriage in the rear of the column, which had stopped while the King talked. "I will vouch for him."

Christopher slipped out of the saddle while Royal snorted and flattened his ears. The horse apparently couldn't tell the difference between a snarling king and a snarling ulvenman. Christopher was humiliatingly trapped, trying to pacify his mount, until Faren walked over and took the tael from him and carried it to the King. To see the highly ranked, dignified old man act as a gofer galled Christopher. But the implements of war made it impossible for Christopher to achieve such a simple task. Not just the warhorse's temperaments, but the arms, armor, and suspicion that must accompany any unexpected encounter.

The King held the gift in his hand, mollified. "You say the danger is over?"

"Yes, my lord," Christopher agreed. "Though the ulvenmen came out of nowhere, so I can't say they won't do it again. But we killed a lot of them."

"How?" Nordland spluttered, finally giving into outrage.

Christopher was in a bind. Half a year ago he had wanted to brag about his rifles. Now he wanted to downplay their power, at least until every peasant had one. He tried to come up with another reason for his victory. "The wizard built us a fort of stone. My riflemen are very strong in a fort."

"Do you take us for *fools*?" Nordland came perilously close to hissing, which was unnerving coming from a man of his dignity.

Wincing, Christopher realized the Duke thought he'd brought up forts as a calculated insult. He really needed Torme here, but the man's head was rotting uselessly in a bucket. The thought that he was arguing with these people instead of reviving his dead annoyed him, and he gave in to anger himself. "Go and see for yourself, then."

"Not likely," the King said. "The swamp is unbearable this time of year, and that wizard is unbearable in any season. We'll take your word for it, since you've put your money behind it." The King, having been paid, was prepared to be satisfied. But Christopher knew Treywan wasn't going to share it with the rest of this army, and so they would resent him for having dragged them out here and then sent them home without even a chance of making a profit.

"I'm sorry to have wasted your time," Christopher said as loudly as he could without shouting, "but I did not expect to survive. The ulvenmen tried to rush us. If they had been more cautious, I would still be trapped in that fort. And then I would have needed your help."

He didn't think they were convinced. And how could they be? He had warned that three thousand slavering monsters were storming toward civilization, and now a dozen dirty men in leather coats were claiming to have cracked the thunder clouds and sent them scuttling. It didn't seem very believable, even to him.

"But any who wish to see for themselves are welcome in my garrison. My men will feed you as best they can. My priestess will heal you. If you want to use my fort as a base to hunt ulvenmen, I'll make you as welcome as I can."

"Does he speak truth?" the King asked Faren, who had been standing quietly to the side.

"For the most part," Faren said. "He doesn't actually want anyone to use his fort as a hunting lodge. He's much too cheap for that."

The King roared in amusement, and a round of laughter went through assembled knights.

"If we hurry, we can make Cannenberry by nightfall," the King said to his mounted entourage. Turning to Faren, he added, "Your Vicar sets a fine table, which I freely confess endears him to me. Will we see you there?"

"Of course, my lord," Faren replied politely. "Although I would have a word with this young jackanapes first."

"Have a basketful," laughed the King. "Then thresh them out until you discover his secret. I would do it myself, but apparently my inquisitors are useless." Casually the King referred to Christopher's brutal torture, reminding everyone of his unimpeachable authority. Christopher found it crass.

But he hung his head in silence and deference while the King turned and galloped off. He was careful to give Nordland no offense as the Duke glowered at him, before following the rest of the entourage. He even avoided staring at the disgruntled feudal levies, as the army disintegrated into angry buzzing chaos and spilled out in random directions. They hadn't been invited to Samerhaven for a meal, and now they would have to find their own ways home.

"Where is Torme?" Faren asked, still smiling his false smile.

"In one of those wagons," Christopher answered, still hanging his head in an approximation of humility. "In a barrel. A small one."

"Do you have many barrels?" Faren nodded like he was agreeing with a comment about the weather.

"Sixty-four. And twenty-four of them are the small ones."

Faren turned his face away from the army and stroked his beard.

"Gods, Christopher. You bring us weeks of labor."

"I can pay," Christopher said, obdurate. "If you need to make a profit, raise your prices."

"As always, you underestimate us. We are not ungrateful to your soldiers for their heroism. But we fear to be seen as your lackeys. For Krellyan to dance to your tune every season is to invite questions."

"That's why I said you can raise your prices. Then people will know you're just taking advantage of my inexhaustible wealth."

Faren stroked Royal's head, and the horse snuffled at him affectionately. Faren softened his face and his voice. "What really happened out there?"

Christopher sighed, letting go of his anger and frustration. "We fought our asses off, Faren. For one terrible night we clung to life by our fingernails. We thought we were dying to give the Kingdom a few hours more preparation for a horde of ulvenmen. And then I come out here and get this. . . ."

"This is better than I had hoped, Christopher. The King did not arrest you, Nordland did not ride you down on the spot, and no one denounced you. You must admit, your victories are suspicious."

Christopher wanted to be offended at their ingratitude, but he couldn't be. He knew perfectly well that the lords should be suspicious of him. He was plotting a democratic upheaval, after all. So he changed the subject.

"I need to get these wagons to the Cathedral. I'm stretched to the limit with preservation spells."

"That would be unwise," Faren mused. "You should not be riding in the same direction as the rest of the peerage of the realm. I will take your wagons. Captain Steuben and his knights accompany me; they will provide adequate protection. Although we won't tell him what he is protecting. I don't think he would be happy."

Christopher managed a weak grin. Steuben would chew his ear off if he knew. The man had already warned Christopher what his generosity to commoners would earn him, and now he would be one big "I told you so."

"Can I go to Knockford first? I need supplies."

Faren sighed, but he didn't say no. "Give Samerhaven a wide berth. And keep your wits sharp. I would warn you of the danger, except it seems you carry danger with you. Dare I ask how Disa and Karl fared?"

"They're fine. I promoted Disa to Prelate, by the way. We thought we would need her healing for the siege."

"On behalf of the Saint, I thank you for your contribution to our Church." Faren was duly impressed.

"Too bad it's not tax-deductible." Christopher tried to make a joke out of it. Faren ignored it with a quirked eyebrow.

"And yourself?"

"Vicar," Christopher admitted, "but after you're done raising my men and restoring Torme's and D'Kan's rank, I won't be able to make seventh."

"Gods." Faren put his hand to his brow, massaged the worry lines there. "You really did kill thousands of ulvenmen."

"About fifteen hundred, we think. But it was the dinosaur riders that really paid off." Those monsters would have eaten Nordland's cavalry for lunch. The only thing that had saved Christopher was fifteen feet of stone.

"Your handful of men have spared the Kingdom a terrible blow. And yet you ride from this meeting in disfavor. Do you know how to avoid this, Christopher? Do you understand how to earn the lords' trust, instead of their suspicion?"

"No," Christopher admitted.

"It is a simple expense of tael. And yet, though I know you to be generous to a fault, I know you will not do it. Simply promote your men. As many as you can, to first-rank. Make them knights, and the mantle of hero will rest comfortably on their shoulders. The realm will admire them, instead of squinting at them through narrowed eyes."

"No," Christopher sighed. He wasn't here to create an elite group of heroes. Trying to find a way to explain it to Faren, he said, "Even if I could afford it, how could I promote the next draft?"

Faren grimaced. "Why would you want to? We cannot give you another regiment. Next year's recruits must serve a different lord, and we cannot even say who. It would be typical of the King to give them to Nordland. Logical, even."

Christopher did some grimacing of his own. "We'll see about that." He still had enough tael left over to promote someone to the fifth-rank. Karl didn't want a promotion, but for the sake of the men, he might reconsider.

With a snort, Faren waved Christopher off. "I have enough of my own problems. I don't need to hear about yours. Keep your head low and do not tarry long from your post. But do not worry about your dead. They are our men, too."

The hostility of the recent encounter put this ready friendship into stark relief. "Thank you," Christopher said, meaning it. Galloping over to his cavalry, he informed them of the change of plans.

They trusted Faren, too. They would have died without hesitation to protect the dead bodies in their care, but they turned them over to one old white-haired man with relief. Only the wagon drivers would accompany Faren.

Freed of the wagons, the horsemen doubled their speed and headed by back roads and byways for the heart of Christopher's empire.

He had been in the swamp so long he had forgotten that the season was changing. Here in Burseberry the mornings were crisp and cool, and soon his training camp would shut down for the harvest season.

But not yet. The lead sergeant, the mercenary turned draftee known as Bondi, had turned the recruits out for inspection. They stood in wobbly lines, hardly more than boys, scared of the future, of Bondi, and, of course, of Christopher. It was hard to remember that his men had been like this only a year ago.

He knew he was supposed to say something inspiring. But all he had was the truth.

"You owe me three years," he told them. "Don't think you'll get out of that by dying. Fix it in your head. No matter what, you're coming back to do your time."

They didn't know what to make of that, and Christopher didn't know how to explain it to them. The memory of snapping jaws and barrels of bodies could not be communicated in words.

But afterward, in private quarters, Bondi could guess. "Another battle, my lord Curate?"

"Over sixty dead. But we won. It's Vicar now."

Bondi nodded in satisfaction while Svengusta laughed.

"Just watching your rise makes me dizzy," the old man said. "It's like you strapped your arse to one of your rockets."

"And Karl?" Helga asked, with more direct interest than she had ever shown before.

"He's fine. Torme and D'Kan bought it this time." He realized they didn't know who D'Kan was. "Niona's brother." Then he realized they didn't know about that either, and he had to tell them the sad news.

Helga burst into tears and ran out of the room. He was a little surprised that she didn't turn to him for comfort, like she used to. Not that he had any to offer.

Svengusta was always thinking of others first. "Lalania will be hard set over this, Christopher. She will blame herself for not predicting his fall and intervening to redirect it. Her College thinks it can influence even the decisions of madmen."

Christopher was far more sympathetic to Lalania's view than Svengusta's. He had encouraged the man to violence, had profited off of his dueling, even when Lalania had warned him that Cannan was shirking his good manners. He had ignored the man's growing brutality, unwilling to see it as long as Niona pretended it wasn't there.

At least he wouldn't have to tell the troubadour. She would almost certainly have ferreted out the news on her own.

Normalcy tried to return. Bondi went back to his duties, and Christopher started in on paperwork. But Svengusta overruled him.

"Set down your rank for a while," the old man said, "and come have a drink in the tavern, like old times. Your duty can wait till tomorrow."

The villagers welcomed him like he had never left, and they didn't ask for news. Instead, they talked about the weather, horses, and pigs. At first, he fretted, feeling like there was something more important he should be doing, but in the end Svengusta was proved right. The evening, with its thoroughly mundane and predictable sameness, was both relaxing and invigorating. Relaxing because no one expected anything of him except a report on how often it rained in the swamp. Invigorating because it reminded him what he was doing all of this for, anyway.

The only notable change was that everyone was drinking lager now, in a sign of solidarity with their weak-bellied favorite priest.

Cantering into Knockford at the head of a column of cavalry was like showing up in a limousine. It made everybody look.

He paid his respects to the Vicar first, including a report on the battle. There wasn't a newspaper printing dispatches from the front. The people back home only heard rumors or what the lords told them. It explained how the draft levees could be treated so badly. Nobody knew what was going on.

He also told her about his assassin. She listened with a stony face to the tale of evil and then shrugged it off.

"You need not worry about us. As long as you spend little time here, she will not risk coming into my lands. Indeed, things have been positively peaceful in your absence." The way she said it made the hint obvious.

Casually he pulled a small lump of tael out of his pocket and set it on the desk in front of her. "One more thing. I need to start making some deposits against those bonds. So I'd like to sell this to the Church, for gold."

Vicar Rana glowered sourly at the shiny purple ball. "I doubt we have so much gold on hand."

"I don't need it now. You can just keep it on account for me. At your usual interest rate."

For a person who was being bought off, Rana was remarkably grumpy. No doubt she hated having to agree with his actions. Just the appearance of approval would prickle her sensibilities; the actuality of profiting from him would stab her like needles.

But she would take it, just the same. They were all on the same side, after all, and the cause needed all the help it could get.

"Are you sure your precipitous advance can spare it?" she said, with exactly as much irony as the words implied.

"Plenty where that came from." He knew it was foolish the instant it left his mouth.

The play-acting vanished, and she spoke with complete seriousness. Not as a cantankerous old woman but as a peer in a world where moral choices were never easy and often fatal. "Do not be flippant, Christopher. This was won at a great price, both to you and to the creatures you slew."

He bit his lip and apologized. "I know that. Believe me, I know."

She stared at him, hard, the annoyance of her previous glowering replaced with critical inspection. Like she was trying to see into his soul. He squirmed a bit under that unsparing glare.

Finally she relaxed and started breathing again.

"If you wanted to know, you could have just cast a spell," he said.

"You rely on magic too much," she told him. He found that ironic and aggravating, but she wasn't interested in arguing anymore. It had passed beyond mere rivalry. With one hand she pointed him out of her office.

From one sharp-tongued woman to the next. Fae was as arch as ever and utterly unapologetic, receiving him in the refurbished magic shop, sitting on overstuffed armchairs while a young girl served tea in fine porcelain and silver. Although Fae had not yet discovered the imposing power of desks, she understood corporate office decor well enough. He felt intimidated by her casual elegance and expensive furniture.

Again it was ironic and aggravating, since he was paying for it all.

"If you wish to inspect the accounts, I can retrieve them for you."

She had headed him off at the pass. If he asked for the accounts now, he would seem graceless and paranoid. Of course, he didn't really care about what he seemed, so it wasn't much of a defense. But luckily for her, he didn't care about the accounts either. As long as she spent his money on things that profited them both, he would look the other way.

"Can you increase production?" he asked instead.

Surprisingly, she gave him a positive answer. "Yes. I can still double the amount of sulfur." And then the hook. "But it would tax me to the limit, and I do have other duties. If you are willing to spare the expense, perhaps I could look for an apprentice."

Christopher tried to hide his automatic wince. Putting someone under Fae's control seemed like a bad idea. But then he remembered she already had dozens of young women who depended on her for their income. He hadn't heard any complaints from them. Fae wasn't a tyrant. Her mistreatment of men was more about payback than unbridled lust for power.

"I would have to approve of whoever you picked. And we would have to agree to a promotion schedule for them." It wouldn't be fair to leave them trapped as apprentices forever. Even if that was all he ever wanted out of them.

"Naturally," she said. Her friendly tone meant she thought she'd won. "One more small detail, Christopher. As my patron, you need to provide for my education. Although you cannot buy spells for me, you can finance my purchase of them. Since these deals are difficult to arrange and secretive by nature, it would be best if you would allocate a budget to my discretion."

Talking to this woman was the most expensive habit he had ever indulged.

"What brought this up?" he asked, stalling for time.

She smiled, becoming the helpful woman who appeared from time to time in her pretty, avaricious body.

"You are rich and famous. This attracts attention, and expectations of profit. I have already had several offers."

"Anything interesting?" He wasn't sure what powers wizards had, especially at her low rank.

"They were overpriced," she sniffed. Grinning, he realized her innate stinginess would protect his purse more than any oversight he could inflict on her.

"Name a reasonable amount, Fae, and I'll think about it."

After all that, the masculine reek of the forge was a relief. Standing in the din of machinery, bellows, fires, and hammers, he nodded approvingly. Dereth yammered on about smelting, but all Christopher could pick out of the noise was that everything was fine.

"More cannons," Christopher shouted. "Especially the big ones."

Jhom had papers for him to sign, new contracts for new men. And the inevitable question about promotions.

"Sure," Christopher said. "Double our staff. Just get me those new rifles."

"A profitable season, my lord?"

Since there was no hope of Christopher reaching seventh, he could afford to be generous. The leap from six to seven was so large that even a fraction of it seemed like profligate spending. The crumbs from his table, indeed.

"You could say that. How is the mill coming along?" Their only sources of power were the four water bottles, and they were already running them in two shifts. Building his own mill farther up the river was the next logical step, even if it would apparently take longer than he planned to stay on this planet.

"Well enough, my lord, but we could use a dozen more."

Christopher would have to invent steam engines soon. He wasn't looking forward to it, since he had only the vaguest idea of how they worked. You heated water, and the steam pushed on something. He was pretty sure it was more involved than that, though.

"So build them. How are the other goods selling?" Wagon axles and stoves were just the beginning.

Jhom grinned, finally on a topic he could brag about.

"We have all but destroyed the smithies of Sprier and Montfort. Their forges cannot compete with our prices. Soon those men will be in our shop."

Another reason for the lords to be pissed at Christopher. This was like bailing out a papier-mâché ship. Every time he dipped the bucket, he knocked another hole in the hull.

"Won't their lords be angry about that?"

"No," Jhom reassured him, "I am not that foolish. I will not hire the lords' armor smiths. Not that I could, since you do not promote men above Senior. And since townsmen do not pay taxes, the lords will not even notice the lesser smiths are gone. If anything, they will appreciate the import taxes on what we ship back."

It was all coming up roses. At least, as long as Christopher kept the money flowing. The bulk of the factory's income was military equipment.

"What about Palek? Is he going broke, too?" The independent smith had reason enough to hate Christopher. He didn't want to give him more.

"No, my lord. The men in this town who do not work for us have adapted. They do not try to make the things our factory does. They have learned to specialize."

They probably weren't happy about it, though. Christopher had taken a profession that was as much artistry as labor and turned it into factory work. All he had to offer in return were regular paychecks and the excitement of powered machinery. He wasn't sure that was enough.

But he didn't have a choice. He needed guns, cheap. This society needed them. It needed lots of things, cheap, so that the many could wield as much influence as the few.

Then Jhom gave him the latest toy, and like any boy, he had to rush back to the village to play with it.

Lalania found him at the shooting range, an hour before sunset.

"There you are," he said, relieved that she had finally shown up. He had no way of contacting her on his own.

"Here I am," she replied. She seemed different somehow, distracted and unfocused.

"Did you hear about Niona?"

"Yes," she answered, and he understood. He had never seen her depressed before.

"I'm going to revive her brother. I paid for it already." It was the only good news he had to offer.

"Do not expect him to return to your call. That is not their way. Not everyone lives by your Church's dogma, Christopher."

Damn but she could take the wind out his sails. The trick was that she was always right.

"Should I send the body back to the Druids, instead?"

A sigh. "It is too late. They have but a week, and you dallied too long."

It wasn't dallying, but he didn't want to argue with her. He hadn't known, and no one had told him, and he probably couldn't have gotten the boy home any quicker anyway. And now, he wasn't even sure he could find the body. They hadn't bothered to label the parts that went in the resurrection barrel. Just making sure there was only one finger-bone from each corpse had seemed adequate at the time.

"Then I'll try it my way. I even paid to restore his rank, Lala. It was the best I could do."

"Does that excuse work for you?" she said, piercing him with her gaze. "*The best you can do?* Is that enough to let you sleep at night?"

"What else is there? We didn't know Cannan would go nuts. We don't even really know what happened." He was arguing with her, though his words were for himself.

"It is your choices I fear, not his. He destroyed only himself and the Lady Niona. Yet look at what you are doing."

He looked at the pistol in his hand. It didn't seem that perilous.

"Not that." She rolled her eyes in frustration, the thespian in her unable to resist dramatics.

"You mean the army?" he asked. She would already know of their victory, of course, and probably of the price.

"I don't think so." The strange Lalania returned, the uncertain and hesitant girl. "I think it's Knockford. I tell myself the changes are merely temporary, the result of your showering of wealth on one little town. I tell myself it's just a local hero made good, and that it means nothing in the long run. But I do not believe it."

"What do you believe?" he asked, genuinely curious.

"I don't know. But I was hoping you would come to the College and explain it to wiser heads than mine."

Her College was the only institution of higher learning he'd ever heard about in this realm. He'd been trying to figure out how to wrangle an invitation out of her, and now she was just offering one.

"Sure. I'd like to talk to some scholars. Especially if their archives go back further than the Church's." He hadn't found very many answers there.

"Just like that, you'll go?"

"Why wouldn't I?"

"You'll have to leave your army behind. We'll be traveling toward Nordland's territory and must rely on discreetness rather than armed force. It could be dangerous."

"I don't think Nordland is going to hunt me down." He'd met the Duke at the crossroads and received nothing worse than insults.

"You have other foes besides Nordland."

Yes, like his assassin. But he was looking forward to meeting her face-to-face. Maybe if he stripped himself of his escort, she would come after him instead of those around him.

"I'll chance it. Unless you know a reason I shouldn't."

She hesitated again, and he almost became worried. But she shook her shiny blonde hair in denial.

"You know, Lala, you're in danger too. Just by being around me."

A wan smile. "Yes, that thought has occurred to me. More than once."

"Then let me give you a present."

"A promotion?" she asked. "I'm only halfway to Minstrel. A dip in your pocket and my lifelong dream comes true."

He winced. He hadn't planned on being that generous.

"I'm joking, Christopher. I can't take a promotion from your hand. That would mark me as your servant, and then I really would be chained to your side. For tradition, and for my own safety."

As always, she let him off easily.

"I was thinking something more personal. Like this," and he put the pistol in her hands. "It's one of a kind." It cost as much as a carbine, since it required just as many steps by magic-wielding smiths to make. He wasn't about to complain about the price now. Although it lacked the range and punch of the big rifle, it was small enough to put in a bread box, and that was a value all its own. "It won't kill a buffalo, but against unranked thugs, it's as good as six dead men. It occurred to me that you might find that useful."

"I might," she admitted. "Although a magic wand would be just as effective, and more convenient."

Without thinking, he explained. "I already gave that to Fae. She probably needs protection, too."

"Fae has a wand?" Lalania shook her head in dismay. "Gods, Christopher, you need to learn to stop giving away secrets so readily. But now that you have, at least name the kind, so I know."

He didn't bother to blush at her admonishment. He already kept the secret of his origin from her, and that was enough. "She called it a wand of fire."

"A clumsy instrument for my tastes. Rarely do I need to vaporize an entire roomful of people. So there, you can stop feeling bad and show me how to use your present."

Standing behind her, he guided her hands to the correct firing position. Eagerly explaining the mechanics and theory of firearms, he did not notice how closely their bodies touched until she fired the first shot. The recoil pushed her back, and for a moment her hair in his face confused him. He remembered standing behind another woman, teaching her how to use a gun. His hands on her soft skin, her arm crooked inside his, shoulders nestled inside the arc of his arms.

She turned her face to his, an inch away. Point-blank range.

"I missed you," she said.

"You mean Gregor. You missed Gregor." He stepped away from her, tried to collect his scattered emotions.

"You're the reason I missed Gregor. I don't know what you said to him, but you must be quite the orator to convince a man to give up sex." She was teasing him now, which was vastly easier to take.

"I didn't convince him. He's crazy about you, Lala. But I think he realized you don't feel the same."

"No," she said, "I don't. He's a good man. No, he's a great man. But he's obviously not my man. I'm not sure I'm meant to have one. I mean, just one." Now she was being salacious. That was not an improvement.

"Seriously," she said, without a trace of seriousness, "if you didn't want me for yourself, why did you chase off Gregor?"

"I didn't chase him off. You let him go."

"He wasn't mine to hold."

"You certainly treated him like yours." He thought of the way she had led Gregor around, a dire beast on an invisible leash.

"Is it any different than how you treat him?"

Now he did the blushing. "He's a volunteer."

"I don't recall any complaints about the wages I paid." She leered in a sultry, sophisticated way. The effect was intoxicating, her clear blue eyes inviting him in for a swim.

He took the pistol, broke open the cylinder, and started reloading it. "Okay, you win. Let's get back to the lesson."

Graciously she let him have the last word and turned her attention to the pistol. Its complexity was no challenge for her, and an hour and several boxes of ammunition later she had mastered the basics. Now all she needed was practice.

What he needed was relief. He found it at dinner, where Lalania became the friend she had always been, just another member of his little group, chattering away with Svengusta and Helga.

The next night Lalania put on a performance for the troops. Armed with a lute, a ridiculously low-cut blouse, and an absurdly short skirt, she reduced his recruits to leering imbeciles. After that, Christopher decided getting her out of town as soon as possible was a priority.

So a few days later he got up at the crack of dawn, saddled his horse, and slipped out with the sunrise. Lala dressed like a man for the trip, with her hair tucked under a pot helm and her bountiful chest wrapped up tight in an overcoat. Christopher was much relieved.

Both of them were armed, if unarmored. Lalania wore her slender, thin sword and had a crossbow strapped to one side of her saddle. Since Christopher was also wearing a sword and helmet, they looked like dangerous people. Lalania assured him this would deter ordinary thugs and ruffians, while still not broadcasting their rank and identity to everyone they passed.

Following her advice, he snuck out of the village and left his escort behind, with only a note of explanation left on his desk to stave off their worry. He knew they would be upset, but Lalania had convinced him that discreetness would be better than a show of force.

15

MIDSUMMER NIGHT'S DREAM

The weather wrecked their disguise. As the sun rose, the temperature followed it, summer not yet ready to yield to autumn's dominion. Lalania slowly shed clothing throughout the morning, stuffing her helmet and eventually her coat into her saddlebags. It didn't seem to matter, though. Since they had left the road after Cannenberry town, traveling through backwoods and open country, they had not seen a single person. A few plowed fields and smoke from distant villages were the only proof that this land was inhabited.

The horses ambled along while Lalania plucked at her lute and told Christopher stories, mostly of the bawdy variety. She assured him they were the popular ones. He was certain she was right, but they weren't the kinds of stories he wanted to hear right now. With her blouse open to the summer heat and her hair loose around her shoulders, the bard's innate attractiveness was impossible to ignore. At this pace it would be four or five long days before they reached her College. The trip could be made in three, with hard riding, but they were swinging south to avoid Kingsrock. Lalania felt the danger of encountering their enemies was too great there.

Christopher was worried about a different danger. His self-control had limits. Lalania wasn't some innocent peasant girl engaging in a distasteful custom. She was a peer, an equal. Her rank put her in the same class as himself, one of the few instead of one of the many. And her affection for him was genuine, born out of her knowledge of his character and not merely his wealth and power. She was intelligent, witty, charming, and thoroughly in control of her own destiny. All of the traits Christopher found attractive in a woman.

All of the things that had drawn him to Maggie.

But he had not known Maggie when she was this young. He had not known her when her skin was still soft and fresh, untouched by the years. He had been so grateful to finally find her that he had not noticed. They had shared their scars and the stories that went with them, the history that had made them who they were. He called them the wasted years, the years they had spent before they had met each other, but Maggie had always looked forward. They would gain the rest of their scars together, she had said.

Except now he had no scars. His skin was more than just unmarked; he could pass for a man half his age, even if he did not glow with youth like Lalania. He was richer, in relative terms, than he could ever have hoped for back home. He had power here that was not even imaginable on Earth. He was respected, for his inner convictions as well as his actions, his moral worth an objective quality like the color of his armor. In all ways this world had been good to him. In all ways but one.

When they made camp for the night, stretching bedrolls under the trees by a cozy fire, Lalania cooked while he brushed down the horses. It had seemed like a reasonable division of duties, until she served him a bowl. He had been too long in this world: a woman cooking for him meant things now that it shouldn't have.

"Was dinner acceptable, my Lord Vicar?" she asked playfully, when they were done. He had felt too awkward to speak while he was eating, but of course it had been acceptable. It had been delicious, and not just in the campfire-everything-tastes-better way. Living with the army had largely removed that effect, anyway. Lalania was simply a better cook than Helga.

Or Maggie.

He grunted something noncommittal and went to check on

the horses. Uselessly, since he'd just finished seeing to them. Royal pricked his ears at his approach, but when he saw it was only Christopher, the stallion put his head down again and went back to sleep. They wouldn't need a guard tonight, Lalania had said. The horses were as good as watchdogs, and in any case, it was unlikely a common brigand could kill Christopher in his sleep.

His mind was wandering, trying to avoid the current topic. Being attacked by murderous thugs would be easier to deal with than Lalania's flirtations. Sighing, he turned back to the camp.

Lalania had stretched her bedroll out next to his, and now she reclined on it, waiting for him. When she saw his gaze on her, she sat up and began to undo her blouse.

"Stop it," he said.

She looked up at him, her blue eyes shining in the firelight, framed in tousled golden hair. "Will you make me beg, Christopher? Because I will."

"Will you make *me* beg? Stop it, Lala. Just stop."

"It's just sex. Just sleep with me, damn it. Just once, Christopher, is that so much to ask?"

"Yes," he said, because it was.

"I know you don't have a pact. That might fool your army, but I know better. I know you find me attractive. So tell me why you won't do what common sense tells you to do."

"Tell me why you're so Darkling insistent on seducing me." She'd been trying from the first moment she'd met him.

"Because you're kind, and generous, and good. Because you're handsome, now that your nose is straight. Because you're the only man who's ever denied me. Because it's been weeks since I've had a good lay. Gods, Christopher, because I *want* you. Isn't that enough?"

"No," he said, because it wasn't.

"Tell me why," she said, and he was startled to see tears in her eyes. "At least tell me why."

"Because I'm not staying. I have a job to do, Lala, and then I'm going to leave. I'm going to go home. To my wife."

"I won't hold you. I just want this one night."

That wasn't a promise he could make. He felt the knife-edge under his feet; he instinctively knew that if he let himself sink too deeply into this world he would never have the strength to tear himself free.

"I told you before. I can't stop at one. So I can't start, or I'll never make it home."

"Then why not stay?" she asked.

"Because this is not who I am. I don't know this person who rides around in armor, giving orders and boiling heads. I don't want to become a lord. I want to stay myself. And Maggie is the only link I have to that."

It had been over a year since he had said her name out loud.

Lalania bit her lip, making her look unsure and vulnerable. "For a man who does not wish to be a lord, you raise a lot of armies." At least she had stopped unbuttoning her clothes.

"That's my task. Do you understand, Lala? Do you understand what I am doing?" He needed to talk to someone about it. Carrying the burden of the god's will alone was making him crazy. And he desperately needed to change the topic.

"No," she admitted. "I do not understand. I thought I did, yet if you are truly planning on leaving, I do not understand."

"You've seen what the rifles do, right?"

"Yes. I see that you have made common men strong enough to kill monsters. I see that you have made the entire profession of warrior irrelevant and have rendered our King obsolete. I thought that you would put a priest on his throne."

Oops. He hadn't thought of that angle. All the time he'd been planning his revolution, it had never occurred to him that other people might think it was simply a coup.

"It's not the King I mean to replace. It's kings. Kingship. The whole Dark damned idea. I don't want to put a priest in charge." Although he had to admit that the idea of the Saint running the Kingdom didn't sound that bad.

"Then what would you put in its place?" she asked, so genuinely curious that he found it arousing again. Lalania the intellectual was harder for him to ignore than Lalania the seductress.

"Law." He remembered a page from Thomas Paine, about how the people should parade the Constitution through the streets every year, so that all the world would know that law ruled in the New World, not crowns.

"You are not Blue." A curious rebuttal that could only make sense on this crazy planet.

"Not Law with a capital L. Not the gods' law. The rule of men. People should make up their own rules, the rules that seem best to them. And then they should all agree to live by those rules. It's called freedom."

"We already do that," she said. "It's called feudalism. Everybody agrees it's the best way to live. The lords collect the tael from the people and spend it to defend the community. And that means spending it on themselves, because a high-ranked lord is worth many low-ranks."

"Black Bart's people didn't agree to live by his rules." The Baron's army had barely agreed to fight for him, surrendering at the first opportunity.

"Bart was a monster, agreed. But he's dead, thanks to you. The system works." Something in the way she said it caught his attention.

"Who replaced Bart?" he asked.

She made a sour face. "The system still has a few . . . kinks. It's not perfect."

Even the Saint had admitted to Christopher that the system was corrupt.

"People are supposed to be equal, Lala. As long as a baron can kill an entire town by himself, they aren't equal. But when a man with a rifle can kill anybody, then they can be equal again." It was hard to believe he was making an argument for the salutary qualities of assassination. "When the barons are afraid of the peasants, then they'll have to bargain with them fairly. That's my goal. I don't care who's in charge when I leave. Just as long as it's whoever the people want to be in charge."

"The people want the strongest man to be in charge. To better protect them."

"When they can protect themselves, then they can want the *best* man in charge. But more to the point, when the leader depends on the will of the people, he has to respect the desires of the people."

"I've met the people," she said. "I'm not sure their desires are as noble as you think."

"The system's not perfect. It has a few kinks." He grinned at her. "But they'll get better. Over time, they'll learn." Democracy had all but conquered Earth, even without foolproof lie detectors. The only thing that had stopped it here was the economics of power.

There was another argument he could use. "Lala . . . you know a woman can use a rifle just as well as a man."

"So you would make heroes out of housewives?" She quirked an eyebrow at him but interrupted him before he could object. "Peace, Christopher. I understand you wish to give women a voice equal to men. But you already are, by keeping men alive. When there are enough men to go around, women will not be reduced to beggars for husbands."

Her grasp of economics was better than he had thought. "So you understand?"

"Yes, I get it. You're not content with destroying our current government. You won't stop until you've upended our entire way of life. But that still doesn't explain why you won't sleep with me."

"Because if I stay, it will be just a coup." The idea of living in wealth and luxury, surrounded by beautiful women like Lalania whose sole goal in life was to make him happy, was definitely alluring. The

notion of running the Kingdom from Kingsrock and making everything *right* was downright intoxicating. It was a cup from which he
dared not sip. The road to Hell was paved with good intentions and
pretty blondes. "So stop it, Lala. Give me your word you won't pull
this crap again. I want your help, I need your help, but I can't deal
with this anymore. I'll send you away if you don't promise to stop."

"I can't leave, Christopher. Whatever you're doing to the Kingdom,
you're doing to *my* Kingdom. For the sake of my people, I have to stay
by your side, to help or even to hinder if you should go astray and seek
to do harm. For their sake I will give you your promise. But understand that you ask no less of me than you ask of yourself."

He didn't understand. "I'm not saying you should be celibate."
He was uncomfortable with her rampant sexuality, true, but he was
pretty certain that was his problem and not hers.

She glared at him. "You are such an idiot." Then she rolled over
and pulled her bedroll tight.

There wasn't anything else to say. He lay down next to her on the
hard ground and tried to sleep.

Late in the night, they pressed up against each other for warmth,
back to back. He pretended she was one of his soldiers. They had
slept huddled against each other on their cold death-march home, like
brothers. It was the least sensual image he could think of.

Lalania was quieter the next day. It wasn't quite somber—her cheerful
personality was incapable of that. But she kept her blouse buttoned
to the top, despite the rising heat. Perversely, that made her more
attractive.

In the middle of the day they had to ford a river. On the other side
Lalania told him to put his helmet on.

"We're in West Undaal now," she said.

He vaguely recalled having seen the name on a map. All he knew for certain was that they weren't anywhere near the Church's territory. "Are they friendly?"

"To the Saint, well enough. To you, well, who knows? Nordland is allied with the White Cathedral and we all know how he feels about you. The Jade Cathedral holds sway here, but it is not a monolithic entity like your Church. Each lord will set his own policy and choose his own allies. But shouldn't you know this already?"

Knowing this stuff was what he paid Torme for. But the man was ash in a barrel at the moment, so he wasn't much help.

"Enough," she said, suspecting his answer would just be another question. "We'll make the town by dark. Tonight we can stay at an inn."

West Undaal was not as bad as he had feared. The villages and hamlets they passed seemed well fed, with plenty of fat livestock and playing children. The ragged edge of fear and hunger that pervaded Carrhill was absent. But then, so was the memory of being overrun by ulvenmen. Lalania told him the worst thing that had happened to West Undaal in the last few decades was their perpetual low-level conflict with Undaal.

"Both houses are convinced the counties should be one county, under one house. Naturally they each have different ideas about which house that should be. Occasionally these ideas bubble up into open warfare. Then a lot of conscripts get killed, a few knights get ransomed, livestock gets slaughtered, women get raped, and in general a good time is had by all. Eventually the King or the Jade Cathedral gets tired of the noise and restores order."

These were supposed to be the good guys. "I thought you said they were Green."

"They are, Christopher. They don't rape children, and they don't murder the helpless. But when 'honor' demands a fight, they don't shirk from violence. And women are always the spoils of war."

She must have seen the disgust on his face.

"Yes, I know," she said. "Under your grand scheme a peasant will be able to stand against rank. Have you realized that then he will be *expected* to? That if he does not put his life on the line at every turn, he'll be counted craven? The knights live and die by the iron code, but until now our peasants have been allowed an easier road. The ravages of the nobility have always been no more or less than a storm, unpredictable, unavoidable, and without any taint of personal condemnation. You would replace that. You would burden every man, and indeed every woman, with the weight of honor."

"Afterward, Lala, you can ask them." He consciously forced his teeth to stop grating. "After they've tried it my way for a few years, you can ask them if they want to go back to the old way."

"I already know the answer. Every boy fancies himself a hero. It's only the thresher that beats it out of them. Every girl pines for a valiant warrior. It's only exposure to a real one that cures them. They'll swallow your gift of honor whole, no matter how sharp the edge. Nobody will count them unwise or unhappy, save for perhaps me."

"Will you?"

"No, I won't. I'm no wiser than they are. An entire Kingdom of men, and I want the only one who won't touch me."

He couldn't respond to that, because they were at the gate now, and a guard had stepped forward to ask their business. Lalania smiled sweetly and told him they were traveling horse-merchants, headed for Palar to inspect the stock.

"I've got something you can inspect," the guard leered at her. Christopher was too surprised to react. He'd become so used to politeness that he'd forgotten what its absence was like.

"I doubt it," she replied, "After all the horses I've seen, I think I'd just be disappointed."

The other soldiers laughed. The guard scowled but stood aside and let her pass with no more than a challenging glare at Christopher. Christopher couldn't afford to glare back. If it came to a fight, his rank would be exposed instantly, and all their stealth would be wasted. Also, despite the crudeness of the guard, he knew it wouldn't be fair. The man was a cretin, but he didn't deserve to be chastised by a super-being. Put a gun in his hands, and then Christopher could give him the beating he deserved.

Lalania found them an inn, a solid-looking timber-framed building with two stories and incredibly narrow windows.

"We have to share a room, Christopher. For security and appearance. And you need to project a little more authority. I don't care to be groped for the rest of the evening." She slid off her horse and handed the reins to the stable-boy.

The boy looked at her and then, reflexively, at Christopher. Christopher lowered his brows. The stable-boy choked back whatever lecherous wisecrack he had been about to make.

"Yes, Goodwoman," he said instead. "If the Goodman would follow me 'round back, I'll show you to a stable for the destrier."

That was one drawback of riding a gigantic warhorse. You had to park it yourself. Fortunately he didn't have to steer. Royal, attracted by the smell of oats, followed Lalania's horse into the barn while Christopher held his nose. The place could do with a good cleaning.

While Christopher was still brushing Royal down, Lalania came in to tell him she'd booked them a room. The price was ridiculous— an entire gold piece—even when you threw in a meal and feed for their horses. That was another drawback of riding around in style. Everything cost more.

"Aren't you forgetting something?" Lalania stood in the doorway and blocked him from leaving the stable. He put on his frown, getting back into tough-guy character, but she just rolled her eyes at him and pointed to their saddlebags.

Christopher decided the stable-boy was definitely not getting a tip. The inn stank only slightly less than the barn. The odor of alcohol and sweat was more nauseating, though, as if to make up for the lack of stench. Christopher's barracks were never like this. For that matter, none of the taverns in Knockford were like this. He'd assumed that Carrhill was an exception, because its level of filth and despair was so unusual to him. He realized now that it was the counties run by the Church that were the exception.

Lalania led him up a flight of narrow stairs to the second floor, where she counted down three doors to find their room. It was small, mostly occupied by a rough wooden frame filled with reeking straw for a bed.

"Gods," she muttered. "This is an insult."

"It's still light out, Lala. We could keep going." Another few hours in the saddle looked more comfortable than that bed.

"To where? It's twenty miles to Undaal, and there isn't an inn between here and there. Every time they build one, it gets burned down in a war. And we can't sleep out in the open on the border. Both sides would consider us fair game."

"They're at war now?" He thought she had been talking about ancient history.

"Not openly. But acts of banditry are becoming unacceptably common. The Vicar of West Undaal refused to cure Undaal's Captain of Horse, suggesting that the Captain frequent a higher class of whores instead of wasting the Vicar's time. The Captain took this as an insult and got his healing from the Vicar of Portia. Now the Gold Throne has its nose in the middle of a family quarrel, and both sides are too stupid to see that it fans the strife for its own profit."

Christopher was a Vicar too. Maybe his rank would let him talk some sense into the local ruler. True, they followed different gods, but they were still on the side of the Bright. When he suggested this plan to Lalania, she rolled her eyes so dramatically she practically lost her balance.

"Do you know where you are?" she asked. "Deep in the terri-
tory of the Gold. Agents of the Iron Throne are thick as fleas here.
Stick your White nose up and somebody will be sure to claim it. No,
Christopher, we'll leave the local politics to cooler hearts than yours.
Tomorrow we'll be sleeping in Feldspar, a county as surely under the
Shadow as the day is long. If they knew a White priest was coming,
they'd be sure to put the kettle on."

That didn't mean they would be serving him a nice cup of tea.

"Cooler hearts? Like your College?"

"Cool hearts make cool blood. We contend always against the
peerage's lust for war."

"Then why haven't I seen any other bards?"

"Because we don't need to do anything in your lands. The Saint is,
well, a saint. He's no threat to the peace."

Belatedly it occurred to him to wonder how much of his grand
scheme she would share with her fellows. Surrounded by the men of
his army and his Church, he had forgotten that she owed her loyalty
to a different institution.

She had not done anything to remind him of it, either. Her
behavior on this trip could even reasonably be construed to have
helped him forget that little fact. He looked at her sideways, and she
sighed in exasperation.

"You could at least pretend to hide your suspicion," she said. "We
are the Saint's allies, even if he does not know it. I do not understand
you, Christopher. Half the time you are as simple-minded and obvious
as a child, and yet only a moment passes before you say or do something completely mystifying."

He understood. The things everyone took for granted in her world
were all new to him, so she could work out every step before he could.
On the other hand, he was from a cultural context she couldn't even
imagine. "If you did understand, you'd stop being interested in me."

"You don't really think I'm that shallow, do you?" When he didn't answer right away, she shook her hair in mock outrage. "I should let you sleep on that rotten mattress alone for that. But I won't. Instead, I'll treat you better than you deserve."

Extracting her lute from its amorphous leather case, she struck a few chords and began to hum in a language that sounded like the one Fae used for her spells. But he stopped thinking about that when he noticed that their erstwhile mattress seemed to be coming alive.

When he realized it was not the straw mattress that had been enchanted into animation, the flowing motion merely a vast horde of bugs crawling out of it, he flinched and retreated, stopping only when he ran into the door. Lalania ignored him, too busy to perform her usual ocular acrobatics. The bugs began falling from the mattress, disappearing in little sparkles of purple light before they hit the floor.

It took a few minutes for her to finish the entire mattress and the ragged heaps of cloth that would serve as their blankets. When she was done, they looked freshly washed and almost inhabitable.

"I have no idea what you just did, but I am extremely grateful for it." Assuming he could get the image of that writhing straw mattress out of his head, he was sure he would sleep much more soundly tonight.

"Yes, that is why I became a troubadour and mastered the arcane arts—so I could impress a man with my laundry skills."

"Well, it's working."

She laughed at him and shook her head.

"And again you confound me. What man has ever before in the history of the world cared for the quality of his bed when there was a woman in it? That's why I'm taking you to the College—so you can confound those more clever than I. Until then, let's go downstairs and ask about our dinner. And . . . if it's as poor as this room, you have my permission to hold the inn-keeper's head in a chamber pot until he stops bleating."

16

BAR BRAWLS AND BETRAYALS

He hadn't held the innkeeper's head in a chamber pot. Last night, the thick cut of beef had been hot, juicy, and heavily spiced. It had gone down easily enough.

But today it lay in the pit of his stomach, causing unpleasant rumblings and eructations every time Royal changed his stride. The juices had turned to cold grease, the tenderness of the cut was probably due to its being on the edge of going rotten, and the spices had been there to hide that unsavory fact. Unfortunately, the spell that would neutralize any and all toxins was still out of his reach. When he complained about this to Lalania, she shook her head at him.

"You could have purified the meal before you ate it, Christopher. It likely would not have given us away. Such a low-level blessing is in the power of an Acolyte, and in any case you could have disguised it as simple religious piety. Plenty of superstitious peasants say a prayer over their evening meal. The alternative is that you could develop a constitution hardier than a girl's." She belched unexpectedly, and a pained look crossed her face. "I take that back. Tonight I suggest you pray over our food, despite the risk. But discreetly, Christopher. We'll be sleeping in a Dark county tonight, one almost certainly under the sway of the Shadow."

He frowned.

"It can't be helped. We'll make Undaal town by noon. Then it's either wait for morning or push on. I don't counsel waiting. It just increases our risk of detection and gives any pursuit we might have a chance to catch up. But if we continue, nightfall will find us in Feldspar, and we absolutely will not camp in the open there. I know a village inn, near the Estvale border, that should be safe enough. The innkeeper is no cleaner than our last one but no more wicked either."

"If this one poisons me, I'm going to have to kill him." A sour thing to say, and probably outside the bounds of strict honesty that his Church demanded. Before he could amend it to be more truthful, another roil of burning garlic-and-clove gas burbled through his belly. As of that moment, he decided his statement was adequately sincere.

Undaal was even shabbier than West Undaal. At least the locals didn't give them a hard time. One look at Christopher's face, wound tight by discomfort and annoyance, a second look at his sword and his horse, and they kept their wisecracks to themselves. The deference was of a different character than back home. In Church lands, people were nice to him as long as he was nice to them. Here, people were only nice to him when he was mean enough to scare them. Christopher was pleased to see that he could tell the difference and was gratified that it still mattered so much to him. He had been impressed before at how the Church could rule without inspiring fear. He was being impressed all over again.

Unfortunately he hadn't memorized the spell needed for cleansing food, so he and Lalania had to risk the local standards for lunch. They settled on the blandest food they could find: fresh bread and a pale, soft cheese. Christopher managed to acquire a few stalks of celery by pretending it was for his horse. The roughage put some solidity into his gut, and he started to feel better.

"Good," Lalania said, "because I think we've dallied too long. We need to pick up the pace."

The so-called road was hardly more than a wagon-track, though wide enough to allow the horses to trot safely. The celery allowed his stomach to survive the bouncing gate. They would cover eight miles in the next few hours, without unduly tiring Royal. Christopher tried not to think about how their three-day journey would have been less than an hour, given a highway and an automobile.

He could tell when they crossed the border into Feldspar. Mostly because there were a handful of ragged soldiers collecting a poll-tax of copper for people and silver for horses, but also because the quality of life went down another notch. The peasants in Church lands were often cheerful, or at least content at their labors. In the Undaals they had been disgruntled and sour. Here, in Feldspar, the few peasants he saw were depressed and skittish, afraid of even looking at him.

"Peace, Christopher," Lalania said, as he was opening his mouth. "Keep your opinions to yourself for now. I already know what you're thinking, and talking about it won't help."

He asked a question instead. "How do you . . . put up with it, Lala?"

The look in her eyes might have been pity. Or disgust. "I've seen worse. Do you know what county lies due south of us now? Baria, once the domain of Bartholomew the Black. Due to Bart's untimely demise at the hands of some white-flocked hooligan, the county has a new master. The Gold Throne has rewarded Prelate Gareth Boniface with the title. But a Prelate is not a peer. He needs another rank before the King will recognize his right. Do you know where the good Prelate can find the tael necessary to make Curate? No? Then I will tell you. The county has been sentenced to decimation."

Christopher didn't have to ask what the term meant. His magical grasp of the language supplied the answer: one out of ten, in the original Roman sense of the word. When a legion had exhibited cowardice in the face of the enemy, it could be sentenced to decimation. The legion would line up, in rows of ten. Each man would draw from a bag of white and black stones. Every tenth stone was black. The man who drew the black stone would die, beaten to death by clubs wielded by the other nine.

In all of Roman history only one legion had ever suffered this punishment. Even for the honor-obsessed Romans, the people who would fall on their own swords rather than face a court trial, the brutality of decimation was too savage to be used more than once every thousand years. Even for the Romans, decimation had really been no more than a legend, a terrifying story from the distant past. On this planet, it was an ordinary fact of life. It was only supposed to be invoked when the community was in serious danger, but, as usual, that determination was up to the lord.

Bart had already liquidated two villages to raise new knights. It was hard to believe the county could survive further depredation. Christopher tried to set aside his revulsion and focus on a legal objection. "Wait a minute. The Prelate doesn't have the title, so he can't just take the tael out of the county. He's got to be Baron first. So he can't do that."

"Strictly speaking, you are correct. When that argument was presented to the Gold Throne, their response was simple. They would decimate one of their current counties to promote the Prelate. Then, once he took possession of Baria, he would decimate it to pay back the loan."

"Gods . . . that's two decimations." Twice as many dead peasants. Twice as many grandparents sent to the chopping block because they were too old to work. Twice as many unpopular people, oddballs who rubbed anyone the wrong way, even a little, sent to the ax. Every curmudgeon, whose only crime was not being disliked but merely lacking enough friends to speak up for them.

And, of course, women. There were twice as many women as there were men, with half as much say in who got chosen. Any woman past childbearing age would be facing a death sentence.

The sickness sank to the pit of his stomach, and Christopher struggled not to throw up.

"We felt pretty much the same way. The objection was withdrawn, and Lord Boniface won his decimation. As I understand it, it won't be quite enough. But the Prelate has graciously agreed to make up the difference out of his own pocket."

"It's happening now?" The thought that such bloodshed should be occurring a few miles away, and due to Christopher's own actions, however well-intentioned or justifiable, made him dizzy with hatred.

"My news is weeks old, Christopher. By now the deed is done. We stalled it for as long as we could: Bart died seasons ago. We gave the peasants what respite we dared and a chance to build up some tael through more . . . natural processes. Now they have a priest who can cure disease. Their lot arguably has improved. But should some amateur paladin waltz in and kill this lord, before he's even pretended to have a chance to save for his replacement, the Gods only know what burden would be dumped on those poor people next."

"Will he? Will he save for his replacement?" It seemed far more likely that a Black priest would pocket it all for his own advance, and the future be damned.

"To suggest otherwise is to lay a charge of treason at his door. And surely no one would be so impertinent as to do that, without both a wealth of evidence and an army to back it up."

Christopher had an army. Lalania must have noticed the calculations writ across his face.

"Do keep in mind that evidence of such a crime is yet impossible to assemble, insomuch as the lord has the right and expectation to advance his own cause, at least until the end of his career is reasonably in sight. Baron Boniface is not yet forty. Spending tael on his own advancement is not yet considered irresponsible. Very convenient for all of us, wouldn't you agree?"

Having a conversation with Fae was expensive. Having one with

Lalania was actively painful. He was pretty sure that his social interactions with attractive young women back on Earth had been no worse than embarrassing.

"Indeed, how lucky for the old codger. Out of pure speculation, motivated by no more than idle curiosity, what would be considered too old to advance one's own rank?"

"Legally, threescore-and-ten, of course." Lalania announced that fact with a tone that marked it as common and obvious knowledge. Which it probably was, to anyone born and raised around tael. "Practically, it depends on how much you fear a knife in the back. If you're still strong enough to paralyze your likely heirs with terror, you can get away with anything. If no one is certain it's their inheritance you're consuming, you can get away with more."

"How about if you'd just like to not offend people of good sense and high moral dudgeon?"

"Then it depends on how much and how long those people can expect to get out of you. As a convenient example, consider Faren Califax, Cardinal of the Church of the Bright Lady. The old geezer is pushing seventy with something less than a ten-foot pole, though his exact age is as well hidden as can be expected by simpleminded doves with a self-righteous fetish for babbling truth, regardless of its effect on themselves or others."

He'd never heard his Church described in quite those terms. Other than the charge of simpleness, he wasn't sure it was an illegitimate description. Lalania was using the necessity of maintaining a disguise to give him a taste of how other people might see his affiliation.

"Were he to advance himself to Prophet, the mewling kittens of the Bright would be horrified. Not only is he old enough that they could expect only a relatively few years of service out of such a huge expense, but he wouldn't gain any particular advantage, since he can already revive the dead. In their eyes a handful of extra spells does not seem worth the price."

"And it's not like the man needs the rank," she continued. "Despite their protestations of benevolence, when was the last time you saw a priest of the White put on armor and take his place at the front lines? No, they always fight from behind a line of low-rank or even unranked meat, brave men who have nothing but bits of metal to face the monsters of the wild."

Christopher almost protested, despite where they were having this conversation. He'd done his share of donning armor and taking hits. He'd seen Vicar Rana face down Black Bart with only two uncertain spells standing between her and his savage blade. And Disa had volunteered for the war, even when she was only first-ranked and completely unarmed. True, he couldn't imagine the Saint or Cardinal Faren in armor, but it didn't make any sense to do that. Their healing power was vastly more useful in the second row, where it could keep the first row standing long past any man's ability to hold the line on his own.

Before he could frame this argument in words, he understood that Lalania had already heard it. Being sensible, she would even agree with it. But not everyone in this world would find a claim of efficiency to be an adequate excuse for what appeared to be cowardice.

"The worst of it is, the Cardinal himself would no doubt hew to these same arguments. Never mind that through personal courage and dedication he has won his way to a rank that befits him. Never mind that he has employed this power in almost selfless devotion to his social inferiors. Never mind all that: he is expected to live like a beggar in his own church, not even having the right to enjoy his own magic for his own purposes. The Saint, his alleged patron, won't even regenerate the old man on a regular basis without charging him the same fee any wandering lickspittle with a fat purse is charged. A fee, mind you, that is out of reach for the Cardinal, since every penny he earns by healing goes straight to the Church's pocket, and he has nothing to live on but a pathetic stipend barely more than a tradesman earns."

Christopher didn't know how much they paid the Cardinal, but he knew it didn't matter; the price of high rank dwarfed all other considerations. As a first-level priest, he had lived comfortably on a fistful of gold. As the master of a commercial empire, he knew his partners in the smithy were earning sacks of the stuff. As a freelance adventurer and head of his own chapter, he'd spent the equivalent of two hundred pounds of gold just for his last promotion.

"And they call this brotherhood?" Lalania said with a polished sneer. "Better to call it hoodwinkery, that a man should do so much and yet profit so little. How wise can such a man be? How hard will he fight for a Church that takes and takes and takes but returns him nothing? Can you blame people for doubting the strength of this Church, when their priests have so little invested and are so far yet untested in battle?"

She didn't have to make her pretend case quite so convincingly.

"No, there is only one explanation for such a man. Weakness, innate and incurable. We should not be surprised that he has only ever fathered daughters, save for one son who fell in his first year of draft, like any weakling."

Christopher hadn't even known Faren had children. Or a wife.

"The Iron Throne is hard, but it is strong. Those who sit in it may bleed, but they will not break. They will not shrink back from harsh deeds, and they will not be deceived. Instead, they will do the deceiving. They will not be beaten; they will administer the beatings. The world is a hard place. Only a fool would put his life in soft hands."

Lalania had a way of making everything she said sound like she believed it. Christopher knew she was only acting. It unnerved him all the same.

"I never quite thought of it that way."

"I know," she said in a softer voice. "We leave the road here. I'll not chance Feldspar town if I don't have to. It's not the kind of place you would want to see, anyway."

No, it probably wasn't.

In the darkening twilight they picked their way through fields and hedgerows. Although he occasionally saw hovels with smoke rising from their chimneys, no one challenged them. Night finally arrived, and still Lalania led him down deer trails and backways through the cooling land. Royal was tired enough and familiar enough with her mare to follow it without argument, a feat he'd never seen before.

The glittering, brilliant stars filled the sky, setting Christopher to wondering. Where was he, in absolute terms? He thought the center of the galaxy was supposed to be a gigantic black hole. But then, he had no reason to assume he was still in the Milky Way. He tried to think of a way to phrase the question so that Lalania's College would understand it. In the absence of any concrete definition his imagination had expanded her College to something akin to Oxford, with orreries and old logbooks full of astronomical observations. Except this College, with access to magic, might well have made the trip to other planets by now.

It was incongruous to be thinking about space travel from the back of a horse, so he stopped. Instead, he tried to pay attention to where he was, but he failed. He was as lost as he had ever been.

Late in the night they finally came across a road. After following it for a few minutes they came to an inn, ramshackle and dirty even in the darkness, yet still promising more comfort than the gloomy night.

Lalania slipped from her saddle and knocked on the front door. Eventually a fat, surly man in a filthy apron opened the door and glared at her.

"We're closed."

"We have gold," she replied. "Send a boy out to see to our horses."

The man wiped his hand on his apron before holding it out, palm up. "You won't like the company. Don't say I didn't warn you."

"I never like the company," she said. A clink of metal and the man's hand disappeared behind his apron.

"Jiminy! We got guests! Get your arse out here!" The innkeeper disappeared. A moment later a tall, lanky man with a shock of orange hair stepped out into the night, holding a light-stone. He stared at Christopher.

"One mare, one destrier. See that you feed it oats." Lalania was talking directly to the man, who seemed to be ignoring her. When she was done, though, he ducked his head in acknowledgment and led them around to the barn.

There were at least a dozen horses already stabled there. Royal perked up his ears and began issuing challenging snorts. Jiminy pointed to the last two empty stalls and started to leave the barn.

"Hey," Lalania called after him. "Leave the light."

Jiminy flipped it through the air at her without breaking stride, and then he was gone.

"I thought you said you liked this inn."

"It appears to be under new management. I don't recognize either of those men. Nonetheless, it's the only choice we have."

"We could sleep in the barn." The stench of horses was overwhelming, but it might be tolerable from the hayloft.

"A right insult that would be to the innkeeper. In fact, so would blessing your food. Tonight, Christopher, we'll just accept what they serve us. The less attention we attract, the better." This time she stayed with him while he squared away Royal, brushing down where the saddle straps crossed his chest and combing the brambles out of his mane.

Loaded down with the saddlebags, he followed Lalania back to the front of the inn. She pushed the door open, and they went inside. Christopher immediately began missing the barn.

Two groups of surly men lounged around the main room, drinking. Christopher dumped his bags at the foot of an empty, rough-hewn table and sat down. Lalania sat next to him, making herself more inconspicuous than he had thought possible.

A timid blonde girl approached them with bowls of stew and mugs of beer on a tray. One of the men pinched her as she passed, and she almost dropped the tray. Christopher started to say something, but Lalania kicked his shin under the table.

"Hey now," called a man from across the room. "Keep your filthy paws off."

The offender glared at his challenger. For an instant Christopher thought a fight would break out on the spot. Then the pincher backed down.

"Nothing worth pawing, anyway. No more meat than a dog's bone." He turned his attention to his table, where his fellows chuckled appreciatively.

After that, Christopher didn't have the heart to tell the serving girl how miserable the stew was. He ate as much as he could bear and tried to wash it down with the bitter, dark beer. Lalania picked at her bowl, equally uninspired.

The girl went around the room with another tray of mugs. Her erstwhile champion stared at the pincher, who pretended to be oblivious to the tension. The man leaned back, apparently casually, just in time to elbow the girl in the backside.

Amazingly, she didn't spill any mugs. The champion glowered even darker; the offender smirked; the girl worked her way to Christopher's table, and now he was the subject of her champion's minatory glare.

He tried to ignore the affair, looking down at his plate and feeling small. He could hardly defend himself, since he hadn't done anything yet. Best to let it slide. Then the serving girl stabbed him in the side of the neck with a dozen feathered darts.

His first reaction was prosaic. "Ow," he said, and reached up to the wound. When he felt his heart begin to slow with every beat, he stood up, reaching for his sword. Lalania drew back in horror, and then he froze.

He could not move. He tried to peer to the side, to see the face of this serving girl who had just poisoned him, but he could not move his head.

"Kill him now," the serving girl hissed. "Hurry!"

Everyone in the room stared at him with surpassing interest.

"Shut up, bitch," the champion said without taking his eyes off Christopher. "You don't rule here. I do."

Lalania darted for the door. She only made three steps before men leapt from their chairs and grabbed her.

The champion laughed and stood up. He was absurdly tall. "Come, my Bloody Mummers, let's treat our guest like the nobility he is. Dinner and a show, lads, what do you say? Can we put on a show for the good Curate?"

"Aye!" chorused the entire room.

"And what shall it be?"

"What it always is," said one of the men standing in front of Lalania. "Rapine and murder." He reached forward and casually tore Lalania's blouse open, the cloth shredding under his brutal strength. "Why, it's the only show we know."

"Wise words, Carruthers, and none truer were ever spoken. I do believe I'll start, as I always do." The tall man crossed the room while the men holding Lalania pinned her to a table. "Never you fear, Curate. You'll not be neglected. Jiminy's like that. Though I fear he will have to make a rush of it, as the poison will only last the hour."

Lalania struggled like a woman on a cliff slowly realizing she had lost her balance and was now doomed to fall.

"That's enough," she said somewhat incongruously. One of the men backhanded her in the face. Her head jerked, blood spilling from her split lip.

The other man reached out with a knife and began to cut away at her trousers. The tall man's eyes were drawn to the girl's peril, as were all the men in the room. Christopher realized that for one second they had forgotten about him.

In the back of his mind, he could feel the presence of the illusionary animated suit of armor that answered his prayers every morning and issued him his spells. It was offering him something now.

Freedom.

It was not fitting that an Acolyte of Travel should have his way impeded. By the grace of his Patron he could walk again, if only for a few steps, for he was only a small servant.

As he drew his sword he muttered the strength spell under his breath. He promised the avatar he would put its gifts to good use.

"Dark damn you," the serving girl cried, and a dagger clipped the side of his neck, thrown from across the room. She had not been distracted by Lalania's nakedness. And now she was throwing knives at him. "Are you proof against every trial?"

He did her the greatest insult he could conceive of. He ignored her.

The tall man realized something was wrong. He instinctively stepped back as Christopher lunged, reaching for his own sword. But the two men holding Lalania down were distracted by her struggles and the promise of getting her trousers off. Christopher gave them something else to think about.

Putting all his weight and divine strength into it, he drove his katana through the back of one man and into the chest of the other. Underneath them Lalania was bathed in a shower of blood.

The room erupted into pandemonium as men drew weapons and shouted. Above them all the tall man shouted loudest.

"Take him, damn it! He's only fifth. We'll feast off his head for a year."

Christopher should have made a telling retort, but he couldn't. His blade had stuck in the first man, and he was struggling not to let the weight of the corpse drag the sword down onto Lalania. The second man, on the other side of the table, had disappeared from view. Gracelessly Christopher wrestled the body on the end of his sword around, put his foot on its back, and shoved it away.

By then it was too late to bluff. Christopher didn't care. Bullies had always been his least favorite kind of people, and now he had a room full of them, a sword, and a perfectly good reason to make sushi. He was filled with a deep and pure hatred for the men who assaulted Lalania, who had planned to destroy her for their transitory amusement. And floating above all was the righteous judgment he would soon dispense on that wicked serving girl.

He knew her, though not her face. He had seen her cloaked form dancing in the snow. He had heard her voice in the deepest darkness of the King's dungeons. He had held the calling card she left him in Carrhill.

And as soon as he had dispensed with these savage beasts, he would pay her a measure of justice.

The Bloody Mummers gang fell on him ravenously, with swords, axes, and daggers clouding around him like buzzing bees. He ignored their stings, his tael binding his wounds in their wake. Eventually he would run out of tael, and then their weapons would kill him. But not yet.

Spinning, he stepped, and the katana lashed out and down. Another man fell, cut open from shoulder to hip, his guts spilling out on the floor. Stepping to put a table between himself and three men, Christopher bought respite from their attacks for a heartbeat. Long enough to terrorize two others not so lucky. With the upstroke of his sword he cut one man's thigh to the bone, blood spurting in a bright-red arc from the severed artery. The man tried to step back, but his leg was only loosely attached. He fell, too much in shock to even whimper.

The other man retreated, holding a pair of daggers in front of him like a shield. Christopher recognized the carrottop. Jiminy.

Men were clambering over the table, spurred on by the tall man. Christopher sprang forward, leaving them behind. Jiminy batted at the katana with his little knives, but magic fueled Christopher's righteous wrath. He pushed the katana into Jiminy's chest, its point sinking deep as the redheaded man's retreat ended abruptly on a table, while Christopher's sword continued its advance.

Jiminy opened his mouth to threaten, to complain, or perhaps to beg. Only blood came out. The redhead slid off the end of the blade and flopped, drowning as his ruptured lungs filled.

Two men leapt on Christopher from behind, high and low, at the knees and shoulders. Miraculously they slid off, as if he were a greased pig. One of his assailants rolled on the ground in front of him. Christopher stepped over him, and in doing so, dragged his sword edge across the man's throat.

A crossbow quarrel whizzed past his head. The men in front of him regrouped, preparing for a charge. Now there were three to tackle him: perhaps too many. He tried to step back, to open some distance.

But failed. The benefits of his faith had run its course, and now he was frozen again, merely mortal.

An explosion, a flash of light, the acrid tang of smoke, and one of the men in front him slumped to the floor. Lalania was behind the bar, the pistol in her hands.

"Kill them both, idiots!" the tall champion roared.

Lalania shot him.

"Dark damned gods, kill the Darkling bitch!" he screamed louder, staggering back from the shot but not falling, a sure sign that had ranks of his own.

Men began to rush her, while others inched toward Christopher. Apparently they thought he was only pretending to be paralyzed, and no one wanted to be the first to die.

He wasn't pretending. He had used his temporary freedom to kill six men, and Lalania had killed one. It wasn't going to be enough. Half a dozen men still stood, and they were beginning to realize that they had won. They had been savage before; now, with half their number dead and dying, they would be psychotic. The best he and Lalania could hope for was to die quickly, while the men still raged. If the tall man regained control, he would torture them in ways that could not be described.

Even if Christopher thought he could still come back from that, the Saint needed at least a hair. And his assassin knew that. The serving girl had disappeared once he started moving, but he knew she would return to burn his corpse and scatter the ashes to eternal death.

None of this mattered to his body, which refused to obey his commands. None of it mattered to his avatar, whose presence was gone, his allotted protection expired for the day. The bright and glowing joy he had taken in destroying these monsters collapsed into fear and grief.

The front door burst open, and a young woman rushed into the room, followed by an army of young men. Christopher's men, led by the stalwart Kennet. They stared, confused and uncertain, until Lalania shot another one of the Mummers. Then the soldiers turned their rifles on the thugs, and in thunder and lightning and smoke the battle ended.

"Colonel!" they shouted at him, saluting, wondering why he did not move.

Find the assassin, he tried to say. His jaw refused to move; his tongue and lips were as numb as a needle-happy dentist could hope for.

"He has been poisoned," Lalania told them, coming out from behind the bar. She clutched her blouse together in the front with one hand, held the still-smoking pistol in the other. "We have to get him to my College. Tonight, or he will die. Only the Loremasters can save him."

The fear in Christopher's stomach lurched and twisted. Lalania had heard the tall man say it would only last an hour. The incongruity of her complaint came back to him. She had been terrified by the attack . . . but not surprised.

The other woman spoke. "I led you here, to succor your lord, on the instructions and guidance of our College. You trusted me for this; now I say, trust us a little further. Give Lalania your fastest horse and let them ride through the night."

His men stared at him, miserable and confused. Kennet's earnest face hung like a sad puppy.

Lalania accepted a coat from one of the men, trying to cover herself. She did a bad job of it, the coat hanging open and revealing a swath of delicate skin from neck to midriff. Christopher knew her well enough to know it was an act. It made her look vulnerable and desirable at the same time. It was a distraction.

"Your foes are destroyed," she said, hugging the other troubadour like a long-lost sister. "Do not dally and let them win by indecision."

His men had no chance. Against ten times as many slavering monsters they could hold forever, but against two pretty, conniving girls they crumbled helplessly. Christopher raged and fumed, to no visible effect.

The smoke seemed to be getting worse, not better. The front door slammed shut, as if in a great wind.

"Damn," Lalania said, and Christopher believed her fear genuine, even while he knew it could only be part of the act.

A man went to the door and found it unyielding. Another joined him, to no avail.

The sound of crackling logs.

"Dark gods," the other troubadour swore. "The inn's on fire!"

Heat leached down from the ceiling, terrifying in its promise.

Three men threw themselves against the door. It held firm, barred by magic. Magic Christopher could have undone, if he could have moved.

"Cut it down," the troubadour cried. Then, when his men looked at her blankly, she swore again. "Not one of you bloody fools has an ax or sword? Not one?"

In one corner of the room, a beam fell from the roof, flames writhing around it. From the hole it left burst light and smoke. Then the smoke reversed, rushing up in the draft, and the flames grew brighter.

Kennet ran to the door, began hammering a grenade into place with the butt of his gun. Other men grabbed Christopher, hauled him bodily out of the way, two flipping over tables. They crouched behind them, dragging Christopher down, sheltering the girls with their bodies. His limbs moved when his men pulled or pushed on them, staying wherever they were left, like a clothing-store mannequin.

An explosion shook the building, shrapnel ripping into the tabletop. The men rose up and carried Christopher through the hanging shards of the door. Behind them the building began to fall.

Outside in the cool air, the heat beat at their backs. When they had retreated far enough, they turned Christopher around so he could see. The inn was in full flame, its second story wreathed in red. As portions of the building fell in, sparks and flames leapt up. In a few more minutes the building would be nothing but a glowing pile of embers.

"The barn!" Lalania shouted over the roar of the flames. Men started running, but it was too late. Even from here Christopher could see the flames rising from it.

Kennet, acting on training and habit, snapped out a report to Christopher. "One casualty, sir. We left Dobbs to watch our horses. Now he's dead and our horses are gone."

"There were a dozen other horses in the barn," Lalania said.

Royal had been in that barn, too.

"The barn is empty now." Kennet ignored her, speaking directly to Christopher. "Whoever loosed our horses loosed those as well. Spooked by fire, they will run for at least a quarter mile. Permission to spread out and search for our mounts, sir?"

Gods, no, Christopher thought. *That's the stupidest thing to do right now.*

"Do it," Lalania said. "But come back when you find the first one. We need to go *now*."

Take your time, Christopher thought.

Then Royal, stupid loyal Royal, came trotting up out of the darkness. He whinnied at Christopher, prodding him with his big stupid head. Lalania scratched his nose, and he whuffled affectionately at her. She stepped to the side of the horse, held up her foot until Kennet reflexively made a stirrup out of his hands for her.

Vaulting onto Royal's back, she stroked his mane.

"Put him up," she told the sergeant. "Wrap his arms around me. Royal can bear us both."

"I will stay with you," the other troubadour said, "until you find your mounts. Then I will lead you to our College, where you will find your lord safe and sound, in honored luxury."

I will beat your Darkling heads in if you fall for this, Christopher fumed. *Can't you see how they are separating us again?* The night was full of dangerous women, and they were going to send him out into it as helpless as a sack of potatoes.

Kennet rubbed his jaw, torn with indecision. Christopher relented. The boy was seventeen years old. He'd seen Christopher treat Lalania like an equal. She'd had the run of his camp, passed on orders from him to the troops. And now she was sitting on top of his warhorse, her coat hanging open to reveal the soft curve of a perfect breast.

Three men boosted Christopher to the back of the horse. Lalania put all of her charms to work, convincing Royal to stand still through these strange shenanigans. Christopher probably couldn't have done that.

Then she wrapped his arms around her tightly, where they stayed of their own accord. Clenching her fists in Royal's mane, she kicked the horse in the ribs, and it lumbered into a gallop.

Once again Christopher rode under the twinkling starlight, but much more uncomfortably than before. His legs hung down, inert and useless. What really bothered him was the feel of Lalania's soft skin on his arms. She had burst loose from her coat and now jiggled and bounced with every step.

"Gods, I am pathetic," she muttered. "I have to paralyze my paramour to get him to cop a feel." She adjusted her coat to cover herself again, no mean feat while they galloped bareback through the murky dark.

"Pathetic" wasn't the word Christopher would have chosen. "Traitorous" seemed more appropriate. The curious pace they had set for the last three days, alternating between hurried and ambling, the choice of route she had taken, all made sense now. She had been a part of this. She had brought him here only when everything was ready and delivered him to his enemies.

He wondered when her plans had turned to ambush. Was it the night she had spent trying to seduce him? When he was teaching her how to use the pistol? Or perhaps weeks ago, after the ulvenmen had failed to kill him.

Perhaps she and her College had been planning it all along.

Royal could not keep this pace for long. But he didn't have to. A mile or so up the road a covered wagon waited, surrounded by armed men and more pretty girls. Lalania pulled to a stop amongst them, calmed Royal while strangers lifted him down. The horse didn't like this. Flattening his ears, he kicked with one rear leg, and a man went flying.

The girls immediately burst into song, lutes and lyres twanging soothingly. Lalania wrapped her arms around the horse's neck, whispering into his ear. Royal turned in a circle, looking for his master, but they had already spirited Christopher into the wagon.

Into a long pine box, padded with straw. They stretched him out, made him as comfortable as possible, arranged his limbs as if he was sleeping.

A beautiful redheaded woman with ivory skin and shockingly green eyes pinched his lips open and fed him three drops of a bitter liquid from a crystal vial. It burned on his lips and tongue.

"Shhh, my lord," she whispered soothingly.

The wagon began to move.

The lights went out.

Christopher, sick with rage, brokenhearted at betrayal, incensed to white-hot fury that these people had cooperated with his child-killing assassin, went to sleep.

17

CONTINUING EDUCATION

He did wake in luxury. After he got over the fact that he had woken at all, he noticed the bed was smooth, the blankets warm and soft, the room discreetly lit by stones in shaded sconces. His first conscious act was to reach to his side, groping the mattress next to him.

His sword was gone.

Seconds later more facts penetrated. His clothes were gone. Tapestries cloaked the walls in tasteful elegance. The bed was huge, a four-poster absurdity out of a Victorian picture book. A fire burned in the hearth at the other side of the room.

He added *waking up naked in a strange place* to the list of things he really, really hated.

Sitting up, he found a set of silk pajamas on the nightstand. Like everything else in the room, they were finely made. He had not experienced such elegance in his time on this planet.

But he knew it existed. Lalania's speech came back to him, about Faren and the Church and the things they chose not to buy. This room was what lords lived like, if they wanted to.

The door opened, and a woman backed into the room, wearing a sheer gown that would have been completely see-through in any stronger light. As it was, it more than hinted at firm curves and fresh skin. When she turned around, he saw why she had entered the room in such a curious fashion. She was carrying a hot kettle that leaked steam, held carefully away from her body by hands bound together with a silver chain.

"My lord is awake," she said, and he looked up at her face. It was the redhead from the night before, the last in a long line of women who kept poisoning him.

She poured the kettle into a large porcelain tub that rested on silvered feet. Steam billowed up, warm and inviting.

"Would my lord like to bathe?"

Of all the luxuries he missed from home, a good hot shower every morning was near the top of the list.

"Sure. I don't suppose you'll tell me where I am, first?"

"Why, at the College of Troubadours, my lord."

She began filling the bath with water from a basin next to the wall. Watching her gown shift and drape around her as she worked was enticing.

As, no doubt, it was supposed to be. Lalania had already tried this and failed. Christopher wasn't about to sit through it again.

"That's enough. You can go."

"My lord? Don't you want me to wash you?"

"I know how to wash myself, thank you."

She stood there with a sponge in her bound hands, looking lost. Hating himself for giving in to his greatest weakness, he sighed.

"Tell me why you're wearing chains."

The woman cast her gaze demurely to the floor.

"I wronged you, my lord. It is your right to chastise me, as you see fit."

Something in the tilt of her head made him look up to the wall behind him. A collection of riding crops and horsewhips hung above the bed.

They were laying it on thick.

"Get Lala," he said through clenched teeth.

"Do you wish two girls, my lord? Because Pia is my favorite."

Very thick indeed.

"Yes, I wish two girls. One of whom must be Lala. Can you do that?"

"As you please, my lord." She curtsied, the gown shimmering next to her skin, and slipped out, the door closing quietly behind her.

He stared wistfully at the bath, unwilling to walk across the room at the moment, since he had to assume he was being watched. Instead he tried to assess the situation. They hadn't killed him in his sleep, which was not as comforting as it should be. It only meant they wanted something more valuable than his life.

Considering that sober fact solved at least one of his problems, and he was just tossing the covers off to get out of bed and into the bath when the door opened again and he had to scuttle back under the blankets.

Lalania and the woman entered, the blonde with an uncertain smile and the redhead with a sultry pout. Lalania wore a ridiculous green kimono-like wrap that barely contained her. She dropped to one knee and bowed, exposing more cleavage. "You wish me to serve, my lord?"

"You made a promise."

The smile disappeared from her face.

"I did. But I cannot promise for others."

"Not even your College?"

"No. Especially not them."

"Then I am done. Get me my clothes and my sword. I'm leaving."

"My lord—" began the redhead, but Christopher cut her off.

"Shut up. I still have a head full of spells, and I will use them. On you. Now either kill me or let me go. I'm sick of this."

"Christopher, I am sorry," Lalania said. "I misled you. You seem to think my College is a gigantic institution swarming with learned scholars in every field. It is not; it is a handful of women trying to pre-serve a Kingdom against its own innate stupidity. If we have wronged you, imposed upon you, it is only because we are weak. We do what we have to."

She had wasted his time, dragging him across the Kingdom to visit a brothel instead of a research institute. He was not going to find answers about interstellar travel here. But that wasn't what bothered him the most.

"Working with child-killing assassins is necessary? Does that excuse work for you?"

That made her angry. "She is not one of ours. We would kill her as quickly as you would."

His face must have betrayed his doubt, because she leaned forward to speak in earnest.

"You know I dare not lie to you. Destroying the Bloody Mummers gang was always our goal. That they had left the road and taken root was an opportunity. That you were on hand to assist was . . . serendipity."

"Then why not just tell me?"

She looked at him with sympathy, and he realized that even though she might never have lied, she had still deceived him many times.

"I cannot answer any more of your questions, Christopher. Put them to the Skald. You have come all this way; I beg you, come a few steps further. Put your questions to the Skald, and if she does not answer them to your satisfaction, I will accept whatever retribution you demand."

"Give me my damn sword."

"Do it," she ordered the redhead.

The other woman bowed and slipped out, her face a perfect mask.

"He's not an idiot," Lalania said to the empty room. "He knows you're watching. Gods, can you not see? You have pushed him to the breaking point, and all he wants to do is escape with his virtue intact."

Christopher stared around the room. Of course, he didn't see anything. "What the hell is going on, Lala?"

"I am putting my career at risk. For you. Again."

He didn't really feel like thanking her, though. There were a lot of answers he wanted about their definition of serendipity before he was in the mood to thank anybody.

"It would have been so much easier if you had just slept with me," she said, trying to smile. "But at least you did not succumb to Uma. For that, my vanity is grateful."

The door opened and Uma returned, carrying a bundle that included his sword. She still hadn't put any more clothes on, but she was followed by a squad of armed men. Christopher decided to make use of their mistake.

"Out," he said.

The leader of the guards, a middle-aged man who exuded competence despite his ridiculous handlebar mustache, spoke deferentially. "We guard the Skald with our lives, Vicar. If you wish to see her while armed, you must tolerate us."

"No, not you, Goodman. You lot." He pointed at the girls and then at the door. "Let a man get dressed in peace."

With the women in retreat he began to relax. The guards were clearly unranked; they neither dressed nor swaggered like knights. More importantly, if they decided to attack him, he knew how to respond. A good clean sword fight might be bloodier than this verbal fencing, but he doubted it would be as painful.

They had cleaned his clothes. Too bad he hadn't gotten a chance to take that bath. Once he was dressed, with boots on his feet and his sword at his side, he began to feel more in control of the situation. Of course, if they still had more tricks up their lacy sleeves, that would be exactly what they wanted him to think.

The guards escorted him from the room, two behind and two in front. Uma fell in beside him, eyes wet.

"You tricked me, my lord. Now the Loremasters will administer my punishment, and I will not even have you to comfort me afterward."

Christopher sighed. "You know what? How about if you just don't talk right now, okay?"

The building was laid out more like a boardinghouse than a

college. The hallways and rooms they passed through were clean, though faded and plain. The room he had been in was a higher standard of luxury than the rest of the building could sustain.

Down a flight of stairs, around and through another hall, and they came to a barred door. Another squad of guards waited there, along with four startlingly attractive women.

"Hello, Loremasters," he guessed.

"Greetings, Vicar," the one in front replied. She had curly black hair and an inviting heart-shaped face, and her friendliness was only slightly compromised by the huge loaded crossbow in her hands. "We apologize for any discomfort we may have put you to. We can only plead foolishness."

"You can punish her, if you want," Uma whispered at his side. "She is as deserving as I."

"I thought we weren't talking," he whispered back. He wondered how long it would be before they started offering him boys.

Down more stairs, of a different quality. If he had to guess, he would expect to find stone or earth behind the fine wooden panels on the wall. The temperature changed subtly, and the echoes of footsteps were dampened. They were underground.

A curved hallway, and at the end of it a small round room, about twenty feet in diameter. Remarkably, real candles burned in holders on the wall, providing real torchlight instead of the magic illusion he had become so accustomed to. The effect was either spooky or romantic, depending on your point of view. A small round wooden table in the center of the room held a large crystal ball, and behind it sat an elderly woman.

She had been a beauty, once. She was still elegant and handsome, wearing a crisp white gown with sparkly bits on it, and her hair was coiffed in an elaborate style. The effect was difficult for Christopher to reconcile. She looked like a dignified society matron sitting at a gypsy fortune-teller's booth.

The woman waited patiently while the first squad of guardsmen filed into the room and took up positions behind her. Then she beckoned for Christopher to approach, leaving the Loremasters and the second squad of guards at his back.

"No doubt my staff has apologized profusely, yet I also must add my apologies. Forgive a foolish old woman for her superstitious fears, my lord."

"Stop apologizing, and start explaining." Any second now, Uma was going to whisper that he could spank the old lady if he wanted, and then he really was going to smack the little minx.

"One more apology, my lord," the woman said sadly, and touched the heavy lead-gray locket hanging from her neck, her lips mouthing the words of a spell.

Instinctively Christopher's hands went to his hip. All around him he heard the rasp of steel, as the guards front and back drew their weapons. There were more behind than in front, so he turned, flinching at what he saw, stepping back and whipping out his sword.

Uma had been transformed, her flawless ivory face turned dull red and stirred like a wax painting partially melted. But the same sharp green eyes stared out at him with accusation. Under the horrible face was Uma's body, still shapely and appealing.

"From lust to loathing in an instant, my lord?" Uma's voice, shorn of seductive pretense, was acidic.

"I'm sorry," he said, once he understood. The woman was disfigured, and he was pointing a sword at her.

Then he realized everyone else in the room was also pointing weapons: swords, crossbows, and in Lalania's case, a pistol. But not at Uma. At him. They stared at each other for an instant, over a sea of sharp and gleaming steel.

Lalania sighed, exasperated, and lowered her gun.

"I *told* you," she said to the Skald.

Christopher was not comforted by her apparent surrender. A fight in these close quarters would be precarious, even without the disadvantage of paralyzing poison. He had not renewed his spells or his tael, both depleted in the last battle. The best magic he had left was the one that made his sword sharper.

They still weren't attacking him yet, so he took advantage of their indecision and cast it. Graceless, yes, but he was greatly outnumbered and possibly outclassed. He didn't know what rank the Skald was, or what her powers were, but he wasn't fooled by her frail appearance. He'd beaten Black Bart by virtue of sneaking in a spell while the man was blustering, and he aimed to claim the same advantage here.

Nothing happened. They didn't attack, and his sword didn't start glowing.

"Um."

The Skald waved her hand. "Let us be at peace. Lala was right all along."

Guards and women lowered their weapons. Christopher decided not to. He'd been fooled too many times by these people.

Repeating the words of his spell had no effect. That was starting to worry him more than being in a small room with a lot of armed people who might or might not be trying to kill him.

"You may go. All of you." The Skald dismissed her entourage.

"My lady," protested the handlebarred sergeant automatically.

The Skald gently shook her head. "We have tried the Vicar's patience long enough. Now I owe him an explanation, and I would rather not have to filter my words for your ears."

Clever old fox. She had hit on the one thing Christopher wanted most. He lowered his sword.

"Yes, I would like an explanation. I would like a Darkling lot of explanations."

"You can go, too, Lala. It will be easier for me to apologize for how we manipulated you if you are not in the room, reminding me of my guilt."

"Shall I also leave?" Uma asked. "I do not wish to cause undue discomfort for our noble guest."

"You may leave, Uma," the Skald said, "because you already know everything I am going to tell him."

The room slowly emptied. Christopher wished he'd memorized his truth-compelling spell. Thinking about it, he wished he could cast the damn thing permanently. Then he remembered that Lalania had said she had never lied to him. These people had lived with truth-spells, and the threat of them, for their whole lives. If there was a way to fool them, then they would know. He would have to rely on logic instead of magic to wring the truth out of them.

"Please, my Lord Vicar. Have a seat." Reaching under the table she produced a bottle of wine and two delicate-stemmed glasses. She set them on the table, next to the crystal ball, and laid out a silver corkscrew. "If you would be so kind. My old hands lack the strength these days."

Automatically, he sheathed his sword so he could pick up the bottle in one hand and the corkscrew in the other. Then he stopped and put the bottle back down, annoyed at having been so easily disarmed. "Questions first. One: why didn't my spell work?"

"What I am about to tell you is one of our best kept secrets. So first I must ask you to promise not to reveal the answer to any other."

"At this point, I really don't feel like I owe you anything."

"No, you don't. But you will be bound by your promise, and I will have it. You can strangle me here with your bare hands, and no one can stop you. But you cannot make me destroy my College."

This was shaping up to be as aggravating as bandying words with Uma, if in a somewhat different way. Only two minutes ago an armed squad had been threatening him with swords, and already he missed them.

"Fine." He pulled out the other chair and sat in it. "I won't tell anybody your secret, unless I determine that doing so would be in the best interests of the Kingdom. Is that good enough?"

"Acceptable, my lord."

"Stop calling me that. Call me Christopher."

"Very well, Christopher. We shall not tread on formality here; you may call me Friea. The locket around my neck is a null-stone. When targeted by a spell, it generates a field that suppresses all magic. You can guess that the range of the effect is the size of this room; indeed, the room was constructed to fit the locket. I apologize for all the preceding theatrics, but this irreplaceable item is of limited charges and we did not wish to use it save for the last resort."

It made sense. In a world with so much magic, there would naturally be an anti-magic defense. It also explained Uma's transformation.

"So that's what happened to Uma—you dispelled the magic she used to disguise herself."

"Yes."

He frowned. The answer seemed somewhat ungenerous. Friea apparently agreed, and volunteered a little more with a concessionary nod.

"Uma has long ago made her peace with her disfigurement. It causes her no physical hardship, and no psychological harm now that she has magic enough to take whatever face she desires."

He almost asked if the Invisible Guild had access to that magic— if so, he could stop trying to fix the serving girl's face in his memory— but he didn't want to waste a question, and anyway the answer was pretty much obvious.

"If it's so valuable, why did you use it just to unmask Uma?"

Friea put her hands together. A subtle signal, but he understood. She thought the question was stupid. "We did not; we used it to unmask you."

He drew back, shocked. Before he could speak again, Friea continued.

"Christopher, you've already asked three questions. I believe it is my turn."

Too late he remembered the very first time he had met Lalania, and how difficult it had been to have a conversation with her without giving away secrets. Now he was talking to the woman who had taught her those skills.

Friea smiled disarmingly at him. "First: are you going to open that wine?"

It was as infuriating as sitting down to play chess with someone, and the first thing they did was knock half their own pieces off the board. The old harridan was toying with him.

Driving the corkscrew into the bottle and yanking out the cork released some frustration. He filled her glass. He left his own glass empty. She was too polite to mention it.

"Second: *why are you here?*"

"Possibly because you kidnapped me and carted me here in a box."

She pursed her lips disapprovingly.

"Seriously, Friea. What do you mean by here? This room? This county? This Kingdom?" He stopped himself before he added, *this planet?*

"We already know you are not from our realm. I have heard your Saint's tale, that you are merely a victim of a random gate. I do not find it terribly convincing."

The last thing he wanted to do was tell these people the one thing the Saint had told him to keep quiet.

"How about if I tell you what I'm trying to do here?" That he could at least answer. "I want to make a change to your society. One I think you'll agree with."

"I have read Lala's report of your cultural revolution. I am not as certain as you that the gain is worth the cost to the small folk; in a clash of titans the grass is always trampled, and yet you seek to change not just our ruler but our rules. But to clarify my question: why have you agreed to do this? What do you get out of it?"

Another easy answer. "I get to go home."

"So you're here to go home." Friea arched an eyebrow at him.

"Yes. I didn't want to come here, and I don't want to stay. I was promised a way home, if I did . . . something."

"By whom? Did what?"

How much could he tell her? On the other hand, how much could the truth hurt?

"By Marcius. And I don't know what. He didn't seem to know, either. So I'm doing what I can. I'm pretty sure I'm on the right track." He had to be. There was nothing else he could offer this world, other than the gift of technology.

"You are still hiding something."

"Yes. But it isn't important. It doesn't affect my task. I'm going to give everybody guns and teach you how to run a democracy. Then I'll get to leave."

He hurried on before she could keep 'clarifying' her ever-expanding question. "That was three questions on your part. My turn. *Unmask?*"

Friea's lips softened into a discreet smile. Finally he had asked a question she thought was sensible.

"Lala says you did not recognize the word *lich*. I trust, then, that you will not recognize the word *hjerne-spica*."

"You trust right." He'd learned this language by magic. It had rarely let him down. But the word she used was utterly foreign to him.

"Try it as two words, Christopher." She repeated the term slowly, so the words became distinct. "Brain. Eater."

The two words hung in the air while his stomach turned.

"OK, I get it. But what does it mean?"

"It means death, doom, and destruction. It means the Black Harvest."

"Um. Yes. About that. What does *that* mean?"

She took a sip of her wine. "Lala did not exaggerate. You are . . . mystifying."

"Trust me, Friea. You're plenty mystifying to me, too." This poised and genteel old lady ran a high-class brothel, a national spy ring, and had recently come perilously close to killing him. Now they sat in a dungeon, chatting. How weird could he be, compared to that?

"Tell me: what is the most horrifying creature you have ever seen?"

Black Bart was at the top of that list, but he knew she didn't mean monsters of the human kind. Ulvenmen weren't that bad: just eight-foot tall wolves that walked on two legs and carried axes. Even their dinosaurs weren't horrifying. Terrifying, yes, with teeth the size of his thumb, yet not truly grotesque. For that appellation he would have to stick with ten feet of slimy, deformed green man-beast, creatures that got up again no matter how many times you shot them and only stayed dead after cleansing fire.

"Trolls."

"Fearsome indeed. You are lucky to have seen one and lived. Yet I tell you, if a troll were to catch sight of a *hjerne-spica*, it would piss itself and run gibbering in terror."

She didn't sound like she was exaggerating.

"Imagine a bushel of tentacles, black and oily, as hard as leather but spongy to the touch. A lopsided sack flops at the root of these limbs, and two dreadful yellow eyes gaze out at you with malevolent intelligence and unadulterated contempt. The creature lurks in the darkness, waiting for you to stumble into its trap, a deadfall, a snare or pit, or worse. When you are helpless, or merely distracted, it springs on you with an unnatural animation. Horned tentacles crush your skull; its greasy skin smothers your face. The creature unfurls its penultimate horror: a slender tentacle tipped with adamantine. With unbelievable force it drives the spike deep into your forehead. You are not dead, not yet: you can still hear the sickening slurping as it begins to suck out your brain. The creature deliberately prolongs the act, allowing your pain and consciousness to persist as long as possible."

Christopher poured himself a glass of wine. He felt a need for some fortifying.

"But the worst is yet to come. Afterwards, it gnaws off your head and discards it, like a crushed and empty eggshell. Now it unveils its most horrifying aspect: a long, thin tentacle with a delicate spider-web of cilia. It inserts this tentacle down your neck, the cilia digging into and meshing with your spine. Then it restarts your heart, your lungs, your vital organs, and your body rises under its new master. You have given the creature legs, arms, hands. All it lacks is a human face, and that it creates with magic. It transforms itself to all appearances as you. It walks in your stead, speaks in your voice, shares in your memories. And there the nightmare truly begins. The Black Harvest; the Feast of Souls. Many will fall before its appetite is sated. And it will feed first on those closest to you."

He poured them both another glass. The first one hadn't lasted long.

"Gods, Friea..."

"No! Not gods. Never that. Monsters of ancient lineage, yes, masters of the underworld, Lords of the Night if you must. But not gods, no matter what tales they spread."

Halfway through his second glass, he finally understood.

"You thought *I* was one of those?"

"It was a possibility, Christopher. You are new to our realm. You have strange ideas and stranger tricks. Your rise to power is swift beyond reckoning, and you are apparently indestructible. It was a possibility."

"So you trapped me in a small room with a null-stone. To dispel my disguise."

She smiled at him. He liked her ever so much more when he was asking intelligent questions.

"It was not our first choice. We would prefer to keep its existence a well-forgotten secret and to preserve it against exhaustion. But when Lala could not seduce you, we had to find another way."

The thought of Lalania striving to sleep with one of those *things* made his stomach clench. With an act of will he stopped himself from throwing up. The wine was first class. It was too expensive to waste.

"Why did you want her to do that?"

"We are certain the creature's control over its stolen body is insufficient to perform such intimacy. When you resisted Lala's every lure, and turned down the woman she connived into your bed, I became convinced that your chastity was merely a cover."

So he had Lalania to thank for his unexpected visitor in the night rather than his innate charm and good looks. The troubadour had been exerting an unknown amount of influence over his every interaction with the people of the realm. He had no idea how much of his fame or trouble was her fault instead of his.

"I watched you on many occasions, but you never let your mask slip. I realized that you must either be innocent, or a fiend of diabolic proportion and discipline."

He almost asked her how she had spied on him, until he glanced down at the crystal ball.

"Next we set you to a test, Christopher. One under our control, instead of deep in the Wild. A band of thugs had seized an inn on the border. We learned of it too late to save the innkeeper's family, but nonetheless resolved to punish the murderers. Our College has few resources: our strength in numbers is little more than what you saw today. Attacking Too Tall Tan and his Bloody Mummers was not a task undertaken lightly. And then you agreed to come to the College, alone, without your screening cloud of boys."

"Friea, did you consider that if I had lost that fight, I would be dead?"

"We did consider it. Our company waited but a short distance away, and I had your own men close at hand as well, led to your rescue by Carala. If you had died, you would have lived again. We would have succored your body and your Saint would have succored your soul. But with the threat posed to you, we assumed you would be forced to reveal your true nature to defeat them. I was watching. I was waiting to see the monster reveal itself."

He was having trouble keeping the wine down. Again.

"You were watching what they were going to do to Lala?"

"Yes." She glared at him. "I have seen worse, and not been in a position to do anything about it. But Lala played her part well. By becoming a victim instead of a threat, she made them toy with her, giving us time to act."

"Did she know you were ready to save her?" He wondered how much of her fear had been acting.

"No," Friea admitted. "She surely must have known we were watching, but she could not know we were close enough to intervene. You must forgive her: she knew only that we wanted her at that inn, that night. If she had known more, you might have plucked it from her mind by spell or craft. And you must forgive us: we were not aware of the assassin's involvement. We did not expect her poison, or that all-consuming fire."

The old witch had played fast and loose with other people's lives. She saw his accusation in his eyes.

"We needed only to save a fingernail, Christopher. Your Saint would have revived you, like he did before. And we would have paid for Lala, too."

"Just a Darkling moment. If I was such a monster, why would the Saint bring me back the first time? Wasn't the fact that he was on my side proof that I wasn't a brain-eating octopus from Hell?"

Friea stared at him earnestly. "Where there can be one *hjerne-spica*, there can be two."

"You can't be serious."

"I can, and I am. My entire life I have been mocked as a superstitious old fool, even when I was young. I saw shadows at noon, they said. A silly girl who could not tell nightmares from nightsoil. And yet, I have watched my College side-lined and reduced, while the reach of the Shadow grows steadily. It falls over the Gold Throne, of course; but that is only to be expected. A truly diabolical plan would corrupt the White Church at the same time. And the *hjerne-spica* are nothing if not the very definition of diabolical."

"Can I take it I passed your tests? And by extension, the Saint as well?"

She bowed her head. "Yes. The null-stone has not only proven you human, but also free of mind-altering enchantment. You are neither the monster we seek nor its servant. We were wrong; *I* was wrong. My only excuse is that my reasons seemed persuasive to me. We will not doubt you or yours again."

A lame surrender, for all the trouble she had caused him.

"It's going to take more than that. I don't want you off my back; I want you on my side. And I won't set any ambushes on you to get it, or ask you to sleep with monsters. All I want is Lala. No, damn it, not her body. Her service. Full-time, as an advisor. You'll keep me out of trouble with the nobles while I teach the peasants how to make trouble. You'll help me find my assassin. You'll tell me things, without making me explain why I need to know them. And you'll send Uma to the Saint get her face fixed."

Friea smiled graciously. "Accepted, my Lord Vicar." Of course she was smiling. He'd just taken her viper to his bosom and buttoned his shirt over it. He'd never have another secret from the conniving old biddy. "Can I render you any other service this day?"

For once, he was out of questions. He'd learned more than he wanted to in the last hour, and this hardly seemed like the time or place to start asking about inter-planar travel, since it would undoubtedly set the Skald on the path to figuring out the one secret he was trying to keep. Then he thought of a tiny detail that had been niggling him for a while. Surely a question this innocent could not lead to a mind-numbing lecture on unspeakable horrors.

"One more thing. How old is the Kingdom?"

Friea stared at him, the whites of her eyes suddenly wide, and her mouth drawn tight like a wire.

"What? What did I say?" Damn, but she was touchy.

"Why would you ask that, Christopher? In all my years as the Skald, in all my years as a Troubadour and Minstrel roaming the land, singing in the courts of lords and spying on them, in all my life I have never heard anyone ask such a curious, pointless, irrelevant question."

"Does that mean you don't know the answer?" That would probably explain why she'd gotten so riled up.

"I know the answer. But before I tell you, understand that if I had not just sworn to never doubt you, I would think you a *hjerne-spica* all over again. No one has ever asked that question, because no one has ever cared. What possible difference could it make to anyone? Anyone, that is, but a *hjerne-spica*, calculating whether our Kingdom is due for the harvest. Only the farmer asks how long the wheat has been in the field."

He wanted to know why there weren't stone fences in the old farmlands. He wanted to know why they hadn't made any technological progress. He wanted to know how long ago they had come over from Earth. But he didn't want to tell her all that.

"Remember the part of the deal where you tell me stuff without making me explain why I asked?"

"Of course, my Lord Vicar. Though it is not widely known, indeed may not be known outside of this building, the Kingdom is precisely two hundred and fifty-seven years old. It was a Sevenday, in the third week of summer, when Varelous the Arch-Mage stepped through a Gate at the foot of the spire of stone that would become Kingsrock. Behind him came his trusted companions, Palence and Byrnia, and a hundred and eighty-seven men, women, and children. They were refugees, fleeing a Kingdom called Attica. That Kingdom had been their home, and it was a place worthy of such heroes as they. Vast numbers of people had lived there, under a wise and just Council, in wealth and plenty, with such a surfeit of strength of arms and magic that monsters were hunted for sport or study, not from fear. Attica had been supreme; Attica was now rubble. Varelous and his pilgrims were the sole survivors, the last out of *millions*. The Black Harvest had come to Attica, and in a day her pride was thrown down, her spine broken, her people devoured."

She paused for breath. Christopher sat open-mouthed, stunned into silence.

"I know all of this, because I have Varelous's diary. At least, the handful of pages he wrote before life in this new land demanded all of his attention. In the last passage, he hints at his greatest fear: that the *hjerne-spica* purposely allowed their tiny band to escape the slaughter. The term he used was 'seed-corn.' Then he set down his pen, wrote no more of his thoughts, and spent the rest of his life struggling to rebuild. We have only legends from that time, adventure stories fit only for children. The people chose to forget the truth. The past was buried; the future birthed in ignorance and hope. But we cannot blame the people. Even Varelous the Arch-Mage could not long bear the burden of this knowledge. It was left to the Skald, one woman in every generation, old and wise and sad, to remember."

"And now," Christopher said sourly, "one man."

"You asked."

Of course he had. Pretty much every lump on his head was there because he'd stuck his noggin in front of somebody's club and asked for it.

"How much time do we have?" If his task was to save this society from the Black Harvest, he was going to need a lot more rifles.

"Varelous wrote of millions of people. Our realm is a fraction of that. We always assumed the harvest would wait until the crop is ripe. And yet, now the enemy moves against us deliberately. The shadow grows over the Gold Throne only as a stepping stone; its goal is the entire realm. Just as we prepare for the resistance, so does the enemy prepare for the onslaught."

The wine bottle was empty. Christopher felt sick, but not from alcohol. He wanted out of here, out of this underground lair of misery and despair. On cue, a knock came from the door. The guard captain spoke from the other side.

"My lady, the Vicar's soldiers are here, and they ask to see him. They are quite insistent."

Christopher stood, ready to leave. At the last instant he remembered his manners.

"Begging your pardon, Lady."

"You no longer need beg my pardon, Christopher. I serve your cause now. Our only hope lies with you and the god Marcius. To that hope, and that alone, I bend the knee that has defied kings for three generations."

He should play the question game more often. If he had done so a year ago, he might have realized that Marcius was seriously underselling the size of his task. He should remember that though all his battles had been with monsters outside the Kingdom, the true war was against monsters within.

He should go and see to his men, because if they were kept waiting any longer they were likely to blow something up.

ACKNOWLEDGMENTS

Thanks for the encouragement of the Loyal Crew who have been with this series since the beginning: nephews David, Alex, Dylan, and honorary nephew Fletcher, and compadre Josh, half a brother half a world away; to my agent Kristin for her inexhaustible patience; to my copyeditor Julia, for her usual magic; to Rene, for believing in the series; to Sophie, for finally starting kindergarten so Mommy and Daddy can have writing time; and always, to Sara.

ABOUT THE AUTHOR

M.C. Planck is the author of *Sword of the Bright Lady* (World of Prime: Book 1) and *The Kassa Gambit*. After a nearly-transient childhood, he hitchhiked across the country and ran out of money in Arizona. So he stayed there for thirty years, raising dogs, getting a degree in philosophy, and founding a scientific instrument company. Having read virtually everything by the old Masters of SF&F, he decided he was ready to write. A decade

Author photo by Dennis Creasy

later, with a little help from the Critters online critique group, he was actually ready. He was relieved to find that writing novels is easier than writing software, as a single punctuation error won't cause your audience to explode and die. When he ran out of dogs, he moved to Australia to raise his daughter with kangaroos.